The Gift of LOVE

The Gift of LOVE

CHRISTINE S. DRAKE

THOMAS NELSON PUBLISHERS
Nashville • Atlanta • London • Vancouver

Sequel to THE PRICE OF LOVE (ISBN 0-8407-6732-3)

Scripture quotations from the Holy Bible—
KING JAMES VERSION

Published in Nashville, Tennessee, by Thomas Nelson, Inc., Publishers, and distributed in Canada by Word Communications, Ltd., Richmond, British Columbia, and in the United Kingdom by Word (UK), Ltd., Milton Keynes, England.

Library of Congress Cataloging-in-Publication Data
Drake, Christine S.
The gift of love / by Christine S. Drake.
    p.   cm.
Sequel to: The price of love.
ISBN 0-7852-7897-4 (pbk.)
I. Title.
PS3554.R195G54   1995
813'.54—dc20   94-48125
                                                                    CIP

PRINTED IN THE UNITED STATES OF AMERICA
1 2 3 4 5 6 7 - 01 00 99 98 97 96 95

In honor of Wade and Nan Drake,
my gracious in-laws

The author wishes to thank the following individuals and organizations:

National Baseball Hall of Fame, Society for American Baseball Research, and the Chicago White Sox; James Franklin Owens; Susan D. Rosso; Sharon Foster; Dr. Gary Laden and Ken Sturdivant; Jim Oxford; Southern International Fireworks, Inc.; Christian Armory; Tracy Haney; David Whipple; Rabbi Robert Solomon; Dr. Jim Collins and Peachtree Christian Church; Southeastern Railway Museum; Museum of Florida History; owners, captain, and crew of the Riverboat *Grand Romance*; Sanford Museum; Eloise Dendy, Lonnie Hull Dupont, Glenna Francis, Beth Gerig, Sharon Gilbert, Ida Grimes, Lynn Kenney, Ami W. McConnell, Julianne Robert, Beth Rollinson, and Joan Waddington.

CHAPTER 1

❧

On the second floor of a rambling Victorian farmhouse a half mile from the Midwestern town of Bethel, in the sultry September dawn of Labor Day in the Year of Our Lord 1908, Jessy Flint was dreaming.

In her panoramic dreamscape, a modern street towered with reinforced concrete skyscrapers, the newest architectural feat. People of all ages and from all walks of life crowded the sidewalks. No sun or moon loomed over her head, just a clutter of telegraph and telephone wires. Trolleys and automobiles sped by. Noise assaulted her from all sides: myriad conversations, shouting newsboys, honking horns, and policemen's whistles.

"Follow Me!" a voice commanded above the din.

There amid the screeching brakes and grinding gears, the thunder of construction, the dust and grime of progress, was Jesus, struggling alone with the weight of His cross. Cruel stripes of blood seeped through His robe. A crown of thorns pierced His scalp. His face, bruised and swollen, attested to the cruelty the created hurled against their Creator, yet Jessy saw no anger in that face, only sorrow and unfailing love.

"Follow Me," came the voice while more blows fell.

"Of course." She nodded and turned for help, but the crowd was too busy to see the Son of God dying to redeem them from their sins. Unlike those who put the Son of God to death two thousand years before and buried Him in a rock-sealed tomb to be rid of Him once and for all, this crowd ignored Him.

"God doesn't exist."

Jessy, turning from them to Him, said, "But here He is, plain as day. What will you do?"

"Why, nothing, silly! We can't get involved. Be quiet!"

Said another, "He'll spoil our fun if we let Him."

Jessy cried, "But He's gone through all this for us. For you!"

1

"Follow Me," Jesus said.

Jessy set out alone, but above the thousand droning objections a strong voice rang out to her: "I'll follow with you!"

Before Jessy could see who had spoken, a scratchy gnawing sent shivers up her spine, waking her against her will. She peered into the dim light of morning, safe in her bed under a light cotton quilt. Fragrant end-of-summer breezes swept into her corner room from the vast fields below. Other than the fluttering curtains, all was calm and drowsy in the farmhouse Jessy shared with her brother, Adam, his wife, Suzanna, and their three children.

Nothing had changed from the previous day, certainly not Jessy's oak dresser, inexpensive but solid. She and Adam had hauled it home from an auction. On hooks were her two hats—the simple straw for farming and another with rose satin streamers she wore for the first time yesterday to church.

Fine art being beyond her means, Jessy had adorned her room with inventive, colorful labels peeled from citrus crates sent by friends in Florida: palm trees, Spanish conquistadors drinking from the Fountain of Youth, pink flamingos standing on one leg, a blissful mermaid with long golden hair, a smiling alligator guarding a box of tangerines, and two pelicans swinging on a silver crescent moon.

Jessy's oil lamp with its misty painted flowers was still on the night-stand, and her Bible too. She reached for it, her dream still pulsing through her brain, but before she could open it she heard that sound again, that strange disturbing scratching. Jessy got out of bed.

When she stepped to the wooden floor with bare feet, the hem of her long cotton nightgown graced her ankles. From her windows she saw the sun about to break above three hundred acres of field corn she had planted and tended that summer. All was calm in the direction of the bright red barn. But then she heard a noise below her. On the roof of the back porch beneath her windows a squirrel flicked his tail and chucked noisily at her. He looked innocent enough, but Jessy knew better than to trust in looks alone.

"Did you wake me up?" Jessy smiled through the screening at the charming critter, but remembered Adam's epithet for all squirrels: *tree rats*. They were forever doing damage to the house.

2

As Jessy made her bed, she contemplated her dream, then read in Deuteronomy of God speaking: *O that there were such a heart in them, that they would fear Me, and keep all My commandments always, that it might be well with them and with their children forever!*

Jessy prayed: "Dear Lord, You speak to us over and through the cares and pleasures of this world. I'll follow You come what may. I want always to know Your truth, love Your truth, and defend Your truth. Please forgive my sins so that I stay close to You."

Jessy beheld the dawn, the fiery orange ball bringing light and heat to this world from the hand of God. She knew the earth orbited around the sun in a most delicate balance. Cosmic changes could reduce the earth to cinders. In Genesis, God spoke the world into existence—He could extinguish it the same way. Jessy hurriedly found the Psalm proclaiming: *The heathen raged, the kingdoms were moved: He uttered His voice, the earth melted.* The earth melted! Jessy swallowed hard.

From below her came sharp young voices punctuated with the slam of the screen door to the back porch—once! twice! three times! Jessy would have liked nothing better than to spend the morning reading the many books on her desk, but there was much to do.

She brushed and wound her waist-length dark auburn hair into a simple knot which she pinned at the nape of her neck, then emptied water from a pitcher into a basin and washed her face. She dressed for her morning's work in a corset, long black stockings, a plain petticoat tied with ribbons at her waist, and, over all, a clean but faded blue-check dress. For now she put on slippers, but before she left the house she would change into work boots left downstairs. It just wouldn't do to drag mud about the house her sister-in-law Suzanna kept fresh as flowers.

While putting on her plain straw hat, Jessy focused on her reflection as if seeing it for the first time—the delicate oval face with a whisper of a dimple in her chin. Then she noticed, wedged between the mirror and its frame, a smashing photograph of Leo Kimball. This holiday she would spend the afternoon with Leo at his family's cookout. Once she had finished her morning's work, she would bathe and dress in proper visiting clothes. Leo would call for her and off they would go. The Kimballs were one of the wealthiest families in the township.

"My whole family will be together on Labor Day," he had said. He also said in his sultry, soft-spoken way that he loved Jessy and they would marry. *Leo said a good many things*, she thought with a smile. He'd had the audacity to propose to her the previous summer, during the heat of threshing, but she hadn't taken him seriously. For one, though Leo was considered a prize catch, Jessy hardly knew him; second, he wasn't a Christian. Eventually, after a heartfelt talk with her, he joined the church, which pleased her so. Now she knew she loved him. Jessy's warm brown eyes glowed with anticipation. This Monday would be unlike any other. Her smile dimmed a bit at the prospect of facing his entire family all at once, but Jessy Flint had braved many a fearsome situation in her twenty-two years.

Jessy had seen some of Leo's numerous kin around Bethel, although she didn't know them all personally. She was especially drawn to his grand-parents and his father, Walter. How kind they had been to help her with farming this season, after her brother Adam's dreadful accident. Leo's mother had a reputation for being aloof. Acacia Kimball seldom ventured from her sanctuary, her home. She was a mystery to Jessy, as were Acacia's three daughters. Jessy felt at a disadvantage, not having been born and schooled in Bethel. Life with her brother under difficult circumstances had isolated her from the social life of the township.

In the mirror, Jessy saw the old wooden steamer trunk at the foot of her bed. She had begun preparing for marriage by filling it with linens bought with some of the reward money the Flints had received that summer, a windfall. How strange it was for them to have money to spend! Since 1904, when the tornado hit, they had been in continual financial difficulty.

While searching for a clean hanky, she found the ragged ticket stub from her outing the previous Saturday to the Tri-County Baseball Park. "This game is so important!" Leo had stressed in dead earnest.

"But you say that about every game!" she had answered in truthful jest.

Leo had called for her in his father's roomy Lozier touring car with a couple of Leo's teammates and his kid sister Emma. Jessy knew Leo hadn't wanted to bring Emma along but had done so to placate Jessy's strict-as-Sabbath brother. Before Leo dashed off with Jessy, Adam had warned him: "Save those fancy hands of yours for pitching baseballs." A girl couldn't be too careful, Adam had warned Jessy often enough.

As it turned out, Emma made a poor chaperone. The teenager watched the game when Leo was pitching, but otherwise she gadded about the rickety bleachers all afternoon, visiting school chums. Not that Leo's behavior that day would have worried Adam. Leo's "fancy hands" had been devoted to baseball. He and his teammates never knew when their big moment might come—a contract offer from a professional club, their ticket to what they called the Big Time. Pro clubs sent scouts, shrewd observers of the game, to parks around the country in search of talented young amateurs.

Unlike Emma, Jessy sat close to home plate watching every inning, pitch, and fielding attempt. Since Jessy began dating Leo, she had watched a good many baseball games. Like all good pitchers, Leo wound up to toss the ball with such artful deception that he could make hitters believe they were getting one pitch while he delivered quite another. And like pitchers of his day, Leo often and secretly covered the ball with spit before hurling it. The spitball, legal in 1908, was made especially effective if the pitcher chewed tobacco, slippery elm, or licorice while pitching. Leo preferred licorice, which he bought by the pound in long strings, the blacker and gooier the better. Deception and licorice-laden spit were not his only weapons. Leo also possessed speed and strength.

"Count Smoke," Leo's friends called him, because his fastballs zipped to home plate and into the catcher's mitt so fast his teammates, as well as the batters opposing him, would shout, "That ball is smoking!"

Leo was quick to pivot, too, to pick a runner off a base to his left, to his right, and behind the pitcher's mound on second base. When he wasn't pitching, he was hitting. He could bunt a ball well enough to throw the other team's pitcher off guard and advance his teammates on base. Leo was considered an excellent all-around player. He could pitch. He could hit. He could run.

All that and incredible good looks too, Jessy sighed. It was no accident Leo's friends dubbed him Count. His nickname referred not only to the count of balls and strikes he pitched—"Count 'Emout" being Leo's other nickname—but also to Leo's maternal grandfather, Count Dimitri Alexandrov, the now-deceased wealthy nineteenth-century émigré to America from imperial Russia. *How wildly exotic*, Jessy thought whenever she looked at grandson Leo, regarded as the most handsome young man in the admittedly unimperial Tri-County baseball realm. Tall and lean, Leo was blessed with thick black wavy hair, piercing blue eyes, and a bright white smile fringed with a bushy black moustache. Leo's olive skin always appeared tanned. He spent all his summers in the sun farming with his father or playing ball. In bad weather Leo pitched baseballs into a peach basket in the family's barn. Now he hurled for a strong bush league.

The bush leagues! Leo "Count Smoke" Kimball dreamed big, desiring nothing less than major league stardom and World Series money. He had yet to hurdle the first step into the minors, but had been playing brilliantly. Even though his Saturday game had gone into extra innings, he had held on for the win. When the cheering stopped, Leo's arm ached so much he could hardly drive the big Lozier home. Still hurting on Sunday morning, he had phoned to break his promise to take Jessy to church but assured her he would come for her this Monday midday.

Jessy dashed downstairs past the battery-operated telephone sitting on Adam's mammoth rolltop desk and toward the toasty aromas of home cooking. "Good morning, Suzanna," she called to her sister-in-law, toiling alone in the country kitchen. Jessy helped herself to tea and a warm sticky roll studded with walnuts. "Mmmm. Perfect! How are you?"

"Tired," the petite blonde answered. "I've spent the entire weekend sewing the children's school clothes and I'm still not done! I'll have to postpone washday till tomorrow. What do you think of these?" Suzanna showed Jessy three lunch pails. With loving care, Suzanna had painted a name on each one: Stephen, Martha, and Taddy.

Tomorrow, Taddy would leave for school with Stephen and Martha for the first time. The house would seem desolate with all three of them gone. Feeling blue, still Jessy managed to say with cheer of Suzanna's handiwork, "Very nice!" Then, sharing Suzanna's stress, Jessy asked in her gentle voice, "How can I help?"

"You can't, but thanks." Smiling through misty blue eyes, the lovely Suzanna sniffed away tears and shook her blonde curls. The dainty mother of three added in her customary, musical soprano voice, "Don't mind me."

"Where are the children, anyway?" Jessy had finished her roll and was putting away clean dishes despite Suzanna's refusal of help.

"They went off to play." Suzanna set a roasting pan in the oven and wiped her hands on her apron. "Stephen wanted to meet with his friends alone at the swimming hole, but Martha and Taddy insisted on tagging along. That boy!"

Jessy smiled as she thought of her oldest nephew. Stephen Flint was independent and highly capable, a big boy like his father, with little patience for his younger sister and brother. "Stephen will come around one of these days, just like my big brother, Adam," Jessy said with assurance. Several years before, Adam Flint hadn't exactly welcomed his orphaned kid sister to his homestead, but in time, he had come to see the good of family ties. In time.

Jessy put a big kettle of water on the stove. "For my bath, after chores," she explained. A mechanical noise interrupted them, a rasping series of lurching, halting cuckoo calls from the hallway.

"That silly clock!" moaned Suzanna, perpetually embarrassed by her impulsive purchase from the mail-order catalog. When it sounded off, everyone within hearing remembered her folly. The cuckoo clock had never worked properly, but she never bothered having it repaired or shipping it back to the dealer. "It's not even seven o'clock and the fool thing thinks it's twelve!"

"In that case, I'd better get busy before it's thirteen o'clock!" Jessy, giggling and shaking her head, left for the barn where her brother was hard at work.

"Morning, Adam!" she called out. "How are you?"

"Mornin'! Say, isn't today your big day? Ready for inspection?"

Jessy could only blush at the prospect of facing so large and important a family as Leo's.

"He'll be lucky to have you for his wife," Adam said with feeling.

Avoiding the topic of marriage and ignoring her butterflies, Jessy saw that the morning's milk was ready to be collected by the farming cooperative, along with more than two hundred hen's eggs the Flints had gathered, washed, and packed over the last several days. From the tidy look of things, the children had helped Adam before going to play. "You must have gotten up early!"

"You know me. Never could sleep past four. Besides, it's sorta my big day too." Without explaining, Adam went off, urging his cows out to pasture. Jessy went to the pens to feed their hogs. Afterward the two cleaned stalls together and lined them with fresh straw. Adam moved slower and slower as the morning progressed, so unlike his normal self.

"Bah!" he complained. "This cane slows me down, but I can't get on without it!"

Jessy looked over at her brother, as tall and good-looking as ever. To her, Adam's rugged face, green-gold eyes, curling hair, and commanding profile had lost none of their appeal. "The doctor's pleased you're getting over that accident so well. He's surprised you're able to walk at all."

"It was the Lord who fixed me up. But look at this flab!" Adam slapped his abdomen. "Used to be flat as a board! Can't use my dumbbells, can't do chin-ups 'cuz my arms won't hold my weight like they used to."

Adam's homemade fitness equipment had been gathering dust in the barn all summer. A champion wrestler and circus strongman until he took up farming in earnest, Adam had enjoyed robust good health until March, when a careless automobile driver had forced him off the road. His two best horses had been destroyed and Adam, badly injured, had taken months to heal during the busiest time of the farming year. Thanks to good neighbors, including Walter and Leo Kimball, Jessy had kept the farm going, and thanks to the Lord, Adam had mended well.

Jessy patted her brother's arm and assured him in gentle tones, "You're still as strong as an ox. I'm thankful to God you're up and around and doing so well."

He patted her hand. Together they continued their endless chores.

"Adam Flint! Hello?" a strong male voice called from outside.

"Hello, Ed!" Adam greeted their neighbor. "Are we all set?"

Jessy wondered what the two men were talking about. Ed Mannon and his sons had found Adam on the road after the accident. It was Ed who had brought Adam home and helped Jessy with some of the work that past spring in addition to tending to his own vast farm down the road from theirs.

"Come see her! My new baby!" Ed told Adam with obvious excitement.

Adam motioned for Jessy to follow, whispering to both of them, "Suzanna don't know a thing about this!"

Jessy and Adam beheld Ed Mannon's shiny new Kissel automobile.

"Got it Saturday," Mr. Mannon exclaimed. "Drives like a baby! Hop in!" When Jessy appeared reluctant, Adam explained in a low voice, "I'm buyin' Ed's used car. Suzanna don't know a thing about it yet!"

"Oh, Adam, is that wise? Cars are so expensive! Shouldn't you discuss buying one first? She may not like the idea because it was a car that caused your accident!"

"Could happen to anyone. Cars is the way of the future! Suzanna will love havin' a car once she drives in it. Come on!"

"But Leo will be calling for me. I'll need time to get ready!" Not even ten in the morning and Jessy's dress was already soiled from work.

"This won't take long. Come on!"

Reluctantly, Jessy obeyed. She had to admit that Ed Mannon's new car was delightful as they chugged down the unpaved country road, leaving a trail of dust as they went. In a few minutes they pulled up to Ed Mannon's farm with its big white house, two silos, and handsome red barn. Parked in the drive was the car Adam wanted, a shiny black gasoline-powered family sedan. Everyone got out of the Kissel.

With his shirtsleeve Ed rubbed an invisible spot from the finish of his old car. "Got her all shined up for you, Adam! I put a full tank of gas in her too. She's ready to roll! The top's up but you can take it down if you want. It's a job, I'll tell you—takes at least two people to do it. Here's the spare tires that fit her. You oughta get a good five thousand miles on these." Ed tugged at a pair of wood-spoked spares standing on the running board, making sure they were secured to the passenger side of the roomy car.

Adam couldn't contain his excitement. His first car! He pulled a wad of folding money from his overalls. "I'll pay you the rest in November, when we sell off the hogs."

"Fine, fine," said Ed, pocketing the money without counting it. "You'll get around better in a car, seeing you were laid up so long."

Jessy had to admit Mr. Mannon was right. Adam had suffered a long, slow recuperation and a car would be a good means of travel. The little automobile travel she had done with Leo had been exhilarating and so much more efficient than real, live horse power. Cleaner too—no droppings to attract flies and vermin. Of course, gasoline fumes were unpleasant, but that was the price of progress, Jessy reasoned in silence.

"Let me show you how to start her up," offered Ed Mannon.

Together the Flints watched Ed pull out the front seat cushion to reveal the gas cap beneath it. Once he removed the cap, he inserted a ruler of sorts into the tank. "Got to make sure you got enough gas, see?" Ed showed them the stick wet with gasoline and marked with gallon indicators. "Full tank. Enough to drive more than a hundred miles easy—twenty-eight miles to the gallon. She'll hold about five gallons tops!"

After Ed replaced the gas cap and seat cushion, he reached under the car, turned a valve, and showed the Flints the oil that dripped out. "Gotta have oil in her, too, don't forget! She's got plenty. Here's how you check the water." At the front of the car, Ed showed them that the big black radiator was full of water. "Now you walk around her and give the grease cups a turn or two." He turned them on all four wheels. "Gotta make sure there's plenty of axle grease in them, and there is. Now comes the fun part."

Ed raised the hood and squirted a few drops of gasoline onto the cylinders. Then he set the spark control inside the car above the steering column. "Play with the throttle a bit; you'll get the hang of it. For starters, it should be set right about here, see?"

Adam and Jessy studied the throttle setting and watched Ed flip on the ignition. Then he walked to the front of the car. "Now it's time to crank her up." A quick jerk of his arm and—miracle—the pretty black car with red leather upholstery and wood trim began quivering all over. Ed hopped inside the car to close down the throttle and advance the spark. "That's it! She's ready to roll! Here're the gears, clutch, and brake. See?"

Once Ed was satisfied that the Flints understood the entire process, Adam and Jessy climbed aboard. As the two rolled down the drive Adam shouted to Ed, "Thanks again, 'n' good luck with your new car! She's a beauty!"

"Be careful!" Ed warned. Still his eyes squinted happily in the sunlight. Once the Flints turned onto the road, the elderly farmer pulled a rag from the bib of his overalls and began polishing the already polished rich blue finish of his new baby.

❦ ❦ ❦

The Flints sat up high in the plush red leather, diamond-tufted seats. "We can see everything!" they said together, laughing.

Indeed the world was clearly visible—at least this grand chunk of it on each side of the road—hedges, creeks, and swelling fields. Industrious farm women were hanging out their Monday wash to dry. Rows of diapers and blue denim overalls snapped and saluted as much as the American flags whipping in the wind this glorious Labor Day.

"Wanna try her out?" Adam pulled over to let Jessy drive.

"It's almost like operating Mr. Kimball's tractor!" Jessy worked the clutch and shifted gears with no difficulty. She liked the feel of the car and enjoyed stepping on the pedals. She took to the new idea of gas-powered engines. How quickly her work went that spring, with the use of the Kimball tractor, when she prepared the earth for plowing and planting while Adam recuperated from his bad accident. Accidents! Jessy watched the road with care and soon let Adam take the wheel again.

"Well done!" he said, proud of Jessy's finesse at the wheel. Once he changed places with her, he squeezed the oomfy rubber horn. A few chickens clucked on the sidelines. Heads of cows and mules turned as the Flints chugged past.

"Gosh, Adam, this is exciting! I'm so happy you bought a car!"

Adam glanced at Jessy with his shrewd green eyes. "You got some money saved from our little windfall," he said, referring to the money the Flints had earned. "Wanna buy a share of the car?"

"No, thanks. I'm saving for marriage," she answered demurely, her growing trousseau uppermost in her mind.

As they enjoyed the pretty views of farmland all around, homes lovingly tended, Jessy remembered how much the Flints had lost a few years ago when a tornado ripped Adam's house away forever.

After the terrible storm, Suzanna's father, George Webb, an attorney who lived in Bethel, had helped the Flints recover. He gave them the home they now occupied, along with its abandoned farm overgrown with weeds and saplings. The old Meredith house had needed repairs inside and out, which Adam did as time and money became available. The rambling two-story had been an empty shell when the Flints moved in. They brought practically nothing with them but the clothes on their backs. Thankfully, the Webbs provided loans and some substantial pieces of furniture. Still, it had been a grinding struggle to recover, slowed by Adam's accident, but eased by the recent reward.

Another horn blast brought Jessy to the present. Over the noise, Jessy shouted, "A wedding, a home, and nice things cost money!"

Adam, husband and father of three, laughed. "A downright fortune!"

Pleased to see him so happy, Jessy shared Adam's laughter. His accident, the tornado, and all the care and worry of the past faded from memory on this beautiful end-of-summer day. Life was good, God graced their lives with the gift of love, and soon Jessy would meet her future husband's family. With Adam driving, the car easily reached the cruising speed of thirty miles an hour Mr. Mannon had promised.

"The car is wonderful!" Jessy said. "But what will Suzanna think?"

"She'll love it," said Adam, brimming with confidence.

However, when they pulled the car up their driveway, the shocked and angry look on Suzanna's face boded no good for Adam Flint's domestic happiness.

CHAPTER 2

❧

"**D**addy, is this ours?" the children cried, thrilled to see the shiny new car. Three golden, curly haired, barefoot youngsters in worn play clothes crowded around the black wonder. Stephen wasted no time opening one of the rear doors and climbing in, with Taddy following. "Wow, Daddy," Stephen said, "this is slick as goose grease!"

"Can we keep it?" Martha wondered as she scrambled up onto her father's lap. "Is it ours forever and ever?"

"Sure is, kids!"

Taddy pushed and wiggled in back, hollering, "Make it go fast, Daddy!"

Eyeing his wife, Adam said, "Later, Taddy. After lunch."

"How fast will it go?" Stephen wondered aloud. "Gee, it's swell!"

The usually melodious Suzanna wailed, "Adam Flint, how could you? Are you out of your mind?"

"Sweetheart, please!" Adam began. He stopped the engine and got out to take her into his arms, but still she refused to calm down.

"It was a car that caused your accident! They're so dangerous! Children, come back here at once! Go inside and wash for lunch!"

As the children reluctantly obeyed, Adam said calmly, "A car's no more dangerous than horses. Come and look." Gently he steered her toward the car. With his big arms around her, he beamed at their reflection in the shiny finish. Everyone who knew them thought they made a most handsome couple—but not today. Suzanna's pretty face contorted with rage. She wriggled out of her husband's arms.

She refused to look at their reflection. "The least you can do is discuss major purchases with me before you make them!" Without letting him speak she fumed, "Lunch is ready, if you're finished touring the country-side!"

"None for me, thanks," said Jessy, climbing out of the car. "I'm going

13

to a cookout!" Once Suzanna returned to the house, Jessy said quietly to Adam, "I told you so."

"Just wait till you get married!" he said with a wink. "A man has a right to buy something nice for his family, don't he?"

"If and when I marry, my husband will talk things over with me—talk and pray." Not wishing to offend, Jessy added tenderly, "It's a really fine car. I'm glad you got it."

Jessy went inside and checked the kettle of water heating for her bath. The cuckoo clock rattled crazily in the hall. She counted the tones, fearful of being late for her date. "Eighteen o'clock!" she thought with a grin. "It's nearly tomorrow and today's not even halfway over!"

❧ ❧ ❧

Once Jessy had bathed and donned a fresh corset, petticoat, and new ecru stockings, she dressed in her prettiest outfit—a tan gored walking skirt that fell just above her ankles, teamed with a graceful ivory blouse that was all tucks and pleats and delicate pink-and-green embroidery. Around her slender waist she fastened a rose belt with upward and downward crests, then slipped into her best, bowed leather dress shoes.

"Now for the hair," she told her reflection. After a furious brushing, she shaped her dark gleaming mane into a long twist she pinned at the back of her head. She pulled a few wispy, curling bangs about her forehead and temples, then pinned on her hat with two seven-inch hat pins. Her beige straw hat had a broad flat brim, pale pink silk flowers, and two rose satin ribbons down the back. Then she checked the contents of her small drawstring bag—a hanky, a hair brush, and a few safety pins.

When Jessy came down the stairs, Adam and Suzanna paused in their heated discussion of money. Suzanna insisted on lending Jessy the cameo set in gold her parents bought in Naples, Italy, a few years before.

In the hall mirror, Jessy fastened the brooch, promising to take good care of it. "Ah, to dream," Jessy said. "Imagine what it would be like to see such wonderful places! Sunny Italy!"

Suzanna hugged her. "Have a glorious day! I'll be thinking of you!"

Jessy beamed warmly at Suzanna. She touched the pin at her throat. "This is really very thoughtful of you. Do I look all right?"

"You look splendid!" Suzanna squeezed Jessy's hand. "Now I must get back to my sewing. School starts tomorrow!" Toward the kitchen she hollered, "You children clean up after yourselves, now, and don't chip those dishes! And Martha, I expect to hear that piano lesson of yours played all the way through!"

A loud, blasting *ahh-ooo-ga* sounded outside. Jessy peeked out to see a sporty new Simplex convertible pulling up the drive with Leo Kimball at the wheel. He was squeezing the rubber ball of an elaborately twisted brass horn. "Ah-*ooo*-ga!" Leo said, mimicking the horn when he caught sight of Jessy coming out the front door.

Inwardly, Jessy ahh-*ooo*-gahed at Leo. What a man, and what taste! She was speechless at the sight of his convertible with its ivory finish, brass fittings, deeply polished wood trim, and French headlights that looked like miniature chandeliers.

"Well, what do you think?" Leo asked, removing his hat and motoring goggles as he stepped out to greet her. His knuckles were bruised from tinkering with the engine, but he beamed with pride. "Isn't she something? Custom built! You look ripping!" He whistled for emphasis.

"Thank you," said Jessy with a modest smile. In a haze she added, "My, what a fantastic car! Is this the one you went to New York to buy?"

"Wait till you ride in it!" Emma Kimball, Leo's fair-haired, delicately freckled young sister, looking dusty, was sitting in the passenger-side front seat. "Leo's been working on it for weeks. It goes like lightning!" Emma crackled something in her mouth for emphasis.

Alarmed, Jessy asked, "What's that you're chewing? Not tobacco, I hope."

"It's Blibber-Blubber," Emma said, giggling. "I can blow bubbles, see?" She demonstrated by forming a gummy ball. Her pale, wide-set eyes grew big as she puffed to make the pink ball swell with air.

"If you get even one speck of that stuff on my car, I'll blubber you," warned Leo, referring to the rich tan leather seats.

"Everything's under control, just like your spitballs! See?" Emma retracted the gooey blubber ball with an expert flick of her pretty pink tongue and merrily continued chewing. "I'm not stupid enough to get this stuff on my clothes, you know. I'd never get it off!" Emma checked over her white dress with long A-line skirt and fresh navy-striped bodice.

When Jessy complimented Emma on her pretty outfit, Emma said, "My sister Laura got it for me last time she was in Chicago, but what I really wanted was a hobble skirt like hers."

Jessy had seen Laura, Emma's and Leo's eldest sister, around Bethel once in a rare while and what a splendid figure she cut, that glamour girl with connections to the Chicago fashion business. Though she lived in rural Bethel, she was always ahead of its women in matters of style.

"Jessy, you should see Laura in that skirt," Emma gushed. "She looks like a mermaid! It's real tight all the way down to her ankles! That's why it's called a hobble skirt, because all she can do is hobble in it. Mum said I get into enough trouble as it is and couldn't have one till I'm eighteen, but by then hobble skirts will probably go out of style!"

"Poor Emma! So deprived!" cried Leo in mock agony. "Woe is she!"

Meanwhile, Adam approached cautiously, his mouth hanging open at the sight of Leo's dazzling new car idling in the drive. He shook hands with Leo and said, "This musta set you back plenty!"

"Six thousand," said Leo with pride. "Six thousand and then some."

"Must ride like a dream," said Adam wistfully.

"It does indeed. I'll take you for a spin sometime if you like. My folks gave it to me for finishing my degree in mechanical engineering."

"You worked on that degree forever!" Emma jeered. "Practically my whole life. Well, almost half my life anyway."

"Six years, more or less, whenever I could take an interest." Leo smoothed his dark, waving hair and adjusted the collar of his black sateen shirt. His engine rumbled in neutral, roaring to go. "Ready, Jessy?"

"Well, I'll be seein' you," said Adam with a polite cough. "All of you be careful now 'n' have a good time." He turned and climbed the porch steps with the aid of his cane.

Jessy, chewing on her lower lip, fought an unbearable aching to be with Leo, while the sight of Adam with his cane tugged at her heartstrings. She went to her brother to ask softly, "Do you want me to stay home today and help you?"

Adam smiled and shook his head. "'Course not! Go on 'n' enjoy your time with Leo 'n' his family."

"I don't have to go, you know. I mean, there's so much to do here and—"

"Everythin's under control," Adam assured her. "I may start on the heatin 'n' wirin' projects today, takin' measurements 'n' makin' a list of supplies I'll need. Think Suzanna'd like a furnace and electricity?"

"Oh, yes, Adam! They would make her life easier!"

"Easier for us all!" Adam's green eyes filled with good humor. "Now you go on. Leo's waitin' for you."

Jessy nodded gently. "Yes, sir." She turned to Leo, asking quietly, "How's your arm? Are you all right?"

"Just fine," he said, shrugging his impressiv shoulders and smiling at Jessy. "You look terrific!"

"Thank you. So do you," she murmured, feeling the fluttering of the most delightful butterflies just looking at Leo.

Emma wasn't quite finished airing family secrets "Daddy and Mum were furious with Leo for flunking out of school that time "

"Hey! No squealing!" Leo warned. His olive face darkened visibly. "Get in the backseat so Jessy can sit up front."

Emma complied, but with a frown. "Well, what's the big secret? They got you back into school on the condition you stopped playing baseball long enough to get your degree, 'so you would have a decent career to fall back on' and then you demanded a bribe to boot—this fancy car! Some deal, huh, Jessy?"

So. Jessy's eyes narrowed at this revelation. Everyone in Bethel, Jessy included, thought Leo left college because he was homesick! She was struck, too, by the irony of her situation. Given the opportunity to attend college, book-loving Jessy would have worked diligently to pay her way through, if only she hadn't been orphaned and then tied to the hard work of farming.

Emma chimed, "Some people get everything on a silver platter!"

"Ignore old Jealous Puss, Jessy. What do you think of my car?"

"It's wonderful, Leo!" Jessy said with feeling.

She knew that, earlier in the summer, before she had given in to Leo's requests that they see each other regularly, he had taken a train to New York City to pick up his fabulous hand-built Simplex directly from the makers. Then he drove it alone the full thousand miles back to Bethel over roads that were hardly roads, very few being paved for automobiles.

After such a rough ride, Leo spent a month working on the car at home, when he wasn't playing ball or helping his father.

Leo pulled a long beige linen coat and veil from the backseat. "Here, Jessy. I brought these so you won't get dusty."

"You better wear them, Jessy. I should've too." Emma shook dust from her clothes and jaunty straw boater.

Jessy put the long linen motoring duster over her clothes, then draped and tied the sheer veil over her face and new hat. Leo put on his cap and goggles and opened the passenger door for Jessy. He helped her into the bright, long, topless, rumbling sportscar, so different from Adam's dark, wide, sedate family sedan.

Leo watched with considerable interest as Jessy lifted her skirt to sit in his car. Horrified that her calf had showed, Jessy quickly smoothed her long gored skirt as she settled into the seat. What must he think?

From his grin, he liked what he had seen. He predicted: "Women's clothes will change because of the automobile. Skirts will get narrower and hems will go up, up, up!" With that he shut the car door.

"Is that so?" Jessy asked once he climbed in.

"They have to." After Leo pulled the car onto the road, he added, "It's impossible to drive a car in those—those things! You women will be wearing bloomers everywhere, just like my bike-riding sister."

Jessy turned to Emma, who was giggling. "Do you wear bloomers?"

"Sure. All the girls in my class do. How could we bike around in long, stupid skirts? Our hems would get all tangled up and greasy in the gears!"

"I see," said Jessy. "I've never tried riding a bicycle."

"You ought to!" said Emma. "After we eat lunch you can practice on mine all you want. I'll even lend you a pair of bloomers!"

Though this really made Leo happy, Jessy disappointed him with her dour response. "Thank you, Emma, but I'm afraid I could have none of that! Why, it's indecent for a woman to—"

As Leo slid the car into higher and higher gears, he said, "You ought to be a nun, Jessy! That's what my teammates say: 'Jessy Flint will have nun of this and nun of that!'" he teased.

"So! You've been talking about me to your friends, have you?"

"Sure! You're a curiosity to them—a good girl! There's so few of them around anymore."

Jessy wanted to answer but sensed this was no time for discussing morality. The fifty-horsepower engine was roaring like the fine-tuned machine that it was and the dust flying about them was intense.

"My car's made of chrome-nickel steel and gun iron!" Leo shouted happily.

"Where are we going, anyway?" Jessy cried.

"To pick up Burl!" Leo shouted.

"Burl Everett," Emma explained. "He's married to our sister Laura."

Jessy nodded. She had seen Burl, the trainmaster, at the Bethel station whenever the Flints shipped fattened livestock to Chicago.

"Burl should be getting off work about now." As Leo gunned the engine, he told Jessy with pride, "My car will do seventy an hour easy. Wanna see?"

"Say yes, Jessy!" Emma shouted from behind. "It's absolutely thrilling!"

In those days before seat belts and other safety features, cars were little more than combustion engines on spidery wheels. Ignoring the danger, Jessy nodded mischievously. Leo, with an adept hand, turned one sharp corner after another hardly slowing the car, until he reached a flat, smooth, deserted straightaway.

"Now watch carefully!" he told the girls as he stepped on the gas. The Simplex nearly flew.

Instead of being scared, Jessy found Leo's car as exciting as its owner. "Wow, Emma, you're right! How thrilling!"

For a short way, Leo let Jessy take the wheel. "What a wonderful car!" she said of Leo's beautiful handcrafted joy. Regardless, she would not admit that her long skirt did interfere with her driving. But Jessy in bloomers?

"Boy, Leo, you must really love Jessy to let her drive!" squealed Emma as Leo and Jessy exchanged places again. "He hasn't let anyone touch this car since he got it, Jessy!"

Jessy blushed but said nothing. Leo looked annoyed at his sister but pleased with Jessy, his car, and himself. He sped along the railroad line until he pulled up to the train station, a square building in the Gothic style. A grain elevator towered nearby. All three passengers got out.

In the hot sun, the station looked deserted. Tall grass, dry and dusty, waved along the tracks. Jessy noticed tiny but brilliant wildflowers growing at her feet, God's little miracles sprouting in the dust. She was about to point them out to Leo, but he had gone on ahead of her.

"Burl? Hey, Burl! You ready to go?" shouted Leo as he entered the station. Jessy followed at a small distance, with Emma close beside her.

The short but powerfully built stationmaster stepped out of his private office and into the passenger waiting room where no one was waiting. They had caught Burl unready; he was hurriedly pulling the navy blue jacket of his uniform over his vest and stiffly starched white shirt. While he readied himself he nodded to the Kimballs: "Hi, Leo. Emma. My replacement hasn't showed up yet—can't leave till he does. Come on inside." From a vest pocket, Burl removed a pocket watch bright as his buttons and compared it to the official railroad clock on the waiting room wall. "He should be here in a few minutes. Have a seat." Burl gestured to the empty mahogany benches.

"Have you met Jessy?" Leo asked him proudly.

Burl Everett tipped his hat to her. "I've seen you around with your brother."

Jessy smiled and nodded politely. She was struck by Burl's deep-lidded, large brown eyes that seemed to drink her in—shoes, motoring duster, corset, high-collared blouse, hat, streamers, veil, hair, body, and all. Blushing, she turned to Leo.

"It's hot in here! Let's wait outside," Leo suggested, taking Jessy's arm. "There are benches out back."

Jessy went with him, grateful to sit in a pleasant breeze, but Emma stayed inside, blowing gummy bubbles and chatting with her brother-in-law. From outside, the two could hear Burl and Emma's laughter echoing in the otherwise empty waiting room.

Once Leo and Jessy sat down, she said, "That Emma is a character!"

"What a pest!" he said. "One good thing about college—besides the collegiate baseball team, that is—was being away from my sisters. All three of them drive me crazy!"

"I didn't know that you finished your degree in mechanical engineering."

"Yes, in May. I like designing things and working with my hands. I repair all my dad's gasoline engines."

"Do you want to be an engineer?"

"Only if I can't play baseball."

The roar of a train drowned out conversation. They watched it pull into the station, all its bells and whistles going, spewing cinders everywhere. The steaming iron monster slowed to a grinding halt near the bench where Jessy sat with Leo. A few passengers got off and a railroad crew unloaded luggage, sacks of mail, a bundle of newspapers, and a citrus crate from Florida with a brilliant label. In a few minutes, the crew got back on board and the train pulled out again, chugging and heaving as it picked up speed along the shiny tracks. Jessy watched all the proceedings with interest.

"You came here from back East, didn't you?" asked Leo.

"Yes, on a train just like that one," Jessy said, her face filled with light. "We roared right into this very station, right to this very spot! I was fourteen at the time and had no idea what I was in for. The price of love! I just had to see my brother, that's all I knew. In faith I stepped off that train and into a whole new way of living. I remember that cold March day as if it were yesterday. I had no idea what to expect, except that God called me to be here, and here I've stayed."

"Think you'll always want to stay in Bethel?"

Beneath the veil, Jessy's delicate ivory face flushed with sudden pleasure. "Always, unless God has something else in mind."

Leo smoothed his full black moustache and pursed his lips. "Well, maybe you might like to travel again. If I get into the majors, we'll be on the road most all the time. Would you mind that?"

Jessy thrilled to the thought of being with Leo always, but with eyes lowered, she said simply, "I'd go wherever my husband wanted."

A horse-drawn carriage approached, driven by the railroad employee scheduled to relieve Burl Everett for the afternoon shift. Leo cranked up his glorious new car as Burl and Emma got into the backseat. This time, when Leo helped Jessy get in, she made sure her skirt covered her legs during the maneuver. Successful, she gave Leo a bemused sidelong glance.

He blew her a little kiss as he shut the door. "The most beautiful nun in the world," Leo said, laughing at her.

"What's so bad about being good?" Jessy asked as he pulled from the station.

"Oh, nothing, nothing at all. Don't change a thing! I love you just the way you are."

"Sure you do," said Burl from the backseat. "And the minute you get married, you'll want everything different!"

"The voice of experience?" Emma teased. "Or doom, maybe?"

Burl Everett's dark, dreamy eyes turned from the teenaged bubble blower to Jessy, silent as a nun, and then to Leo, whose gifted hands worked the car into higher and higher gears down the dusty road.

As they sped along, only Jessy noticed a faded sign posted in front of an abandoned apple orchard. The sign read *Eden*. The iron gates were locked and rusty, but snakes still coiled around its bars.

CHAPTER 3

❦

At the end of the road, the Wilcox Bait and Gun Shop sign read *Closed*, but Leo got out of the car anyway. He rattled a side door that led upstairs to the living quarters of the owners, according to the mailbox, Mr. and Mrs. Chad Wilcox. In a moment Leo returned to the car with a note in his hands. "They've left for our house already. Darlene wrote us a note."

Jessy had seen Leo's middle sister Darlene, and her husband, Chad, once in a while around Bethel, but much of their time they spent here at their combined home and store.

The unpainted wooden building on the edge of Lake Bethel resembled something out of Wild West picture books Jessy had seen, except for the fishing boats and canoes for rent, chained together in stacks to one side of the yard. The shop looked packed with sporting gear.

The second floor living space formed a deep balcony over the first. Visible from the road was a line in back where clothes had been hung to dry from largest to smallest: papa, mama, and little-boy clothes in a row. On the porch were three rocking chairs. Golden dust from the unpaved road rose up lazily in the early afternoon sun, sifting a drowsy haze down over the place.

"Would you like a soda, Jessy?" Leo asked. He gestured to a big tin-lined cooler on the wooden walkway in front of the store.

Jessy declined but Emma yipped, "Yes! Cherry! I'm dying of thirst!"

Sighing, Leo said, "I wasn't talking to you. Got any money?" He stuck out his open palm.

Emma slapped it gently. "Of course not, silly, don't you have a nickel?"

"No, not for you, I don't."

Burl reached into his pocket for coins. "Here, Leo. I'll have a cola while you're at it."

Leo went back to the cooler, dropped the money into a slot, lifted the heavy lid, and fished out a bottle of cola standing in the icy waters. Straightening himself tall and lithe, he snapped off the cap at the side of the machine, taking care not to spatter his gray, neatly pressed pants.

Emma sang out to Jessy loud enough for her brother to hear, "Leo never carries much of anything in his trouser pockets. He doesn't like them looking bumpy!"

From the cooler, Leo called out, "No cherry, blubber mouth!"

Still in the backseat, Emma threw her chewing gum on the dusty ground and stuck out her tongue at him. "Surprise me, then."

Leo grinned devilishly as he returned to the car with two opened bottles. He gave Burl the cola and then, with his piercing blue eyes and white teeth shining in the sun, said to Emma, "Here you are, blubber brains! This should clean out that mouth of yours."

"Sarsaparilla? I *hate* sarsaparilla and you *know* I do! It tastes like medicine! *You* drink it!"

"You asked for soda and you got it! Now be quiet!"

"Emma's about as quiet as fireworks." As they drove away, Burl said to Jessy, "Chad and Darlene have a boy named Billy."

"He's seven years of trouble!" Emma added. "A pip-squeak gunslinger!"

"Jessy," said Burl, "Emma means Billy is seven years old and plays with popguns. Incessantly."

"I call him Wild Billy Wilcox! What a nuisance!" Emma whined.

"Look who's talking!" Leo rejoined.

Burl offered Emma his cola. "I'll swap with you if you like."

"Gee, thanks. *Some* fellas have nice manners," Emma said, kicking Leo's seat directly in front of her.

"Hey, don't mess up my car, blubber foot! What do you think of it, Burl?"

"The car or darling blubber buss here?"

"The car, of course," Leo said. "Who cares about blubber?"

"The car is a beauty, and all for a mere million dollars!" Burl took a long swig of sarsaparilla. "Is it paid for?"

"Of course. Dad sent me to New York with a certified check." Leo turned suddenly to Jessy. "In a few minutes, you'll meet my whole family!"

"I've seen some of them in town," she said, "but I don't know them." Not having been born or schooled in Bethel put Jessy at a disadvantage.

"Laura's just come back from a fashion trip. She goes to Chicago all the time to pose for illustrators." Emma paused to study her nails, so stubby compared to Laura's perfect claws. "She looks just like a cat. Wanna see?" From under the backseat, Emma withdrew a catalog which she handed to Jessy.

Jessy looked at the fashion drawings with considerable interest but was unfamiliar with the mail-order house. "These look like the clothes and accessories college women might buy."

"That's what they are, college clothes and perfumes and stuff like that!" Emma chimed. "Not that Laura's ever been to college."

"Laura barely made it through high school," said Leo, apparently forgetting that Jessy hadn't been to high school or college.

Jessy cringed, feeling suddenly stupid among this accomplished clan—a train master, a mechanical engineer/baseball hopeful, and a fashion model. There was no way Jessy Flint could finish high school, let alone dream of college. Her brother's farming projects had been never-ending. Then there was the tornado, wrecking everything. She was glad to be alive and fortunate to be able to visit the town library now and then. How could she ever fit in with such sophisticates? Jessy's train of thought was broken by a resounding snap of bubble gum.

Emma, having finished her soda, had opened a fresh pack of Blubber. *Bless Emma's strawberry blonde little heart*, thought Jessy, *so breezy and approachable*. Jessy perused the catalog with Emma, who leaned forward from the backseat and provided a running commentary about the delicately tinted drawings. From the look of the varied faces and body types represented, numerous models had posed for the big-city catalog artists.

"That's her! Those illustrations there! I wish I was Laura! She posed in every one of those hats! Look at her in sweaters and skirts, too, starting on page fifty-seven. She doesn't get to keep any of the clothes, except sometimes. Laura's so tall and beautiful. She moves just like a cat! She has such a tiny waist!"

Leo said dryly, "Your waist would be tiny, too, if you didn't sneak around eating that junk you always manage to find, blubber bottom!"

Emma howled, "Is it my fault Mum's so tight with food? You'd think we were poor, the way she makes us starve! Her and her never-ending diets!"

Jessy coughed politely. "Laura has your pretty coloring, Emma. You both favor your father in that regard. Laura does look like a cat, in a way, especially with such dramatic, almond-shaped blue eyes, like a Siamese cat."

Emma agreed. "You're right! She likes sable coats and stuff like that, you know, fuzzy browns and tans and fur, and long turquoise scarves, the kind that get tangled up in everyone's soup. I'd rather wear lip-smacking red!"

Burl and Leo glanced in Emma's direction. Jessy's eyes widened, but she said nothing. She kept turning pages: Laura ignoring a trigonometry book, Laura swinging a golf club, Laura lounging with coeds and lanky football players, Laura smashing a tennis ball. Jessy's eyebrows raised to see Laura up to her creamy shoulders in bubble bath. "She posed for *this?*"

"Yeah, just her head! The artist dreamed up the rest!" Emma laughed.

Leo glanced from the road to the rear passenger seat. "You're not laughing, Burl. How come?"

Sighing, Burl stared at the fast-moving scenery as the car sped along. "If the money wasn't so good I'd tell Laura to stop posing, but she likes fancy clothes, expensive furniture, the works! She never stops shopping."

"Like mother, like daughter," said Leo. "Well, here we are, Jessy. Home sweet home."

"Such a humble abode, don't you think, Jessy?" mused Burl.

"Your place could fit in ours like a bug in a bathtub!" Emma teased Burl, who steamed in silence. "Well, it could, couldn't it?" Emma persisted. "Laura's always saying—"

"I know what she's always saying! You don't have to remind me."

Whether Burl wanted to be reminded or not, Emma said, "Laura likes big spreads. The bigger, the better!"

Leo repeated, "Like mother, like daughter. Shall we?"

Leo had pulled up the drive lined with cars and buggies to a house that looked for all the world like the American dream achieved—signed, sealed, and manicured. The Kimballs owned a vast two-story Victorian cream puff of a house painted gold with soft, gray-blue shutters and matching front door fitted with a solid bronze knob, knocker, and mailbox. The steps leading to the porch were flanked by well-groomed bushes and perky red geraniums in flower boxes. An American flag waved in the breeze, a reminder of this national holiday.

Leo helped Jessy out of the car as Burl and Emma went on ahead. A *showplace*, thought Jessy as she took Leo's hand. The house stood like a queen among numerous well-built, beautifully maintained farm buildings and zigzagging white fences that outlined horse pastures and other grazing fields, with not a weed or sagging blossom in sight.

"You're cold," Leo said, patting her small hand with both of his. "Don't be scared. They'll love you! How can they help it?"

If her throat hadn't been so dry, she would have said she was never afraid because the Lord watched over her, but instead she only smiled as she ascended the stairs with him, pausing a moment to look at the porch flooded with sunlight. The flooring had recently been painted a bright robin's egg blue. Pretty white wicker chairs cushioned with gaily flowered chintz looked inviting but stood empty. A starburst quilt had been casually but artfully draped over a rocker. On a wicker table were roses in a deep green vase and a tray of cookies. Leo helped himself to one.

"I'm starving," he explained. "Emma's right about one thing. Mum's always telling us we shouldn't spoil our appetites. I say, what are appetites for?" Leo offered her the tray.

"No, thanks," said Jessy, sure the butterflies in her stomach weren't hungry for sweets. Under his gaze, she removed, folded, and returned the long linen wrapper. "Thank you, Leo. I really enjoyed our ride!"

"Me, too, but it would have been a whole lot more fun without Emma!" Leo left the dusty motoring cloak on one of the porch chairs and then opened the front door for her. "Ladies first."

For a split second, as Jessy went from the blinding sunlight to the dimly lit vestibule, she felt something was wrong. Dismissing the feeling as nonsense, she entered the cool, stately hall. Alone with Leo, she went to the nearby mirror framed in gilt stucco. While he straightened his hair and collar, she removed the motoring veil.

As her eyes became accustomed to the dark interior, she began to see its detail—the pale green walls, chic black-and-white inlaid floor, chinoiserie urns and umbrella stands, a small but ornately carved black enamel chair with a black-and-white striped seat cushion. On the small marble-topped satinwood table beneath the mirror stood a hand-cut crystal bowl filled with freshly cut flowers.

"Lovely, Leo, really lovely," she said. Without warning, she suddenly felt weak.

"I want to show you something." Leo led her to a grouping of framed pictures on one wall.

"My grandfather—my mother's father," Leo said proudly. He pointed to the oldest picture in the hall, a daguerreotype. "Of all his grandchildren, Mum says I look most like him."

"Count Dimitri Alexandrov!" Jessy cried, remembering how Leo had told her of the imperial Russian who left his homeland for America in the 1850s. Jessy took a long look at the distinguished portrait. Unexpectedly she shivered.

The similarities between Count Dimitri and "Count Smoke" were numerous and striking. Both tall, dark, and slender, they had light eyes, full moustaches, and high cheekbones. Count Dimitri wore a dashing military uniform, a sword at his hip, a sash and swags across his chest, huge epaulets at his shoulders, and numerous medals. His dark hair was shorter than Leo's and he wore it differently—cropped close to his head and brushed forward in flat, comma-shaped curls. Their faces were nearly alike except for a prominent beauty mark on the Count's left cheek.

"I wish he hadn't died before I was born! There's so much I would have asked him. Look at this, Jessy," said Leo, pointing out a recent family photo. "You've met Dad. Here's Mum. She looks like the Count, too, with dark hair and the same blue eyes. And here's Laura, Burl, Darlene, Chad, Billy, and Emma."

As Jessy took in the details of the family, the fashionable females and well-groomed males, a brooding feeling overcame her, a powerful sensation that made her take a deep heavy breath. Without analyzing her thoughts she blurted out, "But where's Peter?"

Astonished, Leo asked coldly, "Who told you about him?"

"No one! I haven't the faintest idea why I said that!" Feeling foolish and seeing she had unintentionally hurt Leo, she put a hand to her tremulous rosebud mouth. "I'm sorry, Leo. I don't know what came over me!" Jessy crossed her arms and clutched her shoulders, trying to warm herself. She began to pace. "I just had this sudden impression. I can't explain it. When we came in the door, I started to feel weak. That's not like me at all. I'm not weak; I don't see things that aren't there." As they both struggled to recover, she asked, "Does someone named Peter live here?"

"No!" Leo, pale as she had ever seen him, whispered, "He's at Fair Haven. He's been there for years—since 1885."

"Fair Haven?" Jessy had heard of the mental institution thirty miles distant, but how did she blurt out Peter's name? No one had ever mentioned him to her, she knew that. Slowly, quietly she said, "As soon as I saw that family portrait, I knew someone was missing—a Kimball who belonged. You said I would meet all your family today. Who's Peter?"

"My older brother," Leo answered flatly, without looking at her.

Learning such a handsome and capable young man as Leo had a brother gladdened Jessy, but also puzzled her. "You never told me you had a brother. You said: three sisters, two brothers-in-law, a nephew, your dad's parents—Grandpa Roy and Grama Flo, the ones who live on the farm here in Bethel where your father grew up—but you never told me you had a brother. Why?"

"We don't ever talk about him. He was born before I was. Laura barely remembers him and she's the oldest—the oldest except for him, that is."

Troubled that Leo didn't speak of his brother by name, Jessy asked, "Why don't you talk about Peter?"

With unveiled annoyance Leo snapped, "Try to understand! He's been locked up for years! It upsets my folks to bring up the subject, so we never do."

"Oh, I see," said Jessy, not seeing at all. "Do you visit Peter?"

"Of course not! He's insane! Let's not stand here talking all day!"

"I'm sorry. It was such a surprise to me, that's all."

Finally aware of the shock Jessy must have experienced, Leo asked, "Are you all right? Do you want to sit down?"

"No, not at all! Let's join the fun! They sound like they're having a grand time." Jessy turned toward the back of the house where, through windows in rooms beyond the vestibule, she could see a crowd of people on the back lawn. Smiling, she said, "Half the world must be here!"

He laughed. "No, not half. Maybe just a quarter. Come on." He led her through the house to the backyard.

Jessy took in the long buffet tables spread with bowls, plates, baking dishes, and trays full of food. Several youngsters—teenage boys and girls from neighboring farms that retained what was known in Bethel as The Old Religion—had been hired by the Kimballs to help prepare and serve the meal. Jessy had seen these modest, hardworking young adults in Bethel, who, like their elders, wore homespun clothes and shunned modernity. The girls wore white, hand-stitched caps covering their hair.

Leo said, "Mum hires them for all sorts of odd jobs—cleaning, quilting, and such. Have some food." He handed Jessy an empty luncheon plate and steered her toward a long table laden with offerings.

As they took dibs and dabs from silver platters and crystal dishes set on tables under the shade trees, Leo introduced Jessy to a host of people she knew by sight. The couple found two seats at a table under a lime green beach umbrella. Jessy ate with relish, enjoying all the fresh, homemade country food. As she sipped lemonade and began eating a creamy confection piled high on her dessert dish, she was interrupted by a silky but authoritative voice.

"Too much of that and your pretty belt won't fit!"

The voice that addressed Jessy rose up out of what fashion writers called a handsome woman, dressed, to Jessy's thinking, inappropriately in a diaphanous chiffon gown that floated over a tightly fitting underdress girded over a stiff, no-nonsense corset. Her dark hair had been piled into an elaborate mélange lacquered to withstand any disturbance this day might bring.

"Mum!" Leo stood at once. "I'd like you to meet Jessy. Jessy Flint!"

Jessy stood too. As soon as Leo finished kissing Mum, Jessy extended her hand to the blue-eyed beauty who looked, without question, to be the daughter of Count Dimitri. "It's an honor to meet you, Mrs. Kimball," said Jessy, awed. Jessy retrieved her rough, hardworking hand from the soft one Acacia had extended. "Thank you for inviting me!"

"Not at all!" Words rolled like satin from the stately woman's mouth. "Have you met everyone?"

"I've met a quarter of the world, I think, but I didn't meet everyone!"

Mrs. Kimball smiled graciously. "There's plenty of time, the whole afternoon and evening, for introductions and—"

"Nope, not for us, Mum. We have a game planned later this afternoon." Leo's matter-of-fact declaration took both women by surprise.

"Co-ed baseball!" chirped the irrepressible Emma Kimball. The strawberry blonde had already changed into bright red bloomers, a sweatshirt, and baseball cap. She held a half-empty plate. "As soon as I finish this and about six different desserts, I'll be ready to batter up, Count Smoke-in-Your-Eye!"

When the two siblings began arguing, Mrs. Kimball intervened. "Stop it, both of you or I'll send you upstairs!" Mrs. Kimball yanked away Emma's plate, saying, "You will confine yourself to one portion of dessert: fresh fruit." Ignoring her whining daughter, who drifted off to another knot of people, Mrs. Kimball turned her attention to Leo. Her tone was softer and richer for her handsome son. "Now, Leo, you know what we said earlier!"

"The guys want to play and I promised."

"But what about your date? Just look at her, so neat and prim."

Jessy, despite feeling slighted without quite knowing why, agreed with Acacia Kimball, saying, "Leo, I'm not dressed for sports. I had no idea! As much as I'd like to, I really couldn't join you and your friends."

"She can borrow some of my old things," said a glorious, towering blue-eyed redhead in a clinging champagne-colored hobble skirt, a silk blouse, and a long turquoise scarf draped over her shoulders. Laura Kimball Everett's enormous hat was adorned with feathers unlike any Jessy had ever seen—long, white, and frothy. In a high-pitched voice, the fashion plate screeched: "Hello, Jessy! Does Leo talk about me? What's he say? What's he say? Tell me!"

"Hi, Laura! Emma showed me the catalog you posed for, the college fashion pictures. I was really amazed!"

Laura fanned her long, manicured nails at Jessy and squeaked: "Shoot, that was nothing! You should see the one I'll be in next—Paris evening gowns! Me in *haute couture*, you know? Can't you just picture me?" With practiced ease, Laura struck an ethereal pose that emphasized her long arms and flawless throat, a vision of pure magic until she grabbed Leo, scruffed up his hair, and screeched, "Isn't he a dream?!"

Jessy, recalling the sobering dream she had that morning, searched her mind for some tactful reply.

"Isn't Leo the berries!" Laura adjusted his black sateen collar and squeezed him by his shoulders. "I could just eat him up! They don't make them like this every day!" Laura's voice scraped the treetops.

Unperturbed, Leo broke free of his eldest sister, smoothed himself all over, and in his best ballpark voice demanded, "Where did you get that stupid hat? You better hang on to something heavy or you'll be taking off in the wind with it! How many birds did you kill for it, Laura? You're a menace to wildlife!"

"Isn't he a scream?"

"Bothering your baby brother again?" Burl said casually, wrapping his arm around Laura's teeny waist. As he did, she squealed like a siren. Laura looked down on her husband, a full head shorter than she. Burl looked up, saying, "Lovely Laura the Lighthouse! You could warn ships in the fog with that voice! What do you think of the family, Jessy?" Burl asked in his casual, drawling way. With his heavy-lidded brown eyes he caressed her as he had at the station.

"I think Jessy Flint is a love!" A peach of a matron in a shapeless cotton frock came near. "A real love!"

"Grama Flo!" Leo kissed and hugged his father's mother.

"How's my baby boy?" Flo Kimball asked, looking up to Leo. "You grow much more and I'll need a ladder to say hello to you! Roy. Roy, honey! Come and look at your grandson, all graduated from college and ready to go in the army!"

"The army? No, no, Grama, I'm going to play baseball!"

"Baseball? They told me you were going to put on a uniform!"

"I am! A baseball uniform!"

Everyone laughed, including Flo Kimball, who was reduced to good-natured tears, a mixture of relief and delight. When the laughter slowed, Flo took Jessy's and Leo's hands and told Leo, "You got yourself a nice, good, decent, Christian girl here! Take special care of her!"

"I will, Grama, I will."

At last Jessy could speak. Addressing Leo's grandmother, she said, "Thank you, Mrs. Kimball. You've been very kind to me, and to my family too. We Flints appreciate everything you did for us when Adam was so badly hurt."

Flo Kimball patted Jessy's hand. "Wasn't nothing at all. You'd have done the same for us if things was reversed."

Jessy said to Laura, Burl, and the others nearby, "When my brother was hurt in an accident, Roy and Flo Kimball sent us food and made sure we were all right. Mr. Kimball and Leo came in their tractor to help me with fieldwork. My family never could have managed this year without help from the Kimballs!"

The uncut gem of a woman was teary once again. Blushing, Flo lifted her glasses to mop her eyes with the hem of her apron. "Wasn't nothing at all, just glad you came through okay! Let us know when you need help!"

"Yes, ma'am. You really are—you really are the *berries!*" Jessy looked to Laura who squealed with delight at hearing her pet expression repeated.

A series of explosions stopped all conversation. "Billy, stop that!" cried a small, dark woman from somewhere out of visible range. Soon, a pint-sized terror in a cowboy hat, gunbelt, and holsters came running through the crowd of adults brandishing a pair of six-shooters. Sweating, the small, rounded woman running after him told the family, "Don't worry, the guns aren't real, just noisy! Billy. Billy! Come back here this instant!"

Burl, watching the woman as she ran away from the crowd, confessed to Jessy, "I never knew that Darlene could run so good!"

"Darlene's no runner!" Laura squeezed Burl's ample waist. "She learned how when she had Billy! What a handful that boy is! She should lock him up!"

"Better be quiet, Laura, or you and Darlene will get into it again," Leo said, cautioning his sister. "You know how she gets when you criticize how she and Chad are raising their boy." Then to Jessy he said, "Billy's daddy deals in guns."

Jessy nodded, remembering the Wilcox Bait and Gun Shop. Billy continued running and firing his guns. Wild Billy Wilcox indeed.

"Has anyone seen Chad?" Leo asked. "He's supposed to play left field."

"Chad's showing Daddy some new firearms and traps he just got in. Hunting season starts soon, you know. They've been inside all morning talking," said Laura. "My own father and he won't even talk to me!" she whined. "How often do we get to see each other?"

"You live just down the road, Laura," Leo reminded her. "Maybe you should stay home more often instead of traipsing off to Chicago every chance you get. Can't you stand being home with your husband once in a while?"

Laura pouted. "Is it my fault we have no kids to keep me occupied? When are you going to give me a baby, Burlie, and a nice big house?" She adjusted Burl's tie, even though it didn't need adjusting. Burl took her busy hands in his to make her stop. "And anyway, I can travel free, seeing as I'm a stationmaster's wife. I have more friends in Chicago than I do in Bethel. And the shopping, well, there's nothing like Chicago for shopping!"

"Looks like you go hunting instead of shopping!" Leo laughed. "Where on earth did you get that hat? It looks like the county dump!"

Hurt, Laura gently probed her veranda of a hat piled with bird wings, fruits, and flowers meshed together with netting—the whole dune shored up with giant feathers. "This hat cost a fortune, Leo. Do you really mean you don't like it? All the girls are wearing them." Laura frowned at Jessy's simple hat, so obviously out of style with its streamers and artificial flowers. Laura touched her own birded wonder. "These plumes are tropical, you know; that's why these hats are so expensive. They have to pay the Indians or the trappers or whoever shoots the birds down South, just to get the feathers!"

"What a shame!" blurted Jessy with more emotion than thought. Everyone stopped to stare at her as she went on: "I mean, why, it's a shame to kill a bird just to wear its feathers. I-I've been reading that the birds in th-the Everglades are hunted down when they get their n-nesting plumage—their longest, prettiest f-feathers. The adult birds are shot while they guard the babies in the nest. Once the parents are dead, the orphaned babies die too." Orphaned herself, Jessy stood tall amidst the crowd around her. "Well, anyway, I think that's horrible, killing hundreds of thousands of beautiful birds just for feathers to decorate women's hats!" When no one spoke, Jessy asked, "Well, I ask you, what good can come from killing birds?"

Leo shushed her.

Jessy apologized. "I meant no offense, Laura, but that's what I've been reading. There are societies forming to protect the birds from—"

"Don't tell me Leo's goin' out with a bird-watcher! Bang-bang-bang!"

"Chad!" shouted Leo, greeting his brother-in-law. Turning to Jessy, Leo said, "Chad Wilcox, proprietor of the Wilcox Bait and Gun Shop."

"That run-down old place," drawled Burl. "It's a wonder a good gust of wind don't blow it away, lock, stock, and gun barrels!"

"I don't see you wearin' yourself out haulin' round sacks o' gold, Burl."

"Good afternoon to you too," Burl casually greeted his brother-in-law. "You use a gun good; how are you with a baseball bat?"

"You'll see," retorted Chad, a tall, fair young man with stick-straight yellow hair and amber eyes, a large version of his son Billy.

Darlene, her hair flying loose and sweating from running after her seven-year-old, joined her husband. "We'll never get him to sleep tonight after a big day like this, Chad, and he's got school tomorrow!"

"Billy in school? Better call out the militia and sound every alarm! Save the poor teachers! Send for the medics!" squeaked Laura. "That kid will burn the schoolhouse down for sure!"

"Seeing as you're not a mother, Laura, you ought to stick to subjects you actually know something about," answered Darlene, "such subjects being few and far between."

A murmur rose up in the crowd at a cold feud gathering heat, a clear case of younger sister becoming a mother sooner than her elder sister. Emma, chewing toffee and wiping her sticky hands on her sweatshirt, had returned to the bosom of her family. While Burl and Chad went off in different directions, Emma asked, "Did someone say that awful word that starts again tomorrow? Summer vacation's over already! I hate school!"

"Speaking of subjects some people know nothing about," started Leo.

Making a face at Leo, Emma struck a Laura-like ethereal pose which looked ludicrous, seeing that she was wearing bloomers and bulky athletic shoes. "I have no need for study," she said loftily. "I just want to get married."

"Married! What a scream!" hooted Laura. "You dumb cluck!"

On the subject of holy matrimony, Laura and Darlene stood in complete agreement. "The drudgery, tedium, frustration . . . " began Darlene.

" . . . that smothering feeling, the lack of romance!" continued Laura.

"Take our advice, kid, and stay free!" both said together to Emma.

Leo clearly wasn't pleased. He said quietly to his intended, "Let's go inside, Jessy. There's something I want to show you."

"Gonna take your girl upstairs to your room, Leo?" Emma teased.

"Watch it, blubber mouth!" Ignoring Emma's jabbing against his arms and back, he turned to lead Jessy inside.

Having witnessed all that had transpired, Jessy looked reluctant to go anywhere at all with Leo. He had to coax her gently along, whispering to her.

"No dirty little secrets, now," cried Emma. "Hey! We're still playing baseball, aren't we?"

"In a while. Al and Mo and Bud and Ryan and Hawk and some of the others will be around later on."

"Shall we dig out our drawers?" asked Laura, screeching with laughter.

"Yes, you should change clothes," Leo said mildly.

Laura, pointing a manicured nail at Jessy, asked Leo in a squeaky echo of their grandmother Flo, "What about this 'nice, good, decent Christian girl' right here? I mean, what's Jessy gonna wear?"

"Bloomers, if you can lend her a pair. And better shoes."

"But, Leo!" Jessy looked down at her pretty shoes. Their bows peeked out from her long skirt. "These are my best shoes!"

"They're adorable, Jessy, but be reasonable. You can't play baseball dressed like that. Borrow some stuff from Laura and Emma. You'll be happier, I promise, and more comfortable."

"I can't wear bloomers, Leo. What would people think?"

"Who cares what they think?" cried Emma, fanning her bloomers around.

"I rest my case," said Jessy, laughing. "Can't I be the umpire or—"

Leo snapped his fingers. "Sure you can ump! Maybe the calls will go my way for a change, with you watching home plate! Come on, let's go inside. There's something I'd like you to see in the parlor!"

"Jessy! Wouldn't you rather ride my bike?" asked Emma. "You can, you know! Wanna see it? It's a Flame Star! Cherry red!"

"Isn't she a scream?" yelled Laura.

Jessy and Leo did their best to ignore his ogling trio of sisters.

CHAPTER 4

❧

In the Kimball parlor all was cool and serene. Acacia played a drowsy, sentimental air on the grand piano. She paused as Jessy and Leo entered the spacious, elegant but irregularly shaped room.

"There's my handsome son," she said, her voice husky velvet. From her open arms the extravagant sleeves of her gown draped nearly to the floor. "Come sit here with me." Acacia made room on the piano bench for Leo.

"Later, Mum. I came to show Jessy our record collection."

While Leo spoke to his mother, Jessy looked over the bookshelves to see what enriched the minds of the Kimballs when they weren't chatting at cookouts. Unfamiliar with any of the titles, she selected a book at random to examine.

"Most of those are Laura's love books," came a familiar voice from a cozy nook. Walter Kimball, the big redheaded farmer and horse trader, was reading in an overstuffed chair.

Startled, but then smiling, Jessy said, "Mr. Kimball! There you are! Sitting all alone, are you?"

Walter chuckled as he joined her on the plush gold-fringed sofa. He flicked the volume in Jessy's hands. "Yep, Laura reads practically nothing but love books from the look of it, and there's some other books of hers up there on the shelves too—the ones she was too lazy to haul over to her place when she got hitched to Burl. Modern drama they call it. European plays, mostly, about well-heeled married women who wish they were dead or in Paris or anyplace but where they're at and wishing they were stuck with anyone else but who they're stuck with, and novellas about potbellied studs trying out fillies that don't belong to 'em, and stories about folks who can't go no place because they got lead in their pants and so they just sit on their porches and gab their lives away, going on and on about what might have been if they could only just pick up their feet and *do* something instead of sitting there and wondering about the millions of other people stuck sitting on porches! And there's some 'studies'—that's what them smart folk call the reports they make up to 'prove' what they think is true about such things as the, ah, well, you got one of them there."

Jessy read aloud the title of the book she held: "*A Study of the Artificial Restraints of Society Concerning Morals with an Exposé on the Folly of Taboos.*" Jessy stopped to say quietly, "But taboos, as I understand them, protect people from harmful activities." Jessy rose to select another book, passing a Bible stand which held instead a hefty volume entitled *Communicating with the Dead: Seances and Other Parlor Amusements*.

Returning to the shelves, Jessy's liquid brown eyes widened with interest as she glanced at title after title: *Telling Fortunes with Cards*; *Hot Jokes for Cold Nights*; *Organized Religion—Who Needs It?*; *The Wit and Wisdom of Charles Darwin*; *Know Your Horoscope—Know Your Future*; *Prudence: Friend or Foe?*; *What You Didn't Tell Me Before We Got Married*; *French in Three Easy Lessons* . . .

Jessy picked up the French book. "I never dreamed a foreign language could be so easy to learn!"

Over the rims of his skinny reading glasses Walter said, laughing, "No one can learn French in three easy lessons unless they're French!"

"Oh," said Jessy, feeling idiotic. She looked back at the shelves.

"Not exactly the Harvard Classics, are they, Jessy?"

She turned to him, laughing and shaking her head. "No, I'm afraid they're not. Tell me, Mr. Kimball, what are you reading?"

"See for yourself!"

Jessy read the title aloud: "*Life Begins at Fifty!*"

Acacia laughed at her husband from her seat at the piano. "I hope for your sake that's true. You're getting old, Walter! Positively ancient!"

Walter, unflustered, answered, "If this writer here's correct, then both of us can expect to wear diapers and crawl around on all fours!"

Acacia shot him a withering glance for revealing her advancing age with so many people about. By this time, Burl, Laura, Darlene, Chad, Billy, Emma, and a clamor of Kimball cousins had joined Acacia at the piano. Soon they were all singing popular songs and playing duets. To the strains of *Sweet Betsy from Pike*, *Clementine*, and *Down in the Valley*, Leo tiptoed to Jessy. "This is what I wanted to show you." Leo led her to a wooden box with a big fluted horn on top. "It's a talking machine. Pick out a record from that rack over there for us to play."

Jessy squealed with delight. "I've read about these in catalogs but I've never heard one!" She looked through the numerous titles: *The Girl I Loved, Fatal Rose of Red, Bagpipes of Scotland* . . . "This one," she said without hesitation, handing the big black disc to Leo.

"*The Talking Barnyard!* Jessy, you can hear that outside any old time!"

Together the two laughed as he played the recording of squealing pigs, mooing cows, clucking hens, and the ringing of a farm triangle signaling that supper was ready. Though she giggled throughout the performance, Jessy was impressed. "My goodness, Leo, it really does sound like those animals are right here in this room! May we try another?"

Leo played one disc after another, popular songs and classics, vaudeville comedians and recitations. Soon everyone had abandoned Acacia at the piano and had surrounded Leo, Jessy, and the talking machine. Even Acacia came to join them when she heard the romantic strains of Chopin recorded by a European virtuoso. After a while, Leo motioned for Jessy to join him in another corner of the room.

"Look through this," he said, handing her a device that looked like binoculars on a stick.

She took it from his hands and gasped. "London! That's Big Ben!" she said with glee at the pretty pictures that glowed inside the stereoscope. "How real everything looks! Show me more!"

"We have hundreds of views. We got Japan! We got Rome! We got the St. Louis Fair! We got Picturesque America! We got the Holy Land!"

"Oh, the Holy Land! Please," said Jessy.

"I've never looked at these myself," Leo admitted.

"Oh, Leo, how wonderful," said Jessy as she gazed at places where Bible personages had been: the Nile, the Sea of Galilee, Bethlehem, and Jerusalem.

Soon the family had migrated from the talking machine to the stereoscope. While Jessy took turns sharing the viewing machine with everyone, Leo whispered to her, "I have something else to show you, too, but not right now. The guys'll be here any minute. I'm going upstairs to change." On his way he asked Acacia, "Can we take a few jugs of lemonade to the game?"

"Oh, you're not going to play ball again today, are you, Leo? You were gone most of Saturday. We're fortunate your right arm didn't fall off at the shoulder. Now, you stay here and rest and visit with your loved ones!"

"Can't, Mum, I promised the guys!" Leo dashed out of the room on his way up the stairs.

Walter and Acacia followed him. Jessy went to the doorway of the parlor.

"Just a minute, son," Walter said to Leo. "Your mother and I don't want you playing ball. Not today."

Leo, halfway up the stairs, beyond the pounding of the piano and all the happy noise from the parlor full of relatives, glared down at his parents. He said quietly, "I have to."

"No, you don't."

"I put off baseball long enough, for six years, just to finish college and make you happy. Now I'm going to do what I want to do!"

"Oh, and what's that?" asked his father of him.

"Three things: become a major league player, pitch another no-hitter like I did a few years ago for the Tri-County League, and marry Jessy!"

Acacia said, "Ballplayers are no better than gunslingers, actors, poolroom hustlers, circus performers, and their kind!"

Jessy felt wounded at this bold attack on Leo and even her brother, Adam, a former circus strongman. She turned to Leo to try to stop this bitter argument, but he wouldn't look at her as he answered his mother.

"As for Mr. Flint, Matt Webb and I watched him wrestle once, a few years ago in Azleton. Jessy's brother was the best—probably always will be! That's what Matt and I thought, and plenty of other people, too, and besides, Adam married Suzanna Webb. She's Matt's brother, and they're both from a good family in Bethel!" Leo nodded to Jessy for emphasis. "As for me, you know I'm a ballplayer and nothing else, not a gangster or anything bad like that. Sure, I like engineering and I'm pretty good at it, but I'm better at baseball than I ever could be at engineering. I have a chance to be a star!"

"You have a chance to throw your life away! We spent a fortune on your college education, Leo, and won't have you wasting that!" roared Walter.

"If I don't make my move to the pros, there's a million guys right behind me dying for the chance!" pleaded Leo, but his parents remained adamant.

"Mr. Kimball. Mrs. Kimball," Jessy said with quiet dignity, "I know you want the best for your son, but as long as Leo glorifies God in whatever he does, well, everything will be all right, truly!"

Acacia's normally marble countenance twisted with contempt at Jessy's words. Steeling herself to regain her composure, she turned to her son. "Leo, you're smart! You understand mechanics, complicated machines I could never hope to understand myself! You are handsome, intelligent, gifted! Why do you throw yourself away on—" Battling mightily not to look at Jessy, Acacia, daughter of far-flung Crimea, said loftily, "Leo, you are of noble blood!"

"Oh, Mum, not that again. I'm a ballplayer! A King of the Mound is about the only royalty I'll ever be, and that's good enough for me. This is America, Mum, not imperial Russia. It's the twentieth century, not the Dark Ages. I can't be a landowning squire and sit here with lead in my pants like Dad was talking about in the parlor a while ago. Now I have to go. Please try to understand." Leo descended the stairs far enough to kiss Acacia on the cheek, but she refused to turn his way. "Dad?"

"Go upstairs, go on with you!" Walter Kimball waved away his son. "Too much has been said already!"

Soon a squad of young sporting men and their girls trooped into the cool green hallway lined with gilt mirrors and pictures of ancestral worthies. Jessy, still smarting from the sharp words Leo and his parents had exchanged, hardly noticed the Al-Mo-Bud-Ryan-Hawk contingent and the Midge-Ruth-Hazel-Marie-Bertha contingent with them.

"Look at all them uniforms, Roy," said Grama Flo. "I just love a fella in a uniform! Wish we could join these nice young folks, don't you?"

Leo's friends tipped their ball caps to the elderly Kimballs, and also to Jessy who stood with the kindly farming couple. She looked from the two warm, pudgy faces of Leo's grandparents, weathered from farming, creased from the laughter and tears of a lifetime, and prayed for understanding. Feeling small, Jessy wanted to love Acacia but she couldn't. She wanted peace but she couldn't have it.

As Jessy waited for Leo, a blessed thought pulsed through her brain, bringing with it peace: *we all have noble blood for all of us have been created in the image of God.*

"Dear Lord, thank You for Your love, Your endless generosity," prayed Jessy quickly, silently, as the group in the hallway discussed the logistics of getting the crowd and all their gear to Lumplyn Memorial Park. "We are all made in Your image. Even Acacia! Even though she doesn't approve of me or my brother, she was made in Your image. Thank You, heavenly Father, for Acacia. In Jesus' name, please bless this home, this family, and all who enter here."

Soon Leo, in his cap and baseball uniform, ran down the steps. As he went, he stuffed his carry bag with his mitt, baseball, and spiked athletic shoes. He smiled to see Laura, Burl, Darlene, and Chad dressed for the game. But his warmest smile was for Jessy, still in her pretty flowered hat, her big bright eyes forgiving and mellow.

Jessy, swept along with the crowd of relatives, friends, children, and the dogs that belonged to Leo's sporting friends, remembered her manners and called out to Walter and Acacia, saying, "Thank you, Mr. and Mrs. Kimball, for a lovely afternoon!"

"Oh, yeah, thanks, it was swell," echoed several of the others.

"In case anyone's looking for us, we'll be playing at Lumplyn Memorial Park," someone shouted.

"Lumpy Land, more likely!" added Emma. "It's got more lumps than Mum's gravy!"

"Is that any way to talk about your own mother, Emma?" questioned one of her friends.

"Mum can't cook a lick! She said her mother told her when she was a girl that if she didn't learn to cook, she'd never have to work in the kitchen!"

Some of the girls giggled, saying, "What a good idea!"

One of Leo's heftiest teammates shouted, "You oughta come to the game, Mrs. Kimball! You've never even seen us guys play! It's fun! Your son's dynamite on the mound! Leo's goin' all the way to the top!"

"What do you say, Acacia?" asked her husband Walter. "Shall we?"

Acacia turned her marble profile from him, from all of them. She glided from their presence, her long chiffon gown billowing behind her, a steel blue locomotive trailing steam and smoke.

Smiling and shrugging his shoulders at Acacia, Grandpa Roy called to the crowd in the hallway: "Can old folks watch this game?"

"Sure! Anyone can watch, only the seats aren't real comfortable!" said Hawk.

"What do you say, Flo?" When Roy offered Flo his arm, she grasped it warmly. "Hey, kids, wait for us, we're coming!"

"Let's go!" someone yelled, and with that, the ragtag crowd trooped out the gray-blue door with the Victorian brass trimming, away from Acacia's dream of gracious living, and into that golden, sultry, all-American late afternoon in the Year of Our Lord 1908.

CHAPTER 5

❦

After a drive, caravan style, from the Kimball home, Jessy—carrying her little drawstring bag, Leo's supply of licorice, and a jug of lemonade—followed their party into the park. Bethel County's Lumpy Land, as Emma so aptly described it, lived up to its name. In addition to the ruts, holes, and stones all over the former cow pasture, the place was littered with the remains of dozens of picnics consumed that holiday. Marching bands had performed, speeches were made, and countless hot dogs consumed. So many games had been played that Monday the grass was nearly worn away. Still, the sight of the field made Jessy and her companions smile. A Labor Day weekend of good weather climaxing in a baseball game seemed the perfectly American way to end the summer.

Leo's friends were young farmers or students or employees of local businesses. Few were as well off as Leo, but they were all young and athletic, with that air of casual confidence that was distinctly American. Some would go to work tomorrow; others would leave for college. On the drive here to the park, Leo had confided to Jessy that he would spend the coming week writing to professional ball clubs in search of a job. Still, the cares of tomorrow seemed far away as the group neared the playing field. Everyone was dressed for sports, except Jessy, still in her Sunday best.

"Oh, no!" moaned Ryan at the sight of two bands of children, the Niners and Ninettes, playing ball on the diamond. "What inning are you at?"

"The fifth!" answered a Niner.

"No, we're still in the fourth," said another.

"I thought we were in the seventh!" chimed a third.

Bud tossed a baseball into his restless mitt. "While we're waiting, we might as well start warming up."

Leo and Al began warming up their pitching arms with their trusty catchers, Hawk and Ryan respectively. Meanwhile Roy and Flo Kimball found two empty seats in the shade. "Aren't they adorable?" they said, watching the wee Niners and Ninettes. "We should come out here more often!"

It was a warm day, at least eighty-five degrees in the shade. While Jessy sipped lemonade, she took in the scenery. Lumplyn resembled any recreational park anywhere in America with its tree-shaded picnic tables and grandstand overlooking the playing field, the far boundary of which was lined with colorful signs advertising tooth polish, shoes, cigars, insurance agencies, chewing tobacco, and the like.

The distant outfield looked imposing. It would take a strong amateur hitter indeed, Jessy knew, to hit a ball out of this park into the woods beyond the signs. A home run! Jessy smiled to see the Ninettes struggling to catch little bouncing grounders. She herself hadn't played ball since her grammar school days, before she moved to Bethel.

As picnickers left the park, new groups arrived and settled into the best grandstand seats to view the fireworks scheduled to start after dark. Billy Wilcox ran around like a boy possessed, easily rounding up pint-sized gunslinging partners among the crowds of families lounging in the park. Meanwhile Mo and Bud began sorting out the playing roster.

"I have to play on Leo's team, I just have to! I'll die if I don't! Let me play right field! I always play right field!" shrieked Laura.

"She plays right field pretty good, believe it or not," said Burl, noting with satisfaction that Mo had given Laura the nod and handed her a glove. "She's so tall and has such long arms no ball gets past her out there in right, that is, unless of course she has to run for one. She hates to sweat."

"I can run!" Laura insisted, smarting at Burl's reference to the surprising quickness her smaller, heavier, younger sister displayed during the cookout.

Darlene made a face. "We're going to beat you, Laura, I've already decided. I insist on being in right field, too, but on Al's team!" Her tone said, I'll show you, Laura!

"Okay, right field's covered. For left, Chad, you're playing on Leo's team, isn't that what you guys decided?"

"Left field it is." Chad put on his baseball glove.

Burl opted for left field too, but on Al's team. Friendly enemies were squaring off tit for tat.

"Fast Emma! Center field?"

"Okay, Mo," she said, still chewing Blubber. "But not on Count Rotten's team. I'm playing with Alsy-Walsey today!"

"It's okay with me if it's okay with Al," said Bud.

Al nodded. "That redhead couldn't hit the side of a barn with a two-by-four, but she can field a ball okay for a girl."

"For a girr-rrl!" whined most of the females, offended. "Watch it, Buddy!"

Al's nine, the Stompers, would pitch first. Leo would pitch for the Grunts. All the positions had been decided. That left Midge and Jessy. Midge had strained her shoulder the week before and couldn't play but, unlike Jessy, she was dressed for action.

"Okay, Midge, you ump home plate," said Mo.

Leo stopped hurling balls. "Jessy umps home plate. Midge can ump the infield." Leo gestured in the direction of second base.

"Why? Midge has way more playing time than Jessy."

"Jessy has no playing time but she's watched every inning of every game Tri-County has played for the last month." Leo gave her a wink and crammed a big chunk of licorice into his mouth.

"Oooh-ooh. Pitcher's preference, huh?" some of the others roared. "Planning on getting some preferential calls for yourself, Leo?"

"Yeah," he said as he spit on the ball. He slammed it repeatedly into his mitt for emphasis. "And if Jessy doesn't work out, she can trade places with Midge."

"Fair enough," said Mo. He turned to the Niners and Ninettes still occupying the field, shouting, "You kids done yet?"

"No!" they shouted back.

"That's what you think!" A host of parents came from the picnic area and nabbed their tiny players, saying, "Done or not, it's time to go home! You have school tomorrow, remember? You need a bath!"

The sight of children being dragged from the diamond reminded Jessy of her own responsibilities. She had chores, lots of them, at this time of day, and the Grunts and Stompers hadn't even started to play. Leo was warming up his pitching arm.

She tiptoed to the sidelines. "Oh, Leo? May I have a word with you please?" Leo stopped in mid-hurl. "I'm sorry to interrupt, but I'll have to go home soon. I have work to do."

"Sure, sure, soon as the game's over." As she continued protesting gently about chores, Leo kept hurling the ball, saying, "Your family's home, aren't they? They can do them."

Leo's response troubled Jessy but she didn't want to create a scene. She estimated Lumpy Land, on the outer edges of Bethel County, to be a fifteen-mile walk from her house. No one else appeared anxious to go. The young farming men and women who had arrived at the Kimballs late in the afternoon had done their work before they left home. Jessy turned to the spot where the elderly Kimballs were sitting, hoping they might give her a lift, but she couldn't see them.

"They're gone. Grandpa and Grama left to do chores," Emma told her. "I'm glad I don't have chores! Daddy can afford to hire help!"

Jessy scanned the crowd but saw no familiar face she could turn to for a ride home. Walking such a distance would take longer than an entire ball game. There was no public telephone, no way to reach Adam or Suzanna. She would just have to bide her time at Lumpy Land. She prayed the game would move along quickly. Fortunately, everyone was eager to let the game begin.

Thundering orders, Mo and Bud, captains of the Grunts and Stompers respectively, readied their players. As Ryan hunkered down to catch at home plate, Al approached the mound to pitch for the Stompers. His teammates—Burl, Darlene, Emma, Bud, and Bertha—took their places on the field, along with Stu and Mike, late arrivals but seasoned players.

Meanwhile the hitting lineup for Leo's team, the Grunts, began swinging bats: Laura just had to hit first. Chad would follow, then Hazel, Mo, Hawk, Marie, Elmer, Ben, and Leo.

"I presume you know the rules, Sister Superior?" the catcher, Ryan, on his haunches at home plate, asked Jessy.

"I played the game in school," she answered, "and I know where the strike zone is."

"If that's the case, then Jessy Flint's the only umpire in the world who does!" laughed Chad, waiting in the on-deck circle.

"I'll be fair, I can promise that much," Jessy said with quiet dignity. She put her drawstring bag on one of the benches and returned to her position behind home plate.

Concentration would not be easy. The sun was in her eyes, for starters, and in the catcher's and the batters' eyes too. Then a troop of pigeons marched around, hunting for leftovers from all the picnics. Stompers playing infield used their ball caps to shoo the birds away.

"Hey, stop it! Leave the birds alone," shouted Leo from the sidelines.

"Why? You wanna start playing, doncha?"

"Sure I do, but if you hurt a bird you'll upset Jessy!"

"Oooh—ooh, listen to him! Forgive us, Sister Superior!" chanted the mighty Stompers. "Excuse us!"

With as much dignity as she could muster without laughing, Jessy cocked her head. "You're excused. But no rough stuff! There are ladies present!"

"There are?" shouted the boisterous boys, laughing. "Where?"

The girls—both Grunts and Stompers—seemed surprised to be considered ladies. They looked at each other and shrugged.

"Jessy's right, guys. No rough stuff. Just a nice friendly game, okay?"

Everyone agreed with Leo. This was not the big leagues by any means, just a casual co-ed game. Still, Al began pitching with a vengeance. He struck out the first three Grunt batters. The Stompers cheered for him.

The game stopped dead when a raccoon ambled into right field in search of picnic leftovers the pigeons had overlooked. Screeching, Laura fled the outfield. It amused Jessy to see a grown woman so frightened of a furry little animal she would gladly have worn as a coat. The bright-eyed, bushy-tailed raccoon, having just wakened for its nocturnal feasting, romped around in abandon among discarded food wrappings with all the time in the world. Jessy groaned; for her, time was of the essence.

"Oh, no, at this rate, we'll never get this inning over with!" shouted the Stompers, impatient to start hitting.

"I'll handle this," volunteered Jessy. On her way to the outfield she grabbed something from a picnic table, but no one could see what she had taken.

"Jessy, don't go out there! That animal might have rabies!" Leo, Darlene, and Laura shouted together.

"Cats can have rabies, too, and no one's afraid of them! I'll be okay.

48

After all, I deal with five-hundred-pound hogs all the time!" With a shrug she marched to the far edge of the outfield. On her haunches she whispered to the stock-still raccoon, "Come on, you racker-squawker!" The dark gray fur ball with the bushy striped ringtail and shining black eyes looked up, fascinated with Jessy, but to her frustration, wouldn't budge from the outfield. Again, Jessy tried reasoning with the adorable masked marauder in her most fetching voice. "Come on! This is no place for you! You might get hurt! Wouldn't you like to go to the woods over there?"

Grunts and Stompers hooted Jessy's performance. "You can't order a raccoon around! They're totally untrainable!"

The jeering stopped when the raccoon began to follow Jessy off the field like a trained show dog. Off it ambled to the trees beyond the advertising signs, far from the playing field, trotting behind Jessy all the way.

"Jessy must've majored in Wild Animal Language 101!" With grudging admiration, the Grunts and Stompers began chanting, "When Sister Superior talks, things happen!"

No one had noticed that she had lured the raccoon away with a donut she had taken to the outfield. Once in the woods, she was delighted the little stranger readily accepted the treat in its able, hand-like paws. It grunted with satisfaction and transferred the donut to its teeth, hauling it away in its mouth like a trophy of war.

Brushing her hands neatly against one another, Jessy resumed her place behind home plate and asked mildly, "Now where were we? Oh, yes. Leo has yet to strike out the third Stomper to retire the side. If I'm not mistaken, the count was two balls and one strike." She motioned for the Grunts to return to their positions and said to Count Smoke, "Please continue pitching, Leo."

And so the game proceeded. Laura played right field superbly, catching every ball that got within a mile of her long arms. She robbed the Stompers of hits, or so they cried when she made seemingly impossible catches. Meanwhile, Darlene—shorter than Laura but faster on her feet—played the same position for the Stompers. She, too, worked hard to chase down ball after ball, robbing the Grunts of fine hits. Their husbands made a strong showing in left field. Chad and Burl played well. By the fourth inning, though, hits were coming on both sides, erratic grounders Hazel couldn't handle, errors Elmer made, fly balls that evaded Stu's straining arms, and balls too well hit for anyone to catch. The score stood two-two after six innings.

By the seventh inning, the game was tied four-four. Jessy made call after call, deciding in split seconds which pitches were balls and which were strikes. More than once players argued with her, but she held her ground. She strived to be fair to pitchers and hitters alike.

In every inning, Jessy studied every pitch, deciding instantly if it was thrown too high, too low, too far inside, or too far outside the invisible strike zone—the imaginary rectangle that reached somewhere between a batter's arms and knees. Was the pitcher throwing low and inside or high and outside that magic, illusory box?

It wasn't long before Jessy developed a sense of timing, a rhythm that kept pace with the motion of the pitcher. As Al or Leo wound up and began to throw, she braced herself to study the path of the speeding ball as it flew toward her and home plate, down into the catcher's mitt, a ball traveling as fast as Leo's new sportscar—and very wet besides.

"This ball is a mess!" she complained to both pitchers repeatedly.

"We like it that way," Leo and Al said, both chewing licorice the entire time, and rubbing their spit on the ball to make it curve. The brown, sopping wet slimeball flew into the catcher's mitt with a messy *splat*!

"Ugh, how unhygienic," Jessy moaned. "There ought to be a law!"

With effort she kept her pretty clothes from getting splattered, but there was no protection from the dust. After the first few pitches, though, she had become so involved in the game she completely ignored how dirty she was getting.

The seventh inning was uneventful except that another delay occurred when Mo split his trousers. Again Jessy came to the rescue with safety pins from her small bag.

"The girl's a regular lifesaver," said Burl again, drinking in Jessy with that all-encompassing look of his.

"Put your eyes back in your head, Burl," warned Leo.

Once the game resumed, a near disaster occurred: Leo hit Mike, one of the Stompers, on the hand with a pitch. Leo was instantly by Mike's side, all apologies. Even if he would get another turn to hit, Mike would be unable to hold a bat for the rest of the game.

During the unscheduled delay, Jessy took the opportunity to tell Leo quietly, to one side, "I really should be going home soon."

"But the game's not over," he protested.

"I have work to do."

"Can't your brother do it? You about killed yourself working all this year while he was laid up. I saw! Besides, it's his farm, isn't it?"

"I'm part-owner. One-third."

"I didn't know that."

"Well, now you do. And besides, it's getting late!" Jessy reminded him.

"Your brother didn't say what time he expected you home, did he?"

"No, but I always do my share of the work. Adam is up and around, but he's still convalescing and should have help."

Leo assured her, "I'll take you straight home after the game; it won't take but twenty minutes for me to drive you there from here."

Dissatisfied, Jessy resigned herself to facing her brother's wrath upon her return home. The eighth inning lasted so long, with so many hitters going to bat, that in the ninth the injured Mike would be due to bat again, the last hitter for the Stompers in the last of the ninth inning, with the Grunts leading the Stompers six to five. The Grunts had it won unless someone could hit for Mike, somehow get on base, and drive Ryan home. The tying run, Ryan, was on second, but he couldn't get home without someone getting a hit. Who could drive Ryan home and score the winning run besides? It would take a miracle to save the Stompers from losing this game.

There were no extra players, no magical unsung, as-yet-undiscovered Babe Ruth waiting in the wings to help the Stompers out of their fix. The injured Midge couldn't take Mike's place. She was hurting just to have umpired in midfield.

Leo, Al, Mo, and Bud approached Jessy in a huddle. "You'll have to take Mike's place at bat and let Mike ump home plate. There's no one else we can send in unless the Stompers forfeit the game right now."

Jessy knew there was no use arguing. If she wanted to see the game end fair and square, she would have to agree to play, even if it did mean making a fool of herself. Silently nodding, she agreed to be the fool, if only to end the game without forfeiting.

Emma ran to Jessy from the sidelines. "Put on my shoes!"

Jessy laughed. "Now what would I need your shoes for?"

Emma looked at Jessy in disbelief. "To help you run faster, of course! It's going to be hard enough for you to run in that long skirt and hat!"

"Run? To where?" Jessy asked. "You don't mean to say you think I can get a hit against Count Smoke, do you?"

Emma pouted. "That rotten brother of mine can't win this one! I've been playing my heart out! I've had to do things in center field I never knew I could do to keep those lousy Grunts from scoring! You have to get a hit! If you can get on, then Burl can try to get something going after you." Both of them turned to see Burl swinging a bat, getting ready to hit, if indeed Jessy was able to get on base. Emma continued her pep talk: "We Stompers have just got to beat the Grunts! Whose side are you on, anyway?"

"No one's! I mean, both sides! I'm the umpire, remember?"

"Not anymore. You're a Stomper now, like Mikey!"

Already Mike, nursing his bruised hand, stood behind home plate, set to take Jessy's place as umpire. She hugged Emma briefly. "All right, I'll do my best, but in my own shoes."

Emma returned to the sidelines to scream for Jessy, the last batter in the bottom of the ninth. A few bystanders elbowed each other, while a few jeered at Jessy.

Someone handed Jessy a bat. She began loosening up like she had seen the other batters do throughout the game. It felt good to move vigorously. Jessy's arms and shoulders had tensed up during the long game she spent hunched over home plate making decisions.

The air was cooler now, as the sun, the fiery orange ball she had seen rise up in the dawn, now sank toward the horizon. A few glorious clouds reflected the rays of the sun. Inwardly, Jessy thanked God for such a magnificent sky over such a magnificent place in the most wonderful country on earth. As she did, a small breeze began to play across the field, cooling her down and steeling her nerves.

She was thankful Billy had finally grown quiet. Since the seventh inning, he had been sitting near home plate, watching the game. Jessy hoped Wild Billy's trigger finger wasn't getting itchy.

Leo pursed his lips, pulled his bright blue Tri-County cap off his head, smoothed and settled it over his long, dark hair, and narrowed his eyes, not really seeing Jessy, but staring down at his target, the catcher's mitt on Hawk's hand. As he prepared to get his last strikeout of the game, assured of the win with a one-point lead, Leo braced to throw to Jessy. It had been an easy day for Leo; he had restrained himself for this friendly little co-ed game and his arm didn't hurt a bit, nothing like the pain he had known from Saturday's marathon effort, men pitted against men.

To him Jessy complained good naturedly, "My feet hurt!"

Sweet Jessy's feet hurt! Leo smiled pleasantly and assured his girl, "We'll go home as soon as I strike you out."

For some reason, Leo's words had the opposite effect than he intended. Sweet Jessy suddenly didn't feel so sweet. Something in her answered, *But I don't want to strike out. Sore feet or not, I want to win!*

Leo's first pitch zipped into the strike zone fair and square. Jessy didn't try for it. Leo bent forward, looked, and threw again with the same result, another strike. Again, Jessy didn't try to hit it. One more strike and she would be out. The Stompers would lose.

"Giving up, huh? Not even bothering to swing!" jeered Hawk. "That's because you know it's useless trying to hit against Count Smoke!"

The Stompers, led by Emma, sang a different tune. "Sister Superior's waiting for the pitch she *really* wants. Why waste her energy until she's ready to hit?" Inwardly, though, the Stompers felt all but defeated.

The next few moments would be forever sealed in the gold of the fading sun over the little town of Bethel. The breeze strengthened. It had changed direction and was now blowing from home plate and against Leo, making his job harder and working in Jessy's favor. Leo wound up fully and threw his body forward, preparing to release the ball from his gifted right hand.

Bang! Bang! Bang! His nephew, Billy Wilcox, chose that moment to blast away with both of his six-shooters. It was a small distraction for big league material, but enough to throw off Leo's timing as he let go of the ball.

The licorice-covered ball was not easy to see in the fading light, but

Jessy had grown so used to following the messy thing with her eyes as umpire that now, as batter, she sighted it easily and adjusted her grip accordingly, waiting for it. Simultaneously, with all her might, she twisted the full length of her torso, putting her full force into the shaft of the bat she gripped with both hands. At that moment, the breeze blew against the ball, slowing it down just enough so, as Jessy brought her full weight to bear, she was able to smash the sluggish fastball hard and solid.

Crack! That sound like no other sound rang out—the unmistakable, crisp snap of a baseball hit squarely with a solid wooden bat. The ball was hit so sharply that someone said, "That girl's not as dainty as she looks! But will the ball go foul?"

The wind that had worked *against* Leo now worked *for* Jessy, carrying the fair ball a long, long, way up and over left field, beyond Chad's outstretched arms, past the commercial signs for dog food and horse liniment, fair-fair-fair!—a perfectly hit solid home run that dropped deep into the woods beyond the outfield.

Ryan, the Stomper on second base, his eyes not believing but his feet moving with practiced speed, needed no one to tell him to race to third and then run home to score the tie, but Jessy could only stare at the arc the ugly, slimy, beautiful, wonderful ball had taken. The bat still vibrated in her hands from hitting the fast-moving ball so hard.

Stompers screamed. Grunts grunted.

"Run, Jessy! Run, for the love of Pete! Run!" Emma hollered.

Jessy's aching feet weren't listening. "I've never hit a ball that hard!" she said. "I've never done this before!"

Leo threw his hat into the dirt, cursing in a smoking blue fury. "That bratty kid! Did Billy have to shoot his stupid toy guns right then? A pitifully easy out and she actually hits the thing! I don't believe it! I can't believe it! I'll never believe it! Done in by a woman!"

"Run, Jessy, run!" the Stompers screamed, the game tied at six-all now that Ryan's spiked shoes had reached home plate.

Emma went to Jessy, screaming, "You've got to touch all the bases! Come on! You've got to touch every one or the game will end in a tie!"

Slowly, Jessy nodded, her mouth hanging open a bit. Feeling something was amiss, she dropped the bat and reached around with her left hand to her right side. The sleeve of her new blouse had torn when she twisted to hit the ball. She barely comprehended what she had accomplished, but realized from Emma's pleading that her job was not yet complete. "Okay, Emma, okay, thank you, you're right. Of course I'll go," she whispered. With one hand holding up her long skirt and the other holding down her hat, Jessy pushed off toward first, touching base gently, moving to step on second, her aching feet in dainty bow shoes not aching anymore, then through the dust toward third, and home where a crowd screamed her name with hysterical joy. They surrounded her and whooped with unbelieving belief. "Hooray team!" she said gently to all of them—to Al, Mike, Burl, Darlene, Bud, Ryan, Bertha, and Stu—the victorious Stompers. They screamed again, roaring their approval of Sister Superior. "Hail Jessy! Hail Stompers!"

"We won! I can't believe it! We won! It's unbelievable!" screamed Darlene, hugging Jessy Flint for sheer joy. "What do you know about that? And Billy, I could kiss you!"

"What for, Mommy?" Billy wondered aloud.

Darlene hugged her little boy. "We beat your Aunt Laura seven to six, that's what!"

"Better yet, we beat that stinkpot Leo!" shouted Emma. She hugged Jessy with all her might. "I've never beaten that stinker in my whole life, not at anything, no matter how hard I've tried, and now you did it single-handed! You beat him at his own game! Jessy Flint, I'll adore you till the day I die!"

Shaking her head and smiling, Jessy said to Emma, "Save your adoration for God!"

"God? What does God have to do with it?" Emma asked, puzzled.

"Don't you see? It was God who made the wind blow hard enough to slow the ball so I could hit it and hard enough to carry it over left field," Jessy answered. "And He kept the ball straight as an arrow, fair all the way into the woods!"

"Well, whoever it was, whatever it was, that ball's gone for good!" said Burl, noticing that Chad, Laura, Mo, Midge, Marie, Elmer, Ben, Hazel, and Leo had returned from the woods beyond the playing field empty-handed. "They'll never find that ball."

"Whatever you want, I'll do!" Emma said to Jessy. "You'll always be my hero!"

Before Emma ran off with the others, Jessy stopped her to ask, "Emma, do you mean that? What you said about doing what I want?"

"Sure I do!"

"Then hear me, Emma," began Jessy in deadly earnest. "You're a bright girl. You're starting school tomorrow. Make the most of the opportunity. It's one I didn't have. Study hard and be the best you can be. Be all our great, good God wants you to be. Will you do that for me, Emma?"

"You're serious!" Emma laughed at Jessy. "I hate school! But you're still my hero! Look at old rot-pot changing his stinky shoes! So there, Count Smoke*less!*"

Alone on a bench, Leo had taken off his spiked shoes and was tying on his oxfords. He looked sourly at Emma, too furious to answer. Jessy walked slowly toward him and to the nearby picnic table where she had left her little drawstring bag.

"You ready to go?" Leo asked her, his voice listless.

"Almost," she said, noticing the fireworks were about to begin.

While Leo stuffed his gear into his carry bag, Jessy paused a moment, alone, at home plate. The same orange sun that had burst in a searing flame over her vision of God early that morning—a thousand years ago, or so it seemed now—was sinking into the horizon. Jessy raised her right arm toward the glorious, spectacular, thrill-bearing sky, proclaiming like the children of Israel centuries before her, *"Behold, I lift up my hand to heaven and say, I live forever!"* Then, pausing reverently Jessy whispered so only He could hear, "Thank you, Jesus, for the victory. For Your joy. How good it feels to win, and when You went to the cross, You won for us the greatest gift of all with Your undying love. I'm so glad I'm on Your team!"

She sniffled the happy tears of a faithful Christian, as she turned from the rapidly darkening sky and headed home with Leo Kimball.

CHAPTER 6

❧

"**I**'m glad you pulled the top up on the car before we left the park, Leo, but aren't we going a bit too fast?" Jessy asked softly.

"I know this road like the back of my hand." Without looking at her, Leo drove on, leaving a cloud of dust behind them as they sped through the fast-falling twilight. The car handled beautifully in his grip, but the imported headlamps hardly illuminated the growing gloom of the unlit country road before them.

Anxious, Jessy glanced from the blackening road to Leo, who had remained silent since they left the park. "I'm sorry if I spoiled your game. I didn't mean to!" When Leo didn't answer, she said, "I can see why you and your friends love to play baseball. It's a wonderful game." Still no answer. "I'll buy you a new ball the next time we order from the catalog, to replace the one I lost."

"Don't be ridiculous."

Her lips parted in apprehension as Leo sped around one corner after another. Jessy rubbed her rough, hardworking hands together in the darkness, and then took a deep breath before saying, "Your mother doesn't like me a bit, does she? What can I do to make things right between us?"

"Nothing. She doesn't like any girl I bring home, even the ones she and Laura insist I meet. The Queen of England, Joan of Arc, and Saint Mary rolled into one wouldn't be good enough for her baby boy. But it really doesn't matter what she thinks."

"Of course it matters! I want her to like me."

"We won't be sticking around Bethel if I get on a pro team. We won't see much of the family at all."

"Still, I'd want to fit in with your family."

"You were a big hit tonight, I'll say that." For the first time since they left the park, Leo smiled. "Darlene thinks you're tops, and she's nearly as impossible to please as Mum. My father has always liked you, and his folks. I get the idea Burl's wild about you, but he likes everything in skirts. And of course Emma adores you because you made me look bad." Without slowing the car, Leo looked at Jessy. "I learned long ago that if I please a fourth of my family half the time, I'm doing as well as possible, so don't worry what they think one way or the other, okay?"

Without answering, Jessy looked down the dark road ahead, as unfathomable as their future together. "Leo, how did your mother and father meet? They seem so different from each other."

"When Dad was young, Grandpa Roy sent him to Chicago to sell some cattle. Afterward, Dad had some time to relax before his train back to Bethel, so he went to a band concert where he met Mum. She's always loved music. Back then Mum lived on her father's—Count Dimitri's—estate. Pretty soon Dad was going to Chicago all the time. They got married two months after they met."

"It must have been love at first sight."

"Something like that." Leo coughed politely and sped up the car.

Blushing in the dark, Jessy squirmed uncomfortably in the plush leather seat. "Oh," she said, realizing Leo's meaning. "Peter?"

"Yeah. My brother was born in Chicago. He and my parents lived there a long while, until he turned ten, I think. Dad helped run Count Dimitri's property."

"Watch out! A deer!" Jessy cried. She strained to see Leo's face in the darkness, then covered her face, sure they would crash.

He swerved madly to avoid a collision and then struggled to regain control of the car. The Simplex roared on, straight down the deserted road.

Once Jessy calmed down, she said, "She's an elegant woman, your mother."

Leo nodded. "She's always been interested in music. Mum loves art and poetry and the theater—big city culture. She's never been happy in Bethel, but after the Count died, she and Dad decided to sell off his property and move back here."

"I see. You have a beautiful home, Leo, a showplace."

"I guess it's okay." Leo had pulled the car into Jessy's drive. He kept his motor running.

Jessy peered up at the old two-story. *The children must already be in bed*, she thought. Only a few lamps were lit, including one left by the front door for her. She felt miserably, terribly late. She said good night and made a move to open the car door.

"No, wait, um, before you go, there's something I want to give you. I've been wanting to give it to you all day, but there never seemed to be a good time to do it." In the dim light Leo handed her a small velvet box.

"Oh, Leo." Jessy was reluctant to take it, but he pressed it into her hands. When she opened it, she gasped. "Leo! This must have cost a fortune!"

"It did. I only paid half of it so far. I got it on the installment plan for you in New York when I picked up the car. I hope you like it. Put it on! Does it fit? Let me help." Leo put the ring on her left hand. "Oh, it's too big! I didn't know your size. We can have it fixed in town."

Even in the dim light, Jessy marveled at the glittering diamond ring. "Oh, Leo, I don't know what to say. What did your parents—"

"They don't know. I'm not telling them till I'm sure I have a decent-paying job on a team. Once I'm established, Mum's bound to come around. I'm her pet. I can always get what I want, sooner or later." Leo pressed his hands around Jessy's. "Do you like the ring?"

"It's wonderful!"

"Just don't wear it when my family might see it."

"Not wear it?"

"I'll tell them when the time is right."

"Somehow I get the feeling the time will never be right. Not the way your mother acted today." Jessy took off the ring and slipped it in the box and held it out to him. "Here. You should keep it till it's paid for and your folks agree to our—your getting married. It's a beautiful ring, though, Leo, truly it is and I thank you for the thought."

Leo gave it back to her. "It's a full carat, and it's perfect, the jewelers in New York told me. I had it appraised after I got it, by another jeweler, to make sure it was genuine, and it's perfect. Like you." Leo pressed the little velvet box into her hands. "I think of you all the time when we're not together. Between you and baseball, I can't sleep nights. I feel so frustrated! All I can think of is you and me and of getting out of Bethel and heading to the big leagues. I wake up sometimes at two in the morning and go outside and look up at the stars and—" Leo sighed mightily.

Jessy held her breath, not knowing what to say or do. Leo was leaning so close to her she could feel his body heat in the darkness. "I-I th-think of you, too, when we're apart," she admitted. How glad she was he couldn't see her blush. He seemed more than ready to kiss her and hold her without ever letting her go. "Please, Leo, not till we're married! Oh, try to understand!"

"You love me, don't you?"

"I love you but I can't—we shouldn't—it wouldn't be right to—"

He leaned back in the driver's seat, letting out the air in his lungs with a sudden burst. "We'll get married soon. I know I can get a berth on a team someplace."

"Look! Someone's coming." They watched a car nearing them.

"Leo? Is that you?" a familiar voice hollered in the dark.

"Hawk? What're you doing here? Spying on us?"

Hawk, still in his sweaty baseball clothes, got out of his car while Hazel remained seated inside. "When we dropped off Emma at your house, your dad asked me to give you this. It was delivered while we were at Lumpy Land."

Leo and Jessy got out of the Simplex. In the glow of headlights, Leo read aloud the telegram addressed to him: "OUR SCOUTS SAW YOU PITCH LAST SAT. 1-YR CONTRACT $150/MO COME NO DELAY PONGO TEXAS-SOUTHERN LEAGUE."

Leo read it once, twice, three times! "Did you hear that?" He motioned for Hazel to get out of Hawk's car. "The best minor league club!"

Everyone congratulated Leo, but Hawk couldn't let the triumphant moment pass without saying, "Good thing that scout didn't see you pitch to Sister Superior today!"

At last Leo could laugh about Jessy's hit. "I guess I didn't look exactly like Walter 'Big Train' Johnson in the ninth, did I?" Everyone laughed at this reference to baseball's greatest living pitcher, the so-called Slingshot on Legs who had been electrifying the baseball world as a Washington Senator.

Still, nothing—not even a lucky home run hit by a girl—could spoil this triumph for Leo. He paused a moment to think. "Next train south out of Bethel leaves at 11:30 tonight. I can just make it if I run home and pack!"

Once Hawk drove away, Leo promised Jessy, "I'll write to you once I get to Texas. Will you write to me? Will you keep the ring? Will you marry me?"

Jessy beheld Leo's face—his bright blue eyes and dazzling white teeth, his smooth olive skin—so inviting, so sensual. "Oh, Leo, this is so sudden! Of course I'll write. But I want your family's approval. I want to know they'll be happy about us. I'll keep the ring if you want me to, but on one condition."

"What's that?" Leo looked so excited he might have agreed to anything.

"I want to visit your brother Peter. Will you take me to see him?"

He frowned and demanded, "Are you out of your mind, Jessy? Why?"

"Because he's part of your family, for one, and because Jesus told His disciples to visit sick people and prisoners, as if He were the one to be visited and helped. The ones who do show they are His followers and the ones who don't aren't. I'm a Christian and I should visit Peter."

Leo bristled with annoyance. "Forget about him, will you? What's he got to do with us? With anything?"

"He might have everything to do with us! He might have everything to do with everything!" Jessy strained to see Leo's face in the darkness. "Don't you understand? How could I face Jesus if I forget about your brother? How could you, a Christian, face Jesus either?" Jessy held out the velvet box. "Here." When Leo didn't take back his ring, she said gently, "I know it upsets you to talk about your brother, but I wouldn't feel right if he were left out of our lives. You and your friends can laugh at me, but I want to do what's right by you and your family—your *whole* family."

With a sigh, Leo nodded. "Okay. I'll take you to Fair Haven when I get back home, whenever that is. Now will you keep the ring? I gotta go!"

"All right," she said, aching with love for Leo. She cried to see him getting into his car. When would they see each other again?

"Love me?"

Jessy nodded as she watched Leo release the parking brake.

"I love you too," he said as he sped away into the night.

Jessy stood there in the swirling dust a long time, until the lights of Leo's car disappeared into the pitch darkness. A train roared past on the line that ran parallel to the road in front of the Flint home, steaming into Bethel with all its lights on. Jessy watched it pass the cemetery across the road, knowing that when the train left Bethel, the man she loved would be on it, bound for distant Texas and a whole new chapter in his life. Sniffing away tears, Jessy put the velvet box into her bag and climbed up the porch steps, wondering what the future held.

CHAPTER 7

❦

Once Jessy stepped inside, she took her shoes from her aching feet. Wiping tears from her face with her dusty hand, she was halfway up the stairs when he caught her.

"So there you are, finally. Where're you headed?"

"Hello, Adam," Jessy answered meekly, clutching her shoes and wiggling her stockinged toes.

"Come back down here. I wanna talk to you."

"Yes, sir." Jessy went cautiously, moving sideways, half twisted away from him. "How are you? Not catching cold, are you? Your voice sounds hoarse."

"Never mind me!" Gesturing toward the second floor with his deeply cleft chin, he asked, "What were you gonna do up there?"

Regarding him with her wide bright eyes, she stammered, "M-me?"

"Course you! I don't see anyone else here but you 'n' me!"

Jessy fidgeted with the shoes in her hands. "I was going to my room to change clothes before I started on my chores."

"Oh. Chores. Them things you do around here, that is, when you *are* around here to do 'em." He nodded for emphasis.

Jessy nodded with him, glad he saw her point. My, *he was acting especially thick-headed tonight*, she thought, going over everything with his extra-fine-toothed Grade AAA comb, and Jessy with her mouth as dry as dirt. "So if you'll excuse me, please, I'll just run upstairs and get changed so I can get started. On the chores, I mean, the ones I do around here."

"Don't bother. When you didn't show up by five, me 'n' Suzy 'n' the kids did your chores for you."

"Oh, thank you. That was very nice of you and Suzanna! I'd thank the children, but I guess they're—" She glanced up toward their rooms.

"They went up to bed hours ago. They got school tomorrow, you know."

Jessy nodded and lowered her eyes, feeling miserable. *Why doesn't Adam just go ahead and kill me and get it over with?* she wondered.

"When eight o'clock came 'n' went without a sign of you, I kinda started to think you 'n' Leo ran off to get married."

Jessy's head came up with a jerk. Clutching her shoes to her heart with both arms, she said, "No, never! If and when I marry, I'd want the service in our church with the minister to officiate, and the beautiful organ music and fresh flowers and, afterward, everyone here for a party, if it wouldn't be too much trouble. And I'd want you to give me away, that is, if you wouldn't mind, I mean, I w-would want it that way, with you there, and Suzanna and Stephen and Martha and Taddy, of course, and all our friends, too, and neighbors, and George and Rachel Webb, not just me running off to who knows where to—" Too late Jessy remembered Adam Flint's elopement and the uproar that followed when Suzanna's father, the illustrious George Webb, Esquire, found out. The fallout from the familial explosion took a full three years to settle. Struggling to remove her foot from her mouth, Jessy stammered, "Oh, d-dear, what I m-mean is, I won't go off without your permission and elope, no matter how much in love I am."

"Glad to hear it." Adam's green eyes lost none of their sharpness.

Smiling weakly, Jessy said, "Well, I-ah, it's been a long day. G-good night." Though she turned her head toward the top of the stairs, her brother was far from finished giving her the third degree.

Now he continued in his assumed role as prosecuting attorney. "Then I wondered, when I came to the window just now 'n' saw Leo dump you off down in the driveway without even botherin' to make sure you got inside the house okay, I figured maybe you 'n' him was through. From what I saw, he didn't even bother gettin' outta the car he was in such a hurry to speed off."

"Oh, I can explain. I'm sure—I mean, I'm *pretty* sure—in fact, I'm almost positive Leo would have shown me in, but he had to be someplace in a hurry."

"It's a wonder he didn't kill somebody the way he took off in that car of his. You tell him to shove off 'n' hit the road 'n' never come back or somethin'?"

Jessy smiled and shook her head, "No, of course not." As she untwisted herself and relaxed at last, turning to go up the stairs, Adam roared at her to "come straight back downstairs this instant!" Trembling and sweating, she did so. He grabbed her right arm and made her turn sideways, smack into the very direction she had been avoiding ever since he first caught her trying to climb the stairs unnoticed.

Flicking at the long rip in her blouse with his free hand and holding her arm so tight with the other that it hurt, he looked her over from head to foot, at all the dust and dirt. Through clenched teeth and with nostrils flaring, he asked in his deadly quiet voice, "What'd Leo do to you? I'll kill him. And maybe you too. What've the two of you been up to all this time, rollin' around in the dirt in an alley somewheres?"

Horrified and flushing crimson, Jessy stammered, "N-no! Absolutely, positively no!"

Adam's voice rose slowly to thunder. "That musta been some cookout! You been gone a good nine hours! Where'd you go with Leo in that hot car of his, a hotel?"

"Adam!" Jessy shrieked. "How can you even think such a thing?"

"Jessy, you're home at last!" Suzanna came from the far back of the house asking, "Adam, what are you hollering about this time? You'll wake the children! Haven't we had enough for one—"

"Stay outta this!" Adam snarled at his wife in a cold fury. Turning back to the sister still in his iron grip, he asked again, "You tell me what happened." He jerked her arm hard without letting go of her. "What did that Fancy Hands Leo do to you?"

Crying, Jessy blurted out, "He made me play baseball!"

"I'm not in a jokin' mood. You tell me the truth or I'll knock your teeth loose!" Adam raised a hand to wallop her.

Under the shadow of his arm she wailed, "I am telling you the truth!" Jessy sobbed miserably, her glorious victory at the park evaporating in the blaze of Adam's fury. "Leo's friends wanted to play co-ed baseball all the way out at Lumpy Land, I mean Lumplyn Memorial Park. And one thing and another kept us out there later and later and I asked Leo several times to take me home but he didn't want to go until the game was over and it would have taken hours for me to walk home so I just stayed and that's why I'm so late getting home and I'm sorry but I couldn't help it, honestly I couldn't, and I'm sorry not to have been here to help you because I know you're still not well." Jessy paused to swallow tears and catch her breath. She looked to her upper arm. The pain of being caught in Adam's iron grip was ferocious. She'd be black and blue in the morning, she just knew it.

In a low rumble, Adam demanded, "You look at me." It took all her strength, every ounce of will to meet his eyes, but she managed it, just for a moment. He jerked her arm again. "I said look at me."

She nodded and tried again. "Yes, sir." This was too much; she started crying again. "You're hurting me."

"I'll hurt you worse if you don't quit bawlin' like a kid 'n' tell me the truth. What took you so long? From the look of you, you didn't spend the day at a prayer vigil! What've you been doin'? And don't you dare lie to me."

Now she faced him squarely without tears. "I'm not lying. I've been at the ballpark since about four o'clock this afternoon. Right after the game Leo took me straight home as fast as he could." Jessy started crying again to think of her Leo gone to Texas without warning. "He drove here so fast it's a wonder we didn't have an accident. We were saying good night when his friend Hawk drove up and Leo got the news that he's been offered a one-year contract with the Trans-Southern League down in Pongo, Texas, wherever that is, and they need him to come immediately—tonight—and that's why he headed off so fast, so he could go home and pack and get on the next train out of Bethel." She reached around, feeling the tear in her blouse. She owned so few clothes and now she had ruined her one pretty blouse. "Oh, dear, I hope it can be fixed."

Suzanna took a close look at Jessy's torn blouse. "Your seam split, that's all. I can fix that easily enough."

Adam asked quietly but still angrily, "What else happened?"

"Nothing. Not a thing. I tore my blouse when I took a swing at the ball. I felt my sleeve pull in the ninth inning. Afterward I would have pinned it so it would stop tearing, but I didn't have any more safety pins in my bag because in the seventh, I gave all the ones I had to Mo. He split his trousers." Seeing imminent danger flaring up in Adam's face, Jessy added fast, "When Mo tagged a runner out at third base, he tore his pants."

"Oh." Adam loosened his hold on her a little and looked her up and down, apparently deciding that even though she was dusty all over, her clothing did not appear to have been disturbed since she left the house at lunchtime. Finally he let go of her, saying, "For now, I guess you're off the hook, though you got home way too late to suit me 'n' your alibi sounds crazy. You playin' baseball?" He began laughing at her.

Relieved, she wiped away her tears and laughed too. "I know it sounds ridiculous, but you know what?" Jessy looked impish.

"What?" Adam asked, the golden lights in his green eyes dancing.

"I got the winning homer."

"Not off Leo."

"Yes, off Leo! It was wonderful. It was a miracle!"

Suzanna's cuckoo-quail clock began rattling crazily, reporting the time as quarter-to-twenty-six.

"Goodness gracious, I really am late!" Jessy said.

The three of them laughed together. Suzanna said, "I started to worry when you didn't come home by supper time."

"I miss you when you're not around," Adam told his sister.

Jessy eyed him sardonically. "I'm sure you must, just like the Romans missed the slaves after their empire collapsed."

"Jessy, come and sit down and tell me how your day went with the Kimballs!" Suzanna took a seat where she liked to sew by hand.

Adam turned to retrieve the cane he had propped in the entryway when Jessy first walked in. With it he limped to the sofa in the sitting room. He signaled for Jessy to join him by patting the empty seat cushion beside him. "Come tell me about your day," he said with a grin.

"All right," said Jessy. She continued to wonder why he sounded so hoarse. Before Jessy sat down, she went to the hall mirror and removed her hat, saying, "What a relief to take this off at long last!" Once she settled onto the sofa, she sniffled to Adam, "It's good to be home, even though you nearly broke my arm. Can't you behave?"

"Me behave? The way you look don't make a man who's been around like I have think you spent the day at Buck'n'ham Palace sippin' tea with the queen."

"Speaking of which, do tell about your day! I can't wait to hear!" Suzanna said over her sewing. It was clear from her frazzled appearance she had spent a hard day working on this holiday meant to honor those who labor.

Jessy looked to her sister-in-law and then to her brother, thinking over the long and eventful day in a blinding series of images: the wild ride in that wild car and all that wild talk of Emma's, the way Burl studied Jessy so intently, Jessy's defense of birds wasted on a throng of bird hunters, Acacia's utter contempt for Jessy, the odd assortment of books the Kimballs kept in the parlor for all the world to see—but no Bible in sight—that eerie moment when Jessy realized someone was missing from the house that otherwise epitomized the American dream, the argument Leo and Jessy had with his parents, her thrilling home run, and then the telegram that took Leo away so suddenly, without a moment to think things through. All this flashed through her mind as she answered, "It was a strange day—very strange. In many ways, simply horrible. What I can't understand is the way the Kimballs act when there's no rhyme nor reason to—"

"The Kimballs are one of the finest, most successful—" began Suzanna.

"I know! And they have a beautiful house and money and all, but—" Jessy tried to collect her thoughts and explain without appearing critical or disloyal. "They're always at each other, like a bunch of hens cooped up together and not at all happy about the arrangements. They're forever taking swipes at each other and competing with each other." She thought of the ongoing rivalry between Emma and Leo, and Darlene snapping at Laura, and Laura criticizing Billy, and Burl putting down Chad, and Chad criticizing Leo for dating bird-loving Jessy, and on and on.

Jessy looked with kindness at her loved ones. "Why, I'd do anything I could for both of you. I'm so fortunate to have a brother who loves me and cares what happens to me and takes an interest in what I do and who I'm with, and who wants what's best for me."

Adam sniffled at this.

Remembering the cameo at her throat, Jessy unpinned it and returned it to Suzanna. "If I had a sister, I'd love her like I love you, and I hope I would never say bad things to her or wish her ill." Jessy tried to understand the Kimballs. "Of course, maybe it's not so easy to be loving under some circumstances, in some families. I shouldn't judge people, but the whole tone of things today made me wonder. All that sniping—one thing led to another and another until—" Jessy stopped to ask, "Did you know Leo has a brother in an institution?"

"No!" Adam and Suzanna said as one.

"Yes, an older brother. He's been locked up at Fair Haven since 1885 and no one ever talks about him or goes to see him."

In the ensuing quiet, Jessy pulled the little velvet box out of her drawstring bag. "Leo gave me this."

Gasping, Suzanna took the ring from her. "Oh, my, Jessy, this must be worth a fortune! It's beautiful! Why aren't you wearing it?" Suzanna's own left hand bore a plain gold band, the only ring Adam had ever given her. "Leo must think the world of you to give you something this valuable!"

"I suppose." Jessy said with discomfort, "But his mother doesn't like me at all."

"Not like you? Why?" Adam was incensed at the very idea.

"Well," Jessy began, trying herself to understand what lay behind the look Acacia had given her, a look that welled up, she sensed, from a blistering anger that could peel paint off walls at fifty paces. "Acacia is a very fashionable, elegant lady, and I'm just a country bumpkin by comparison. She's the daughter of an imperial Russian count who owned an estate in Chicago, which she inherited. Back in the old country, Count Dimitri was practically royalty. He owned forty thousand serfs, that's what Leo told me once. Imagine *owning* living, breathing people who did everything for you and cheered you like a king? Acacia would be a countess if her father had stayed in the Crimea."

"And what are we, dirt?" Adam asked casually.

Jessy sighed and looked up at the ceiling. "No one rolled out the red carpet for our ancestors. They didn't exactly come over on the Mayflower!"

"No, but they came by ship. Great Gramps stowed away and got arrested!" Adam found this very funny.

"He did?" Jessy asked, horrified.

"Sure, when he was a boy. Didn't you ever hear the story?"

Jessy shook her head miserably. No wonder Acacia looked down on Jessy with such contempt. "That proves my point. We Flints are nothings compared to Acacia and her father."

"I wouldn't say that! Once Great Gramps was able to, he signed on a whaler from New Bedford round Cape Horn and was gone from home three years. He went to sea a boy and came back a man. Most of our family was in the New England shippin' business. There's no shame in bein' ship's carpenters. A hard life but a crucial job." With his sharp green eyes sparkling, Adam said, "Way back when, the Count's ancestors probably stole cattle or the Holy Grail or whatever else they could lay their hands on like most people's ancestors did, doin' anything they could to get a fortune for themselves 'n' lordin' over other people to get them to do their dirty work. There's no royalty in America and for good reason: here we're all equal." Adam, in that superior way of his, raised his handsome head crowned with curls. "Course, I'm more equal than everyone in this house."

Suzanna looked up from her sewing to glare at her husband, but Jessy said with a big grin, "Of course, your royal highness!" Adam's perpetual cynicism about everything, coupled with his robust American sense of liberty, made Jessy feel better, but still she felt beneath the Kimballs. "You should see the picture they have of Leo's grandfather, the Count. He had medals and epaulets and everything. He looked just like Leo."

From her chair, Suzanna leaned toward Jessy to return the ring. "Now, why isn't this gorgeous rock sitting on the third finger of your left hand?"

Jessy took it back from her. "I'm not supposed to wear it because Acacia might find out. Besides, it's way too big for me. What would I tell Leo if it fell into a slop pail and one of our hogs swallowed it? You know they eat everything in sight." She put the ring in the box. "I'll just keep it safe until Leo finishes paying for it. The jeweler gave it to him on the installment plan—can you imagine? I won't wear it until it's all paid for and after Leo tells his parents officially we're getting married. He told them unofficially today and I thought the roof would cave in. What a day!"

"That's too bad!" Suzanna said. After a few moments she asked, "Are you hungry? I saved a plate of supper for you."

"I would like some nice cold milk."

Adam and Suzanna went with her to the kitchen. When Jessy helped herself to a glass of milk, she noticed a colorfully labeled crate on the floor beside the icebox. "From Bo? Oh, my, did he send us a letter too?"

"Yeah, and some orange blossom honey," said Adam. "Crate came today on the train up from Florida."

Remembering that she had seen this crate being unloaded at the station, Jessy peeked inside. Every few months Bo Bally, Adam's good friend, shipped the best fruits in season to the Flints—this time grapefruit, juice oranges, limes, and a well-padded jar of orange blossom honey. Each fruit had been wrapped in pretty tissue paper and every nook of the crate stuffed with excelsior. Jessy marveled at all the colorful fruits.

As had all the other shipments from Bo, this one, too, arrived with beautiful labels on all sides, evocative images that conjured up in Jessy the wonders of a faraway, magical land where farmers basked in semitropical splendor, tending trees that bore glorious fruits. The orchards and fruits had names the likes of Crown Jewels, Romance, and Celebrate.

"The illustrations get prettier all the time," Jessy said, admiring the latest arrival, an Indian princess with long braids canoeing up a river under a canopy of Spanish moss. "Bo and Beatrice must live in a grand place!"

When neither Adam nor Suzanna answered, Jessy picked up the letter addressed to all the family. In it Bo and Beatrice invited the Flints to Florida for a vacation after the Christmas holidays. Bo expressed concern about "the sick Yankee," as he referred to Adam, insisting as he had in previous letters that his old friend would recuperate from his accident much faster if he could spend the worst of the cold Midwestern winter in sunny Florida. They could stay with the Ballys free of charge. All the trip would cost would be transportation and related expenses. Jessy wondered aloud, "Wouldn't it be nice to visit the Ballys sometime?"

Adam glared at Suzanna and Suzanna glared back at him. Although not a word had been spoken, Suzanna smashed a pot hard on the counter for emphasis. "Did I say something wrong?" Jessy asked. "This seems to be my day for putting my foot in my mouth."

"Don't say another word to me, Adam! We've been over this and over this and all day I have said no a thousand times! Over my dead body!" shouted Suzanna.

Any other day, the anger in Suzanna's normally musical voice would have been surprising, but after the kind of day this had been, nothing would surprise Jessy. Still, not wanting to offend, she asked, "Did I say something wrong, Suzanna? I didn't mean to make you mad."

Adam interrupted before Suzanna could answer: "Aw, she's got this crazy idea that if we go down there to see Bo—"

"I am *not* crazy! We simply cannot go off in the middle of winter and that's final!" Turning from Adam, Suzanna wailed to Jessy, "After New

Year's, your brother wants to take the train to Florida and spend four or five *weeks* there! Can you imagine?"

Jessy beamed with pleasure. "Oh, how wonderful!" To Adam she said, "It would be so good for you to recuperate, rest, relax, and get your strength back!"

"That's what I said, but do you think she'll listen?" Adam added furiously, "Pig-headed female I went 'n' married!"

More to Suzanna than to Adam, Jessy said, "I could take care of the place while you're gone and look after the children, if that's what you're concerned about. You two need a vacation. You never even had a honeymoon!"

Adam shook his head. "No. I been thinkin' we all could go, the six of us."

Jessy said, delighted, "Really, Adam? Are you serious? Me and the children too? But who would look after the farm—our animals and all?"

"Ed Mannon. I talked to him this afternoon. I figure by New Year's, after we sell off the feeder pigs, there wouldn't be a whole lot to do 'cept care for the cows 'n' horses 'n' hens. All Ed would want is a coupl'a crates of fruit for his trouble. I'd give him more'n' that, of course."

"Oh, how wonderful!" cried Jessy. "It's been years since I've seen the ocean, ever since I came to Bethel to live with you. How delightful Florida must be! You know, I read once that—"

"It's a horrid idea," said Suzanna tartly. "Disrupting the children's school year, ruining our routine, leaving our home and all our nice things."

"Couldn't the children take their books along? We could see that they keep up their studies while we're gone. And besides, traveling is an education." Jessy, very happy now, said, "I remember that long trip I took by myself, all the way here to be with you, Adam. It was so exciting being on the train five whole days! And then that time we took the train to Azleton, when you fought The Gunboat. Remember?" Jessy beamed with delight.

Adam remembered and smiled too. "It would be wonderful to see Bo again. We've never visited him or met his wife and children. They got three now, about the age of my own."

Suzanna was livid. "There *are* other concerns, you know."

"Oh, of course!" Adam shouted. "Everythin' you gotta do is more important than anythin' I gotta do."

"That's ridiculous. You only think of yourself." Suzanna began to cry. She ran out of the kitchen.

Limping after her, Adam hollered, "I'm not just thinkin' of me. It's you 'n' the kids 'n' Jessy I'm thinkin' about too! We work like dogs 'n' I'm sick of it. I need a break 'n' so do you 'n' Jessy."

Puzzled by the battle in progress, Jessy put down her empty glass and followed them. She could hardly believe her ears. She wondered if they had been fighting since lunchtime, first about the car, and then, after the crate of fruit arrived, about the trip Adam wanted to take. In the hall, at the bottom of the stairs, Adam, Suzanna, and Jessy looked up to see all three children in ankle-length nightshirts, standing at the top of the staircase in their bare feet, rubbing their sleepy eyes and looking downward.

"There! Are you happy now?" Suzanna shouted at Adam. "You've disturbed the children and they have school tomorrow! How will they get back to sleep after hearing you raise your voice?"

"My voice? What about yours? You been screamin' like a banshee all day!" Adam reminded her in a roar. "And anyway, them kids of yours better mind their own business or I'll wipe up the floor with 'em!"

Suzanna brushed tears from her eyes.

"You're making Mama cry again," Taddy moaned to his father.

Again! Now Jessy knew for certain that this struggle must have raged all day and she had stirred things up again by making a fuss over the crate. She would have to put things right, she knew, and as soon as possible.

To his children Adam bawled, "Shuddup or I'll knock your heads together!"

"Now, Adam," Jessy said calmly. Changing the topic to something happy and bright she said to her beloved nephews and niece, "We were just talking about all of us going to Florida. Wouldn't that be wonderf—" The response was dismal.

"We don't wanna go to Florida!" groaned Martha.

"We don't wanna go to school!" moaned Taddy.

"We don't wanna go to bed!" shouted Stephen.

Stunned, Jessy asked, "Do you *all* not want to go to Florida?"

The three blond and dimpled children wagged their heads in unison. "I can't understand this. Why not?" Jessy demanded.

"Because, Aunty," Stephen began as if she were a child and he her professor. "Granddaddy George promised me fifty cents every time it snows and I shovel the sidewalks in front of his house and law office. It snows a lot in January and February and if we go away, we won't be here!"

Taddy said, "And we won't be here to build snow forts neither!"

Martha chipped in, "I can't leave LuLu. I just can't!"

Adam, gazing upward, wondered aloud, "And who, may I ask, is LuLu?"

Jessy knew. "LuLu is the daughter of Martha's piano teacher."

Martha nodded. "LuLu has the best dollhouse and she lets me play with it when I go for my piano lesson!"

"No wonder you ain't makin' progress!" Adam bellowed in disgust. "Playin' instead of learnin' somethin' at the teacher's house! Two months a' music lessons 'n' you can't play a note!"

From his nightshirt pocket, Stephen whipped out his harmonica and played a haunting little tune. Taddy tried grabbing the magical musical instrument from his big brother's hands, but Stephen was too fast and strong for him. "It's mine," Stephen shouted, triumphant. "I saved up for it and it's all mine!"

"You should share with your brother, son," Adam said, but he added with a smirk, "Martha's had two months a' music lessons 'n' she can't play a note on the piano, while her brother's had no lessons 'n' can play anythin' he hears just once, and all on a thirty-nine-cent harmonica!"

"It's a good thing you and Suzanna ordered the piano with the customized muffler," said Jessy. Even so, for months her ears had been assaulted by Martha's pathetic attempts at making music.

"What a waste," said Adam. To his oldest son, he called out, "You want music lessons, Stephen?"

"Nope! I got other things to do!"

Adam turned to Taddy. "What about you, short stuff?"

Taddy shook his head, his entire body, saying, "I'm busy!"

Adam thought a moment and said, "Well, no more piano lessons for Martha."

"How selfish can you be?" Suzanna railed. "You would deprive a little child—your own daughter—of the joy of music!"

74

"Face facts, woman. That ain't music your kid's makin'. Martha's scarin' the hogs!" Adam folded his hefty arms across his chest. "No more piano lessons."

Suzanna's eyes narrowed at him. "I see right through you, Adam Flint. You just want to cut back on expenses now that you've bought yourself a fancy automobile and you want to go off on this stupid vacation!"

"Oh, stupid, is it? Look at all the stuff you bought lately with our windfall, besides that piano you said you couldn't live without!"

Fighting tears, Suzanna raged, "You heartless brute! You know we lost my piano in the tornado! You agreed we should buy a new one for the children!"

Ignoring her and counting on the fingers of both hands, Adam tallied Suzanna's purchases: "First there was the cast-iron stove. Then you had to have a sewin' machine. Then an icebox. Then drapes. Then carpets for the livin' room—what's wrong with bare floors? And if that wasn't enough, you had to have a machine to wash clothes, as if the old way of washin' wasn't good enough for you!"

Such extravagance! thought Jessy of this last item. She imagined women—her and Suzanna included—beating laundry with rocks on the banks of a river in the Stone Age. This primitive image made her break into a fit of giggling, but her laughter came at a most inappropriate moment. Adam and Suzanna both glared at her, neither of them in the mood for gaiety. Forcing her face to be serious, Jessy looked back up to the banister where the children still stood in their night clothes. "Now, Stephen, tell me, just what would you do with the money you earn shoveling snow?"

"I'd get a baseball, a bat, and a uniform out of the catalog, that's what! And maybe a football, too, and a go-cart or a bicycle!"

Jessy regarded Stephen and his younger siblings and also her own brother. Strong-willed as he was, Adam appeared to have his hands full trying to govern his equally willful family. Still, she sided with Adam in this great debate, saying to the children, "I'm disappointed in you. In all three of you. How can you disappoint your father so, who wants to recuperate down South? To hear you, you care more about your selves and your petty pleasures than you care about your own father who loves you."

Adam muttered, "That's right. God made them kids through me 'n'

75

Suzy, and there they stand talkin' back like they know everythin'! Why, I oughta—"

Still addressing the children, Jessy added calmly, "You can play fort and shovel snow before and after we visit Florida. Martha, you can play with LuLu and her dollies any time. But all of you can only go once to Florida when your daddy needs to recuperate from the bad accident he had. The nice people in Florida who care about your daddy have been very gracious to invite us all for a visit out of pure friendship and love."

Jessy's well-spoken defense pleased Adam immensely, but his pleasure vanished to hear his children whining again, but on a different track.

"We can't go to Florida. They have hurricanes," declared Taddy.

"Sure they do, but not in January!" laughed Jessy. "Your daddy and I used to have hurricanes in New England when we were your age. They weren't fun, but we survived. And anyway, we have tornadoes right here in Bethel and you don't mind living here, do you?"

Martha twisted around inside her little nightie while saying, "We could get sunstroke!"

"You could get sunstroke here if you stayed out in the sun too much!"

"What about the alligators? They eat children," said Stephen. His big green eyes looked deeply troubled.

"I'll protect you! Didn't I save your life when you were little?" Jessy reminded her nephew.

"Not against alligators!"

"Bo wrestles alligators. For fun!" Jessy retorted. "He owns—or used to own—a share of a place called Cowboy Joe's Birdland, or some such thing, and once he told your daddy and me that he wrestled alligators for the fun of it!"

Stephen appeared a trifle impressed but was still frowning. "But Florida's got bugs!"

"You love bugs! You spent half the summer catching grasshoppers and letting them go!" Jessy laughed. "Bugs are no excuse!"

"The bugs are bigger there. And they have snakes," said Taddy.

Jessy trained a fishy eye on Taddy. "You love snakes."

"Only little snakes." Taddy swayed in time with his sidekick Martha.

"Mama said the rattlers in Florida are as long as a man and as thick around as Daddy's arms!" Martha held out her childish arms for emphasis.

Getting exasperated, Jessy replied, "But children just like you live in Florida—Indian children and white children and black children and Bo's children—and they grow up tall and strong just like children do right here in Bethel! Don't you think your mom and dad and aunty and Bo and his kin and God up in heaven will take care of you? Don't you want to take a nice long ride on the choo-choo train? You love to see the trains go by the house!"

"There's train wrecks and train robbers too," Stephen reminded her gravely.

"Train robbing went out in the nineteenth century," Jessy cried. "And for every train wreck there's hundreds of trains that reach their destinations with no problem whatever!" Now Jessy's throat was getting as hoarse as Adam's, debating all this silly worrying of theirs.

Martha answered, "We'll get killed on the train, that's what Mama said."

Speechless, Jessy looked to Suzanna, but Suzanna turned away.

Adam, looking pitiful, said gently to his sister, "You'd think I was forcin' 'em to a death march the way they're carryin' on! All I wanna do is have a little vacation! Even Jesus took time off to go apart 'n' pray 'n' think 'n' relax, didn't He?"

"Of course He did," Jessy affirmed under her breath. "Often! He was divine but He was human, too, and He got tired just like us."

As their elders conferred, the children fretted on the landing.

"If the alligators and hot sun and hurricanes and snakes and bugs don't get us, we'll die in a train crash for sure!" Stephen said.

Jessy laughed. "So? We're all Christians, aren't we? If we die, then we'll all go to heaven together! Won't that be fun?"

"Stop it! All of you!" Suzanna interrupted. "I won't hear another word! This is my home and we're not leaving and that's final!"

Adam grabbed his wife as she tried to leave the hall. "Hey! Just a minute! Number one, this is our home, not yours alone. Two, you don't have the final say, and three, since when do little kids have the brass to tell their elders what to do? This is your doin', Suzanna, the shameful way you raise your kids, makin' 'em fearful and fretful!"

"My kids? They're yours too, you know. And besides, they may be children, but they have rights."

Fuming, Adam turned from her to their children. "They're gonna have the right to get whipped if they don't shut their mouths 'n' get back in bed. Fine buncha brats you're raisin', Mrs. High 'n' Mighty!" Adam glared alternately at his wayward children and his suddenly all-too-mouthy wife. When the children failed to move, he roared, "You hear me? Either get to bed or get me my strap!"

"Uh-oh." The three children needed no further urging. Quickly and quietly they went to their rooms.

"You brute," Suzanna said in a furor. "So this is your idea of a family meeting! Despicable! You're an ogre, that's what you are!"

Before he could defend himself, the cuckoo clock began chirping a nonsensical number of times.

That was all the ammunition Adam needed. "That stupid clock you bought! You talk about me wastin' money! I hate that dumb clock, and that other one, that ratchet striker you ordered for our bedroom. Before I got married, I never needed an alarm clock. I got up just fine without one, me 'n' the rooster! But no, you gotta have this 'n' you gotta have that! When I was single I was always flush with cash 'n' now I'm always broke 'n' it's your doin', Suzanna!"

Jessy intervened. "Ever since you two got married, I've always tried to be fair and never take sides, but this time I must speak out," Jessy began. "Now, Adam, you know we've needed things. I mean, certain purchases we've made lately have been a real help to us, don't you think?"

"Who needs a cuckoo clock?" Adam raged without looking at his wife.

"All right, so the clock is foolish, I agree, but it didn't cost much and it makes us all laugh and what's wrong with laughing? And anyway, most of the things we've bought are useful and worth having, especially the washing machine. Scrubbing clothes and filthy overalls and towels and sheets for six people by hand with nothing but a tub and a washboard is really hard work, slave labor if you ask me. Before you got married I had to do your washing, ever since I was fourteen, with no help from you, you big muscle man! No doubt about it, Suzanna and I need that washing machine!" Jessy turned from Adam. "Now Suzanna, what I can't understand is why you don't want to take such a wonderful trip. Sure it costs money and sure the children will miss a little school, but it's the chance of a lifetime."

Suzanna flew up the stairs without a word.

Adam, his craggy face dark with anger, watched his wife abandon him. "Go ahead, be stubborn! You'd drive a man to drink! Stay here all winter 'n' freeze to death for all I care, you 'n' them bratty, scaredy-cat kids of yours. Me 'n' Jessy'll go to Florida 'n' have a good time. My sister ain't afraid of nothin'!" With that, he turned and, with the aid of his cane, limped outside into the night.

CHAPTER 8

❦

Without hesitating—indeed without shoes—Jessy ran out in search of her brother, alarmed at what he might do to himself or to others. Would he go off and never come back? Armed with nothing but faith and love and the benefit of past experience, she ran into the darkness after him, a thousand thoughts flying through her harried brain.

Adam had been a heavy drinker several years before. Jessy had rescued her brother from his destructive ways. Would he take up drink now? He had fought men as big and powerful as himself, and nearly killed them—often for prize money—smashing heads like walnuts, cracking ribs like breadsticks! Had Adam gone off tonight on a rampage looking for whiskey? Would he leave in his new car looking for trouble? Or take his own life by driving off a cliff? Not that Bethel abounded in cliffs, being rolling flat prairie, but still, he could drive off one of the docks at Lake Bethel and drown! They'd never find any trace of him!

Jessy ran outside into the darkness, thinking of nothing but Adam Flint, the dearest brother on the face of this earth. Even though Adam was an adult, he was a baby Christian, a new believer who had only just begun worshiping God and reading His Word. *Where could Adam have gone*, she wondered, *out into the dead of night without a lantern, without a jacket, without—*

She nearly tripped over him on the porch. He was sitting there alone in the darkness, not two feet from the front door. "Adam! There you are! Oh, thank heaven!" she said, relieved.

"Hi." Adam sniffed a little in the breezy night air.

"Mind if I sit with you?"

"No. Not at all. I'd like some company that ain't screamin' at me."

"Poor Adam!" she said with a smile. *Poor, dear Adam*, Jessy thought, remembering her silly girlish ideas, her long train trip from New England at the tender age of fourteen, to be with the brother who had left home before she had been born. Thrilled that he hadn't run amok tonight as the old Adam would have, she sat in peace in the rocker next to his. She couldn't help but glory in the beauty of God's gracious night sky. After a long while she said, "What a gorgeous evening. Look at all those stars!"

"Yeah. They're nice, ain't they? So many of 'em. Should be pretty tomorrow, no rain." Adam could always tell about rain. After a deep, mellow pause, he asked, "You like that Leo?"

Leo! With all the ruckus Jessy had forgotten about him. "Yes, I do, and I'll miss him terribly. He's probably getting on the train right now, heading for Texas. Texas is so far away from here!" Jessy sniffled at the thought.

"Been a long time since I took a trip. I miss travel sometimes. I miss bein' on the move like I was when I was performin' six days a week, and twice on Saturdays, all over creation! It's hard bein' married sometimes, not that I regret it any, even though sometimes things don't go right. I love my wife. I love my kids too. But I'm still a man, after all, and I feel the need to travel."

Jessy groped for the right words. "What do you suppose upsets Suzy so much about taking a vacation? I know how much she loves you and wants you to be well. That's why I could hardly understand the fuss she was making. She must have told the children about the bugs and snakes! Such silly reasons not to go to Florida! I couldn't believe my ears!"

"Well, for one thing, she's upset about the kids growin' up, now that all three of 'em will be goin' off to school. She's been upset for the last few days." Adam sighed deeply. "But worse than that, fear makes people do crazy things. Back when Suzy was a kid, just a schoolgirl, one of her cousins was killed in a train accident. He was only twenty-five. Suzy saw the body all mangled up when they brought him back here for the funeral. He was still wearin' the tie her 'n' her mother gave him before he left Bethel for medical school. A doctor, almost. She 'n' her brothers 'n' her parents had seen him off at the train station the day before he was killed. She's never been on a train since."

"How horrible!" Jessy breathed in the darkness. "But we Christians have such hope!"

"Fear makes people act strange, makes 'em think strange, and believe strange ideas. You 'n' me ain't fearful so we don't get all paralyzed like the fearful do." Adam paused before saying, "'Perfect love drives out fear,' that's what the Bible says, and it's true. I'm beginnin' to think it works the other way 'round too: perfect fear drives out love. Look at how Suzanna acted tonight. She's been carryin' on like that all day, ever since that crate arrived from Florida. And this ain't the first time we argued about takin' a trip—any trip. Every time I ask her if she'd like to go with me anyplace she gives me one excuse after another. She won't listen to reason. My accident back in the spring didn't help matters; she thinks cars are as bad as trains!" Adam sighed in the darkness. "But this time I won't give into her. I'm goin' to Florida with her or without her. Course, it won't be as much fun as it would be with her 'n' the kids along, but you 'n' me 'n' Bo'll have a good time, don't you think?"

"Of course we will! Thank you for asking me! I can't wait!" Jessy beamed in the dark, thinking of the sunlight, the birds, the orange trees, the colorful flowers, peaceful rivers, misty blue lakes, giant live oaks dripping with Spanish moss. Who wouldn't want to go? "Of course, I'll need some things," she said slowly.

"I knew it! No woman can't go two feet without spendin' money!" Adam was laughing at her.

"I'm not asking you for money! I'll buy what I need. But what I was getting at was, well, do you think it would be all right if I bought a bathing suit? I saw one in the catalog the other day. It costs $2.98 and comes with a cap. I'll pay for it out of my savings, but I wouldn't order it if you didn't approve of me wearing such a thing in public." The "thing" Jessy described would cover her from her neck to her knees and still she fretted. Would it be too risqué?

"I guess it's okay."

"All right. I'll order it tomorrow, then. The catalog showed swimsuits for men, too," Jessy remembered. "They only cost sixty-five cents, as I recall, and they look like union suits except the arms and legs are short, up to the elbow and over the knee. They pull on from the leg and button at the shoulder."

"Yeah, I better get one. Show me the pictures in the mornin', okay?"

"Okay," Jessy said in a happy dementia. They were going to ride the train to the beach! "Remember what fun we had in Azleton when Bo arranged that wrestling match between you and The Gunboat? It was all so exciting, riding the train with you to Azleton and seeing the big road show and meeting your old friends and getting to know Ruby—how she adored you! And seeing the baby elephants and that sweet little flea circus! Remember?"

"Sure do. I was single then, the summer before me 'n' Suzy got married."

"And Bo had to leave before your match. He had to go to Florida, remember? And then later we got that letter telling us he had married Beatrice and you said—I'll never forget it, Adam—that when a man marries, everything changes."

"It's true. Now, I know you would go anywhere. You're that kind of woman—brave, fearless, good through 'n' through. Sometimes I think you're even more courageous than me."

Laughing, Jessy said, "I doubt that! You're full of courage!" She patted his arm gently.

"You'll make a good wife, the best. That Leo will be blessed to have you by his side."

"If we ever get to the altar. I'm not so sure, Adam."

"You'll get there. True love don't run smooth."

"I've noticed! Think you can smooth things over with Suzanna?"

"How can I if she won't even speak to me? All she did today was yell. You saw. The only time she was calm was when you came home."

"I hate to see you both unhappy. It reminds me of when our parents fought, and Mother was such a strong Christian too. I never could understand why our parents fought so much. Of course, they were upset after you left home as a boy, but still, they never worshiped or prayed together. Father just wouldn't put his trust in God. I wouldn't want to live like that. When and if I get married, I want to pray and worship with my husband, and with our children, if we are so blessed."

"That was a good sermon yesterday about the power of prayer," Adam said.

"Yes, it was." She reached out her hand to him. "Shall we pray now?"

"Okay, if you want. That'd be a comfort to me." He took her hand awkwardly, but gave it a pleasant little squeeze.

Bowing her head under the starry sky, she said aloud, "Dear heavenly Father, please bless this home with openness and much love. Thank You for the deep love Adam and Suzanna share. Bless their little ones, too, the three you gave in love. They start school tomorrow. Please watch over them so they grow up to be good and decent with faith and trust in You. Please help them and all of us conquer fear and clear up misunderstandings. We can't live without You."

"And please, dear Lord," said Adam, "help me be a good father 'n' husband 'n' brother." Adam squeezed Jessy's hand gently. "Bless my good girl here 'n' her Leo as he goes to Texas."

"Oh, yes, Father," Jessy said, "please keep Leo safe, and help him be a good pitcher wherever he goes, and help his sister Emma as she starts school, and all the Kimball family, Peter included."

"And forgive our sins," pleaded Adam. "We don't always do what's right but we're down here tryin'!"

At this Jessy smiled and said, "In the name of Your loving son, Jesus, we pray! Amen!"

"Amen!" said Adam with a burst of joy welling up within him. To her he said, "That was good to do. We oughta pray together every day, you 'n' me and Suzy 'n' the kids."

"Yes, I think we should. Maybe we could read a chapter of the Bible every day together, and pray for understanding, to help us stay together in spirit, especially now that all the children will be going off every day to school."

"Good idea."

They sat together in silence for a few minutes, gazing into the darkness. Stifling a tiny yawn, Jessy asked, "You're not staying out here all night are you?"

"I should say not!" Still hoarse but refreshed, Adam stood and struggled to get his footing with his cane.

Jessy stood too, and helped him as he lifted his foot over the threshold. "Gosh, Adam, I sure am sorry you had to do all your work tonight and mine too. I really didn't want to get home so late. Forgive me?"

"Think nothin' of it. I'm only glad you're all right. You had me worried. I thought somethin' bad had happened to you."

Together they extinguished the lamps and climbed the stairs to their rooms. He nodded good night to Jessy before he closed the door to the master bedroom behind him.

When Jessy went to her room, she could almost feel the heavy, stony silence that had descended over the house.

CHAPTER 9

❦

Jessy wakened groaning. Below her windows, in the hushed darkness over Bethel, a crabby rooster crowed. Jessy lay there alone, struggling with sensual thoughts of Leo. Her comfortable room yielded no peace. Leo was gone but hardly forgotten. How he had yearned for her before he left for Texas so abruptly. What good were diamonds if they had to be apart like this?

She hurriedly dressed and ran to find Suzanna, voice of experience, married to Adam—the rogue of her dreams—after being forbidden by her parents to see him. Suzanna, wife and mother, could advise Jessy in this, her hour of need. Jessy found Suzanna busy in the upstairs bathroom scrubbing children who were protesting this new, disorienting, and unwelcome routine: preparing for school.

Only yesterday—glorious yesterday—they had risen willingly far earlier than this and had romped barefoot all day in good brown dirt and thick grass that left impossible stains on their rugged playclothes. Only yesterday they had splashed about with friends in a hidden cove, reveling in the joys of summer.

Now, today, there was a hint of fall in the air and with it, a new schedule and work, endless work every day for the whole school year. Torture! The children weren't alone in feeling tortured. Jessy stood there flustered, wanting and needing to speak to Suzanna privately—now, this minute— about the fire raging within her as hot as the kerosene heater warming the bathroom.

"Jessy! Thank heaven!" Suzanna looked up from soapy washrags and a counter dripping with puddles and sodden towels, and then back to the unwieldy task of preparing three grumpy, groggy youngsters for school. "Could you put on the coffee? I haven't had a minute! Thanks."

With that, Jessy had been dismissed. She stood in the hallway fuming, anger welling up in her. *Make coffee? At a time like this? The nerve of Suzanna!* Jessy thought.

Soon enough, though, she realized she had started the day all wrong, without prayer. She paused to reflect. How close she felt to the ancient writer who cried, "Oh that I had wings like a dove for then would I fly away!" "Lead me to the rock that is higher than I!" God's Word reached her, alive with meaning, fresh as the dew but old as time. Her task was as clear as was her ultimate reward: "Delight in the Lord and He shall give thee the desires of thine heart."

"You will, Father, I just know You will. You've never failed me!" Jessy prayed fervently, hopefully, joyfully. God's people had always found comfort in His word. Calmed that He and His people knew how she felt and assured God was watching over her, Jessy went downstairs prepared to face the day.

Coffee. Jessy hunted for the various pieces of the coffee pot. This morning why was nothing in its place? Suzanna's usually neat counters were littered with school lunch makings and, on the table, three cold breakfasts left half eaten.

With difficulty Jessy found the pieces and assembled the pot, which she filled with water she pumped at the sink and coffee beans she ground by hand. Tea. She needed tea to rouse herself for the jobs at hand. Tea required hot water, but the kettle was cold, as was the stove. Worse, the firebox usually piled high with wood was empty. Moreover, the ash pan in Suzanna's wood-burning range was so jammed full it would need to be emptied before a fire could be started and any cooking done.

Fuming, she slid the ash pan out of the stove as carefully as she could to avoid dirtying the floor. With a practiced hand she raked out the ashes still inside the stove. Holding her breath while she carried the overly full ash pan outside, she dumped it and went to the woodpile for a load of kindling. All these were Stephen's jobs, she knew. Last evening he must have been so busy doing his Aunt Jessy's chores he hadn't had time to do his own, not with the early bedtime school had required. Feeding three hundred hogs was a big chore for a small boy.

Jessy thought back to the cause of this state of affairs: Leo, who made her late last night. Leo! Jessy sighed again, but not with the poignant longing of dawn. Now, in the cold light of day, she was angry.

86

At this same moment, Leo would be rising from a comfortable Pullman berth on a sleek, luxurious passenger train speeding to rip-roaring Texas, where he would spend sun-filled days playing a little-boy game for adult pay. Jessy fumed to remember, at Tri-County games, how male spectators tossed money to Leo after a great performance on the mound, while females flung themselves! Shocking, positively shocking.

About now Leo would be making his way to the dining car where his piercing blue eyes would be studying a gilt-edged menu and sending messages to his fertile, mechanical-engineering brain regarding the merits of eggs cooked to order with hashbrowns, a rasher of bacon, a stack of warm buttered toast with three different kinds of jam, and a china pot of cocoa served with a silver spoon. There would be fresh flowers on the table, breathtaking views of America rolling past his window, and a waiter (or two or three) making sure *Monsieur* had everything his heart desired. Some people! Jessy poked herself in the hand so hard with a sharp piece of wood she dropped the load of kindling she was carrying. Again, some people! Jessy regathered the wood and, with arms full, stormed up the steps to the back porch and into the kitchen.

After starting the fire in the range, Jessy ran to the barn where Adam was slowly milking cow after cow. "Morning!" she shouted. "Sorry I'm late!"

"Mornin'. Help me with Bessie, will ya?"

"Of course," Jessy answered. Bessie was mindlessly flinging her tail in her poor brother's face while he milked her.

"Bessie's already stepped on my foot once," Adam complained. "What would Bessie do if we didn't milk her? No gratitude in this world, you know?"

"I know." Jessy held the balky cow's tail. "Hey! Stop swaying or you'll knock me over!"

It was going to be a long, nasty morning, Jessy felt. She proceeded to work through it in silence.

❦ ❦ ❦

About eight, a horn tooted. Adam and Jessy paused in their efforts to stop a pig fight to see Jeb Williamson, a farming neighbor, in their driveway at the wheel of a makeshift school bus: a grain truck that had been scrubbed inside and out, fitted with benches, and covered with canvas for this new purpose. Inside were a half-dozen neatly dressed elementary school children. From the look of them, they were at least as groggy and disoriented as the Flint children and everyone else this morning.

Adam nodded hello to Jeb. "Makin' a few bucks on the side?"

"Yep. I run the mornin' route and one of my sons takes over in the afternoon. Ain't bad, when the kids behave." Jeb Williamson, father of nine, shot a menacing glance over his shoulder which produced a miraculous effect of quiet and order amongst the younger generation.

Soon Suzanna appeared, spotlessly dressed in a starched white cotton dress with a full bell skirt, sprinkled all over with tiny golden roses. The three Flint children came forward with her, making their way to the school bus, lunch pails in hand, as well as paper and pencils in carrying kits. "Good morning, Mr. Williamson," they chanted at Suzanna's prompting.

"They look adorable," Jessy said, shamelessly complimenting the three youngsters so smartly turned out, thanks to Suzanna's tireless sewing marathon and frenetic bathing activities. Each child was neatly attired: plaid shirts for the boys, a plaid dress for Martha. The trio made quite a picture: hair cut and combed, and three pairs of clean feet in brand-squeaky-new shoes. Taddy whimpered in pain. Only yesterday he romped through fields in bare feet and now, he suffered shoes and a scratchy pair of brown corduroy knickers. It was too much! Only yesterday his bare feet had become happily, joyously filthy and now, disgusting shoes and socks and pain! "My feet hurt, Mama!"

Adam raised one eyebrow in reply as Suzanna kneeled to poke the toe of Taddy's shoe. The fit was adequate for the boy's weed-like, fast-growing feet. She stood, satisfied the boy would not only survive but also flourish.

Still, Taddy whimpered so much that his father barked, "Are you a puppy or a man?"

"I'm a man with sore feet!" Taddy exclaimed.

Suzanna demanded quiet, saying, "You'll be all right, Taddy. You'll be sitting most of the day. Did you remember to take a handkerchief?"

"Yes, Mama," Taddy said for the dozenth time already that morning.

"Well, then, use it to wipe your nose, you crybaby!" chided his father. "I certainly hope no son of mine'll spend the day in public sobbin' like a sissy!"

"Oh, Mama, my ribbon's falling off again!" wailed Martha.

"Oh, dear, not again!" Suzanna deftly tied the ribbon and smoothed Martha's beautiful flowing mane. "There!"

"Mama, can I bring my frog to school?" Stephen asked. "He'll be lonely here at home all day without me to 'ribbet' to."

"No, absolutely not. What are you hiding? Not your slingshot! Give it to me! Don't tell me you've filled your pockets with stones! Do you want to be thrown out of school? You know better! You're supposed to set a good example for your younger sister and brother!"

Jessy thought, *How quick we are to run to mischief, how slow to goodness!*

With a frown, Stephen handed over the weapon and ammunition. "You won't throw my stuff away, will you, Mama?"

"I'll throw you away if you don't behave," barked Adam.

Their mother said, "Well, you'd better get on board, all of you. You're keeping Mr. Williamson and the other children waiting."

Jessy stood on the sidelines, crying. "It seems only yesterday I watched them all being born and now—" Suzanna's anxiety of the previous days had finally engulfed Jessy.

Adam didn't feel sentimental in the least. Leaning on his cane and frowning with furrowed brows, he said to his three youngsters, "Stay outta trouble, hear me? One bad report from school 'n'—"

"Yes, Daddy," the three said as one.

Jessy poked her head in the back of the bus. "I'll tell you a secret of life, if you like."

All the children looked at her quizzically, not only her own little relatives.

Looking at each small sweet face, Jessy told them all, "Learn to love what's good for you."

Judging from their expressions, all the children, the Flints included, regarded the wisdom Jessy imparted with deaf ears, dumb mouths, and dull brains. *Education is wasted on the wrong people*, she thought.

"Aunty?" asked Martha. "Will you miss me?"

"Of course, honey! Will you miss me?"

All three of the Flint children nodded. Perhaps they would heed her words of wisdom after all, if not today, then perhaps some day.

"You kids'd better stay out of trouble," Adam reminded his brood.

As soon as the makeshift bus pulled away, Suzanna shouted at Adam, "Your children may get into trouble, but not mine!" In a huff, she was gone.

"You know, Adam," said Jessy, "I think your wife has a point there somehow."

Adam gave his sister one of his most contrary schoolboy looks. "Let's go in 'n' eat. I'm starved."

"I'm not."

"You should be. You didn't get any supper last night."

"I may never eat again. I'm—" Jessy couldn't stop the confession. In sheer, utter misery she blurted out, "I'm lovesick."

Adam began laughing at her.

"It isn't funny," she said, half crying and half laughing.

"You ain't a little girl anymore."

"You only just noticed? I'm practically ancient and a spinster!"

Adam found this all very amusing. "Good thing Leo pulled outta here in a hurry. Nothin' worse than a lovesick female doggin' after a man." Adam knew of which he spoke, having been dogged by more than his share of temptresses the world over during his wild bachelorhood.

"It's not easy being a woman."

"You're more than a woman, Jessy." Adam had suddenly grown quite serious. He looked from her to the vast horizon, the big sky all around them, trees laden with nuts towering near fields of ripening corn. "You're a lady, Jessy, and that's the least easy thing to be in this world."

Jessy felt better somehow. At least one person appreciated the effort it took, but how odd that one person was her brother, of all people, a man who had sown bushels of wild oats as a bachelor. Her stomach growled so loud he heard and began laughing at her again. It was impossible, somehow, to appear dignified and superior around Adam Flint. She was human, despite her high calling.

"Even the lovelorn gotta eat," he said.

Inside on the kitchen table was a stack of hotcakes, waiting to be slathered with butter and syrup. Suzanna banged noisily around the cabinets, the sink, the stove, and the icebox. With an unceremonious burst of energy, she turned and slammed forks, knives, and spoons on the table before turning her back on Adam and Jessy again.

Knowing Suzanna was not paying the least attention to him but nevertheless observing all the good table manners she had taught him, Adam spread his napkin on his lap before helping himself to a generous portion of pancakes. As he handed Jessy the serving dish, he said to her above the clatter his wife was making, "While Leo's gone do you intend to get to know his family better? Meet with his sisters maybe?"

"I'd like to, but that won't be easy." Laura was so often out of town and so unlike Jessy in every way. Darlene lived on the far side of the lake. With a business to run, a husband to care for, and a small son to raise, what time would she have for chitchatting with Jessy? And Emma was a schoolgirl with friends her own age. "There's so much work coming up—the field corn will be ready to harvest before long." Jessy thought a moment of what she faced, she and Adam together.

Picking the garden crop of sweet corn, the fine ears Suzanna creamed and sealed in glass packing jars for the family's winter dining, was work enough, but it couldn't compare to picking three hundred acres of field corn destined to fatten their hogs and cows and beef cattle. Corn husking was one of the most demanding, lengthy, and nasty of all farm chores. Soon Adam and Jessy would begin work outside before the sun came up and would continue working till nightfall, day after day, week after week, in rain, early snow, and long after the ground began to freeze solid under their feet. There would hardly be time for rest, much less recreation.

"Where's that orange blossom honey? It'd be good on pancakes," Adam said.

Suzanna's arms were up to the elbow in dishwater, so Jessy got up to find the jar from Bo. While Adam pried off the lid, Jessy sliced a grapefruit and arranged the half-wheels on a platter which she put on the table before resuming her seat.

Adam winked at Jessy. "Florida honey sure is sweet, like them mermaids they got down there. Maybe I'll find a few to keep me company. A pair o' sea urchins! What do you think, Jessy?"

"I'm sure Bo knows where to find them," Jessy added, enjoying the juicy grapefruit Bo Bally had sent to them. *Vacation! What a wonderful idea,* she thought, *a rare treat after putting in such long, hard, slave labor.*

"Oh, yes. Two shapely bathing beauties—one for each of my arms."

Suzanna flipped pancakes at the stove with as much noise as possible.

"Definitely a pair of urchins. Sea bunnies," Adam said, pouring more honey on thick. "A man gets lonely in the tropical latitudes. Real lonely."

Jessy was snickering now. Her snickering came to a sudden end as Suzanna turned and slammed more pancakes on the table. She looked angrily at both of them, her pretty blonde curls dancing around her face, then she returned to the sink and snapped, "Will you two be wanting anything else?"

"Nothing for me, thank you," answered Jessy politely. "Those pancakes were delicious." She dabbed her lips with her napkin.

Adam pursed his cupid's-bow lips. Big dimples appeared in his otherwise craggy face. "Oh, I guess I do want somethin' else." Carefully he coated another stack of pancakes with butter and honey and cut into them with all the care Suzanna had taught him.

Suzanna worked away without looking at him. She snapped, "Well, what is it you want, Adam? Make it quick, will you? I have a lot to do today, laundry I didn't have time to do yesterday, and many other—"

"I know, I know. I'll tell you what I want." Adam breathed deeply and put down his fork. "I want for the woman I love best in all the world to put her fears aside long enough to trust our Lord 'n' me 'n' have a trip that can bring us closer together. I want for the woman I love most in this world to let go of things 'n' schedules 'n' routines long enough to go away with me 'n' enjoy my company 'n' let me enjoy her company. I want my wife to show me that her love 'n' her faith are bigger 'n' stronger than fear."

Suzanna stood like a stone with her back to the table.

Adam continued in his tender, rumbling voice, "When you married me you promised you'd go where I go. Don't you feel that way about me anymore?"

Suzanna turned slowly toward him, her golden hair reflected in the numerous golden roses of her fine cotton dress. To Jessy, Suzanna looked like a gorgeous porcelain doll, fragile and lovely.

"You meant what you promised, didn't you? You still love me, don't you?" Adam asked, as frank and open as a child. He reached out to her. "Let's show our children we're not so afraid of death that we're too scared to live!"

Jessy held her breath, watching and hoping.

Suzanna went to him, her eyes swimming with tears. She sat on his lap and let him wrap his wonderfully strong arms around her. He cradled her like a child, a beautiful, glorious golden child but with all the grace and charm of a woman. Jessy marveled to hear them murmuring together in the language God gives to all who love deeply, endlessly, forgivingly. Over her grapefruit section, Jessy said merrily, "Florida, here we come!"

Suzanna and Adam began to giggle.

"Now I won't go unless you promise me . . . " began Suzanna to Adam.

"Uh-oh. What sort of bribes do I have to offer m'lady?"

"First, we need to talk with Daddy about our wills. You should update yours and I don't even have one! I won't get on that infernal train unless our wills are in order."

"Okay," said Adam. "What else?"

"Let's talk with the children's teachers about their lessons. I insist they keep up with their schooling even when we're traveling."

"Okay," said Adam again. He reached for his mug and took a sip of coffee but never let her go. "What else?"

"We should pray together daily between now and January for a safe trip."

"Absolutely."

"And you'll have to tell me you forgive me."

Adam pursed his lips to hers and whispered that he did, absolutely and unconditionally. Suzanna nestled close, murmuring to him.

Jessy raised her eyes toward the high ceiling of the kitchen. "It's awfully quiet around here without the children."

Adam glowed with the thought. "As much as I love 'em, they're newcomers! I loved my wife long before they came on the scene 'n' I'll love her long after they're grown 'n' gone away!" Adam gave his wife a rousing squeeze. "What do you say, sweetheart? The kids'll be gone till three o'clock!"

"Three forty-five!" she corrected him with glee.

"We have the whole house to ourselves for a change!" the couple said together.

The ever-imprecise cuckoo clock announced the time: one o'clock.

Laughing, Adam said to Suzanna, "Tell you what, Mrs. Flint. Let's pretend like it's really one o'clock last night!"

"Yes!" But quickly Suzanna's smile faded. "Oh, pooh! The laundry!"

A huge pot of water, nearly at the boil on the stove, would have to be hauled with care to the cellar where the washing machine awaited. Despite its cost and newness, there was nothing automatic about the washing machine which required hand agitation with a crank and hand wringing. Every piece of laundry required several turns through the mangle, also operated by hand. And that was just the sudsing portion of the process; more cranking and wringing and mangling were required for rinsing. Every wet item would be hauled outside and hung to dry, an all-day job.

Sighing but sensing her cue, Jessy brought her dishes to the sink and began washing them, saying over her shoulder, "Shall I start the laundry?"

Suzanna peeled, "Oh, would you? What an angel you are, Jessy! I'll join you downstairs in a few minutes."

Downstairs! *Down to the cellar and its various instruments of household torture*, thought Jessy. A full day of washing, and, tomorrow, a full day of ironing for a family of six. She turned to Adam and Suzanna, snuggling together in a fond embrace, sighing sweetly. Together the two went upstairs, happy as newlyweds. Jessy doubted she'd see either of the lovebirds for hours.

❦ ❦ ❦

Once Jessy began soaking the first load of laundry, she studied the mail-order catalog. While she agitated dirty clothes with one hand on the crank, she turned pages with the other, studying the illustrations. Jessy couldn't decide what color her bathing suit should be: black, navy, or white? Some had red collars. Red! Perhaps for Emma Kimball, but not for Jessy Flint. She selected the sensible all-navy bathing suit.

The family would need insect repellent, too, and broad pith helmets, judging from the pictures Bo sent regularly of jungle depths and swamps.

They must write to the Ballys for advice about what to purchase in advance. Travel books suggested mosquito netting, tinted spectacles, hatchets, sporting gear, maps, canned milk, and meat.

Jessy studied drawings and prices of dollhouses, go-carts, and sporting gear. Christmas wasn't all that far away. Christmas, then New Year's, then Florida! She tingled with excitement.

After Jessy washed, rinsed, and wrung the first load, she began another. As she agitated sheets and towels she searched the catalog for books. She decided to give Peter Kimball a Bible. Perhaps a priest or minister had already given him one. If so, someone else at Fair Haven could benefit from having her gift. She couldn't imagine what Peter's life must be like at Fair Haven. Was the place a pesthole like those she had read about? When would she meet him? She had no idea, but decided to pray for him every day. The Bible she selected cost nearly $4.00, a good deal on Jessy's budget, but well worth any price. She selected two more, one for Leo and another for Emma. She would give them the precious books for Christmas, she decided.

While the children's playclothes and Adam's dirty overalls soaked in suds, Jessy tidied the cellar which had become cluttered with junk. It was then she noticed a sack torn open with seed spilling onto the floor. When she knelt for a better look, she saw animal droppings had ruined the costly seed. A squirrel must have gotten into the house. Adam would have to be told once he emerged from seclusion with Suzanna.

Before too long, Suzanna came down to the cellar, explaining, "Adam just had to go see what the hogs were up to!"

Jessy nodded. The pig fight earlier that morning weighed heavily on Adam's mind. It wouldn't do for the animals to harm one another so close to the time they would be shipped to Chicago meat processors. "What happened to your day of, ah . . . romance?" Jessy asked with a grin.

Suzanna returned Jessy's grin. "There's just too much to do around here to take a day for ourselves. I don't know how we'll manage an entire vacation!"

"We'll force ourselves to relax!" said Jessy with a wry smile.

While Suzanna relieved Jessy of the hand-cranking, she studied sporting illustrations in the catalog. "Let's remember to take Adam's fishing gear, and the boys' too. Maybe Martha would like to go fishing too. I'll ask her. Remember the letter the Ballys sent a few months ago, where they described all the good fishing near their home?"

"Yes, I do. We'd better get plenty of mosquito repellent too."

Jessy hauled a heavy basket full of wet laundry upstairs and hung it outside to dry with wooden clothespins. Out in the fresh breezy fall day, while she thought about the Ballys in Florida and Leo in Texas, Jessy entirely forgot about the intruder who had invaded their cellar and contaminated their good seed.

CHAPTER 10

❧

Leo had been thinking of Jessy ever since their sudden separation, for he began writing a letter to her on the train to Pongo, Texas. Jessy read and reread his casual, newsy letters with her heart doing flip-flops.

Life as a rookie ballplayer was harder than the general public might have imagined. Veteran players pulled incessant practical jokes on the newest arrivals. Leo, with several other newcomers, had been jeered, short-sheeted, and teased without mercy from his first day on the team. Their salt had been mixed with sugar; their sugar had been ruined by salt. Their baseball gloves had been filled with sand; their bats were sawn in two.

Leo took all the joking in stride, writing, "Half the players grew up on farms and the rest are from cities—some from slums. A bunch of us are from the Midwest. One is a member of the bar but he'd rather hit fungoes with us bushers than practice law. One teammate is a pharmacist by trade. Most of the guys tell me their families thumb their noses at baseball, so the guys know how I feel.

"I'm pitching pretty good for the Rowdies. I've won two and lost one so far. The game I lost was close: three to two. If our second baseman hadn't dropped a grounder we would've won for sure.

"For now, we play local Nines, but pretty soon we go to California for exhibition games against Trans-Western teams. We work out every day. We walk to the ballpark from our sleeping rooms—a good eight miles. It's hot and dry here. Our uniforms are white with blue trim. They're beautiful (but not as beautiful as you!). We won't be staying in Pongo much longer. I love you and think of you every day."

In his next letter, postmarked California, Leo described the harrowing trip the Rowdies made from a cheap downtown hotel to the ballpark in an open, horse-drawn bus. The Rowdies, who had no dressing room at the park, put on their uniforms before they left the hotel, making them handy targets. The locals booed the Rowdies and threw rotten apples and eggs at them in the streets. Someone even took a few shots at the bus. The Rowdies got their revenge by shellacking the locals eleven to two. The Rowdies swept the series, winning all four games. Leo pitched one of those games, all nine innings.

Leo described without complaint his new living conditions. Baseball players of 1908, major and minor leagues included, were not welcome at the finer hotels and restaurants as they toured the country by train. Acacia Kimball had been right to say that ballplayers were held in low esteem. Teams stayed in third-rate hotels and were seated in the dimmest corners of cheap restaurants, where they came to expect poor service and unwholesome meals.

The Rowdies, like all ball teams of those days, traveled on a tight budget. They went about on stifling hot trains to potholed fields that dotted the bigger cities of America. After a game played in scorching hot sun, there would be one shower stall for the entire team and a long line of dirty, sore players waiting to use it. Players either washed their own uniforms or wore them smelly, damp, and dirty, game after game. Players on a winning streak might be superstitious enough to avoid washing their uniforms as long as their lucky streak lasted.

Saloons and poolhalls abounded near their lodgings—dark, beer-swilling places Leo didn't especially like, but he went along with his teammates unless he was due to pitch. There were no trainers, no team doctors (or truss-fixers as some players called them), no beautifully manicured ball grounds. There were hardly any rules governing pitchers, either, so Leo and his mates could cover a ball in spit, rub it and rough it up on their spikes or belt buckles, and otherwise mangle it any way they liked to achieve the desired curve when it was thrown. In 1906 at least one board of health discouraged pitchers from wetting balls with spit because of the threat of spreading tuberculosis. By 1908, however, the only rule, if one could call it a rule, guiding pitchers was to apply spit in as genteel a fashion as possible. A player with a cough was always looked upon with concern. Did he have TB?

An umpire's life was hard. The few who worked the games in those days suffered so much abuse from players, managers, and disgruntled fans that they often carried loaded handguns to the park. They were routinely spat upon and jeered without mercy. Fans threw trash or empty pop bottles at them and at players too. It was not unusual for players to scramble up the stands during a game to punch unruly spectators in their loud mouths.

Reading Leo's letters between the lines, Jessy sensed there were girls everywhere the Rowdies went—on trains, at games, in hotel lobbies, dance halls, and gin joints. Girls everywhere, and here sat Jessy, the virginal homebody. What could she write about? Leo knew all about her life, dull as it was, the endless round of work she did, the hassles, the weather now turning cool, the ripened corn to be harvested, the amusing things her little niece and nephews said and did. When would Leo come home again? In October, the baseball season ended in the United States, but the winter season began south of the border.

Leo would return for a few days in early November. Then he and the Rowdies would go back to the West Coast and perhaps Japan. They might instead tour the Caribbean dominated by numerous clubs with powerful players. Leo could not plan to be home at Christmas, nor would he be seeing Jessy and her family off as they departed for Florida in January. By the time the Flints returned to Bethel, Leo would be on his way to spring practice. He wrote often that once he got a major league contract he'd tell his parents of their engagement.

His letters sometimes arrived in batches, but often nothing came for long stretches. Leo had to stay in a perpetually combative mental state, fighting for his job on the mound and keeping his wits about him when off the field. As he traveled, his letters became sketchy at best; he had to concentrate on his game. He promised to spend as much time as he could with her when he came home in November. Jessy counted the days.

Leo finally returned during a week filled with brisk, balmy days, the last good days for outings before the severe winter began. Corn husking was going on full swing when the telephone rang at the Flint home.

It didn't ring often; when it did, it was usually Suzanna's parents or dealers selling farm equipment. But this Friday lunchtime, the telephone rang, and, surprisingly, it was for Jessy. She held the heavy black receiver to her ear and put her mouth close to the speaker of the boxy wooden phone. "Hello?"

"Jessy! I'm home! I just got in on the 12:20 from Birmingham!"

"Leo! Is it really you?" Her unexpected joy was frustrated by the work she had to do. "I wasn't expecting you until tomorrow!"

"Our playing schedule changed—everything's moved up a day! Can I come and see you? We could go for a drive, or come back to my parents' house."

Jessy looked down on herself: grimy as usual and unprepared for romance. She had finished lunch. Adam was lingering with Suzanna at the table, taking a break from his arduous work.

"Jessy? Are you there? Were we cut off?" Leo tapped the switchhook on his phone set a few times. "Hello? Hello!"

Jessy looked back at the telephone. "I'm sorry, Leo. It's wonderful to hear your voice, but there's so much to do." She fretted silently.

"Can I come over? I don't have much time—I leave for Texas on— hello?"

"Yes, Leo. I'm listening. Please hold a moment." Jessy went into the kitchen. She saw, through the windows, acre upon acre of field corn waiting to be husked. "Adam? Leo's just gotten home and wants to know if—"

"Let me guess. Leo wants to know if he can spend the day with you, and tomorrow 'n' the next 'n' the next 'n' so on until—?"

Jessy looked miserable, torn between her duties, her family, her livelihood, and the love of her life. "Leo will only be home a few days, Adam," she said softly.

Adam studied his sister's simple silhouette: her long, dark hair tied and pinned away from her face; her modest, hard-worn work clothes; hands raw from husking; her sweet face struggling with conflicting drives and needs. From his chair at the head of the table, he said, "Of course you can see him. I can manage without you this afternoon, but you'll need to be back by five."

"Oh, thank you, Adam!" Jessy ran back to the phone.

Leo said he'd be right over. With her stomach in knots, Jessy raced upstairs to freshen herself and change into her good mulberry wool suit with its gently gored skirt. From her upstairs windows she could see Adam making his way alone to a distant field, driving his team, seated at an empty wagon that he would spend the afternoon filling with field corn. So much work and him all alone and still not entirely well. Jessy sighed and looked away, concentrating on getting dressed. Leo would be here soon. Leo! Her heart beat a confused rhythm. Had he changed these two months he had been gone?

As she waited for Leo in the parlor, she could hardly sit, she was so excited. She kept jumping up to look for his car and checking the small watch pinned to her lapel. When a full hour and a half passed after his call, Jessy began to fret. Had something happened to Leo? Now she paced about, glancing at the front door, the telephone, and her watch, getting more upset every minute. The cuckoo hadn't made any announcements in what seemed like hours, not that it had even a vague notion of the true time.

As Jessy paced, she caught a glimpse of herself in the hall mirror. She appeared worried. She never felt like this before, worrying and waiting for a man. During the summer, Leo had always been so prompt, but then he was rushing to the Tri-County baseall park for scheduled games.

Jessy sighed and tried to relax. "Dear God, are Leo and I right for each other? I love him, but I feel so unsure sometimes! Please show me Your way. What could be keeping him? Where is he?" The cuckoo sounded eight times, totally incorrect, but still a reminder that time was, in one form or another, flying. Jessy could have picked and stripped several bushels of field corn in the time she had wasted pacing about. In a slow-growing anger, she started upstairs to change into work clothes again. There was a knock at the front door.

"Leo!" She flew down and looked at him through the lace curtain over the glass while she fumbled with the knob. "Leo!" She flung open the door and beamed at him.

"Did you give up on me? I'm sorry I'm late. Some friends stopped by just as I was on my way out." He looked genuinely delighted to see her.

Jessy forgave all in her happiness at seeing Leo again, even more handsome than ever but tougher, tanner, leaner, prouder, with the look of up-and-coming success about him. He was dressed in a new deep blue suit and vest with a rich red silk tie.

"Come in, please." Before closing the door, she peeked at the unoccupied Simplex in the drive. "Where's Emma?"

"In school."

"Oh, of course!" Jessy's own niece and nephews were in school, too, this Friday afternoon. "How are all the Kimballs? And especially you?"

"Everyone's dandy. I was thinking we could go for a drive." Leo admired Jessy's slender, shapely figure and wholesome, pretty face. "Miss me?"

She looked into his shining blue eyes. "Like mad!"

"Me too! Let's take a nice long drive, just the two of us."

Apprehension overtook Jessy. She swallowed hard, fighting primal urges to give Leo all a woman can give a man. *A long lonely drive*, she thought, *and then*. And then! What if she gave in to such urges? What if every woman did, without the benefit of marriage? What would the world be like then?

Jessy looked away from him, searching for her gloves. Leo came up behind her, so warm and so close she could feel the life force pulsing within him. Instinctively they both turned and looked at their combined reflection in the hall mirror. They made a striking, vibrant couple. He put his face near hers and closed his eyes, murmuring hotly to her, "Oh, how I've missed you . . . "

"Leo? Leo Kimball, is that you?" Suzanna was calling from the kitchen.

Pulling away from Jessy as if he'd been shot, he hollered in his booming pitcher's voice, "Yeah, Suzy, *the* Leo Kimball, in person!" He took Jessy's hand and followed the voice in the kitchen. "We're deciding how to spend the day."

"Hi, Leo! You look well!" Suzanna said, her hands and arms white with flour as she kneaded bread. "How's life in baseball?"

"Greatest thing in the world. Hear from your brother lately?"

"Matt is no letter writer!" Suzanna's younger brother and Leo had been great friends as boys growing up in Bethel. "As soon as he finished college, off he went to California. He writes to our folks once every six months—two sentences on a postcard!"

"Next time you write, tell him I said hello, will you, Suzy?"

"Of course. I have his address somewhere around here if you want it. Maybe you could visit him when you're out his way."

"I'd like that." Leo stood with Jessy, still holding her hand. Together they watched Suzanna search through recipes and mail piled on her kitchen desk.

As Suzanna hunted for Matt's address, she asked "Are you hungry, Leo?"

"Nope, ate on the train. The cooking's great but not as good as your mother's."

"She was asking for you the other day. Drop by and say hello! Now where is Matt's address! It's here somewhere!" Suzanna talked as she dug around.

"If you find it," Leo suggested as he put gentle pressure on Jessy's hand, "just let Jessy know and she can put it in one of her letters to me."

Letters, pleasant, interesting letters! How hard it had been, at first, for Jessy to be separated from Leo, but their romance by mail was so safe compared to Leo's earthy presence. He squeezed her hand again and met her eyes in a way that set her pulse racing. As Suzanna continued hunting, Jessy told Leo, "I—um—Adam expects me back by five."

"We'd better get started then." Leo couldn't take his eyes off of her, wrapped in deep reddish purple with cream lace peeking out at her throat, all in all, a most delicately poised and arresting face and form.

Lest Leo be thinking about a lonely drive, Jessy stammered, "On th-the phone you m-mentioned spending the afternoon with your p-parents?"

Leo looked surprised. "Is that really what you'd like to do?"

She nodded vigorously. Facing her future in-laws was preferable to the trouble she could get into with Leo on a lonely country road.

❧ ❧ ❧

The next morning, a Saturday, Jessy rose early and picked corn with Adam until eleven o'clock when she returned to the house to prepare a picnic lunch, with Suzanna's help, for her afternoon with Leo. During the ride home from his house the previous day, Leo and Jessy decided to make the long-awaited trip to Fair Haven this afternoon. Emma would chaperone.

"We can't tell Mum and Dad we're going to Fair Haven," Leo had told Jessy. "They're upset enough about my playing baseball! Don't mention Fair Haven to Suzy or your brother either."

Jessy felt uncomfortable about Leo's need for deception but agreed. She told her family they would take an afternoon drive and enjoy a picnic lunch. Still, Jessy had felt better about Leo's family now than she did during the Labor Day cookout. Their Friday afternoon together had been pleasant enough because Jessy remained in the background, allowing Acacia and Walter ample time to visit with Leo. After all, Jessy reasoned, they, as she, hadn't seen Leo in two months. Emma didn't come home from school until nearly five, as Jessy was ready to return home. The redheaded teenager seemed unusally distant. Now Jessy and Suzanna prepared a bountiful picnic lunch.

Suzanna laughed remembering: "Leo ate at our house all the time when he and Matt were in school. Leo was always hungry! He was almost a boarder!"

"Acacia doesn't cook, according to Emma," Jessy said. "Oh, look! My cake!" Jessy pulled a lopsided devil's food cake from the oven.

"Oh, dear, I told the boys not to peek! I'm sorry!"

"It'll taste fine, I'm sure," said Jessy as she took her misshapen cake to the counter. While she creamed a bowl of frosting, Suzanna searched for the picnic basket.

When Leo came for Jessy, it was cool enough to keep the top on the Simplex convertible. Jessy put on the motoring veil and duster Leo offered as protection for her rose-colored wool coat and matching felt hat. The duster would keep her warm in those days before cars came equipped with heaters.

Leo very nearly lifted the veil and kissed Jessy's lips there in the hall but changed his mind when he heard Adam thumping above the landing. "Hi, Mr. Flint. How's everything?"

"Fine, just fine. I'm still thinkin' about wirin' the house for electricity." As he spoke, Adam tapped walls and dug around inside the upstairs hall closet. He poked his head out and said abruptly, "Now, Leo, don't you bring Jessy home too late. I expect her back by supper time. We got field work to do 'n' we're way behind schedule."

"Yes, sir," said Leo as he ushered Jessy out the door.

❧ ❧ ❧

The long drive that Saturday afternoon was lovely in every way. Leo behaved like a perfect gentleman. Even Emma had been well behaved, or at least subdued. She seemed more interested in getting out of the house than seeing her brother Peter. Emma had visited him once when she was a small child but remembered little about him.

Still, Jessy found it strange that Emma had remained so quiet in the backseat, staring at the scenery as they drove the thirty miles to Fair Haven. Jessy thought perhaps Emma was growing contemplative as she matured into a young lady. She turned to Emma, dressed warmly and well in a royal blue coat. Strawberry curls twisted from her pretty blue velvet hat.

"Emma, you've been so quiet! What are you thinking about?" Jessy asked.

"Nothing," she answered.

"That's probably true," joked Leo.

Jessy wasn't about to give up. "How's school?"

"I dunno," murmured Emma.

"She's about to flunk out," Leo said quietly.

"Really? Emma, is that so?" asked Jessy, truly concerned.

Emma shrugged. "Who cares? I hate school. I wish I could get away."

"Maybe you can move into Fair Haven," Leo said. "We'll leave you there."

"Leo!" Jessy said, her voice troubled. "It's bad enough we've all gone sneaking off like this without telling anyone where we're going."

"We didn't go sneaking off, as you put it. I didn't lie to my parents. I told them I wanted to take a long drive on a beautiful day, and enjoy a picnic lunch with my girl."

"What you didn't bother telling them is that we're all going to the nuthouse," Emma snapped at Leo with some of her old sparkle.

"Has Laura been posing again?" Jessy asked. "I'm looking forward to seeing that new catalog with the latest Paris fashions."

"It isn't out yet," Emma said flatly as she stared at the scenery.

Jessy remembered being Emma's age, not so long ago. For some, Jessy reasoned, moodiness was just part of growing up. In her warmest voice Jessy said, "You know, Emma, you're always welcome to visit me anytime at all."

Emma nodded to show that she had heard.

"Are you upset about seeing Peter?" Jessy asked.

"No," said Emma. "I just came for the ride."

Why did Emma's toneless voice make Jessy quiver inside? Jessy shrank down deep into her warm wrappings and burrowed her gloved hands into her muff. In the silence, Jessy thought ahead. She had read about insane asylums. She pictured the place where Peter lived, as more of a prisoner than a patient, in more of a madhouse than a hospital. She could get little out of Leo in the way of a description but sensed that Peter had been treated humanely during his long illness. According to Leo, their parents spared no expense for Peter's care. Fair Haven was considered one of the most advanced institutions of its kind for men in the nation, nothing like the nineteenth-century snake pits where the mentally ill were routinely caged.

As they neared Fair Haven, Jessy took the gift Bible out of her carry bag, hoping Peter would receive it in the spirit it would be given. "Do you think your brother might like to read this?" she asked Leo.

"I don't have any idea. I don't know what he likes to do or doesn't like to do. I know he's asked for books in the past."

He, always *he*, never Peter! It troubled Jessy that Leo either would not or could not refer to his own brother as a thirty-three-year-old man with a name. For the first time, though, Jessy felt a ray of hope. Peter liked books. At last she said, "I hope he likes fried chicken too."

They neared a red stone building surrounded by a tall wrought-iron fence that had no beginning and no end. Beyond the high fence, vast lawns surrounded the place, with a few well-pruned trees for shade.

Leo told Jessy and Emma, "He'll want to come with us. He got pretty violent last time we were here so whatever you two do, don't give him any false hope, either of you!"

Leo stopped at the gate and explained to the guard the reason for their visit. The gates were opened to allow Leo entry. As soon as he drove through, the gates were closed and locked behind them.

Jessy's eyes widened to hear the gates being shut behind them and see the view opening up before her. Male nurses and doctors walked about among their patients, tending men in wheelchairs and those who moved slowly on foot. None of the patients moved with decisiveness. Men of all ages, so many ill and lost-looking men! Jessy nearly cried to see them, each one lost to family and friends and the world beyond the wrought-iron gates. Men, she thought, *yes, despite their illness they are men, all of them, each one created in the image of God.* But, oh, so very lost. One struggling lad was restrained by his nurses.

Had she done right, insisting on visiting this strange place, making this visit a condition of her continuing relationship with Leo? Was God's will in this? For two months she had prayed about this moment, but now she faltered.

Jessy remembered the story of Jesus confronted by the madman who dwelled among the tombs, crying and cutting himself on sharp rocks, a man so strong and violent no chains or fetters could hold him. Yet, even in his madness, he cried to Jesus and worshiped Him, and Jesus, with great compassion, healed the man and made him whole. Over and over, Jesus had not only brought love and healing but even identified with the lost, the needy, the wounded.

Calmed and reassured, Jessy thanked the Lord for the brilliant light that glowed over all of them—patients, visitors, and medical staff alike. With a heart full of hope she walked with Leo and Emma to the visiting wing.

While Leo talked with the administrative staff, Jessy watched him at a small distance, thinking he had never looked more handsome, more virile. Leo was wearing another new suit and rich silk tie. She saw him sign a form and hand the pen to his sister. Emma signed her name, as did Jessy. Would the staff report to Mr. and Mrs. Kimball about this visit? Jessy had never considered such a possibility. Was she ruining her chances for a happy marriage by this insane trip? Insane! What was she thinking?

The three waited in an oversized parlor flooded with sunshine and furnished with comfortable chairs. In another room not too far away a pianist was playing a stirring but unidentifiable etude echoing the beauty of the day.

The sitting room overlooked a lawn that rolled and swelled away from the complex. Trees had turned yellow and gold and orange, but the grass was still bright green. In silence Jessy pondered the majestic view while praying, "Dear Lord, forgive me for not telling my family about this trip. If this visit is wrong, if it isn't Your will, let it be forgotten, but oh God, if this is Your will, guide us with love and caring, with the right word spoken at the right moment and the right outcome for all. In Christ's name, I ask this. Amen."

When Jessy lifted her eyes, Peter Kimball was standing before her, Leo, and Emma. He was wearing carpet slippers and warm but casual clothing. The colors and patterns he was wearing didn't go together, but Jessy decided that he was probably color-blind like so many men. She couldn't help but compare Peter to Leo, two brothers from the same parents, and yet so different: Peter so fair, so pale and vulnerable; and Leo, so swarthy, athletic, and successful. Leo resembled their mother's side of the family, and Peter resembled their father's. While Leo had only just reached the threshold of manhood, his older brother looked past his prime. Had Peter ever looked young?

Peter was flanked by two hefty attendants. Jessy got to her feet and reached for Peter's hand. Leo and Emma also rose but were unsure of what to do.

After the attendants stepped away a little, Leo spoke first, asking, "How are—" Leo paused to bite his upper lip hidden under his bushy dark moustache. How was Peter? Well, crazy, that's how Peter was and how he always would be!

While Leo stood there wondering what to say, Jessy filled the void by introducing herself. "Hello, Mr. Kimball. I'm Jessy Flint." They shook hands. "I'm so glad to meet you. I live in Bethel, where your family lives." She paused, her delicate face upturned to Peter's. He was tall, at least as tall as Walter Kimball, but not at all bulky, with Walter's coloring and wide-set pale eyes like Laura's and Emma's. He had good, thick reddish-brown hair.

"Peter," Emma said slowly. "Do you remember me? I'm your sister."

Peter shook his head. No, he wouldn't remember this girl less than half his age. He took Emma's hand even though she didn't offer it to him. "I'm glad you came." His glance included all of them in what he said next: "I don't know why you came, all of you, but I'm glad you did. Can we sit down?"

Relieved that Peter seemed so normal, everyone sighed, took off their coats, and sat with Peter. Jessy and Emma sat close together on a sofa, with Leo and Peter in separate lounge chairs. The attendants sat at a distance, watching but not eavesdropping.

Jessy smiled at Peter, saying, "I'm glad we came too. We brought a picnic with us." She gestured to the basket beside her seat. "Are you hungry?"

Peter regarded her with his wide quizzical eyes. "Not now, but maybe later. Can you stay?"

"Only for a little while." Leo fidgeted in the deep leather chair. "We have to be back in Bethel by five and it's a pretty long drive."

Peter looked to the clock on the wall. "It's early."

"I'm getting married," Leo said, "to Jessy." Leo reached for her hand. "It was Jessy who wanted to meet you. She wanted to meet the whole family."

Peter nodded. "I see. I wish you both every happiness."

"Thank you," Jessy said. "We didn't interrupt you, did we? Your friends are taking exercise." From her seat, Jessy could see a half-dozen patients roaming aimlessly about the lawn.

Peter followed her gaze toward the windows. "I was out earlier today. I came inside to practice."

"Practice?" Jessy asked.

"The piano. I was playing down the hall when they told me I had visitors."

Jessy beamed. "Oh, so that was you we heard just now! That was a lovely melody you were playing, but I didn't recognize it."

"Oh, it's just something I made up," Peter said. "I learned to read music when I was a boy, in Chi-Chicago, but I never did much with what I learned until I came here. When I began to play, the staff gave me sheet music. That's mostly what I do here, play music and read." Apparently Peter enjoyed reading as much as music, for though he was glad to have company, his eyes wandered to the magazines and books strewn on the table nearby.

"Oh, that reminds me. I brought you something to read." Jessy pulled the Bible from her bag. "You probably have one already, but I—well, I wanted to give you the very best gift in the world, seeing as you're Leo's brother."

Peter took the book in his extraordinarily long hands and opened it carefully, turning the thin pages loaded with text.

Jessy admired Peter's hands, *the hands of a concert pianist for sure*, she thought. Then she laughed a little self-consciously. "I'm sure there must be Bibles all around this place. I hope you don't mind my—"

"No, not at all. You're right, there are Bibles around, but I've never had one of my own." He tore his eyes from the book to look at Jessy. "Thank you. I'll read it, I promise you. I've been meaning to."

"How wonderful! I'm so glad!" Jessy said. "It's the truth the Lord wants all of us to know."

Peter's face darkened with fear, as if some unnatural, irrational panic had seized him.

"What is it, Peter?" Jessy asked with alarm.

Without looking at her or anything around him, Peter said in a stiff, toneless voice, "It was truth that undid me. Truth is a killing gypsy."

This strange and chilling remark gave them all pause. The attendants stood and prepared to take hold of Peter. Leo raised his hand to keep them at a distance for the moment. Jessy closed her eyes to pray and think. In a few seconds she said, looking at Peter's feet, "Aren't you cold without socks?"

It seemed a silly thing for Jessy to say, but the tender concern in her sweet voice touched Peter in a way that chased the anguish from his eyes. He looked down at his feet and shrugged. "I don't mind the cold. I don't feel it much." Suddenly his eyes went blank. Without looking at anyone among their party, he said in a flat monotone, "I don't feel things."

To this Jessy had to object. "But you play the piano with such feeling! I heard you. I felt your emotion when you played. You moved me."

"I feel music. Inside me. But not—" Peter could not continue.

"Will you play more music for us?" Emma asked.

"If you like. You're Emma," he said. "But your voice is different."

"I'm Emma, that's right. Emma Kimball," she affirmed.

Jessy thought for a moment that Peter's mind was clouding over, but then she realized why he might be confused. "I suppose you think Emma looks like Laura! They do look something alike in their coloring and features but their voices are very different!"

"That's it! You're probably thinking of Laura," said Leo, relieved. "Laura and I came out to see you once, with Dad. Back then Laura was about Emma's age now. They do look alike, at least a little, but their voices are entirely different."

Emma appeared flattered to be confused with her glamorous older sister, but her youthfulness poked out when she announced in a petulant manner: "I'm hungry. Can't we eat now? I didn't eat breakfast and it's nearly two o'clock!"

"You haven't eaten?" Again, Peter seemed to look wild. "You should eat. You must eat if you want to live. Do you understand?" Peter sounded angry. "You must eat!"

Jessy was about to shrug off Peter's especially strong reaction as a symptom of his mental imbalance when Emma began to speak as if waking from a deep trance. Peter, Leo, and Jessy gazed at Emma as she recollected something from deep within her subconsciousness.

Emma began slowly, in a voice that seemed to come from a far distance, "Mum had a pet bird, a budgie I think it was. I was little, maybe five years old at the time, and I wondered why the bird stopped singing. It didn't move. I poked at it with a pencil through the bars of the cage and saw it was dead. The pretty little blue bird lay there at the bottom of the cage, dead and stiff, with its scrawny little legs sticking up." Now Emma's voice rose, and as it did she shut her eyes tight, crying and saying, "I ran and told Mum and she put her hand to her forehead, like she had just remembered something. I felt so angry at her, angrier than I've ever felt toward anyone in my whole life. I wished I were big enough to punish her. I wanted to hit her, but I knew I mustn't! Oh, how I wanted her to suffer!"

Everyone looked stunned to hear this story of Emma's. Jessy spoke first. "But, Emma, pets die sometimes, no matter how much we love them and care for them."

"You don't understand, Jessy!" Emma wailed. "Mum forgot to feed the bird and that's why it died! It starved to death right in the cage, right in the middle of the sitting room because she forgot to feed it, and no one else in the house paid any attention! After Daddy took the bird away, I took the seed cup out of the cage and puffed on it. There was nothing in it but hulls, empty hulls! A bird doesn't eat much, but it can't live on nothing! No food at all! The water cup was all slimy, as if it had never been washed or refilled. Just a tiny bit of fresh water would have kept the bird from dying of thirst! How could my own mother have been so careless? The animal couldn't ask for help. It depended on her for nourishment and look what happened to it!"

Bird-loving Jessy nearly cried. "That's horrible!" To herself, she wondered why Emma would tell that story now, of all times, in all places! Even odder, why did Jessy suddenly recall a small portion of Scripture about cisterns, broken cisterns? Later, alone in her room, she would search the Old Testament to find the complete verse, but for now, she said in an effort to comfort Emma, "No wonder you don't like dieting! You're afraid you'll end up like that poor little bird."

"That's for sure!" Emma began fidgeting with the long leather gloves in her lap. "No one wants to die of hunger and thirst."

"I'm curious, Emma. Why did you tell us that story?" Leo asked. "We weren't talking about birds."

"I don't know. I hadn't thought about that poor little bird in years."

Peter had been listening with rapt attention to all of this. "You remembered because I said you must eat."

Emma nodded readily, glad Peter had understood. "Mum and her stupid diets! She about starves us to death. Did she make you diet too?"

Peter shrugged. "Probably, but it's been so long since I've seen her I hardly remember."

"Mum never could cook worth a flip!" Leo said with a laugh, "When I was still living at home, I solved my hunger problem by eating at my friends' houses! There's nothing like country cooking."

Peter steepled his wondrously long fingers and peered over them at his visitors. "Here I can eat all I want. Sometimes visitors come to see the other patients and leave home-cooked food for us. It's often better than what we get to eat here. What did you bring?" He indicated Jessy's basket.

With a smile, Jessy said, "All sorts of good things. My sister-in-law makes the best fried chicken. It's my brother's favorite. She made lots! And potato salad, and sweet corn she put up from our garden, and biscuits. We made fresh cider from the apples we grow—they're small but sweet. And a cake. Don't laugh when you see it." Leo helped Jessy put the basket on a table and started passing plates to everyone, including the guards and other patients. "I made the cake," Jessy confessed. "It's a little lopsided, but it should taste all right. This morning I thought I should pack candles for the cake—so we could celebrate—but I couldn't find any."

"We'll celebrate anyway," said Peter as he began munching on a drumstick.

Emma joined in, eating ravenously, as if she had never before seen food.

CHAPTER 11

❦

"What a Monday." Adam reported the reading he had just noted on the outdoor thermometer: "Two feet below zero."

"You hardly exaggerate," Jessy said, her laughter turning to puffs of steam in the cutting cold of that dark November dawn.

They were riding through newly fallen snow to the rear eighty with an empty horse-drawn wagon they would fill and empty several times before dusk. The harvesting process that had begun in early fall was slowly grinding to its backbreaking conclusion. They were far behind schedule in their corn husking. Adam's slow recuperation prevented him from working at his usual brisk pace.

Since mid-September he and Jessy had worked from dawn until dusk picking and husking corn, a killing job. The work was hard on clothing and harder on the hands, and the harvest bigger than any year before this. So far they had refused to hire help, preferring to save what remained of their windfall to enjoy in Florida.

Before starting out, they had already done the morning work by lamplight, caring for all their livestock. Now corn-loving crows took flight from the field as Adam and Jessy approached. Dawn was just breaking as they arrived at the spot where they had stopped on Saturday night. After Jessy had returned from Fair Haven and eaten supper, she had changed clothes and gone straight to this field with her brother. They had worked by lantern light until their hands began to freeze.

During all the years before this, Adam would have worked on Sunday, not keeping the Sabbath holy and expecting Jessy to work without ceasing, especially if the harvest had been as vast as this. But after his Christian conversion that summer, Adam looked forward to their day of worship and rest, a time to be with his family enjoying simple pleasures.

It had been a beautiful Sunday. After church the Flints enjoyed Sunday dinner with Suzanna's parents. How George and Rachel Webb looked forward to these visits and seeing their daughter Suzanna happily married with children of her own.

Afterward, the Flints had returned home to relax in their parlor. While Suzanna embroidered, Adam read about Florida. Jessy searched her Bible, without success, for that verse about cisterns. The children played with their Sunday toys, those special gifts meant for the Sabbath: a hand-carved brightly painted Noah's ark filled with animals that Granddaddy George and Grandmother Rachel had given to them the previous Christmas.

Stephen, Martha, and Taddy played with other special toys, too, taken from the closet every Sunday and scattered over the carpet: a tiny tea party set; a metal windup baseball pitcher, catcher, and batter; a scale model general store with tiny merchandise for sale and a wee lady and gent to run the tiny cash register; and the sturdy firehouse Adam had made for his boys.

Adam sketched a dollhouse while his little Martha made suggestions: she wanted a Victorian two-story painted yellow just like Mommy's and Daddy's, she told him, and "a barn with snowflake-shaped windows just like ours."

Adam nodded, smiling as he thought he might never be done with all of this miniature construction under the supervision of his miniature boss lady. Adam gave her a hug and kept sketching. Martha ran for her coloring set, to help with the planning of her tiny estate. "You'd better order customized carpets 'n' drapes from your mother," Adam called to her. Suzanna looked up at him with a wry, knowing smile. She put aside her embroidery and began fashioning teeny clothes for Martha's dolls and wee curtains for doll windows.

The whole day had been perfect, but for Jessy there was one important element missing: Leo Kimball. After their Saturday at Fair Haven, she had hoped they could worship together, but Leo had to catch a train back to Texas. Now, this frigid Monday morning, Jessy thought about him.

She and Adam dropped to the ground and began picking corn, tossing every ear of it up into the wagon Adam had fitted with a bang board. The stalks were stiff and dry and tore at clothes and flesh. Before leaving the house they had rubbed their hands in salve, and then put on gloves and mittens and old stockings over their arms for added protection against cuts. On their right hands they each wore a husking hook, a metal device strapped across the palm. Automatically, they reached with their left hands into the stiff dry stalks, grabbed an ear of corn, stripped its husk with the hook on the right hand, and snapped the cob free. Bang! The first ears of corn were thrown into the big, empty wagon. Bang! The sound would go on nonstop till nightfall.

"You never did tell me about your Saturday with Leo," Adam reminded Jessy over the noise they both made. He knew Leo, Emma, and Jessy had picnicked together, but ever since, Jessy had been uncharacteristically quiet.

Jessy eyed him sidelong, watching his noble profile silhouetted in the rosy dawn. He tossed an ear of corn upward without looking. It hit the bang board dead center and slid down into the empty wagon. Together they would repeat that maneuver countless times.

"So? What'd you do?" he pressed.

Jessy stripped and tossed a few frozen ears of corn into the wagon before saying, "It was interesting. Most interesting. I wish Leo had taken me to church. He didn't have time." Jessy stood still in the cold, facing the brittle morning sun. "I believe no matter what work we do, our lives should honor God, whether it's playing ball or picking corn, leading the country, digging ditches, building churches, or raising children."

Adam nodded. "Leo's busy, that's all. I'm sure he'd take you to church if he wasn't on the road all the time."

Her mind wandered as she mechanically picked ear after ear of corn. She was in a jungle, hacking her way through the tangled undergrowth of disbelief, shoulder to shoulder with Leo. They were missionaries in pith helmets—she with her Bible and Leo with his baseball bat. But his face went all fuzzy. The bat fell from his hands. She swooned in the tropical heat, but a strong, insistent voice called out her name.

"Jessy! Jessy? You okay?"

"Oh. Adam. I must have been daydreaming."

"You looked like you were a million miles away. Tell me what happened Saturday." He shot her a piercing glance with his sharp green eyes. "You did more than eat fried chicken. You can't fool me."

She knew her brother wouldn't stop interrogating her until she told him. Snow filtered down over them. Their wool hats and eyelashes were sprinkled with white that soon melted from the heat of their bodies.

"I wish someone would invent a machine to pick corn," she muttered.

"They got 'em but they don't work so good from what I hear. Maybe someday a decent one'll come on the market."

Jessy felt stiff and sore in the cold. Her hands ached. She felt sleepy. She yawned and moaned a little.

"Poor Cinderella! Take our minds off all this drudgery 'n' tell me about you 'n' Prince Charmin' at the ball."

"Well, if you must know, we went to see Leo's brother in the insane asylum." Bang! The cob she threw hit dead center again.

Adam stood there, thunderstruck in the cold. "Is Leo outta his mind, takin' you to a place like that?"

Jessy shrugged and kept working. "It was my idea, not Leo's. I wanted to meet his brother. Peter's really very normal, most of the time anyway, at least I thought so." Jessy frowned as she bent to break more corn from the stalks hidden amid dry, razor-sharp leaves. She took care not to cut her face. "He sounds fine one minute, and then the next, something snaps in his mind and he says strange things. Later, Leo said Peter had to be institutionalized because of the wild talking he did as a boy. He would rant and rave for no reason, day or night, starting when he was about ten years old—before Leo was born."

"Until then Peter was normal?"

Jessy straightened up and nodded. "Yes. It's strange, but Peter can play the piano beautifully—complicated works by Bach and Mozart. He writes music too. He played for us after we had our picnic with him. When we started to put on our coats he begged for us to take him home. He started crying! The guards had to hold on to him really hard to get him to stop lunging and yelling. He was thrashing around like a child having a tantrum. They had to put him in a—" Jessy could hardly talk, she felt so sorry for the grown man who had begged like a child to be brought home but was tied into a straitjacket instead. "I pray for him. I don't know what else to do. You won't tell anyone where we went, will you?"

Adam stopped working a moment to look at her. "What's the big secret? I don't like you goin' off without tellin' me what you're up to. I don't like it when you hide things from me."

116

"You're right. I don't like deception either! But I believe it was important that I meet Peter, and I'm very glad I did. Sometimes I think people are less embarrassed about their relatives in jail than in mental hospitals. Leo didn't want his parents to know we went to Fair Haven because it upsets them even to talk about Peter. They feel very strongly that Peter's condition should not interfere with the lives of all the rest of the Kimballs. Acacia has heart palpitations whenever she hears the name Peter, even if the reference isn't being made to her son."

Adam nodded. "I'll keep quiet. I don't want to be the cause of some woman havin' a heart attack. It must be awful, havin' your kid locked up in a looney bin. What if somethin' like that happened to Stephen or Martha or Taddy?"

"I know! But Peter's well taken care of, from what I could see. He has his music and books." Still, she knew he was living in a strange prison of sorts, barred from a normal life, that is, if he were capable of living like other people—working and raising a family—without depending on others to care for him. Who knows what sort of man Peter could have been, a great concert pianist locked up in a mental hospital when all the world craved beautiful music. Jessy looked into the sun that had risen through the morning mists. It was burning away the clouds. The snow had stopped falling.

Adam and Jessy worked rapidly until Suzanna came out with hot broth for them to drink and lotions for their aching hands. By lunchtime, the wagon had been loaded, unloaded, and reloaded with corn. Suzanna had taken time from housework to help, and as soon as the children arrived home from school, they helped, too, but had to stop to do homework. After taking time for evening chores and a quick supper, Adam and Jessy returned to their bitter cold field. Deep night had settled over their farm when at last they stopped and returned to the house for sleep.

It was only then, as Jessy dragged herself to her bedside, aching from the strain of a long day's hard work, that she found the verse from Jeremiah that had come to her mind at Fair Haven: *They have forsaken Me the fountain of living waters, and hewed them out cisterns, broken cisterns, that can hold no water*. Why had Jessy been reminded of broken cisterns at Fair Haven? She connected this verse to Acacia. How Jessy wanted to like her! Jessy prayed for good relations with her future mother-in-law.

❦ ❦ ❦

On a brisk, cold, brilliantly sunny Saturday in mid-December, the Flints were busy packing the sleigh with gifts for Kem Curtis and his motherless children: a smoked turkey Stephen and Taddy had raised for food, and Suzanna's preserves and home-baked delights.

When Suzanna handed Adam the generous basket, she said, "Please tell Kem I'm praying for him, but the children and I just can't go by there today with you, Adam. Will you do that for me, please?"

"Okay! We'll eat lunch when we get back; don't wait for us," Adam said.

"Let's not forget this sack of clothes for the Curtis family. The bin at church was loaded with things for them this week." Jessy hauled the big sack out to the sleigh.

Since the previous December, the Church of Bethel had targeted Kem Curtis, a widower, and his five young children for assistance of any and all kinds. Each member of the church had been asked to donate something: time, help, child care, food, clothing, prayers. Each week, members took turns delivering whatever had been collected during the previous seven days. Special efforts were made as Christmas drew near, but the church members had agreed to provide help as long as Kem Curtis needed it.

Kem Curtis. As Jessy and Adam loaded the sleigh with gifts for the widower and his needy children, she remembered the previous December, a stormy day she tried leaving home. Adam had stopped her in his mocking, casual way, thinking she was running off to meet Kem, as if Jessy could do such a thing. She hardly knew Kem at the time. After finally meeting him she knew they wouldn't be the best possible match, though she liked him and his children.

The widower had once asked Adam if he could court Jessy and take her to church, but Adam—the old God-scoffing Adam—had refused without informing Jessy of Kem's interest and allowing her the opportunity to make up her own mind about Kem. A most unfortunate man indeed, Kem had lost his wife shortly after she gave birth to their fifth child. At the same time, their prize Black Angus cattle sickened and died. Surely, Jessy hoped, life would improve for Kem Curtis and his children.

Jessy made her way back into the house on the path packed down hard with brilliant white snow. As she picked up more bundles, she remembered the first description she had ever heard of Kem's place. Adam thought Kem's farm was an eyesore. The pigs had the mange. The chickens ran around out in the rain, picking through trash in the yard. The house was falling apart for want of repair. Even their one remaining cow looked desperate.

Still, Kem Curtis attended church with his children regularly, all six family members poorly dressed but present to worship. The Flints had been unable to help until Adam was back on his feet. Then he and Kem had become friends. Jessy looked forward to visiting Kem's family and little farm.

True, the place still looked run down. It had for a long time. Kem's wife had passed on after a lengthy illness, leaving the house in dire need of care. Kem had little time for its upkeep, being occupied with the farm and his small children. He did all he could, but death and disasters hovered over Kem's place like a pox.

The first time the Flints visited, the oldest child—Gina, age nine—wearing a ragged dress missing buttons, her hair uncombed and unwashed, was hauling a heavy feed bucket in each hand. The two younger children, Tom and Cathy, ages seven and five, were feverish. Brad, a toddler, and Dana, the baby, lay unattended in cribs that needed cleaning, which was what Jessy did that first visit. Suzanna saw to the sick children while Adam helped Kem with farm work. After the Flints returned home, Adam couldn't stop talking about the shambles the Curtis place had been in: boards, old sacks, broken ladders, cats prowling through the clutter, rats nesting under cover wherever they could hide.

The Flint homestead, in marked contrast, was kept in good repair and improved as time and money allowed. Adam often thought about Kem living in a house that might cave in any minute.

"Not everyone is as blessed as we are," Jessy had said quietly to Adam.

"I thought we had it rough, with my accident 'n' all," Adam whispered back.

The Flints, with their church members, had prayed something good would come out of such suffering.

Such were Jessy's thoughts that frosty Saturday morning. She and

Adam were ready to depart in their sleigh when a familiar figure walked toward them from the direction of town, a pretty redhead in a bright blue coat and hat.

"Emma!" Jessy said, delighted. "What are you doing here?"

Emma shrugged and said, "Some friends of Dad's dropped me off in town and I decided to visit you. Here." She handed Jessy a present wrapped in pretty Christmas paper.

"So soon! Thank you! I have your gift in the house, but I haven't wrapped it yet." Jessy said happily, "I'm so glad to see you! Listen, we're on our way to the Curtis farm. Why don't you come with us?"

Emma, her hands deep in her pockets, looked from Adam, to the sleigh, and back to Jessy. "I was hoping I could talk to you."

"We can talk on the way to the Curtis place." Seeing that Emma still looked unsure, she added, "We won't be long. We're dropping off clothes and food. They don't live far away."

Emma nodded. "I don't care. I'm always in the mood for a ride."

Adam, who had hitched a horse to his Russian bobsleigh, was seated up front with things for the Curtis family stacked around him. Emma and Jessy rode together in the back seat. The bright green sleigh with its merry bells made a charming picture as the horse trotted briskly over the road packed with shimmering new snow.

"Have you heard from Leo lately?" Emma asked Jessy.

"Two days ago. He's going to Cuba for a long series of games." Jessy paused, certain Emma and her parents received letters with the same news.

"That's Leo, lucky as usual, in a warm place. What else did he write?"

"Doesn't he send you letters?" Jessy asked.

"No." Emma gave Jessy a knowing look. "He must write you more often, seeing how much he loves you. You'll get married and live happily ever after!"

Jessy wasn't so sure. "In letters we can't discuss our future, but I hope and pray things will work out for the best, if we seek God's will for us."

At the mention of God, Emma sucked in her breath and looked out at the road. The whole earth was covered by a thick dazzling white crust of snow that sparkled but could not melt under the brittle winter sun.

Adam pulled up to the Curtis home decorated with lopsided but cheerful Christmas ornaments the children had made in school. Jessy got out of the sleigh, but Emma sat still with her hands in her pockets. "I'll wait here for you," she said to Jessy.

"Oh, please come in and say hello to everyone." Jessy picked up the turkey with two hands. It must have weighed twenty pounds, she estimated, proud of her young nephews' farming abilities.

Emma frowned at the Curtis place. "Pitiful, isn't it?"

"A lot has been done, but a lot more needs to be done. Coming?" With her warm brown eyes, Jessy cast a beckoning glance at Emma.

"Oh, all right. I hope they have a fire going."

"They do. Smoke's coming out of the chimney," Jessy noted. "Can you carry in the clothes? Those sacks there."

Emma took her usually idle hands out of her pockets and put them to good use. Loaded down, she followed Adam and Jessy along the path crunchy with thick, packed white snow.

Kem Curtis opened the door with his hands full. The tall, brown-eyed widower with dark hair thinning at the temples was holding his youngest child, Dana. He smiled to see Adam and welcomed everyone inside, but his warmest greeting was for Jessy. She always felt a little flustered around Kem, knowing he had once expressed romantic interest in her. Thankfully, Kem, an absolute gentleman, devout and reserved, never brought up the fact.

"Turkey, raised on our farm, fattened on our corn, and smoked to perfection!" Jessy put the turkey on the kitchen counter and pulled a doll from her coat pocket. "From Martha for your girls!"

Jessy was glad to see that the house was tidy. The women's guild had been by earlier that week. "Mr. Curtis, I'd like you to meet Emma Kimball."

"Hi," Emma said, looking up at the balding farmer who stood a good head taller than she. "I've seen you in town."

Kem smiled and nodded in agreement before setting his little girl on her own two feet. He said to his guests, "Please, let me take your coats."

"Oh, we weren't planning to stay," said Adam, "unless you need help."

"I have things under control for the first time in a long while. I've been doing some plumbing." Kem went with Adam to show off his handiwork.

"Isn't she adorable?" Jessy said. She picked up little Dana at once and cuddled her.

"I s'pose." Emma looked around in distaste. "What a dump."

"It's really much improved now. Kem's had hard times—one bad thing after another."

"What's in there?" Emma gestured toward a small room off the kitchen.

"The nursery. Come on." Jessy led the way, with Dana still in her arms. The child was sucking her thumb and ready to fall asleep.

Two of her young siblings, Cathy and Brad, were taking a nap on a child's bed. Jessy laid Dana in the crib. She checked the foreheads of the two sleeping children. No fever. She brushed the thick dark hair away from their small faces and led Emma away on tiptoe. "They all look like their father, same dark hair and brown eyes."

Emma nodded in a noncommittal sort of way. She was looking at the badly stained ceiling.

"The last time we came here, Adam helped Kem fix the roof. It was leaking something awful," Jessy confided in low tones. "It's fine now."

Gina and Tom came in the front door, a gust of cold air following them inside the toasty little house. They gave Jessy a hug and then everyone gathered around the crackling fire. Jessy helped Gina set another log on the grate.

"Coffee's on, if you want some!" shouted Kem from the bathroom where he was running water, showing the wonders of indoor plumbing to Adam.

"No, thanks!" Emma shouted.

The shout awakened Dana, who began whimpering. Wordlessly, Jessy and Emma went back to the nursery. Emma reached Dana first. "Don't cry, baby. I'm sorry I woke you up. Shhhh. Go to sleep!" When the child continued to fuss, Emma said, "When I go home I'll go up into our attic. We have so many things—toys and clothes and books from when my brother and sisters and I were little. You kids would love having it all." She patted the groggy tot in her crib.

"That's awfully good of you," Jessy told Emma.

Emma shrugged. "Mum and Dad would never miss the stuff. We have lots of Christmas ornaments, too, enough for three Christmas trees. We never use them all. I'll bring some of them, too, before Christmas."

"Oh, that would be wonderful!" cried Jessy. "That's really very thoughtful of you, Emma. Really." Except for Leo, Jessy had never seen the Kimballs in church, yet here was Emma, admitting that they decorated their home lavishly. Jessy considered the idea preposterous: Christmas without Christ? And they had an attic full of clothes and other useful things that could help the needy. Jessy wondered what other bountiful resources went untapped in Bethel township, languishing in the attics and basements of homes as fine as Emma's. Jessy's prayers had resulted, so far, in no apparent effect on the Kimball family, but that Emma would be generous at Christmas gave Jessy reason to be thankful.

Adam, having returned from his plumbing tour with Kem, had a brainstorm. He turned to Kem with a grin. "I might have a job for you, if you're interested. I want to wire our house and barn for electricity and put a furnace in the house, too, but with all the corn to pick, I haven't started either job. I could use your help, say, after the holidays, when we get back from Florida some time in February. I can pay you for your time."

Kem looked as excited as the Flints had ever seen him. "I've been thinking of starting a business—plumbing, heating, wiring. With all these new conveniences, people want to modernize their places but so many of them don't have the time or interest in doing the work themselves. I like tinkering. I'm better at it than farming!"

"Great," said Adam. "Let's plan on it." He turned to go. "We'll be back to see you before Christmas. In the meantime, let us know if you need anythin', okay?" Adam shook Kem's hand.

"Before Christmas, Emma's going to round up some things for the children," Jessy said.

"Thank you, Emma!" Kem looked delighted with the fair-skinned, natural beauty. "Thanks very much."

Without answering, Emma put her hands back in her pockets and turned away from him and went out into the cold.

"Emma's usually so cheerful," Jessy told Kem. "I don't know what's come over her lately."

Jessy was soon to find out.

CHAPTER 12

❧

"**A**re you hungry, Emma?" Jessy asked. "Let's have lunch."

Together they took off their coats and hats in the hall of the Flint home. "I'm so glad you came by today, I really am!" Jessy led Emma to the big country kitchen where a cast-iron pot of ham and bean soup was slowly simmering on the range. "Would you like soup and crackers? There are corn sticks too."

"I don't care." Emma looked around at the room that mirrored Suzanna's country tastes brought to a fine level of sophistication.

"Want some cheese on your soup?" Jessy asked as she ladled out two bowls full of thick steaming soup and looked for the tin of soda crackers. As they sat waiting for their soup to cool a bit, Jessy asked, "Would you like a glass of milk?"

"I don't care."

Jessy eyed Emma warily. "I never know what that means. Does it mean you want milk or you don't?"

Emma smiled for the first time that day. "I mean yes, as long as you're offering it, I wouldn't mind having some milk."

Jessy filled two glasses. "I'm hungry! Before dawn I was out with Adam and the children picking corn. This year's crop is huge! I'll need to get back to it straight after lunch." Jessy sat down again and looked at Emma. "How have you been doing? How's school?"

Emma paused, spoon halfway to her mouth. "I'm pregnant."

At this Jessy's cheerfulness evaporated. "Oh, Emma!"

"Don't worry. Everything's under control."

Jessy cheered up. "So you're getting married!"

"No. That's what I came here to talk to you about." Emma looked around uneasily. Doors leading to other rooms in the house were wide open.

Jessy put aside her napkin, got up to close the doors, and sat down again, saying, "There. Now we can talk in private."

"Good. Because what I wanted to ask you was," Emma began, sipping soup and munching crackers, "I need your help."

"Of course, Emma. Whatever I can do, I'll do."

"That's a relief! Everyone's so busy this time of year with Christmas and everything. Of course, if you have fieldwork, you may not have time either, but I was wondering if you'd go with me to Cranstock next week. It's an hour by train. I'll pay all your expenses."

"What's in Cranstock?" Jessy had never been to the city due north of them. She hazarded a guess. "Is that where your boyfriend lives?"

"Boyfriend? No, silly! That's where the doctor is!"

"There are doctors right here in Bethel!" Jessy said.

"Jessy, honestly, you're so naïve sometimes!" Emma paused, hoping Jessy would comprehend what she was trying to say. Once Emma saw that her meaning was penetrating Jessy's brain, she continued, still nibbling on lunch. "Mum gave me the money for the operation, but she said she wouldn't go with me again, not after last time. She said if I was foolish enough to get into trouble again, then I'd have to get out of it without her."

Jessy had lost all her appetite. "You've been pregnant before?"

"Yes, but the doctor fixed me up in no time. He can do it again, just like before, but afterward, I'll need to rest a couple of days in Cranstock, in the hotel near his operating place. I'll pay for your meals and everything. I'd rather not go there alone, that's all."

Slowly, Jessy put down her spoon. Her heart was racing, as if in a panic to jump out of her body. After a long silence, Jessy asked, "Won't the boy marry you?"

"I don't want to marry him. And he's not a boy, he's a man. It was a boy last time. His parents paid for my operation and gave me some extra money for keeping quiet about the whole affair! But no such luck now. Last time, my boyfriend was sent off to private school someplace and I never saw him again." Emma paused to drink her milk. "So, can you go with me? You can take your books along and read. It'd be a nice rest for you, don't you think? Can you get away without explaining to your family?

I'd prefer it that way, nice and quiet, and it'll be over before anyone knows about it."

It, it, it. Jessy picked through a minefield of reactions. Finally, she asked, "Have you talked to your father about—it?"

"Of course not!"

"But he may be able to arrange a marriage for you."

"I don't want to marry the man. I don't love him. Once I thought I did, but now I don't."

Jessy's face flushed with color. "Then neither you nor this man is interested in marriage?"

"He's already married."

"Married?" Jessy struggled to remain calm. "You're only fifteen! A man can go to prison for a long, long time for—"

"Sure he could, if I press charges, but I won't. I wanted to do it as much as he did and so we did it."

It again. It, it, it. Jessy sat quietly, trying to think while gaining her composure.

"Don't act shocked," said Emma with a sly, knowing look. "You must have done plenty with Leo!"

"I certainly have not! I've never let Leo kiss me, let alone—"

"No wonder Leo calls you his greatest challenge!" Before Jessy could comment, Emma said, "I'm not like you, I guess. I get these urges."

Jessy sputtered, "I get them too! We all do, Emma, but none of us has to act on them."

"Why not? They're perfectly natural."

"Of course, they're natural, but sexual relations are for marriage—for holy matrimony—and for that purpose only, as the Bible teaches. Otherwise we're to remain celibate."

"Oh, I see!" Emma cried. "You're 'saving' yourself! How quaint! Our family's modern! Mum says people should ignore musty old books and do what they feel is best."

As Emma finished her milk, she rolled her pretty pale eyes around at the comfortable country kitchen: the colorful chintz curtains Suzanna had sewn, the string of mama and baby ducklings Adam had whittled and painted for her, the handsome cupboard he had built that Suzanna had filled with baskets—all evidence of a life built together, the fruits of a

126

marriage with both husband and wife working in harmony. Jessy's view was quite different: the promiscuous Emma framed by closed doors, keeping countless secrets.

"I'll ask someone else to go with me when I do it," said Emma.

"It! We're not—at least I'm not—talking about an *it*. We're talking about the life of your child or the death of your child!" Jessy was furious now, and then mad at herself for speaking harshly to Emma whom she loved.

"It's not a child. It's like a-a tooth the dentist pulls out or a tumor. One snip and it's gone. No problem."

"No problem for you, perhaps, but what about your child?"

"It isn't a child, Jessy, it's a-a blob!"

"It isn't a blob! We all start out tiny and helpless inside our mothers' bodies. God forms us in the womb."

"God didn't have anything to do with this." Emma clutched her abdomen. "I created this-this thing and I'm going to get rid of it!"

"Mothers don't create babies! People don't give life—God does! Think of what you're saying, Emma."

"Think of what *you're* saying! Having a baby would ruin me."

"Having relations with men is what's ruining you! If you think killing a child is the right answer, you're asking the wrong question."

"Why should I have a baby I don't want?" Emma cried.

"Because abortion is murder. When you have an abortion you've snuffed out a life. *There's got to be a better way.*"

"This is America and I'm free to do as I please."

"You're confusing freedom with license. You're irresponsible, that's what you are. God gives us freedom within limits for our own protection. Ignore His limits at your own peril. Abortion is illegal. Doctors are supposed to uphold life, not end it."

"The doctor in Cranstock has friends in the government."

Jessy said thoughtfully, "Even if abortion were legal, it isn't right, no matter how many friends in high places that doctor has."

"No one's telling you to have an abortion if you don't approve! And anyway, what business is it of yours?"

"According to the Bible, Emma, God hates hands that shed innocent blood. If I just sit quietly by and let you do such a thing, I'm not living up to my responsibility as a Christian. If I saw you about to step into the path of a moving train and I didn't warn you, I couldn't live with myself when you were hurt, as you surely would be. It's the same with your moral life, Emma. Do you see? *There's got to be a better way*."

"My friend Sally—she goes to the Free Thinkers Church—she says there's nothing in the Bible about abortion one way or the other."

"Then Sally hasn't read her Bible carefully. It says murder is wrong. So surely abortion is also wrong." Jessy softened at the sight of Emma, so young and ill informed. "You're a beautiful girl, Emma, but beauty without virtue is ruinous. In the Bible, in Exodus, a man would be put to death if he hurt a pregnant woman." Sensing that none of Jessy's reasoning was having any apparent effect on Emma, Jessy cried, "Where would this world be if the mother of Jesus decided to have some doctor like the one in Cranstock operate on her so she wouldn't give birth?"

Emma looked puzzled but still unconvinced. "Women go to Cranstock all the time. This doctor's got a long list of women waiting for him to operate!"

"High numbers of people doing wrong doesn't make it right." Jessy added, "Jesus wasn't just some 'it,' a bit of tissue in Mary's womb that could be tossed away like a rotted tooth! And neither were you nor I nor any other human being on this earth!" The defiant look on Emma's face made Jessy cry in exasperation, "I can't help you that way. I'm sorry. It would go against everything I believe in."

"Don't get all upset about it. This soup's good. I'd like some more." Emma laughed. "I guess it's hungry!"

Jessy fought the combined urge to cry and slug Emma in her pretty pink mouth. She got up and took Emma's bowl to the stove. "More cheese?"

"Sure! And milk too. I'm starving, for some reason."

"It's that house you live in, Emma," Jessy muttered to this girl who starved amid plenty, living in a moral and spiritual vacuum. Jessy sensed the sureness of the Bible verse: *Without a vision the people perish*.

Just then Adam burst in, all six feet four inches and two hundred plus pounds, glowing with cold from the great outdoors, his craggy face ruddy from the effort of unhitching his horse from the sleigh. "So, what's goin' on in here with all these doors closed?" he boomed, looking from his sister to her guest with one interrogational eyebrow upraised.

"Couldn't you knock?" Jessy asked.

"What for? It's my house 'n' my kitchen 'n' I'm hungry." Adam turned a chair around backward and sat cowboy style at the table with his legs stretched under it. "We've never closed the doors to the kitchen, not that I ever recall. What're you two talkin' about?"

"You missed your calling, Adam," Jessy said as she ladled some soup for her brother. "You should have been a prosecuting attorney."

"Now that's an idea! We'd be rollin' in greenbacks!"

Jessy gave Emma her brimming bowl, refilled both glasses with milk, and then sat down again. Both women watched Adam break crackers all over the top of his soup and then begin slurping heartily. "No milk for me? After all, it's mine. I squeezed it with my own hands from my own cows."

"Sorry." Jessy obediently rose and poured him some milk.

Adam laughed at Jessy. He had her flustered and he knew it. "You girls haven't answered my question."

Jessy confided to Emma. "Adam will keep on and on until he finds out what we've been talking about. We can go upstairs if you want, to my room."

"Find out what?" Adam asked as he ate.

Emma seemed unwilling to leave the table with so much good food left to finish. "I want to stay here, Jessy."

"Should we tell Adam?" Jessy asked.

"Tell me what?" Adam helped himself to a corn stick.

"I don't care," said Emma.

Jessy couldn't help but laugh. "There's that phrase of yours again. Should we tell Adam or not?"

Emma found this amusing too. "I didn't realize how often I say I don't care. Would it do any good to tell Adam?"

Jessy regarded her brother, former rogue who had left a wake of brokenhearted females in his past, before saying to Emma: "Adam has had some general experience in these matters."

Adam paused in his soup slurping and cracker cracking. "Oh. You're talkin' 'bout guys! I should've guessed. How 'bout closin' them doors again, Jessy."

While Jessy did so, Emma said simply, "I'm pregnant and I want to have an abortion and Jessy thinks I shouldn't."

"Jessy's right. If you were my kid I'dve beaten some sense into you 'n' the guy too. Who is he anyway?"

Adam's first comment so irritated Emma she hardly heard what else he had said. She asked, "Why do you say *Jessy's* right?"

"'Cause kids're worth havin'."

At that moment, not too far from where they sat quietly talking, Stephen and Taddy began hollering at each other and Martha decided to practice her piano lesson in the most dreadful way possible. Wincing in pain, Adam continued, "Like I was sayin', kids're worth havin'. *Mosta* the time."

Emma eyed Adam with a half-serious expression. "Like when?"

"Like all the time. We were all kids at one time, even you 'n' me."

"Gee, you're cute," said Emma boldly.

"Emma! Adam is a married m—" Jessy paused, wondering which married man might have fathered Emma's child. Thinking the unthinkable but hoping it couldn't be so, Jessy stared at her brother.

Adam looked righteously indignant. "Don't look at me that way with them big cow eyes, Jessy! I'm innocent for once."

Emma reassured Jessy. "Adam Flint's not the father." Still, Emma sized him up for future reference.

"Don't even think it, Emma. Please," said Jessy. "Remember how you swore your undying loyalty to me after I hit that home run off Leo?"

Reluctantly, Emma nodded. "Okay, if you feel that way about it."

Adam said to Jessy, "I can take care of myself." To Emma he said, "I wouldn't have truck with a kid like you if you came wrapped in pure gold."

"Why not?"

"You're jailbait 'n' I'm not goin' to jail! Even if you were of age, I love my wife 'n' kids too much to hurt 'em havin' affairs."

"So you like kids, Mr. Flint?"

"Sure."

"You didn't always, as I recall," Jessy reminded him. "When I first came to live with you, you didn't want to take me in. And when Ollie Gaad—bless his soul!—told you that children were a gift of God, as the Bible says, you told him children were no gift you ever wanted."

"I felt that way then but I don't feel that way now. A man can change his mind from wrong to right." Adam handed his bowl to Jessy for refilling. "What would I have done without you?"

"That's true," Jessy said, remembering all that they had endured, and triumphed over, together. "You'd really be in the soup, instead of eating it! Want cheese on yours?"

"Nope. Gotta watch my weight. So who's the guy?" Adam asked Emma, his eyebrow cocked in his prosecuting mode once more.

Emma looked up from her bowl. "I won't tell either of you, but that's not important."

"Sure it is. The guy broke the law. You're a minor."

"She doesn't intend to press charges, Adam," Jessy said. "She just wants to get rid of the baby."

"Stop calling it a baby!" Emma cried.

Jessy could only say, "Kill that baby and you're killing me in a way."

Emma snickered. "What's that supposed to mean?"

Adam spoke up. "Jessy means she almost ended up dead when she was born." To his sister he said, "Will you tell Emma or should I?"

"I will. Maybe it will help Emma understand." Jessy began, "After Adam left home—he was about your age, Emma, when he did—my mother and father longed for another child to take Adam's place." She smiled at her brother. "Not that anyone could take Adam's place. And so, here I am, but—" Jessy wasn't sure how to phrase this next part. "My mother told me that on the day I was born my father decided he didn't want a girl, that he would rather have no child than a daughter. While she was recuperating, he took me outside and put me in a garbage can and put the lid on tight. He might have finished me off right then, but my mother got out of her sick bed and found me and brought me inside. My father had probably been drinking, I don't know."

"That's horrible!" Emma said.

"It is, isn't it?" Jessy asked with a shudder. "I don't know why parents can be so hateful to their own children, but eventually I forgave him. It wasn't easy, but I did."

"I'd never forgive anyone who did that to me!" Emma said.

"I forgave my father because I want God's forgiveness. If we don't

131

forgive others, God won't forgive us," Jessy explained. "And how will your baby feel about you if you end its life? Have you thought about that?"

"It isn't a person who can think or feel."

"How does anyone know what a tiny, growing baby feels? But God knows. And whether we believe in God or not, He sees what we do, everything, every sin and every good work." Jessy added softly, "If my mother hadn't cared enough to rescue me, I would have died long ago." For a long while, Jessy gazed at Emma. Finally she said, "Your soup's getting cold. Want me to heat it up?"

Emma was too deep in thought to respond.

Adam roused her from her reverie, saying, "If Pa had had his way, Jessy'd be dead 'n' so would I 'cuz, see, Emma, Jessy saved my life. She led me to Christ, the most important thing she could do for me—or for anyone. It was no easy job, I can tell you. I didn't want to listen. I thought I knew best. I was lost and didn't know it. Not only that, if that wasn't enough, Jessy saved my wife 'n' Stephen when he was still in diapers. She saved Martha, too, 'cuz when Jessy saved my wife, Suzanna was pregnant with Martha at the time. And then, after all that, Jessy figured out some things that saved my reputation in Bethel, 'n' well, that's why no one should ever put a kid out to die. There's no tellin' what good that child will accomplish in life if given the chance to live and grow up. All children should be conceived 'n' raised in love by both parents. That's what God intended. That's what marriage is for."

"I'm glad your mother saved you, Jessy!" Emma said in her immature but sincerest way. "Why, if you had died, we Stompers would have lost the baseball game on Labor Day!"

"See?" said Jessy, laughing. "God was watching out for me. He always is. He's watching you, too, Emma. Not to make your life miserable but to help you, to give you an abundant life if you will follow Him." Jessy, concentrating on Emma's lovely eyes, said, "Don't dishonor God by throwing a life away. You may not care much about the child's father, but don't take out your anger on the child. You made a mistake, but don't make a worse one by going to Cranstock. I'd be sad to know a beautiful little Emma-baby died there. You might have a wonderful teacher or a pianist or a president growing in your womb!"

At this mention of a pianist, Emma's eyes went dull. "Mum said she wished she had gotten rid of Peter when she had the chance. She didn't want a baby, especially out of wedlock, so she and Dad got married and she had Peter, and then look what happened to him. That's why she wants me to nip the problem in the bud rather than go through all sorts of trouble later. Last night she told me: 'Do away with the little devil while you have the chance!'"

"Is that what your mother said?" asked Jessy, aghast. Slowly she added, "Peter is a wonderful man and very talented. I don't know why Peter ended up where he did, but there's no good reason to hurt your baby."

"But, Jessy, I can't have a baby, not if I want to marry well and keep on living in Bethel. I thought about going to Chicago with the money my mother gave me, but—" Emma sighed. "I thought about killing myself too. No one cares about me." Emma eyed the knives on the table. "Life's unbearable sometimes!"

"No! Oh, Emma, promise me you'll never do such a thing," cried Jessy. "Pray to God with all your might to live, to hold on no matter what! Life is a gift from God and far too precious to throw away, whether it's yours or your child's! Promise me you won't take your life!" Jessy took Emma's hand and wouldn't let go. "You never know what tomorrow may bring, what wonderful gifts God has in store for you!"

"For you, maybe, but not for me. I was about to do myself in that day you and Leo and I went to Fair Haven," Emma admitted. "I never told anyone, but I was thinking about it all the time. I couldn't decide how to do it. After I saw Peter, I thought that if he could survive in such a place, then I could survive too. But soon after that I knew for sure I was pregnant. I began thinking of killing myself again. I hate school. I'm flunking out. I'm not going back after New Year's."

"If you've been thinking about a trip, why not come with us to Florida and have the baby there? We'll ask Bo if there's room for an extra guest. Maybe they know a couple that would adopt your child. Then you can come back here and go on with your life." Jessy turned from Emma to Adam. "You don't think Bo and Beatrice would mind if Emma came along with us, do you? I'd be glad for Emma's company, that is if Emma—"

"Florida? Me?" Some of the misery left Emma's voice now.

"I don't see why not," Adam said. "Write 'n' ask. Speakin' of which, what'd Suzy do with them oranges Bo sent? I want one."

Jessy went to find the crate that had arrived a few days before. Suzanna had put it out of sight, under a counter. "Here," Jessy said, tossing a bright orange to Adam. While she was down on her knees, she said, "I think I'll have one too. Would you like one, Emma?"

"They're too big."

"Will you share one with me, then?" Jessy asked. "They're delicious!"

"I don't care—I mean, all right," Emma relented.

"They got seeds," Adam said as he ate.

"You're not mad at me, are you, Emma, for what I said?" Jessy asked as she sliced the big bright orange in half.

"No," Emma said, "but you always surprise me. You don't react like everybody else I know. I never know what to expect from you."

From Jessy's hand Emma took the blazing orange half loaded with tangy juice. "A gift from God," Jessy said.

Emma tasted it. "This *is* good." She picked a seed from the orange pulp but before discarding it, she looked at it with more care than she had ever taken about anything: such a tiny thing from which a tree could sprout and go on to produce so much fruit.

Jessy said: "No human being has ever created a seed. Or an orange."

Now Emma looked hard at the orange. The juicy sweet reddish-yellow treasure had been plucked from a tree that had grown from a tiny seed until it blazed like glory in the brilliance of God's sun, where it produced good fruits year after year.

"No question about it," Jessy said. "Life is a gift from God."

The light started in Emma's eyes.

CHAPTER 13

❦

For the Flints, Friday, Christmas day 1908 proved merry indeed. In the brilliant but frigid sunny morning, the family rode in their charming sleigh to church to celebrate the great miracle—God taking on the form of a child and dwelling among us and for us and within us. Then, with the grand music of the season ringing in their hearts, they returned home for a noisy, happy time of swapping gifts in the parlor beside a festive tree close to the toastiest fire Adam could build.

Considering their upcoming trip to Florida present enough for themselves, the parents of three had spent a fair sum on presents for the children. They gave each of their sons a complete baseball outfit with bat, ball, and glove. Martha loved the two-story yellow Victorian dollhouse her daddy had made for her. A new bicycle arrived, too, but only one for all three children—"an experiment" as Adam put it—to see if the children could learn to share it fairly and enjoy riding it.

Adam and Suzanna gave Jessy a typewriter that arrived from Chicago in a heavy wooden crate. Jessy, thrilled recipient, was eager to learn the latest craze: typewriting. In turn Jessy had given each of her loved ones practical gifts—train cases filled with travel necessities. The Flints planned to borrow larger pieces of luggage and steamer trunks from Suzanna's parents who had spent four months on a European grand tour a few years earlier. The Webbs were so pleased their daughter and son-in-law were taking a much-needed trip they donated a significant cash gift this Christmas to the Flint travel fund.

While Martha plunked Christmas tunes on the piano, Jessy opened gifts from Leo. Along with a vial of costly perfume he had sent her an illustrated book about North American birds and wildlife. Jessy knew she would enjoy the book, but was troubled by his inscription: "To my best brown-eyed girl." Did Leo have other brown-eyed girls? And blue-eyed

135

girls too? Jessy felt uneasy as she considered the possibility, but then put the matter out of her mind, praying he would enjoy the Bible and travel case she had sent to him.

Jessy prayed for Emma, too, hoping she would not be offended by the Bible Jessy had given her. Jessy believed with all her heart that she had given Emma, the girl who had nearly everything, the truth she needed above all else. She opened Emma's gift last: a pretty fringed shawl of the finest ivory wool, imported and embroidered with brilliantly colored flowers and leaves.

It was only a matter of days until the Flints and Emma Kimball would depart for Florida, busy days after Christmas crammed with packing. Adam and Suzanna visited school to be sure their children would take with them all the lessons they would need to cover during the coming weeks. After Adam and Suzanna left the big new schoolhouse, Adam confessed, "Wish I'd gotten more schoolin' myself, but it's too late for me."

"It's never too late! Would you like to finish public school?"

Adam nodded. A grown man, married and a father, a successful farmer and world-class wrestler, Adam felt awkward discussing his lack of formal schooling with his accomplished wife, but was pleased at her reaction. At the dinner table that night, when Adam raised the topic, again he was pleased his suggestion was so readily accepted, this time by Jessy.

"Could I go with you?" she asked. "I feel so inadequate around Leo and his family. Maybe finishing school would help."

Suzanna said, "I've heard that the Bethel school system offers high school certification to adults who pass equivalency exams. The program bypasses most classes children normally take." There and then, Jessy resolved to finish high school and learn the correct method of typing. She and Adam agreed to look into the school program after vacation. Adam felt glad for her company.

On that note of optimism, the Flints made last-minute preparations for their trip and bid farewell to their nearest neighbor, Ed Mannon, who, with his sons, would look after the Flint homestead and tend their animals while they were gone.

On a bright but bitter cold afternoon in early January, while Adam and Suzanna discussed their wills with George Webb at his law office, Jessy visited Emma. In her excitement over the trip, Jessy had given no thought to the effect her influence over Emma had been having on the Kimballs. Alone, Jessy drove the sleigh to their home, unprepared for the assault awaiting her.

"Mr. Kimball! Happy New Year! I've come to see Emma about our trip."

"Oh, yes, I'll get her for you." Walter Kimball was friendly as always, Jessy thought, but he looked troubled as he let her in.

While Jessy waited in the hall, she looked at family photographs, marveling once again at the resemblance between Count Dimitri and Leo Kimball, separated by two generations. At the sound of rustling taffeta, Jessy looked up to see Acacia, beautifully groomed, descending the staircase. "Mrs. Kimball! How are you? Well, I hope?"

"Miss Flint, I don't like emotional outbursts. I can hardly believe I became so outspoken during your Labor Day visit." Acacia paused, giving Jessy the opportunity to remember the argument that took place in this very same hall. Mrs. Kimball, her usual serenity veiling strong irritation, warmed to her subject. With her hands clasped primly together, she railed against the enemy. "Miss Flint, I find your interference in my family's affairs intolerable! You've encouraged Leo in this insane baseball business—"

"Nothing anyone could have said would have stopped Leo from playing baseball!" Jessy exclaimed, reeling at this unexpected attack. "He loves the game and is a great player. On Labor Day I was only trying to make the point that if we honor God in all we do—"

"I am speaking! You will please allow me to continue!"

"I'm sorry," Jessy said at once. "Please excuse me."

Above them on the stairway a pale Emma Kimball appeared in a dark, deep plaid dress with a long bustle skirt. Despite her condition she looked gaunt. She stood still, clutching the plaid, pleated ruffles of her standup collar as if she were deathly cold.

Acacia held out her arm to her youngest daughter. "Don't stand there eavesdropping, Emma! It's most impolite! Do come down here this instant!"

Moving cautiously, Emma obeyed. Acacia clutched her daughter's hand once it was within reach, and continued to Jessy, saying, "I understand you have convinced my daughter to run off to Florida."

"I wouldn't call it running off, Mrs. Kimball. We invited Emma to join us on our visit to my brother's old friend in Florida. The Ballys are glad to have Emma. We've heard from them." Jessy added quietly, "Besides, Emma doesn't especially like cold weather and in her condition—"

"My daughter wouldn't be in this condition, as you call it, if she had listened to me and had the operation as I advised. Instead you've beguiled her to travel to Florida with you!" Once Acacia reined in her anger she added, "I've contacted some friends of mine, good friends from my youth spent in Chicago, people of wealth and influence who winter in Florida. I expect that, once there, Emma will be well treated by the right people."

With quiet dignity, Jessy said, "I assure you, Mrs. Kimball, that as long as your daughter is with us, she'll be with the right people."

Acacia Kimball glared at Jessy with her blue eyes glittering ice. "You think you can ride away with my daughter and marry my son, just like that!" She snapped her elegant fingers on air. "Emma will go to Florida, yes, she must if she insists upon the foolhardy notion of giving birth out of wedlock, but mark my words: you will never marry my son. Leo shall have the best, the most illustrious—"

As Acacia paused in her groping for superlatives hardly adequate to describe the lofty ambitions she held for her son, Jessy said quietly, "You may be right, Mrs. Kimball. Leo and I might never marry. But the matter isn't in your hands, or mine, or Leo's either, but in God's. Because I'll wed only if that is His will, and I'll marry only the man God wants me to marry. And now, if you will please allow me, I only have a few minutes, and I would like to speak with Emma about our travel arrangements, if I could."

Acacia turned from the two young women. The tower of formidable strength mounted the stairs and soon vanished.

"Oh, Jessy!" Emma let out a held-in breath as she spoke. "You rile my mother like nobody I've ever seen!"

"I certainly don't mean to," Jessy said in a haze, hating herself for muddling everything with the very woman she'd been praying to befriend. Like a naughty boy, Walter peeked out to Jessy from the opposite end of the hall. "Mr. Kimball!"

Emma turned to him, crying, "Oh, Daddy!"

Walter Kimball came and hugged his daughter. "My baby! I'll miss you!"

"It's just for a few months, Daddy. I'll be all right, won't I, Jessy?"

"Of course you will!" Through tears, Jessy smiled at the tall, red-haired father and daughter. "Of course!" Jessy wrapped her arms around both of them. Though Jessy appeared calm on the outside, she was shaking within.

CHAPTER 14

❦

The glorious but blustery day of departure had finally arrived, a January day as cold as cold gets. The snow was thick everywhere in Bethel, but the railroad tracks were clear and the afternoon sky bright. The wind had calmed since morning. During their usual round of chores in a gale force that threatened to bowl them over, Adam had predicted the winds would calm soon enough, roaring with sardonic good humor to Jessy, "There ain't that much air left to blow!"

Jessy had giggled at her brother's remark for a long time afterward, but she was simply too excited to think of a suitably amusing reply. Even though Adam had teased his family all day, with his spirits soaring higher and higher as the time of departure approached, Suzanna grew increasingly grim. At least twice she attempted to call off the trip. While she made frantic references to the dangers of travel, Adam had only laughed and held her and told her how much he adored her and how excited he was about this long-awaited honeymoon of sorts. Adam had lifted Suzanna off the floor more than once with gigantic bear hugs, but nothing placated her.

"This is calamitous!" Suzanna declared with her pretty round mouth.

"This is goin' to be fun!" Adam had said repeatedly.

"How can you say that?" Suzanna railed back.

With the rigors of packing, rushing up and down the long flight of stairs, and venturing in and out in the cold, the sparring duo was at last reduced to arguing silently by mouthing words back and forth to each other. "Calamitous!" and "fun!" became two invisible tennis balls rallied on air until Suzanna changed her silent litany to "You don't love me" to which Adam mouthed silently and repeatedly, "Yes, I do love you!"

Now the afternoon sun was beginning to wane as the Flints, dressed in their warmest Sunday best, waited at the Bethel station for their train,

The Midwest Express. After traveling south, it would link up the next day with The Dixie Special. Dixie! Jessy could hardly contain herself. At last she would venture past the Mason-Dixon line for a sun-filled holiday. For weeks, the Flints had been showered with requests from neighbors for Florida collectibles—baby alligator teeth and oranges ranking high on everyone's list.

Near departure time Emma Kimball arrived looking sedate, mature, and proper in a deep blue suit and new veiled hat, new gloves, new everything. Hundreds of tiny jet beads glimmered on the shoulders of her darkly elegant traveling suit. Looking slender, her secret safe and tiny within her womb, Emma entered the crowded waiting room and casually greeted the six Flints. "You look so excited."

"We are!" said Stephen. He and Taddy took hold of Emma's hands and ogled her. "Gosh, you're beautiful!"

Emma went limp at this. "I hardly feel beautiful!" she admitted to the two small boys. She looked around with sudden apprehension.

"Have you got your ticket?" Jessy asked Emma.

"Daddy's buying it for me. He's seeing to my luggage too." Emma clutched her handbag. "I've got the cash Mum gave me and a bank draft, too, to exchange when we get to Florida." She had packed an overnight case and a trunk for her extended stay. Her baby was due in May. Emma would be unable to return to Bethel until July at the earliest, long after the Flints had completed their vacation.

The waiting room was crowded with travelers of every sort: farmers, salesmen, and families leaving for vacations in warmer climes—points south. A few soldiers tipped their hats to the Flint party. In a corner, a pair of newlyweds stood holding hands, lost to the world but joyously overwhelmed by one another. Jessy admired the pair—the bride wearing a corsage and the groom a flower boutonniere—thinking how it must be for Emma without a husband, bound on a voyage fraught with sadness.

Have I done right, dear Lord? Jessy prayed in silence. *Encouraging Emma to go through with having this child? Is it Acacia who is right and me who is wrong? Please guide us and bless us and, oh dear Lord, please be with Emma and her child!*

When a twenty-car train roared in amid white steam, black smoke, and screaming whistles, an announcement was made as to its numerous destinations: one stop after another down through the American Midwest from north to south. Jessy's heart stopped for a moment; she could hardly stand the excitement. She rushed forward to see the train that would carry them southward.

Unlike the eager, elated Jessy, Emma stood well back behind the Flints as if wanting to be lost in the crowd and out of everyone's sight. The children, fearing this monster train ready to engulf them, held back to clutch Adam's and Suzanna's hands. As they stood in line waiting to board, Walter Kimball came forward, along with the Webbs. They hugged their departing loved ones and waved teary good-byes as the Flints and Emma Kimball climbed the steps and found their seats on The Midwest Express.

Once aboard the comfortable passenger car, the seven tucked their train cases under their seats and removed their coats. Jessy admired the rich interior—paneling of mahogany, and carpets and upholstery of deepest umber. Jessy and Emma sat together, facing Martha and her dolls in one four-seater, and in another four-seater across the aisle, Stephen and Taddy sat facing Adam and Suzanna. Martha couldn't resist getting up on her knees and peeking over her seat to see who was sitting behind her. The young newlyweds beamed at the little girl in the bright velvet dress trimmed with lace, a big white bow pinned to her curls. Martha slid down in her seat, blushing and giggling at Aunt Jessy and Miss Emma. As they readied to depart the Bethel train station, delicious aromas wafted through the air, promising a wonderful meal that would be served in the car adjoining this one.

"Those are our beds," Adam told his children. He gestured over their heads to metal panels that curved above their seats.

"How can we sleep up there?" Taddy wondered aloud.

"At bedtime, porters will come and pull those panels down for us. When they do, you'll see our beds unfolded and ready for us!" Adam explained. "I really miss travelin'!"

"You've traveled some, too, haven't you, Emma?" Jessy asked.

"Oh, sure. Lots of times. Last year Daddy and Mum took Leo and me to Washington. The year before that, we went to New York. It's fun." Emma smiled at Suzanna, but Suzanna was too nervous to smile in return. She squeezed Adam's arm when the train jolted as railroad workers

142

prepared to leave the station. Some cars were being loaded with boxes and others with coal and timber. A jumble of noises assaulted them: slamming doors, clanging metal against metal, shuddering jolts beneath the car in which they were seated. Jessy fought her fears in silence.

"It's normal," Adam, the most seasoned traveler among them, assured everyone, but still he reached out to his loved ones. Without a word, the Flints linked hands as they had so many times in the preceding weeks, praying silently together for a safe trip. Jessy took Emma's hand, wordlessly but lovingly including her in their circle. Emma's hand felt as cold as snow.

Once the train began to roll, everyone started to relax, even Suzanna. She straightened her dark green suit and smoothed the collar of her white blouse. Her boys tried interesting her in the views on all sides as the train began picking up speed. "Wonderful," she murmured, and indeed it was—the broad Midwestern prairie billowing in all directions, vast and white and clean, an endless shimmering blanket of snow poked through with leafless trees and evergreens under a cloudless late afternoon sky. Suzanna looked out the window quietly, wordlessly, as Adam and Jessy did, all three lost in thoughts of the home they were leaving behind and their destination far south.

While other passengers occupied themselves with newspapers, books, and games, Jessy said to Emma, "I packed the shawl you gave me. I love it!"

Emma said slyly, "I packed your present too." She pulled the Bible from her carry bag. "It's hard to read," she admitted, opening it to the ribbon marker at Genesis. "I keep trying, but I'm not getting very far!"

"Then why not start someplace else. John, perhaps? Or Psalms?" Jessy glowed to think of all the treasures contained between those dark covers in Emma's hands. She helped Emma find a new place, a new beginning in her reading.

Once Emma had settled into her book, the grandest book of all, Jessy began reading about the flora and fauna of Florida. Martha read her storybook illustrated with flamingos, pelicans, and the long-legged white ibis. Across the aisle, Adam and Suzanna were reading too; Adam with his newspaper and Suzanna with her poetry, both quietly enjoying the ride, being lulled along, forgetting with every mile the care and worry of their lives in Bethel. Stephen and Taddy remarked on every new sight, every snow-covered tree and ice-thickened creek. Soon the train rounded the track into a river valley, winding along the equally winding river. In the midst of watching this scenic splendor, passengers were invited to enter the adjoining car for the evening meal.

Waiters dressed in immaculate linen jackets and black trousers brought menus to the passengers, now seated at tables in the dining car. Electric lights came on, dainty little things shaded in yellow, illuminating every table. Jessy settled in her dining chair and read the menu: Maine lobster, Alaska salmon, Canadian trout, Texas sirloin, Louisiana jambalaya, Boston baked beans, Idaho potatoes, stewed tomatoes, crab bisque, hot biscuits, curried fruit compote, Hawaiian pineapple, French vanilla ice cream . . . Everyone had a hard time deciding what to order. Soon, steaming foods prepared fresh on the train arrived in heavy silver serving dishes. The Flints and Emma enjoyed nibbling everything, sharing from the hearty platters and covered pots.

Gradually a violet dusk and then darkness settled over the land around them, but the train sped on, stopping every so often at one station and another, dropping off mail and picking up more, but only spending a few minutes in any one place. On and on they went into the dark night.

The steam heat of the train kept the passengers toasty as they settled once again into their seats to read and rest. Adam sat with the boys while Suzanna, Emma, Jessy, and Martha went together to the maze of ladies' rooms linked together and equipped with commodes, sinks, vanities, and a bathtub, as well as hot water, fresh towels, and fine hand soaps. Jessy's heart felt full to bursting. How many years had she, with Adam and Suzanna, slaved away? No matter. This trip more than balanced all that hard work.

Refreshed and changed into nightgowns and robes, the ladies made their way back to their seats which had, in their absence, been converted, as Adam had predicted, into beds. The porters had been by to pull down the Pullmans—beds for the overnight passengers. Heavy drapes would provide privacy for all the double-deck sleeping berths. The group would occupy three bays: Jessy and Emma would share one set of beds, Suzanna and Martha another, and Adam would take a lower berth with his two sons above him.

Emma insisted on climbing to the upper berth in their bay, allowing

Jessy the privilege of the bed with the windows, now covered by tiny pull-down shades. Between the windows was a small electric light the porters had thoughtfully turned on. Once Jessy climbed in and closed the drapes, she marveled at how cozy the bed felt, how warm and comforting, surrounded in all this luxury while roaring south at a hundred miles an hour.

Once Emma had settled in above her, Jessy turned off the light. In the darkness, Jessy asked quietly, "Will you be all right up there?"

"Sure," said Emma, still shifting around and settling in. "It's nice and warm up here."

"It's nice and warm down here too."

"I always take the upper berth whenever we travel. Mum always wants the lower berth."

At this mention of Acacia Kimball, Jessy felt edgy. Chewing her lower lip, she asked Emma, "Are you sorry you came? Do you wish you had gone to Cranstock instead? Do you hate me, Emma? Tell me the truth. Please."

Emma sighed and stretched. "Of course I don't hate you! You're the best friend I've ever had. I'm glad I'm going with you. It's an adventure. Mum's sent telegrams to people she knows who vacation in Florida. They stay at a really swank resort. I guess it might be fun to visit them. Leo stopped by to see some of them on his way to Cuba."

Leo! Jessy shut her eyes, imagining Leo traveling to the islands and south of the border with the Rowdies playing *el beisbol*. Unlike Americans, Hispanic baseball players had two full seasons, summer and winter. Where was he now, she wondered, and what of that cryptic inscription he wrote to her, his best brown-eyed girl? In a hushed voice, hating herself for asking, Jessy ventured: "Emma, does Leo see other girls, do you know?"

"Leo likes girls, but he loves you . . ." Emma sounded groggy. The train was rocking her off to sleep.

Worry won't help me or anyone else, Jessy thought, *but prayer can do wonders*. As she prayed, the soothing rhythm of the train lulled her to sleep.

❦ ❦ ❦

By the next morning, the train had reached Tennessee. Their flat, snowy world had grown mountainous and wintry brown, accented with tall evergreens. Everyone rose, washed, dressed, and then met for breakfast in the dining car. Again the choice was astonishing: Scottish oats, scrambled eggs, Virginia ham, home fries, fresh Florida fruits, steaming Brazilian coffee, Indian tea, Dutch cocoa, and Georgia hominy grits. Jessy was determined to sample new foods. With no effort whatever she polished off a batch of grits laced with golden hoop cheese and melted butter.

"An adopted Southerner?" Adam asked his sister. He too had ordered grits, along with a Western omelette, O'Brion potatoes, and a tower of wheat toast.

"Maybe so," said Jessy as she dipped into preserved figs with cream.

The children enjoyed their sausages and pancakes, while Suzanna, looking rested and happy, had French toast with jam and confectioner's sugar. "This is all so good, and the best part is I didn't have to do the cooking!"

In silence, Adam mouthed an oft-repeated refrain: *I love you and this is going to be fun!* He made Suzanna laugh.

While the passengers enjoyed their leisurely breakfast and the expanding panoramic view of the Deep South unfolding beyond the windows all around them, the porters closed the Pullman berths and restored the sleeping car to its seating format. The Flints decided to spend the day in the lounge, a coach adjoining the dining car but furnished like a living room, equipped with a library, soft comfortable chairs, and game tables. The lounge connected to the observation deck, an outdoor platform where, weather permitting, rail passengers could enjoy the fresh air as the train sped ever southward.

Before Suzanna took her seat in the parlor car, she asked Adam, "Would you join me outside? I think the boys would like to—"

Adam stood at once, surprised and pleased at Suzanna's daring. "I'll get my hat!" he said as he rushed back to the passenger car. Soon he was leading her and their two boys outside to the observation deck. Jessy put her books aside, and Emma and Martha did too, in their eagerness to see the South—*the sunny South so dear*—for the first time unhampered by glass windows and steel doors. Standing outside in the fast-moving air, they squeezed each other's hands as they beheld immense mountain

146

ranges, gray and sweeping, rounded and mellowed by centuries of rainfall, studded with bare hardwoods and towering evergreens, veiled in purple mists. "It's all too wonderful!" cried Jessy.

Without fear, without worry, Suzanna nodded. She let go of Adam's hand long enough to take Jessy's and say, "You were right and I was wrong! How silly I was to object to taking such a wonderful trip! How glad I am we've come!"

"It wouldn't have been nearly so much fun without you!" Jessy shouted above the roaring train and wind. "Or you," she cried to Emma.

"This sure beats home!" Emma said with a big smile.

The strain and worries of the past, the perils of the future, all paled now in the overwhelming majesty of America viewed from a speeding train.

CHAPTER 15

❧

After lunch in the dining car—yet another round of glorious goodies including Canadian meat pies, stuffed Italian zucchini, salad with Pennsylvania dressing, plantation shortcake, and apricot-almond custard, The Midwest Express linked up with The Dixie Special—the major stopover of the trip came in Atlanta, Georgia—an opportunity for everyone to disembark and see what could be seen in two hours. The Flints didn't stray far from the station, but managed to do what Atlantans and their visitors love doing most—shop.

Emma, with Jessy and Martha's approval, came away with a white lacy hat with a big frilly brim. With part of her small travel allowance, Martha selected a pink parasol. Adam bought a map atlas. Stephen and Taddy bought heavy misshapen bullets fired during the great War Between the States, and Suzanna purchased a book compiled by the Daughters of the Confederacy. Jessy bought a big sack of fresh roasted peanuts. As The Dixie Special pulled out of Atlanta, everyone sang the glories of goober peas: Georgia peanuts. *Goodness how delicious, eating goober peas!*

The air grew warmer. They were riding amid green mountains now. From their speeding train they could see flowers in full bloom, camellias, they were told by Southerners on board, in all varieties: white, pink, and candy-stripe. The Flints, with Emma Kimball, were far beyond their white world. Now in south Georgia, the land was flat again. Red clay fields opened on each side of the train, sometimes studded with white. *Snow?* they wondered. *Not in this heat, surely.* Again the Southerners on board explained that this was cotton, what had been left from harvesting the fall crop, acre upon acre of short twiggy bushes.

"My back hurts just looking at those low bushes!" Jessy said with compassion for Southern farmhands who picked acres of cotton each year.

As they approached Florida, Adam told the group about his long friendship with Bo Bally when both were boys on their first adventures away from home, how they worked road shows together, how much territory they had covered in this country and abroad. Bo had eventually become part-owner of a circus and had married and settled in Florida.

Now Jessy, like her nephews and niece, and indeed everyone on board, could not find interest in books or games, not with this new world opening before them. With every mile the earth grew greener, lusher, richer with vegetation, tangled with vines, flooded with sunshine, even as daylight began to fade. The warm air was thick with moisture. When passengers prepared for bed, they gladly changed out of heavy clothing and put on light sleepwear.

"Cotton," Jessy noted as she slipped into a white nightdress. She marveled at the fabric with newfound appreciation for the intense labor cotton required. Tomorrow, blessed tomorrow, they would reach their destination.

In mid-morning The Dixie Special puffed into a Florida station shaded by royal palms. Palm trees! Once Jessy and the other passengers had disembarked, she gawked at the scenery, especially the flowering bushes all around them. A stand of trees waved to her in a tropical breeze. She neared them to learn their identity: the small trees with dark green almond-shaped leaves laden with ponderous, slowly ripening grapefruit. Jessy pinched herself to make sure she wasn't dreaming—and she wasn't. Here she was in January among palm trees and flowering bushes and a brilliant sun so hot she put on her tinted spectacles.

The boys, meanwhile, bid farewell to the train, the iron monster they had once feared but had grown to love. Suzanna thanked the Lord for *terra firma* but had to endure Adam's teasing: "Looks like we survived the calamity!"

Jessy picked up where Adam left off. "The misery of it all—catching up on our reading and eating rich food!"

With the apologetic and contented Suzanna clutching his arm, Adam went about finding transportation to the Bally home—two open horse-drawn carriages for them and their luggage.

As they rode along, the ladies hid from the intense noon sun under cotton parasols that matched their dresses. Gone were thick woolen coats and felt hats in favor of delicate cotton, cool linen, breathable lace and straw. Emma was wearing her bright white two-piece dress and navy striped blouse, the outfit she had worn on Labor Day and one of Jessy's favorites, but Emma's waist looked more than a trifle thick. Suzanna and Martha wore matching outfits of white eyelet. The boys wore short pants, suspenders, and white shirts with ties. Adam had donned a dapper white flannel suit and straw boater. For this day Jessy had chosen a peach-colored cotton dress that accentuated her slender, pretty figure, wholesome coloring, and darkly vibrant hair. "I'm so excited!" she confessed. "Just think! It's probably snowing back home!"

Oddly enough, now that Suzanna felt relaxed, Adam looked nervous. As his excited children clamored to sit on his lap and take hold of his hands, he wondered, would he and Bo still get along now that they both had families and numerous responsibilities? Would the Flints be imposing on the Ballys? All sorts of vague doubts clouded Adam's mind as he hugged his young ones close.

The horse-drawn carriage moved slowly in the noonday heat with the baggage wagon following close behind. The party noticed fine hotels and smaller boarding houses along their route—white and mint green and powder blue stucco buildings, nothing taller than two stories, with broad verandas decked with rattan rockers and potted plants, full-story windows overlooking yards lush with palms and ferns, mango trees, and a profusion of lovingly cultivated flowers. The air was heavy with perfume. Adam lifted up each of his children in turn so they could see the peaceful, pretty, colorful town.

Signs welcomed them to Garden Springs with its numerous therapeutic, natural bathing spas for invalids, where hundreds of thousands of gallons of fresh water gushed to the earth's surface from deep below every minute, every hour, every day. From other signs, Garden Springs offered boating, fishing, hunting, pecans in the shell, oysters and shrimp by the bucket, fresh produce, and more. Above all, the beach! Jessy and Adam breathed deep and long as soon as they recognized that special scent. Everyone took notice, but only Adam and Jessy remembered it fondly from their childhood. To the landlocked Emma, Suzanna, and the children, it was a totally new sensation. Ah, no childhood was complete without tripping to the beach!

Their carriage stopped at a rambling pale coral stucco house with light turquoise shutters shaded by banyan trees whose long limbs had, over many years, sent roots downward to the ground from a good thirty feet or more above the earth. Private yards extended on each side of the house for a great distance.

In awe together they beheld the Bally residence with its two-story wraparound porch that overlooked the street and, in back, faced the pounding surf. From their carriage the Flints could see a shimmering wedge of ocean. At one side of the Bally property, an empty rowboat bobbed about on a freshwater inlet. A hand-shaped sign pointed to a golf course *thataway*. Adam's face glowed with anticipation. Golf!

"Dear? Dear!" Suzanna had to tug her husband's sleeve to rouse him.

Their driver stood ready to help everyone out of the carriage. He and the driver of the rig bearing their luggage readied to unload all the Flints and Emma Kimball had brought: hat boxes, steamer trunks, luggage, fishing poles, everything for an extended holiday at the seaside. Before both drivers began unloading, though, Adam asked them to wait until he knew for certain the arrival of seven people would still meet with the approval of the Ballys. Then Adam took in a deep breath, steadied himself with his cane, reached for his wife's arm, and headed with her up the crushed tabby path to the front door.

Adam knocked and waited with Suzanna in the shade of the veranda, grateful for a tiny breeze and the cool lush greenery all around them that blocked the burning tropical sun. Jessy came up behind them, quietly, enthralled by their surroundings. The door soon creaked open on its hinges.

A small, pretty woman dressed in black despite the heat, with a peaches-and-cream complexion, stood in the hall. A lazy ceiling fan circled slowly over her gracious head. "Don't tell me! Adam and Suzanna Flint! And this must be Jessy!" The delicate woman with the pleasant drawl gently exploded with good humor at the sight of them, so pale and wan from their life in the cold bitter North. "Come in, come in all of you! Oh, please!"

To a boy a bit older than Stephen she said, "Billy! Run fetch your father!" To a boy and girl about the ages of Martha and Taddy she said, "Bobby and Betty, come greet your cousins!" Smoothing her skirts and dark lovely hair, the lady turned back to her guests. "Do come in, all of you! You must be exhausted after that long train ride! You've come just in time—we're having lunch! Here, straight through to the dining room. Oh, and your luggage! Why, can your drivers just carry it all right up these stairs?"

She turned and called out, "Jerome! Roberto! Come help if you please! Our guests have arrived!" Two stalwart servants appeared and began working on the baggage with the two drivers outside.

"If we're too much company for you we'll take rooms in a hotel!" Adam said in his forthright way.

"A hotel? We wouldn't dream of it! We have plenty of room! We've been wanting you to visit us for so long and here you are at last!" Beatrice declared. "We've set aside a big room upstairs for you and Suzanna overlooking the banyan trees, and another room with a balcony for Jessy, Emma, and Martha. Your boys can bunk with our two. How does that sound?"

"It sounds wonderful! But you'll tell us if we're in the way, won't you?" Suzanna asked.

"There'll be no need, I promise you!" Beatrice Bally's gentle patter, gilded Southern honey, soothed everyone's nerves.

Emma and Jessy stared at the interior: the rich mahogany paneling, the high ceilings, flowered wallpapers, parquet floors, and dense green views beyond the tall windows. They passed a parlor, a library, a sun room, a sitting room—the place was huge.

"Bo!" Adam took hold of his old friend's arm. "Bo! It's been years!" Adam was too overcome with emotion to say more.

"Too many years!" agreed Bo, grasping his old friend warmly. "And Jessy! My, you're not a kid anymore!" Bo reached out to Jessy.

She delighted to see the big mellow acrobat, Adam's friend whom she had come to know during his Midwestern travels with his circus. Part owner of a big traveling show, the wealthy self-made Bo Bally had put on weight since she had seen him last. On this Saturday, he looked perfectly comfortable lounging in his magnificent home wearing an old shirt and baggy trousers held up by colorful suspenders—a pattern of trained seals balancing balls on their noses. Barefoot, as were his youngsters, they stood together, arm in arm, three redheaded children to match their acrobatic father.

When Adam finally found his voice again, he introduced his wife and children. Bo and Beatrice introduced their three children: Bill, Bob, and Betty. Jessy introduced Emma Kimball.

As Bo must have done countless times before their arrival, Bo bragged to his wife and children about his old friend and traveling companion, Adam "Man of Iron" Flint. With a showman's flourish, Bo announced, "Why, here before your very eyes stands the greatest strongman and wrestler in the history of the sport!"

Adam leaned on his cane, basking in all the attention, but quietly shaking his head. "I'm still recuperatin'," he said to Bo.

"I guarantee you'll be good as new in no time!" said Bo. "Plenty of rest, sunshine, fishing—"

"And golf?" Adam asked.

"We'll golf all you want!" Bo agreed. "Golf, dips in the springs hereabouts, swimming, fresh-squeezed juices, and Bea's home cooking and you'll be good as new!"

"Speaking of which," said Beatrice, leading everyone to their seats in the dining room as she spoke, "Do have lunch! There's plenty: macaroni and cheese, fried bass, Savannah red rice—don't you just love it loaded with tomatoes and bacon? Here's the tray of celery sticks. How about some fried okra and cornbread? There's watermelon and wild lime pie afterward if you like." Beatrice carried out fresh luncheon plates and silverware to her guests.

A hush settled over the group. Even Emma, who had seen some lovely places in her travels, was in awe at genuine Southern hospitality.

"As soon as we finish lunch, we'll give you a tour of the house and then we can go to the beach if you like. It's a beautiful day, if you don't mind the heat!" said Beatrice.

"I was hoping you'd help me catch dinner," Bo said to Adam.

"I'd love to!" Adam said. "Soon as I change out of this suit."

After lunch they toured the walled gardens that sheltered a tree house in the shape of a pirate ship. "Bo had it built for the children! One of his circus cronies did the wood carving," Beatrice explained to Suzanna.

"Wanna see?" asked Bill, Bob, and Betty.

Stephen, Martha, and Taddy rushed with the Bally children to take a closer look at the ship-shaped tree house high in the banyan glade. Its brightly painted prow was adorned with a figurehead: a raving brunette sea urchin amid a school of leaping blue dolphins.

"We'll hardly be able to drag the children to the beach," Suzanna confided to Beatrice. "What a wonderful place you have, Mrs. Bally!"

"Thank you, but please call me Bea. The swimming pool is this way."

Together they ambled over pebbled walkways to another courtyard with pink blooming hibiscus, a splashing fountain, and a swimming pool. "You'll be sorry you invited us!" Jessy called out to Bo. "We may never want to go home!"

"I can't get over how you've grown up, Jessy!" Bo said over his cigar. "How come you're not married, a sweet girl like you?"

"Oh, she's workin' on it," said Adam.

"What about a swim? Or a walk on the beach? Let's take a vote!" the Ballys asked.

And so it was decided: Bo and Adam would go fishing, and the women and children would go to the beach. Emma, feeling suddenly weak, decided to stay behind. Bea and Suzanna ushered her up to her room, with Jessy asking the two mothers, "Will Emma be all right?"

"Yes, Emma must be feeling the effects of her pregnancy," confided Suzanna.

"The change in climate could also be affecting Emma. It's awfully warm for January, even in Florida!" Beatrice closed the broad wooden hurricane shutters to ward off the bright midday sun and then pulled the cord to turn on the electric ceiling fan over the bed. In the slow, steady breeze, the women helped Emma out of her corset and clothing. "Here, lie down and put your feet up, honey!"

Emma regarded her abdomen. "Looks like I'm starting to show all of a sudden." She leaned back on the pillows and closed her eyes. "I feel dizzy."

"Oh, you dear girl!" said Beatrice. "You know, just a few months ago I had a miscarriage. I'm not over it yet. I may never be! How we will miss that dear child! I'll wear black as long as I feel such a loss as this, the loss of my child!"

"Child?" Emma said, one hand on her forehead and one on her abdomen.

Each woman contemplated the differences of opinion. In the early stages of pregnancy, was a child involved or not? Would a child—could a child—be missed if it is never born?

CHAPTER 16

❧

In the cool, shaded room, Martha changed from her pink pinafore into her bathing suit. Jessy unpacked a few things, careful not to disturb the sleeping Emma. As she rooted through her things, she found her new navy bathing suit, more like a uniform, with its detachable skirt, bloomers, long black stockings, short-sleeved blouse, and hat. The purchase that seemed so right last September now made her feel uneasy.

"You look adorable!" Jessy whispered to her young niece who had just wriggled into her own suit, a smaller version of Jessy's, but in pink and white. Jessy helped Martha put on her white cotton hat. "Remember to take a shirt with you. You don't want too much sun, now."

"Yes, Aunty. Aren't you changing clothes too?"

Jessy shook her head. "For today I'll just stay as I am," she said, indicating her peach of a dress with its bolero jacket and soft flowing sleeves. Wearing her sun hat, she left behind only her long stockings and high-buttoned shoes. Before Jessy went downstairs she filled her shoulder bag with roasted peanuts.

Jessy and Martha beheld the shore. Such a vision it was, such thrilling sounds it made, and that bracing aroma! The brilliant sun sparkled over the churning turquoise sea. Offshore, tiny sailboats breezed along in the wind. Tireless gulls and sanderlings policed the water's edge in search of edibles. The Bally children were giving fresh bread to the birds. Everyone delighted in seeing the dauntless crying gulls scoop up their easy meal. Jessy marveled at her first sighting of a pelican gliding effortlessly along the horizon, inches above the ocean surface but well beyond the waves breaking on shore.

While Suzanna, fit and stylish in her new bathing suit, ventured toward the water with her sons, Jessy held back with her hand in Martha's. "It's been so long since I—" Jessy paused, looking intently at the ocean, letting it fill her senses with its overwhelming force, its reminders of her past.

"If you like," said young Betty Bally to Martha Flint in a shy voice, "we can go swimming together."

Gratefully, Jessy released Martha's hand and entrusted the girl to Betty, who was well adapted to life by the seashore. Jessy watched both girls, dressed in pink bathing suits, testing the water's temperature with their small bare feet. The four boys in briefs were already soaked and crying for more. A colorful ball quickly became the object of great desire as the children bounced it amid the waves.

Suzanna, thoroughly soaked, returned to the shore laughing and wiping salt water from her face. "The ocean is so different from Lake Bethel!"

Beatrice had spread out a blanket and stood a big umbrella in the sand. She and Suzanna sat together talking and watching their children. "They get along just fine!" said Beatrice. "We're so glad you've come! Tell me all about your trip."

As Suzanna recounted the wonders of train travel, Jessy dug her toes deep in the sand soft as confectioner's sugar. When she approached the water, to her surprise it felt as warm as a bath, nothing like the icy waters of New England. New England! This place was so far from the rocky, barnacle-encrusted shores of her home. Instinctively she looked northward, remembering her childhood home gone forever. Oh, the bitterness, the loss and sadness of that old life of hers before she left for the Midwest. A young woman now, Jessy was as different from the girl she once was as an oak is from the acorn.

Jessy began to walk along the shore, moving farther away from the others, up the deserted beach. Somehow she felt drawn away, apart, to think and to remember, to pray and to hope—but for what she knew not. A gull's sharp cry pierced her thoughts. Quickly turning, she looked back. Suzanna and the children waved to her. Above the roaring surf she shouted, "I need to walk! Please excuse me!"

Suzanna and Beatrice smiled and nodded. Jessy waved to them and turned away, lost in thought once more. It had been a long train ride, and restful, but Jessy was used to hard work and active days spent laboring with her brother. She rejoiced for Adam renewing his old friendship with Bo. How good of the Ballys to invite them all to such a glorious place.

She thought of Adam, the first time she ever met him, on that cold winter day in March several winters past, how bitter he had been, how angry she'd made a thousand-mile trip to be with him. And yet, how fortunate they had both been since then, drawn together, two siblings without parents. Mother and Father, Jessy thought, remembering them. Her father had died when she was a small girl; her mother followed a few years later, leaving Jessy orphaned, alone. Alone! Jessy raised her eyes to the sky, praying, "I'm never really alone because I have You, dear heavenly Father! What wonders You have made, what treasures—from the biggest to the smallest—all formed in Your loving hands!"

Jessy reached down for tiny wet shells and teeny pebbles. Smooth and worn from being tossed by the sea, they glowed with sea water like diamonds in her hands. She was letting them slip through her fingers when she noticed a struggling white crab the size of her smallest fingernail several yards from the water's edge. "You need to go back to the sea! Let me help you before the gulls eat you for lunch!" Gently she put the tiny sidewinding critter out of harm's way into the wet sand and watched to see what it would do. It burrowed under. Jessy concentrated on the spot. After a big wave broke over the hiding place, a tiny breathing hole poked through the sand. Satisfied the tiny crab was safe, Jessy continued walking.

No one was about now except tireless sanderlings at her feet, and, above her head, a task force of pelicans gliding along on a fishing expedition. Jessy came to a ruined cabana on the shore with a scrawled, roughly painted sign by an unknown, unseen author who filled her with unspoken joy. The scrawling paint read: *Something good's going to happen to you.* "It already has!" she shouted.

The wind picked up so much Jessy had to hold on to her hat. She looked around. A rambling white stucco house stood behind a sea wall. She had walked more than a mile in her bare feet. Now she reached a dead end of sorts where a river met the sea. In the brackish waters she could see scores of fish, more fish than she had ever seen in one spot.

The water was deep here. The ocean swirled around Jessy, pounding at her legs and tugging her long skirt and petticoats, soaking them through. *How wonderful the ocean feels*, she thought. How alive she felt in this place. Jessy closed her eyes, glad for the sun and the beauty of the day, even her memories of the dead, glad for blissful solitude.

"All will be right, have no fear! All all awl y'awl!"

Jessy's eyes snapped open. Startled by this curious message spoken in the most rasping voice imaginable, she looked around to see, hopping about on the thick retaining wall, a bright green parrot with soulful black eyes. The bird did a little dance, whirling around and picking up one leg, and then the other, up and down, and around. He cocked his head at her. "Hey, y'awl!"

"Well, hello!" Jessy said, laughing, in the voice she reserved for toddlers. "And who, may I ask, are you?"

"Gorgeous!" rasped the parrot. "Gooooor-juss!"

"You *are* gorgeous!" she laughed. Jessy admired the Christmas-colored bird with his kelly green body, blazing red forehead, and violet feathers cascading like eyebrows over his bright black eyes. The edges of his wings were tipped in pale yellow, the color of his generous curving beak. "But how did you know I needed consolation? How did you know I was mourning on such a beautiful day? You are sweet to wish for right, you pretty bird."

"Walllk the plaaaank!" Again the bird went into his lively dance.

"Oh, now, don't be threatening people, Plato Q!" crooned a man whose voice was unfamiliar to Jessy but, at the same time, familiar. "Don't mind Mr. Snaggletooth, Miss. I'm afraid he is incurably ill-mannered."

Jessy waded closer to the source of the male voice where the sea wall ended and a wrought-iron fence began. Beyond the open gate, the man was untangling a mound of fishing line near a small craft anchored in the shallows. The sun behind the man obscured small details to her, but from his silhouette, Jessy could see that he had a physique that could withstand anything.

"Hello," the man said to her, glancing up from the heap of tangles. "I like untangling things."

"I see," she said, squinting in the sun. "I didn't mean to trespass but I had been walking along the beach and it suddenly ended somehow and—"

"No need to apologize," he said with his mild and sonorous voice. "Tourists wander up here all the time."

"How did you know I was a tourist?" Jessy wondered.

He looked her over before resuming his work of untangling the line. "White feet!"

Jessy glanced down at her small bare feet, a sickly pale white indeed, but from the tone of the man's voice, he must have liked what was attached to them. Mystified and a trifle flustered, Jessy said, "I *am* a tourist, as a matter of fact, here for the first time."

"Welcome to Florida! And how was your trip from New England by way of the Midwest?"

"My goodness, how did you know that?" Jessy looked around to see what miraculous device had described her so completely to this total stranger.

"I'm right, aren't I?" he said with a smile. "You are originally from New England but somehow ended up in the Midwest and, well, here you are!"

"Yes, exactly!" Jessy, squinting in the sun at the stranger, babbled affably. "I was born in New England. When I was fourteen I went to live with my brother. We live on a farm in the Midwest; we raise hogs and dairy cows and field corn mostly. Adam's friend Bo Bally from the circus invited us down for a visit. We just arrived on the train. It's wonderful here."

The stranger nodded wisely as she verified his assumptions. He shifted so that she wasn't blinded by the sun looking in his direction.

"But how did you know all that about me? You and I have never met. I would have remembered." Jessy's voice slowed and quieted. "I know I would have remembered seeing you before. I just know I would have."

How familiar he seemed, yet she knew they had never met, not ever. Jessy admired this well-spoken fellow in his thirties, dressed more for a prayer meeting than the beach, in a dark suit, vest, and tie. Beyond him in the yard, on the outdoor extension of an indoor loggia, an older couple sat in the sun, the woman bound to a wheelchair.

"My parents," said the man. "My mother's recuperating from a fall."

"Oh. I'm sorry." Jessy, parents uppermost in her mind, added, "You're fortunate you have your parents. Mine died several years ago. I ache to think of all that might have been." When Jessy rubbed her hand against her mouth, she tasted sea salt. It tasted good. "Still life has its many joys despite the sorrows."

She studied the man now, taking him in fully, every detail: the formal black suit, long-sleeved white shirt, the loose artist's tie, his thick sandy brown hair whipping in the wind. But his eyes most arrested her attention—large, luminous, soulful gray, and full of wisdom. His coloring was fair and fresh, his skin smooth, pale ivory. She thought he looked like more of a tourist himself than a sun-bronzed local.

He turned suddenly and called out, "Dad, this boat needs an overhaul!" The man's father nodded and waved in the distance. Jessy found the stranger's way of speaking splendid. His voice was clear and resonant, polished, capable of carrying a great distance without losing its mellowness, a voice that had been tamed and modulated like a fine musical instrument played by a master.

Never before had Jessy encountered a man like him. That he might not have appealed to every girl made him all the more appealing to Jessy Flint. Surely he was one of a kind, she thought. Then she noticed the wedding ring on his left hand, a simple band of solid gold that had the power to send Jessy's world crashing down and crushing over her. She felt foolish to have fallen in love and out of it all in a moment. She turned to go but stopped when she heard a wolf whistle. She turned abruptly to the man who laughed and explained, "That bird! It's the sailor in him."

"Sailor?" she wondered aloud. She turned again to the showy, comic parrot. "What did you say your name is and why don't you fly away?"

"Plato Q. Snaggletooth!" the man began and the bird finished. The man explained, "Q is for Question. He never stops asking! He can't fly away because I keep his wings clipped. He couldn't manage in the wild, the spoiled pet that he is." The fellow fussed over his parrot and smiled at Jessy.

She smiled too, hoping the man's lucky wife rejoiced in the treasure she had married. The man had finished unsnarling the line and was digging around in a toolbox at his feet in the patchy grass.

"You untangle things very well," Jessy said.

With unhesitating assurance he said, "We can't catch fish if we're all tangled up in knots, now, can we?"

"No," she agreed, sensing deep theological intent in the man's remark. Before she could comment, something distracted her. As he moved about she noticed the front of his vest, a gorgeous thing of deepest night sky blue embroidered with the planets, the sun, and a sprinkling of silver shooting stars. "That's a work of art, your vest!"

"Thank you," he said, slowly, sadly. "My wife's handiwork."

160

His wife! *Fortunate, blessed, talented,* Jessy thought, *and married to this splendid fellow.* "She must be an artist to do such magnificent work!"

"She was an artist indeed."

"Was!" Jessy cringed.

"I've just come back from her grave." With his head he gestured to pots of flowers on an outdoor table. "I brought too many. I always do, but how she loved flowers! She loved them as much as I love the stars." He spoke haltingly now. "Gone two years already," he sighed. "You'd think I'd be able to talk about her without—" The man with the glorious voice now couldn't speak at all.

Sharing his sorrow, Jessy drew near him again. She said nothing, but the expression on her face revealed volumes about her caring heart.

In a moment, he composed himself enough to say, "Hope and I made good use of the short time we had together. Without warning, her memory rises up in me. She was only twenty-six when—"

"Oh, I *am* sorry! Please forgive me for chattering on and on about my own losses so long ago. I'm sure they can't compare to losing a spouse— your dear young wife! I'm so very sorry, I truly am."

His face suddenly filled with peace. "I'm glad you came along!" he assured her. "There are so many good things in life. God sends healing, in time. When Hope and I married we thought we had so much time, a world of time, an eternity. But—" The man's large gray eyes shined with the memory of love now lost. "No one knew she had an aneurysm. Took her like that!" The man snapped his fingers. "We never knew how little time we had."

"It's a matter of time for us all," Jessy said. "We never know what the future holds."

"It holds sorrow, true, but also much joy, as you know."

"Yes, of course." Softly Jessy murmured, *"Eye hath not seen, nor ear heard, nor entered into the heart of man—"*

"—the things that God has prepared for them that love Him," he said, finishing the exquisite verse of Scripture she had begun.

The two, gazing into each other's eyes, stood where salt water and fresh met and mingled and teemed with life. They might have stood there together poised for eternity, on the very precipice of love, but they were interrupted.

Three visitors paddled a dugout canoe to the dock beside the house: a powerfully built, graying, soft-spoken black man with two younger men. The older man called out, "Dr. Fisher!"

With great reluctance the stranger, now a stranger no more—Dr. Fisher—turned from Jessy to greet his visitors. "Hello, my good men! It must be three o'clock!" Dr. Fisher turned to Jessy and explained: "Leviticus Tye and his sons come by at three every day except Sundays, rain or shine. Mr. Tye always has something good to sell. He grows vegetables and what he doesn't grow he buys from Caribbean shippers. Come and have a look! What's your name by the way? I'm Nathan Fisher—Isaac Nathan Fisher."

"Pleased to meet you, Dr. Fisher. I'm Jessy Flint." She followed him to the dugout canoe loaded with fresh vegetables and exotic fruits Jessy had never before seen.

"You like banana, Miss Flint?" Leviticus asked her with his charming West Indies accent.

"I don't know, Mr. Tye. I've never tried one."

Soon enough Leviticus and his two sons, Moses and Aaron, had peeled and cut two bananas for sampling. Mr. Tye set them on a palm leaf he used for a platter. "Fresh from Jamaica. We get this morning. We have many more; we sell them too fast! We grow strawberry. Here, if you like. The bird, he loves them. And the mango, too, try her, Miss! She is perfect!"

She *was* perfect. The tart, juicy mango tingled in Jessy's mouth. She enjoyed her first taste of banana too. "How wonderful!" she exclaimed. "These fruits must come from paradise!"

"That's certainly where their Designer lives," Nathan murmured.

Nathan's father, the elder Fisher, joined them, pushing his wife's wheelchair to the dock. Mrs. Fisher selected some produce—celery, greens, bell peppers, and bananas—and sampled the mangoes too. While they were all nibbling there under the palms, Jessy remembered the peanuts in her bag. As everyone sampled some, she asked Nathan Fisher, "Would Mr. Snaggletooth like a peanut?"

"That bird can never get enough of them!"

Jessy took one to the dancing bird. "Shall I peel it for him?"

"Oh, no, he'll get it open with that beak of his. Watch!"

Holding the peanut in one talon, Plato Q. Snaggletooth ripped open the shell with no difficulty. Soon the peanuts inside were gone and he was begging for more. Jessy obliged.

"Now you've spoiled him. You'll have to stop by every day to give him more peanuts!" Nathan Fisher said to Jessy. He turned back to Mr. Tye and his capable-looking sons. "There's paying work at Hope's place, if you're interested." When Leviticus Tye appeared interested indeed, Dr. Fisher continued: "The stairway and back entrance need painting."

"You finally decide to sell?" Mr. Tye asked.

"Yes, finally. It's time I found a buyer. I keep postponing the inevitable. Could you meet me there at five today? Is that convenient?"

"Sure, sure, Dr. Fisher."

Jessy enjoyed the cordial exchange. Mr. Tye and his sons insisted on loading Jessy's arms with gifts wrapped in coarse paper—bananas, strawberries, celery, fresh cut flowers for "you and them nice folk, the Ballys." To her surprise, Leviticus Tye, preparing to move on, refused all payment, saying the peanuts were payment enough.

The doctor reassured her again, "You've spoiled us. We'll want peanuts every day!" Pulling out his pocket watch, he said to the Tyes, "Meet you at five, then, at Hope's place?"

The Tyes nodded and resumed their journey upriver by dugout canoe. Meanwhile, the doctor's parents chatted with Jessy Flint.

In his expansive way, their son said, "Mother, Dad, the good Miss Flint has arrived on our doorstep like a gift from the sea, washed ashore after a perilous long journey from New England by way of the Midwestern prairie! This barefoot girl has had to hack her way through snow-covered forests and vine-tangled jungles just to grace our doorstep! Think of it for a moment if you will, the effort her journeys must have required! And all to give us fresh roasted peanuts! It's not every tourist who comes bearing gifts, now is it, I ask you? Don't you think the dear lass deserves a tall glass of iced tea flavored with lime and sweetened with plenty of sugar!"

"Oh, really, I couldn't impose!" Jessy cried, her arms overloaded with gifts from Leviticus Tye. "I should be going!"

"Oh, but you must have some tea!" exclaimed Mrs. Fisher. As she spoke she smoothed her soft gray hair away from her pleasant face. "Cyrus made a jug of it for us right after lunch, didn't you, dear?" She reached out to her husband from her wheelchair before turning to Jessy, saying, "Just set those vegetables and fruits down in the shade; they'll be fine right over there. Yes, that's right, dear."

Cyrus Fisher went off at once and soon waved his son and Jessy toward the loggia where a frosty pitcher of tea awaited them. Reluctant but thirsty from her walk in the sun, Jessy thanked the Fishers for their hospitality before sitting down with them and taking a sip from her tall glass. "How delicious! I've never had iced tea with lime before. It's so refreshing!"

"We drink it by the bucketful down here," said Nathan, taking a seat and eyeing her with a sudden healthy and all-consuming relish: her simple straw hat, the peach dress with soft billowing sleeves, her sweet hands and feet, her delicate oval face, and especially her tender brown eyes.

His father explained, "It's a very Southern thing to do, you know. Iced tea and hot grits are as Southern as mockingbirds and magnolia trees."

Mrs. Fisher added, "And down here we like our greens laden with hot pepper sauce. How long will you and your family be staying in Garden Springs?"

"Oh, ah—" With a jolt she remembered her family members who must be wondering what had become of her. "I, ah—"

"You'll have to go on a river cruise. I do hope you've time enough in your schedule," Nathan intoned.

"A river cruise?" Jessy said, her eyebrows raised. "We hadn't—"

"You hadn't? Oh, but you must!" Nathan Fisher smiled at Jessy, in her eyes, his face the very face of love. He waxed eloquent on what was obviously a pet topic, his rich-timbred voice saying, "It would be unthinkable to come to Florida and leave again without seeing one of the greatest wonders of the world—a river that flows northward—the only other river to do so in the entire world being the Nile! And not only that, but the river leads to Laguna Springs! Have you not heard of Laguna Springs?"

Jessy shook her head, all apologies at being ignorant of such scenic wonders.

"Doctor! Doctor!" A small barefoot boy in ragged short pants and a broken straw hat ran to them. He pulled a small rusted wagon behind him. In his wake were two silent little barefoot girls in sleeveless sundresses. "Doctor, it's nearly a goner! Can you help?"

Jessy followed Nathan and Cyrus to where the boy stood. Nathan took off his jacket and vest and put them aside before bending down to examine a bird caught in some sort of web.

"Oh, my, what a shame!" Nathan moaned.

"My papa won't touch birds. He's scared of 'em," wailed the boy, "But soon as I found him I knew you could make him right!" With that the boy and his little girlfriends ran off with their wagon.

Nathan wasted no time rolling up his shirt sleeves and picking up the pelican. Holding the big brown bird with the long bill in his arms, he turned to his father. "Would you care to do the honors or shall I?"

"I'll get the scissors, but I can't do any cutting till my glasses are fixed. Maybe Miss Flint could—"

The two men looked expectantly to Jessy. She peered at the pelican's legs twisted in cutting, cruel knots. "Looks like the poor thing's gotten all tangled up in a fishing line!"

"Exactly," said Nathan as he took a seat on a bench under the trees and waited for his father to return with the scissors. "A careless fisherman tosses away a fishing line and a bird belonging to a species especially trusting of humans is in danger of losing its life."

Jessy couldn't help but be touched to see Nathan holding the big brown bird in his arms. "You like untangling things," she said.

"We'll make it right, have no fear!" screeched Mr. Snaggletooth.

"Yes, Plato Q, we will!" said Nathan in the reassuring tones of one who performed good deeds on a routine basis. "Ah, here comes Dad with the scissors. Would you mind, Miss Flint? Considering the size of this bird, this is a two-person operation. I'll hold our patient if you would be so good as to perform the cutting ceremonies."

"Of course," said Jessy, her maternal instincts aroused. Sitting beside Nathan, she asked of the big-billed, web-footed bird, "Will he bite?"

"Not if I hold his jaw while you snip. I've had a great deal of practice holding Plato Q whenever his nails need trimming!"

Jessy began snipping, but went slowly so as not to injure the bird's legs. "The poor thing! His legs are cut from struggling against the line."

"Fishing wire's tough as nails," said Nathan, speaking in hushed, thrilling tones close to Jessy's ear. "You're not afraid of birds, I take it."

"No." Jessy looked up from the pelican into Nathan's eyes. "I'm not afraid of anyone or anything except the Lord who is all powerful."

"And all-loving too," said Nathan.

Jessy, her heart aflutter, asked, "Are you a Christian, then?"

"Certainly! A Christian is the only sane thing to be in this world!"

Their eyes met, brown and gray merging together in sweet harmony.

Turning back to her snipping, she asked, "And you're a medical doctor?"

"No, but my father is. A number of years ago he and my mother began visiting Florida. They bought this place and began collecting treasures from shipwrecks and salvage operations. They love auctions and museums. We're planning to donate a good many things to get a museum started here in Garden Springs. Hope's father was a collector too; he got interested in shipwrecks while running a trading business on the coast. Hope's family place is jammed with antiquities. That's why I keep putting off selling her house, but I really need to do something soon. I'm here on an extended winter break. To answer your question, I'm a doctor of philosophy. I teach college in the Mid-Atlantic, up in the mountains. It's a small college. Perhaps you've heard of it: St. Azarias, near a place called Enigma."

"St. Azarias? Really?" College, the unattainable, but nevertheless Jessy's fond desire! Her eyes widened as she asked, "What do you teach?"

"Oh, a little of everything: history, geography, geology, theology, archaeology, biology, mineralogy, ornithology, museology, ecclesiology, epistemology, hydrology, spectrology, cartology, the classic apology, and the inevitable euology. Which reminds me. I like dabbling in technology and criminology."

The pelican had relaxed completely at this lengthy monology. Laughing, Jessy claimed, "I take it you're a prodigy! Such mental efforts must be positively exhausting!"

"Yes, I admit, sometimes I am simply involved in lethargy." By now Nathan was laughing, as was his father standing under a nearby palm.

Jessy giggled as she said, "So, as I understand, Dr. Fisher, you teach the History of Western Civilization. About ancient things and new, and things in between, and scientific and mechanical things and literary things and philosophical things, and spiritual things, and holy things— um, Scripture?"

"Ah, yes! Scripture, sculpture, architecture—" he said, his grin never fading. "I'm interested in everything from the rudimental to the cosmological."

Warily Jessy paused in her snipping to say, "Of course this could all be conjectural!"

"By no means! I'm interested in athletics, physics, statistics, ballistics, harmonics, economics, mathematics, civics, linguistics, phonetics—"

"Ah! Phonetics!" Jessy said wisely. "So that's how you could tell about my origins! My accent gave me away!"

"Exactly!"

"Extraordinary!" Now they both were snickering so much the poor bird became restless. "Almost done, Mr. Pelican," Jessy assured the bird.

"Everything will be all right," said Nathan, gently rocking the big bird in his arms and saying to Jessy, "I'm so glad you aren't afraid of birds. My wife loved birds, but from a distance. Hope worked tirelessly to save them in the wild but she would have been terrified to get close enough to touch one."

"Oh, I like animals of all kinds," Jessy said, smiling warmly at Nathan. "Living as I do on a farm, I tend to animals all the time. They get into all kinds of things." Jessy paused as she brought the scissors very close to the brown bird's tender underbelly. "Hold still now, Mr. Pelican. I don't want to clip your feathers by mistake!" She continued snipping. "You have some wonderful animals here in Florida."

"Yes, we do, a paradise! But it'll be Paradise Lost if the developers have their way, cutting into the earth the way they do without a thought for the animals or the ways of water. The Lord gave us dominion over the earth but, my heavens, I'm sure He didn't intend for us to ruin the place! And the poor birds! Hope devoted her life to saving them from poachers."

Jessy remembered Laura Kimball Everett's elaborately feathered hats. "I'm glad to know efforts are being made to protect the birds. It's awful the way they're being killed just to decorate hats!" Jessy stopped in mid-snip. "There should be a law!"

"Oh, there are laws and more laws coming, but poachers pay no attention. There's a good many people trying to establish wildlife sanctuaries, but too many more who have no regard for anyone or anything. If man insists on ruining the earth, the earth will ruin man. It's something we're all concerned about, my family included. Hope's work will go on. Numerous groups are seeing to it."

"We'll make things right, have no fear!" squawked the parrot.

"Yes, Plato Q, yes of course!" Nathan pursed his lips at his pet. "Speaking of boorish behavior, I rescued that parrot from an abusive sailor down in the Keys last winter."

"Ka-boom! Ka-baaam! Blamm-blamm-blamm!"

Jessy thought the beach was under attack. "What was that?!"

Nathan, laughing, said, "Oh, just old Plato Q! From the sounds he can imitate, I've decided he must have survived the Spanish-American War! He can imitate bombs bursting in air, rifle fire, rockets exploding—he loves sitting in my laboratory up at school, waiting for some experiment or other of mine to backfire!"

"Blam! Ka-boom!" Plato Q. Snaggletooth was warming to his subject now.

"There," Jessy said, examining her handiwork. "Oh, our poor patient's bleeding a bit, I'm afraid. This line has really cut into him."

"Dad! Could you fetch some antiseptic?" Nathan called out.

Cyrus Fisher nodded and went off toward the house. Soon Jessy was daubing the pelican's wounds.

"Poor fellow! All because some fisherman was careless! We should always be mindful of our actions, that's what I'm forever telling my students—be mindful of others, including wildlife, and all the earth's resources!" Nathan carried the pelican to the inlet. "Now, we're going to put you down, Sir Pelicanus Occidentalis, and see if you can manage on your own! If not, you'll just have to stay with us for a while."

At the inlet where the river met the ocean, Nathan stood the pelican on a floating board that became a mini-raft under the bird's webbed feet. The bird took a moment to get his balance, and then yawned heartily and began preening his rumpled feathers with his considerable bill as he bobbled along on his makeshift raft. Nathan rubbed his hands together in satisfaction, saying, "The operation is a complete success thanks to you, Miss Flint!"

"Please, call me Jessy. All my friends do."

"And call me Nathan. Looks like we have company." Nathan shielded his eyes from the sun. A gang of noisy children was coming their way.

Jessy gasped, remembering everyone she left on the beach.

"Aunty! Are you all right? Mama sent us looking for you!" Stephen, flushed with the sun and barefoot, still in his bathing suit, gathered close to her as did Taddy and Martha, and Bill, Bob, and Betty too.

Jessy hugged them all, saying, "Yes, I'm fine, loves, just fine! Look down there! See that pelican? Dr. Fisher and I have been operating!" As the children ran to get a closer look at the bird commanding its little raft, Jessy turned to her newfound friend. "Well, I suppose I should be going now, Dr. Fisher, I mean Nathan. It was so nice to have met you and your parents and the Tyes." She retrieved the fresh produce and flowers Leviticus had given her.

"You're staying with the Ballys, then?" Nathan nodded to the Bally children, whom he obviously recognized.

"Yes, for a few weeks, unless we drive them crazy and they send us packing to a hotel!"

"A hotel? Nonsense! We have plenty of room here! And there's always Hope's place. It's enormous, and perfect for company! It just wouldn't do for you and your loved ones to stay in a hotel, not with all the room we have."

"That's really very kind of you!" Jessy gazed up into those luminous gray eyes of his. How she hated leaving this madcap professor of everything, this Renaissance man.

"Funny, just now," he admitted. "This is the first day in two years I've been able to say Hope's name without breaking down. I have you to thank for that."

Jessy looked down in modesty. "Oh, to everything there is a season—a time to mourn, and a time to dance."

"Yes, a time for every purpose under heaven."

Nathan watched as the children spirited her away from him, Jessy in the center, happily chatting with youngsters on all sides. When she turned to wave good-bye to him, Nathan shouted in his best public speaking voice, "You won't forget to bring more peanuts, will you, Jessy?"

Snaggletooth seconded the motion with a cheery screech.

Jessy laughed and waved good-bye to the pair of them and to the elder Fishers still sipping tea on their loggia. Nathan stood watching until the little crowd disappeared entirely from view, walking down the unpaved road to the Bally home.

In the shade of the loggia, Cyrus and Grace Fisher exchanged knowing looks. How long had it been since they had seen their eldest son, their genius Nathan, as happy as he had been this afternoon?

CHAPTER 17

❦

"**N**athan Fisher!" exclaimed Bea Bally over dinner that evening.

"Yes, do you know him?" Jessy, who had since rinsed her clothes of saltwater and had pinned them on the line outside, was now dressed in dark cotton for dinner with both families and Emma gathered round the big mahogany table. "Nathan Fisher knows everything! When he heard me speak just a few words he could tell where I was born and where I live now. And whenever I started a Scripture verse he could finish it! I was so impressed!"

Adam frowned. "Just where did you go today?"

"For a walk down the beach. I met the Fishers and rescued a pelican." Jessy dug into sweet potatoes baked with honey. "How was your fishing trip?"

"Bo caught most everythin' there was to catch!" said Adam.

"Your brother will be catching everything too, when he begins to relax!" Bo drawled.

"I'm already relaxed," said Adam, who had begun to acquire a tan.

"I've totally forgotten our home, our farm, everything!" said Suzanna. "I never dreamed how much we needed to get away. This is so splendid of you, Bea and Bo. After dinner we want to give you the presents we brought."

"Presents! Now you didn't have to go and do that!" drawled Bea.

"Why, yes we did!" Suzanna answered, her blue eyes sparkling in the soft light. "This chicken is delicious, Beatrice. Just how do you prepare it?"

"Oh, we slow-bake it for hours and fix a lime sauce with the drippings. Here, have some more of that sauce," Bea said, passing the gravy boat. "It's an old family recipe I adapted to the citrus fruits we have here in Florida."

Accepting the sauce boat, Suzanna admired the lovely china, an old, exquisite pattern banded in royal blue that had been in Bea's family for generations.

"Yes, my family was deeply cultured, up in Savannah, but because of the War of Yankee Aggression, of course, we had no money! Poor as church mice, all of us! But, my, we surely have culture!" Beatrice laughed about her predicament. "Then Bo came into my life and rescued me from the poorhouse! And to think, him a Yankee!"

Bo added, "Now, honey, my first name is Beauregard, after all! That's about as Southern as Southern gets! Besides, I'm from the South—Southern Iowa!"

Everyone tittered at this. The ceiling fan lazily cooled the room. Electric lights glowed softly in their pink frosted glass shades. A large mural over the buffet depicted spectacular wading birds and wildlife of the Everglades: pink flamingos, roseate spoonbills, white-plumed egrets, tiny scrub jays, and a pair of alligators.

"Where are the alligators?" Stephen wondered aloud. "We didn't see even one and we were at the beach all afternoon!"

"Oh, you won't see them at the beach, son, that's for sure," explained Bo. "And this time of year, you may not see them on the river, either, if the temperature drops too low. They like sunny, warm weather because they're cold-blooded."

"Nathan Fisher told me about a river cruise," said Jessy.

"Bo mentioned the same thing while we were out fishin'," said Adam.

"Oh, you really should go! Everyone should!" said Bea. "Bo and I cruised the river before the children were born." She sighed happily. "It was so romantic, just dripping with charm—the Spanish moss, the wading birds, the peace and quiet, the beauty of it all! And how we danced at the hotel when our steamboat stopped for the night! Oh, do go if you can!"

"A steamboat trip?" Suzanna said with alarm. "But surely everyone remembers the sinking of the steamer *General Slocum* in the East River a few years ago? Oh, it was dreadf—"

Adam, with eyebrow raised, mouthed a silent, "I love you."

"Now what do you know about Nathan Fisher?" Bea asked Jessy.

Jessy paused in her languid dining. "He teaches at a college."

"Yes, that's true, he's a professor and a scholar. But above all he is a brave spirit, that one. Why, do you know Nathan Fisher—" When Beatrice lowered her voice to a confidential hush, all ten seated with her at the table stopped eating and leaned forward to hear more. "Nathan Fisher risked his life facing down a lynch mob last winter right here in Garden Springs?"

"No!" said Jessy, her eyes bright with terror. "What happened?"

"Well, it was almost a disaster, that's what it was! A human tragedy in the making! A man—a white man—a prominent local politician by the name of Ambrose Polk was found in his carriage house dead of a bullet wound. A neighbor had stopped by to visit and well, Ambrose lived alone and there he was, dead as Abraham Lincoln and quick as lightning a mob formed demanding justice at once. They went with torches to the home of Leviticus Tye."

"Why, I met Mr. Tye today!" Jessy eyed the lovely fruits on the table, compliments of Leviticus Tye. When Jessy brought the fresh produce to the kitchen, Beatrice had told Jessy to remind her to tell a story, and here it was. "Oh, what happened?" Jessy asked her hostess.

"Well, Leviticus Tye did landscaping and home repairs for the deceased Mr. Polk and an eyewitness said he thought he had seen Tye at the Polk residence earlier that day. The mob dragged the unfortunate Mr. Tye out of his bed in the middle of the night. They had a rope with them! It was horrid! No trial, no jury, just a mob ready to hang the man then and there!"

Bo continued the story. "I was there. I heard the commotion and got out of bed. The mob came right past this house and went up the street toward the train station. Nathan Fisher scrambled ahead of me, stood up on a bench, and demanded quiet. I'll never forget. He said the accused couldn't have been at Polk's house because he'd been doing landscaping for the elder Fishers all that day and the day before, he and his two sons! This gave the mob something to think about—it's not every day a white man will brave a lynch mob defending a black man, and an immigrant at that. But of course, there's always some trigger-happy fool in a crowd and—*bang*!"

Jessy's eyes popped open. "Someone shot Nathan Fisher?" Jessy's protective instincts raced in high gear. "Was he badly injured?"

"Not injured in the least! Bullet went right past Nathan's face—just missed blowing his jaw away by an inch, we guessed, we who were standing close enough to see what happened. Even that didn't stop Nathan! Bravest fellow I ever did see, and him unarmed! Some of the other men and me grabbed the gun from the coward and let Nathan finish speaking his mind. He told the mob he'd hold Leviticus till all the facts were known. He begged the men not to shed innocent blood, like the Bible warns against. Gives me goosebumps to think about that night!"

"Then what happened, Mr. Bally?" Stephen asked.

"Well, true to his word, Nathan brought Leviticus home and waited all night while his father, Cyrus, talked to his lawyer. The law was considering putting Tye behind bars in the next county just to keep him safe from the mob, but in the end it wasn't necessary at all." Bo pushed away from his plate and lit up a Tampa Star. "The next morning at Polk's office, his staff opened the safe first thing, like they always do, and they found a suicide note in Polk's own handwriting explaining that he planned to take his own life because he'd been embezzling county funds and was soon to be found out!"

"Gosh," said Jessy, still wide-eyed. "So Nathan saved an innocent man's life." As the conversation continued, everyone talking and laughing now, Jessy became lost in her thoughts about Nathan Fisher, a man who would risk his life for the truth.

🍂 🍂 🍂

Conversations continued in the parlor where Bea and Betty began playing the piano. Bo strummed a few merry tunes on his banjo before letting his sons have a try. Stephen and Taddy tried playing the banjo too, delighting in its sound. Martha sat at the piano with Bea and Betty, picking out tunes from memory. Soon the group was singing one tune after another, with various accompaniments, Adam singing the lead with his rich bass voice.

Suzanna, Jessy, and Emma volunteered to do dishes, but found the job lighter than expected with the help of Jerome and Roberto, the two menservants. While they all worked putting the kitchen aright, Jessy heard a feeble scratching at the back door. She found a raccoon there, up on its hind legs begging. "Well, what did you do, follow us down here from

Lumpy Land?" Laughing she called out, "Emma, come see our old friend Mr. Racker-Squwacker!"

"No, Miss Jessy, that no mister, she be the Mama Tropic Queen!" said Roberto. He put a goodly mound of table scraps outside for the small ringtail.

Emma stood there, dish towel in hand, ooing and aahhing. "How cute!"

"She got babies—two. See?" Jerome indicated where two smaller raccoons were climbing headfirst down a big tree in the backyard.

"We feed them year-round. They come every night. If they hear us work inside, the Queen she bang on door! She smartest animal I ever saw. Fussy too! She got a sweet tooth that for sure!" He grinned about his wild pet. "We no let the chilrun play with them, they be wild, but they sure be sweet."

Emma watched the bright-eyed babes eat heartily with their mother. Jessy too enjoyed the sight. Quietly she asked, "Did you rest today, Emma? Are you feeling better?"

"A little. Look." Emma handed Jessy a telegram from her pocket. "Orders. From Mum."

"Do you want to go to Palm Beach?" Jessy asked.

"Not especially. I'd rather stay here with you and the Ballys, but I suppose I'd better do what Mum says. Her friends are sending a car around for me Wednesday. They phoned while you were on the beach this afternoon."

"How long will you be gone?" Jessy wondered.

"I don't know. I don't want them to know I'm pregnant but they probably can guess why I'm down here. I talked with Mrs. Bally before you came back this afternoon. She's just as nice as can be! She said I could stay here as long as I wanted."

Together Jessy and Emma went out into the rapidly cooling night, to the dense trees in the courtyard. The raccoons, having finished their meal, were scampering away. A delicate sea breeze drifted up from the beach. "I suppose we should join the others," Jessy said at last.

In the parlor, during a pause in the singing, Beatrice said to her guests, "We'll be going to church tomorrow. Now y'all are certainly welcome to join us, but if you'd rather sleep in, why—"

Suzanna said, "We'd love to worship with you!"

Adam nodded, saying, "We want to praise God for good friends and a safe trip. What time is the service?"

"Eleven," said Bo. "We can walk, the church is so close. And after lunch, we usually spend Sunday at the beach, but we can do whatever you like. It's your vacation, after all!"

"And then the children will have school on Monday. It seems a shame they can't stay home and enjoy playing with their new cousins!" said Bea, smiling at the six children gathered around her.

"The Flints have schoolwork too!" said Suzanna amid a chorus of whines.

"Emma, what would you like to do tomorrow?" asked Jessy in a whisper.

"I'd like to go with you. I've never been to church."

"Never?"

"Never. What do I do?"

Jessy hugged her friend. Before she realized she was crying, the whole party broke into song again, a rousing version of *Crown Him with Many Crowns*.

❧ ❧ ❧

Early the next morning, Jessy dared putting on her new bathing suit. Covered from neck to toe in it, she tiptoed down the stairs from the room she shared with Emma and Martha, still sleeping, and then out the back door. Expecting to have the swimming pool to herself at such an early hour, she was surprised to see Adam swimming strongly and well.

"Well, look at you!" he called out, laughing.

Jessy clutched herself, feeling ridiculous.

"Come on in! The water's wonderful!"

Slowly Jessy waded into the shallow end. Adam kept encouraging her deeper but watched to make sure she would be all right. With difficulty, Jessy paddled to the deep end with her head out of the water. Her swimming skills were limited, gained only from girlhood trips to the shore and wading in Bethel's creeks, but she managed a fair sidestroke.

Adam's powerful arms stroked cleanly and well through the water. His breathing came in great relaxed puffs. Jessy was so intent on imitating his good strokes she stopped feeling self-conscious. The cool morning air felt grand, and the sight over their heads was glorious: the warm morning sun breaking over Florida in January. "Did we take the train to heaven?" he asked Jessy. Soon the children joined them, one by one, splashing and screaming with abandon.

When Adam and Jessy got out of the pool and sat on the patio beside it, drying off with towels, she asked him, "Feeling better?"

"Absolutely! I'm gettin' more use of my bad leg. Look." He flexed it easily. "Bo keeps sayin' the springs down here can do wonders. People come from all over the country to get the benefit of 'em."

"Let's try them," said Jessy. Having wrapped a big towel around herself, she asked, "You don't think I look too silly in this suit, now do you?"

"Nah. You look fine!" He called to his children. "Stay at the shallow end! Later today I'll give you a swimmin' lesson!"

"Adam?" Jessy said in a hush, "You know, yesterday I didn't just go for a walk and befriend a pelican."

"Uh-oh," Adam said good-naturedly. "What've you been up to?"

"Promise you won't tell a soul? Especially not Emma?" Jessy confided. Sure her secret would be safe with her brother, she said, "I met a man who has so many of the traits I would want in a husband."

"Nathan Fisher?"

"Yes," she said timidly. "But I have no hopes about Nathan. A man of his stature wouldn't be interested in someone like me. We come from two different worlds. I've been trying not to think about him, but I can't get him out of my mind. I've never felt this way before about anyone."

"Not even Leo?" Adam asked in a gentle undertone.

As they watched the children splashing about in the pool, Jessy said, "I love Leo, but he's not like Nathan. Dr. Fisher is a widower, so he knows what it is to suffer. Leo can be so brash! Nathan believes in God, but I wonder sometimes what Leo believes. And he won't tell his parents about the ring. Is he unsure of our future? Or ashamed of me? It's things like that I wonder about." Jessy shivered in her wet clothing. "I feel so confused! Please promise you won't say a word to anyone!"

"I promise," Adam said. He gave her a most reassuring look before calling to his children. "Time to go inside and get ready for church!" As he stood and helped his sister up, he said, "This is somethin' we should pray about."

Jessy nodded. "Oh, yes, of course!" Gratefully she took the hand her brother offered, feeling better for having shared her secret with her best friend.

At church Jessy spotted the Fishers. She did her best not to stare at Isaac Nathan Fisher, knowing nothing could come of her attraction to him. She was, after all, practically engaged to Leo Kimball.

CHAPTER 18

❧

On Monday morning at poolside, after the Bally children had left for school, Adam and Suzanna planned their stay, deciding their children should study each weekday after breakfast or before dinner. Repeatedly, Adam and Suzanna reminded the Ballys they didn't wish to interrupt the normal routine of the household. It was agreed the two families would spend time together and time apart, giving everyone breathing space.

Stephen and Taddy couldn't wait to learn how to cycle on the flat, straight Florida roads all around Garden Springs. Bo offered to lend the family's bicycles, but Adam preferred to rent them from a nearby shop rather than inconvenience anyone.

The Flints discussed what they could do that day—visit therapeutic springs or citrus groves, or golf. Sand racing on the beach was another possibility; Bo owned a sort of sailboat on wheels that flew across the windy shore at speeds upward of forty miles an hour. There was also a Seminole Indian festival, musical entertainment, and inland fishing. Suzanna was slowly warming to the idea of a river cruise.

In the midst of these discussions, the group was interrupted by a knock at the front door. Dr. Cyrus Fisher, in the neighborhood making house calls, had come to see his patient, Mrs. Bally.

Although she was smiling, still Beatrice wore black, a reminder of the loss of her unborn child. "I'm fine, but since you're here, would you talk with our guest?" Bea led the doctor to Emma's bedside and held the girl's hand to reassure her.

"I've had other patients in your condition, Miss Kimball," the doctor told Emma. "You may experience considerable difficulty due to a buildup of scar tissue that formed after your abortion. While I'm not suggesting an extended hospital stay, would you consider a hostel for your confinement?" Seeing the perplexity in the girl's face, he explained: "There's an

179

excellent convent hospital nearby. The nuns sometimes have a waiting list; young women like you come to stay with them from all over the country. Patients receive excellent prenatal and postnatal care, and the sisters work hard to place the newborns in good homes. If you encounter medical problems, you couldn't be in better hands. What do you think, Miss Kimball?"

Emma looked to Bea before saying, "Ever since I got here, I've been worrying about what to do when the baby comes. I can't bring it home with me and I can't leave it in a basket on a doorstep someplace, I know that for sure!" Emma clutched her abdomen. "But, doctor, I'm not a Catholic. I'm not a Protestant, either. I'm not anything! Those nuns wouldn't take me in."

"Being a church member isn't a requirement, but St. Catherine's does have house rules which patients are expected to follow. The fee is based on what each patient can afford to pay."

"My family gave me some money, but I'd want to see St. Catherine's before I decided."

"Of course you should. I could arrange a visit for you, say tomorrow morning? Would that be convenient?"

"All right, but—" Biting her lower lip, Emma asked, "Could my friend Jessy come with me?"

"If you like. I'll make the arrangements. In the meantime, I want you to rest. No strenuous activities, no excitement."

"But I'm supposed to go to Palm Beach later this week. My mother wants me to see some of her friends there."

"As long as you avoid strenuous activity, you should be all right." The doctor began writing. "Here are the names of some specialists in Palm Beach, and my own telephone number." Before the doctor left, he called St. Catherine's to schedule a visit the next morning at ten.

Jessy was concerned for her friend. Until now she hadn't considered the possibility of complications. *Life is fraught with peril at every turn*, she thought, resolving to pray for Emma and her unborn child. Was Acacia justified urging her daughter to have an abortion instead of giving birth? Jessy couldn't agree, but she did pray for Acacia, Emma, and the unborn child.

❧ ❧ ❧

All the Flints spent that Monday at the therapeutic waters of Garden Springs, enjoying the warm bubbling waters and rich scenic splendor of the place—lush greenery and deep waters so clear that their thirty-foot depth seemed only inches from their fingers. Already Adam was looking stronger than he had in all the months following his accident. How happy he looked with his wife and children splashing and wading with him. Their laughter rocked the grotto. Jessy, too, delighted in their day at the springs but thought it a pity the springs could do nothing for Emma.

Now, Tuesday morning, Jessy and Emma waited for Dr. Fisher to arrive. He came at nine with his son Nathan in a vivid green convertible. Nathan was dressed casually but well in a worn, pale linen suit with lots of pockets and a shapeless loose brimmed cotton hat that gave him the look of a savvy traveler. After Jessy introduced him to her family, the foursome left for St. Catherine's. Emma was so caught up in her own predicament and so interested in the countryside surrounding Garden Springs, she failed to notice the great attraction Jessy felt for Nathan. Jessy did her best to hide her feelings.

The ride was splendid. Cyrus and Nathan provided the two young women seated behind them with a running commentary about their surroundings: the quaint town with its public square beneath magnificent palms; the main street no bigger than Bethel's, but with broader, breezier streets; pretty country roads dotted with hazy blue lakes and vast orange groves; all under a brilliant hot sun. "Is it January?" Jessy and Emma wondered together.

At the convent, the foursome went to the gate where Cyrus Fisher rang the bell. While they waited, they admired the clean white stucco complex, colorful plants, and clock tower. It was almost ten. A fragile breeze met them, perfumed with flowers. A nun, shrouded in white from head to ankles, came to open the gate. A long string of rosary beads dangled from the woman's waist, the heavy crucifix at the end of it banging against her calf with every step.

Emma, never having seen a nun before, clutched Jessy's hand. Jessy wrapped her arm around Emma's waist and whispered, "Everything's all right, Emma, really."

Jessy hadn't seen a nun since her childhood in New England. *How fortunate, how blessed!* Jessy thought, in awe of such women who devoted their lives so totally to God, giving up all—freedom, relatives, marriage, motherhood, friends, fashion—and yet, how much they must gain! It was on the tip of Jessy's tongue to ask how she might join them.

"This way," said Dr. Cyrus Fisher to Emma.

"Dad, Miss Flint and I will wait for you here, if that's all right," Nathan said, indicating a bench in the courtyard.

The elder doctor nodded to his son. Once Cyrus and Emma went inside, Jessy turned to Nathan saying, "It's lovely here! How kind of your father to suggest this! If Emma chooses to stay, I know she'll be in good hands; I've been praying for her ever since she told me about—" Jessy paused, blushing. How could she discuss such an intimate subject with a man she hardly knew? Still Nathan looked at her with such an open, thoughtful expression in his gray eyes, she knew she could tell him anything. She continued, "Emma prides herself in being modern. She thinks I'm terribly old-fashioned—and I am. She laughed at me when I told her I've never even been kissed by a man." Jessy, embarrassed by what she'd just said, covered her mouth with one gloved hand.

Just then the clock towering over their heads sounded ten times. Looking around her, Jessy said thoughtfully, "I've never told anyone, but for some time now I've been wrestling with the question of how I should serve God. A few months ago, I had the most vivid dream of Christ! The Lord called me to follow Him, but a sound wakened me before I could see what happened next. Perhaps this is the best way of serving Him, here without distractions, in a convent apart from the world, praying and working among like-thinking women."

Nathan breathed deeply before answering, "No question about it, the Good Sisters do excellent work, and so do monks in monasteries, but there's a crying need for dedicated, devout Christian men and women outside cloistered walls as well as inside them." His luminous gray eyes moved from her own eyes down to her lips—delicate rosebuds untouched by man.

"I suppose you're right." Jessy's lips widened into a glorious smile. "God leads us to where He needs us, yes?"

"Yes!"

Together they smiled and admired the fragrant herb garden. For a few moments they took in the beauty of the place so carefully tended, the flowering vines and shrubs, and, beyond them, several heavy wooden doors barring they knew not what. No one was moving about in the sun but one chapel door was ajar.

Nathan asked, "Would you like to see the chapel?" He offered his arm.

As Jessy reached out, she hoped she'd stop feeling such a powerful attraction to Nathan, but once she put her hand on his arm, she felt it belonged there. "Thank you," she murmured. He reinforced his hold as if bracing to protect her from all harm.

Jessy was unprepared for what happened in the overwhelming beauty of that tiny chapel with its blue cloudlike dome, the life-size wooden crucifix at the altar portraying the dying Christ in all His agony, brass kneeling rails, marble basins filled with holy water, countless burning candles lit by the faithful, and everywhere, images of saints triumphing over the world, the flesh, and the devil. Alone in an alcove above them, a woman blessed with a glorious voice sang a hymn of praise. Overcome with emotions too deep, too exalted for words, Jessy walked forward to the rail and kneeled. She covered her face to weep and pray.

It was a long while before she was aware of Nathan kneeling beside her. As she wiped tears from her face she whispered, "The Lord has done so much for us! We owe Him our all!" Again she began to cry. "I'm so concerned for Emma! I don't know her very well. We've only been friends a few months. She has such a hard road ahead of her and no faith to carry her through!"

"How dearly we pay for the wrong choices we make in life," he said quietly. "Would you like to light a candle?"

Jessy nodded, too overcome to speak. Together they lit white candles that glowed within rich red glass cups. Afterward they dropped their offering into the metal box beneath the candle tray.

They left the cool, dark interior so deeply imbued with meaning, and returned to the brilliant sunny morning out of doors filled with singing birds. The whole world was His, they knew, inside and out. Together they delighted in watching big bees bumbling from one flower to the next, rolling in yellow, dusty pollen.

"Wouldn't the fellow marry Emma?" Nathan asked at last. When Jessy shook her head, he said, "The cad! Men should honor women and not disgrace them, or themselves. They should always strive to do right. There was a time when a fellow would be horsewhipped for seducing a girl and then abandoning her in that condition!"

"Emma belongs to a prominent family in our community, but she's had so little guidance!" Without mentioning Emma's involvement with a married man, Jessy added, "If husbands honored their wives and wives their husbands, and both honored the Lord, so much pain could be avoided!" Sniffling, Jessy took a hanky from her bag. "Oh, but I'm not married. Certainly I'm no expert!"

"It isn't every couple who understands that marriage is a three-way arrangement. The best marriages entwine a husband, a wife, and God in all their decisions, in all the thousand deeds of love and kindness." In the peaceful beauty of that cloister, Nathan said, "The other day you told me that you and your family live on a farm."

"Yes." Jessy smiled, remembering the snowy farm that now seemed so remote, a mere figment of her imagination as she basked in the warm Florida sun. "This is the first time we've been away."

"Do you like farming? You were concerned about serving God."

"Oh, yes, I think of God all the time, no matter what I'm doing. Some people might think I'm a religious fanatic!" Jessy made Nathan laugh. Referring to the life she shared with Adam, she said, "I know that despite all sorts of obstacles, the Lord drew me close to Himself and to my brother. God gave me faith for that mission."

She remembered all that had happened when she stepped out in faith, to follow God and love her brother, who had been, for so long, so very hard to love. Jessy's faith had confronted the full force of Adam's unbelieving fury. The price of love! The tremendous struggle they had endured—the whirlwind of heathen rage and then childlike, humble trust—led, in time, through that narrow gate Jesus described, and into the great, green pastureland of God's promise.

"I have no regrets, for I am convinced no price is too great to pay for the Lord," Jessy affirmed. "When we allow ourselves to be filled and used by God, that's when we are most truly alive."

"That's the irony of the Christian life—when we submit our free will to God's, then we are truly free. Ah, Jessy," Nathan said softly so only she could hear, "do you know that you are absolutely glowing?"

Jessy's eyes widened at this. She shook her head. "No."

"Well, you are." Nathan looked at her face, sheathed as she was in delicate blue from head to foot with the glowing light shimmering around her. "A most extraordinary effect!"

"You're joking!"

"No, I'm not. Quite extraordinary! There are so many things in this world we can't explain. We can merely believe and marvel and give thanks."

Glancing down at her gloved hands, Jessy said modestly, "If it's light you see in me, it isn't mine—it's His. He uses me when it pleases Him."

"You don't mind the Lord's intrusion into your life? A good many people your age would resent it."

"Not at all! Why, I'd be hopeless and helpless without Him!"

"So would we all," Nathan said with assurance.

Looking up into Nathan's loving face, Jessy said with more than a hint of innocent daring in her tender brown eyes, "I like to think of my life as a thrilling *adventure* with God."

Before they could say more, Nathan's father appeared with Emma. A pair of nuns led them to the gate. Nathan and Jessy rose to join them but, together, they turned just for a moment to admire once again the lovely grounds.

Emma looked calm now, reassured and comforted. "Oh, Jessy, this place is right for me, I just know it! A girl staying here told me everyone had helped her in so many ways. I would like to stay when they have a place for me."

Dr. Cyrus Fisher nodded to her. "Since you're sure you want to stay here, I'll talk with Sister Elizabeth on your behalf."

"Oh, yes, I want to as soon as I get back from Palm Beach."

As they drove to the Bally home, Emma confided to Jessy, "I feel so much better now than before. Everything's going to be all right, I just know it."

Jessy's smile was radiant now. "Yes, Emma, I believe you're right."

For now, everything was right with the world. For now.

CHAPTER 19

❦

After Emma left for Palm Beach in what everyone thought must have been the most elegant touring car in Florida, the days moved languidly along at the Bally household and took on a loose pattern of sorts. After everyone breakfasted together, the Bally children left for school and the Flint children spent the morning studying, then went swimming or biking until lunch. While his children studied, Adam spent mornings with Bo swimming, fishing, or golfing. Suzanna and Beatrice grew close, spending a great deal of their time with the children or in the kitchen, sharing recipes and talking about everything imaginable. Sometimes the two couples went off in the Bally car, exploring and shopping for treasures.

The Flints took side trips to citrus groves. They picked oranges and grapefruit to ship home to friends and neighbors in Bethel. Adam went to the springs twice each week, benefitting from the fresh churning waters.

Afternoons, when the Bally children came home from school, the Flint children joined them in the tree house, on the beach, in the pool, or up in the attic to hunt through trunks for treasures. While the girls donned ladies' dresses and clopped about in grown-up shoes, the boys played soldier with helmets, canteens, swords, gunpowder flasks, and a stack of Confederate paper money. No matter how the day had been spent, evenings drew to a pleasant close around the dinner table and then in the parlor for music and singing.

Jessy believed she was having the best vacation of all. Sometimes she joined the ladies in the kitchen or on excursions, or the men when they went fishing or golfing. Adam, a born athlete, excelled at golf. Still walking with the aid of a cane, he competed keenly with Bo game after game on the course near the Bally home, usually shooting near par, and growing stronger with each passing day. Then came the day on the dirt road in front of the house, with all manner of instructions being shouted

186

at her by the Bally children and even her own niece and nephews, that Jessy learned, after a few mishaps, how to ride a bicycle.

During all the hours Jessy spent with Adam in the water at the pool, the beach, and the springs, she was becoming a fair swimmer. When no one was about, Jessy sat on the Ballys' shady veranda, reading to her heart's content.

Emma telephoned from Palm Beach once or twice. Jessy didn't tell her about the lovely afternoon she had dared to fill her pockets with peanuts and walk up the beach alone to the Fisher home. Although his parents were in and most cordial, Nathan was working at Hope's house, preparing for its sale. He had a great deal to do before returning to his college teaching and administrative duties. "But he left this for you," the Fishers had said, handing Jessy a brochure about the riverboat cruise. "Nathan hopes you and your family will go. So do we!"

Jessy studied the illustrated brochure of the *True Heart*, a three-decker, side-wheel riverboat with an American flag flying, smokestacks streaming, and people waving. Nathan had circled a certain cruise date and train schedule.

"We're hoping to go, if my doctor approves," said Mrs. Fisher, looking to her husband, Cyrus. "I've been trying to learn how to walk with crutches," she said with a groan, still confined to her wheelchair.

When Jessy stood to leave, Cyrus confided, "Emma's stay at St. Catherine's is arranged. I'm sure she'll receive excellent care."

"I know she will. Thank you very much, Doctor." Before she left, Jessy emptied her pockets of peanuts for Nathan's parrot, and, in their place, she put the cruise brochure.

❦ ❦ ❦

January was fast fading. Emma would soon return to Garden Springs, relieved to know she would have a safe haven, good medical care, and adoption services. With reluctance, Jessy told her that the adorable raccoon mother continued making her nightly visits, but with only one baby.

"A baby died?" Emma asked. "Oh, no!"

"Yes, I'm afraid so. There's just one baby now." Both girls were silent as the thought overtook them: the loss of one baby *did* make a difference.

❦ ❦ ❦

Between Adam's gentle cajoling, Bea's and Bo's pleasant travel anecdotes, and the enticing brochure from Nathan, Suzanna finally succumbed to the romantic lure of a riverboat cruise.

It was still dark when the Ballys took the Flints to meet their train bound for Vitrina. The Ballys promised to meet them upon their return in two days. "We know you'll just adore it!" said Beatrice, smiling and waving good-bye. With a wink to the Flint children she added, "Especially those alligators!"

When Jessy didn't see the Fishers on the train, she kept her disappointment to herself. A mist had settled over the land. In the dim light, after their train ride in the early morning fog, the Flints, each carrying a small overnight bag, crossed the street from Vitrina Station to the wharf in search of their riverboat, the *True Heart*. Jessy was too sleepy to feel the excitement of this new day.

A porter in a black cap with a red band bearing the name *True Heart* asked, "Check your bag, ma'am?"

Jessy, surprised to be called a *ma'am*, smiled politely but sleepily and gave the man her carrying case.

As the porter tied a tag on the handle he promised, "Your bag will be in your room when you get to your hotel tonight upriver."

"Yes, sir," she said, "Thank you."

The morning was cool enough for Jessy to wrap herself in the shawl Emma had given her for Christmas. She knew Emma was settling in well with the Good Sisters. Jessy, with Suzanna and Mrs. Bally, had visited Emma the day before the cruise. Emma would have eleven other girls, all in similar straits as she, for company.

Missing Emma, but assured that her friend was in God's loving hands, Jessy stood with her family in the shrouded mists. Porters continued tagging bags belonging to other passengers gathering at the wharf. The fog was so heavy they could hardly see the river, much less their riverboat.

The contented quacking of ducks offered reassurance that the water was close and calm. However, there was another bird about, a raucous one.

"Walk the plaaank!" a familiar voice squawked.

Jessy finally woke up. She knew that squawk! "Mr. Snaggletooth!"

"Ka-baaaam!" came the parrot's energetic reply. Tourists looked alarmed. Were they being bombed? "Blam-blam-blam!"

"Oh, now you behave, Plato Q, or we'll leave you here at the dock!"

"Nathan!" shouted Jessy, in tones hardly suited to a *ma'am*.

"Jessy?" Nathan's distinguished voice cut through the fog.

"We're over here!" she shouted happily, feeling joyously awake.

Nathan made his way to her side. "How delightful! So glad you and your family could make the trip!"

"You'll enjoy this, I promise," said Mrs. Fisher, just visible in the fog, leaning on crutches with Cyrus standing beside her. "We came up yesterday to do some visiting."

"Shame about the fog," said Nathan. "This is the prettiest part of the river, where it's narrow and twisting. It widens further along into a lake."

A foghorn blasted through the mist. Soon the damp air cleared enough to see the *True Heart*. Sailors eased a sturdy gangway from the ship to the wharf. In a few minutes, passengers began boarding.

"Where are the alligators?" Stephen wanted to know.

"Hiding in the mud," said Nathan. "If the sun warms them up you'll see them today, but you'll have to keep a sharp lookout!"

Stephen had spent a restless night in anticipation of spotting such primitive creatures. "I can't wait!"

"Are you ready to walk the plank?" Jessy asked her nephew. When he nodded vigorously, she took his hand and together they joined the long line of passengers moving slowly up the gangway.

Once on board, the beauty and spaciousness of the ship surprised Jessy. A broad interior salon furnished with dining tables was set for breakfast. The sweet aroma of hot baking bread filled the air. The interior was lit by delicate crystal chandeliers. Porters explained that, for the entire cruise, all passengers were assigned seating at indoor tables where they could leave their personal belongings. Meals and snacks would be served inside during the day, but everyone on board would be free to wander the entire riverboat throughout the cruise, moving inside or outside through the glass-paneled doors as they desired. Soon the *True Heart*, with foghorn blasting, pulled away from the dock and chugged gently and slowly upriver.

Jessy went out to the forward deck where she beheld the spectacle unfolding before her: the ancient river, gray and misty, swirling as the *True Heart* cut through water and fog. The fog played tricks—one moment Jessy would think she had spotted a wading bird, but then if she blinked, it was gone and in its place she would see a buoy. In the cool mist, porters served passengers hot beverages—broths, coffee, and steaming tea. In time the sun emerged through the low-hanging mists. Birds of all sorts were visible on either bank. The river was narrow here and winding, as Nathan had said.

A wise old passenger in pink flannel trousers and an outrageous top hat entertained all the children with stories of fifteen-foot-long alligators, the denizens of Florida's lakes and rivers, and alligator mothers who carried babies in their mouths and who were sometimes careless enough to eat one.

When an osprey perched on a roost above the highest deck near the pilot's cabin, a crewman said, "That bird's an old friend who follows this ship at the start of every trip. He'll fly back to the wharf after a few hours. Watch!"

In one swift flash the hawklike bird swooped down to the water to nab a fish in his big claws. The masterful white-breasted hunting bird soon returned to his high perch, but not before showing off the fish he had caught in a blinding second—no simple matter in the fog. Around and around the deck he flew, showing off his catch to the passengers. Eventually he perched on the *True Heart* mast to eat his fish.

"Now, why can't you catch your dinner?" Nathan asked Plato Q.

"Where's my peanuts?" the parrot asked. He danced roundabout Nathan's broad shoulders and gave Jessy a wolf whistle. "Hey, baby!"

"Rude bird, isn't he?" With one eyebrow raised and in his smoothest seminar voice, Nathan said to Jessy, "I didn't teach him that, I assure you!" Still, Nathan's mischievous smile made Jessy wonder.

Plato Q kept up his volley of wolf whistles, imitation bomb blasts, and general nonsense. The passengers nearby made sure Plato Q had an attentive audience. "Pea-nnnnnuts! Roast pea-nuuuuts!"

Laughing, Jessy fumbled through her bag. "Here you are!"

After the birds ate, both domesticated and wild, and once breakfast had been served to the humans, some passengers stayed inside to enjoy live music: banjo, piano, harmonica, and guitars. The children just had to go in and listen, but not before extracting promises from their parents, Aunt Jessy, and Dr. Nathan Fisher to call them immediately if alligators were sighted.

Out on deck, Jessy and Nathan enjoyed the slowly clearing view as the ship moved forward, gently plying upriver. Cyrus read to Mrs. Fisher from a guidebook about the sights they were soon to see.

Suzanna and Adam sat together on the forward deck, holding hands like newlyweds, enjoying the relaxing cruise. Jessy was content to sit in her deck chair between Nathan's and Adam's, looking at the river and listening to conversations on all sides. Suzanna murmured happily to her husband. Jessy could hardly remember a time when she felt so at peace, there among loved ones and friends, in the midst of God's creation.

If the world is a stage, now the curtain went up. The sun grew hot enough to evaporate the fog, revealing all at once a lodge, a hall, a bridge, a cabin. In a canoe an Indian woman wearing a brilliantly colored frock was fishing—a small, dark, pretty woman with a weathered but serene face. Palm trees grew in thickets along the low banks. Everywhere anhingas dried themselves, a most common sight that day on both sides of the river: big blackish birds with long snake-like necks, their wings spread open like fans. Cypress trees rich with tannin had turned the river water as brown as strong-brewed tea.

The passengers on deck thrilled to come upon a channel filled with little fishing craft and dozens of other boats big enough to hold only two or three people. Adam called out, "Any luck?"

All the fishermen shook their heads glumly.

Nathan said quietly to Adam, "If the fish *were* biting, they'd be sure not to tell us!"

Adam nodded and roared with laughter.

The side-wheeler they were on must have made quite a picture because those in smaller boats waved to the *True Heart* passengers as they glided along at a gentle twenty miles an hour, never disrupting the wildlife. A few eagles appeared, with their unmistakable white heads and dark brown bodies. Their nests sat high on treetops like tubs or vats. Pileated wood-peckers beat sharp rat-tat-tats against tree trunks and punctuated the stillness with their maniacal laughter. High in the trees grew balls of bright green mistletoe. In one place the faithful had planted a big cross at the river's edge. Just beyond it, on a green lawn, stood a simple white church basking in the morning sun.

"Oh, darling, to think I didn't want to leave home!" murmured Suzanna, renewing her grip on Adam's hand. "Thank you, love!" Even-tually the pair rose from their chairs, and, with their children, toured the *True Heart* up and down.

Once they were gone, Nathan asked Jessy, "Is this your first cruise?"

"Yes, and it's splendid."

"Someday you must see the Greek Islands—magnificent!"

"You've traveled abroad?" asked Jessy.

"Oh, yes, some, during my studies. I spent a good deal of time in England, and was able to visit Europe. Some of my favorite destinations are Italy, Greece, and the Holy Land."

"I can hardly imagine such splendor!" she said, and she could not.

"Such sights are meant for those who appreciate beauty, history, and theology. You strike me as one who would be greatly enriched by travel."

"I know so little about the world. I didn't finish school."

"Would you like to, Jessy?"

"Yes. Very much." Jessy would have liked to reach for Nathan's hand, but she was too much a lady. She felt guilty remembering Leo and the ring he had given her, still hidden in the velvet box in a drawer back at home. Would she ever wear it? Quietly, as other passengers drifted away, Jessy told Nathan about Leo—that he was Emma's brother. Jessy expressed her concern as to her future with Leo.

Nathan's fair and noble face darkened as he listened to her. With a tension rare for Nathan, he asked, "Do you love him?" When she didn't answer at once, he pressed on, asking, "Could you vow before God and the world to love, honor, and obey Leo Kimball as long as you live?"

Jessy's face became a thoughtful question mark. "I'm not at all sure that Leo is the man God wants me to marry."

"When the right man comes along, you'll know."

"Yes. When I marry—and if—are matters I trust to God."

Light and warmth returned to Nathan's face. "Amen to that, Jessy."

Huge poinsettias brightened the banks, red, flaring, and tall as trees. Jessy borrowed Nathan's binoculars to view the distant shore. She laughed when she spotted a lady looking back at Jessy through binoculars of her own. They waved to each other. A pelican appeared, flying perpendicular to the *True Heart*'s course, gliding like an airship. Nathan and Jessy saw it at the same moment. Together they exclaimed, "I hope it's *our* pelican!" They laughed together, remembering the pelican they had rescued at Garden Springs.

The view changed and expanded. Mean shacks and grand estates dotted the banks, and the hulks of ruined ships poked out of the water. Plato Q, who all this time had been perched on the railback of an empty deck chair, had become so sleepy Nathan went off to tuck him in his carrying cage and put him in a safe corner to nap.

In Nathan's absence, Jessy looked for Suzanna. "Are you glad you came?"

"Oh, yes, Jessy. It's grand! Everyone should see the river!" Suzanna lowered her voice and added, "I've been talking with Mrs. Fisher. I told her you're the finest girl I know and good clear through. I told her how you saved my life and led me to Christ!"

"My goodness, you told her all that?"

"She was asking about you! She's a devout Christian, too, and is most impressed with you!" Suzanna smiled knowingly in Nathan's direction. "A mother knows! Trust me, Jessy."

Jessy's face flushed crimson. She whispered back, "Nathan wouldn't be interested in me."

"Adam and I want the best for you! And the Fishers want the best for their son!"

"Alligator starboard!" came the call.

Most of the passengers, including Jessy and all the children on board, raced to a side deck to see what appeared at first as a knotty, bumpy log of varying widths floating in the water close to shore. Amid the water lilies, the log studied the *True Heart* with two bulging eyes protruding just above the water. Stephen, Martha, and Taddy screamed their hellos to the creature that had eluded them so long. The huge brownish green reptile wriggled its mighty tail toward the muddy bank, the leathery beast's home sweet home, then yawned heartily, exposing ridged masses of teeth. One eye winked at the children.

"It's so big, Daddy!" Martha said. "Can we have it for a pet?"

Before Adam could answer, shots were fired. As Adam grabbed his children, Nathan reached for Jessy to protect her. "Get inside, Jessy, at once!"

"But you and the others—"

"Please go inside!" Against her protests, Nathan urged her inside while he remained out on deck. Jessy peeked out through the glass. Crewmen had come running from all directions to the source of the shooting. She heard her brother shouting: "Any more shots fired and you'll answer to me, Adam Flint!"

A ripple of excitement went through the crowd: *the* Adam Flint was on board, "Man of Iron" in person, the greatest professional strongman and wrestler of his day.

Once the gunman had been disarmed, the captain warned everyone that shooting at wildlife from riverboats, once a popular entertainment, was now against the law. Thankfully, no one had been injured, including the alligator. The crowd dispersed, but a knot of men stood around Adam Flint, excited to be in the presence of an athlete of his stature. Adam, with his children under his protective arms, spoke at length with his crowd of admirers.

❦ ❦ ❦

As the *True Heart* moved along, passengers shifted about, mixing and mingling with one another, reading or napping or enjoying the river views on all sides—starboard, port, fore, and aft.

By midday they entered a broad lake. Hundreds of gulls of all varieties followed the *True Heart*, looking for a snack of fresh fish in the riverboat's wake. While Adam and Suzanna were inside enjoying a songfest with the children and most of the other passengers, Jessy wandered to a railing on a rear deck where she could watch the gulls who were having no luck in catching a fish. She saw one lone eagle swoop down to the water and snatch up a fish in its claws. What a sight! But how surprised she was to see the more common birds chase him until he dropped his prey. Soon the mean gulls had picked the fish apart. The lone eagle flew off to a far bank, high to its nest—outnumbered, outwitted, and hungry. One day Jessy would have reason to remember this moment on the river, when the sharp-tongued gulls robbed an eagle of its prey.

Jessy looked around her, wondering if anyone else witnessed the eagle's plight. Wise, all-observant Nathan had seen. She studied his noble profile. His large gray eyes looked somber as he gazed out steadily at the lone eagle. The rest of the passengers had wandered away, finding other amusements, but Nathan and Jessy stood together, watching, remembering, lost in their private reverie. Would the eagle ever have his reward? Hoping he would, Jessy stood close to Nathan, as close as she dared, but said nothing.

❦ ❦ ❦

At twilight, once the *True Heart* docked for the night, the passengers disembarked and made their way up a torch-lit wooden walkway under waving palms to their hotel, the Grand Araby.

"Abracadabra! Aladdin must have been the architect, eh, Jessy?" teased Nathan.

"It's wonderful! Oh, for a magic carpet!" Jessy beheld the new hotel that had been purposely designed to look old, ancient, magical—a fantasy in stone and plaster castworks suited to tales of Scheherazade's thousand-and-one nights. In her room she found her luggage waiting for her, as promised at the start of the trip—and such an elegant room it was with marble vanities, Moorish tiles, and steaming bath waters.

Once she and the other passengers had time to relax and change clothes, they assembled for dinner, music, and dancing. Jessy had never seen her brother dance, but dance he did with his wife, and not awkwardly in the least. His limp had nearly disappeared. How handsome he looked, Jessy thought, in a pearl gray suit and black tie, tall and broad shouldered, his lovely Suzanna in his arms. She wore an opal gown of frosty delicate chiffon that reflected the blue of her eyes and sheen of her blonde upswept curls. The Flint children danced, too, like small curly haired elephants, with a herd of equally noisy children they had befriended on the *True Heart*.

For a while, Jessy sat alone, admiring the crowd of dancers dressed their best. Her delicate face, tinged with the faint natural rose of her cheeks and lips, was crowned with her wealth of auburn hair piled in a soft chignon graced with a few loose curls at her temples. To those who did not know Jessy Flint, her appearance, especially her wide and warm brown eyes, radiated fragility, yet there was nothing fragile about her physical and moral courage. Tonight, though, she felt vulnerable. Did her sapphire velvet dress look too home-sewn, too Northern, too heavy for this magical salon that recalled a luxuriant Persian miniature? She peeked at her shoes. The dark satin flowers on them were just visible at the edge of her hem.

"Would you do me the honor?" murmured a warm, thrilling voice very close to Jessy's ear.

Nathan's two hands braced the back of her chair. A warm glow rushed through her at the sight of him, looking impressive in his black tuxedo, white waistcoat, white tie, and white shirt. Nathan's clothes, ivory skin, and thick hair the color of spiced ginger gave him the look of a virtuoso, a young, golden conductor who might bring the world into harmony. As always, to Jessy's mind, his face, lit by those extraordinary gray eyes that radiated tenderness and wisdom, was the very face of love. She sat there speechless, too bashful to move.

His glowing smile warmed her so she forgot her shyness. With gentle authority he helped her to her feet. Even in her heeled satin pumps, she had to look up into his eyes, but not too far up, she decided—just exactly far up enough. Nathan was just the right height and width for Jessy, with protective arms that wrapped well around her waist without crushing her soft, billowing velvet sleeves. His hands and fingers, though longer and larger than hers, meshed perfectly with her own. With one fluid motion, Nathan led her to the dance floor.

In their dancing embrace, Nathan didn't merely hold Jessy's right hand in his left, but gently enfolded his hand over hers. His right hand braced the small of her back to guide her, not to intrude. Her left hand, close to his collar, accidentally brushed his thick shining hair. How wonderful it was, Jessy thought, to be enfolded by such a man, so good, so true, so courageous and bright. Too bashful to speak in such circumstances, she was thankful for the music, a lovely waltz. Then she remembered. "But

196

Nathan," she said, alarmed, "I've never danced. I don't know how to waltz!"

"My heavens, *everyone* knows how to waltz! It's as easy as breathing!"

And Jessy *was* waltzing, to her own amazement. "I can because you can!" she said to him over the music, laughing with a full heart.

"A time for everything under heaven, including a time to dance," he reminded her. Triumphant, Nathan held Jessy close and gently as a fragile bouquet, with care for the jewel she was—a lovely young woman, strong in her faith, but innocently unaware of her own manifold charms.

Once the waltz was over, a lively reel began. Following Nathan's lead, Jessy kept up, just barely, laughing and breathless when the music came to a sudden stop. She readily agreed to step outside on the balcony when Nathan suggested they do so. There the night air was wonderfully cool and breezy; the architecture, utterly fantastic, was framed by a colonnade of Moorish horseshoe arches that shielded walls and floors of brilliantly colored tiles.

"Oh, for a magic carpet!" Jessy cried as she regained her breath after dancing. "I wonder if this is how Cairo looks!"

"Mmm, not quite," said Nathan with an infectious grin. "Did you know you can see the *True Heart* from here? It's quite a sight." Steering Jessy away from the bright lights inside, Nathan brought her to a far curve of the balcony that overlooked the river. "Look there!"

Jessy peered into the midnight blue darkness where, beyond the waving palm trees, the *True Heart* waited for them until morning. Tiny lights outlined her broad low decks.

Turning from the twinkling ship to the vast twinkling night sky, Nathan threw his head back, saying, "Great night for star gazing! How many stars and constellations can you name?"

"None, I'm ashamed to say!" Looking in the same direction with him, Jessy thrilled to hear Nathan call out in his rich-timbred voice the names of his old friends.

With his arm pointing for her benefit, he said, "There are the twins: Castor and Pollux. Do you see Perseus and Pegasus? And near Perseus, there's Auriga the Charioteer with Capella glowing bright tonight!" His arm outlined an arc as he called out, "There's Orion, the Pleiades, and Cassiopeia! And our faithful Polaris! We'd be lost without Polaris."

"Can you name all the stars?" Jessy asked.

"My heavens, no!" he laughed, looking at her now with a captivating smile that quickened her pulse, "But I know the ones I rely on when I'm wandering on land and sea. I always take comfort in their steadying presence, especially old Polaris up there, showing me the way home. We're led home by the light."

"Yes, the light," Jessy said softly, thinking of Christ, the great light of the world. Slowly she asked Nathan, "Were you ever lost?"

"Oh, a few times." His lively eyes grew distant at the memory. "Before I became a Christian, I was lost. But I suspect you're asking about world travel. Once, up in Canada, a snowstorm obscured the stars for days. I was cold, hungry, and lost, but I wasn't alone.

"During a school vacation, my younger brothers and I decided to hunt for caribou, not that I wanted to shoot one, mind you. I went with my camera, not a gun. After hiking for days deep into the woods in twenty below zero temperatures, our guide twisted his ankle and couldn't walk a step! My brothers and I had to leave him where he was and go looking for help. We spent three days wandering through the wilderness, but eventually we got out all right—or nearly all right, thanks to the stars.

"I led my brothers out—both of them big bears of men now, but quite young then and scared. Mark and Freddie got a bit of frostbite in their fingers and toes. I left them at our base camp with my father who was busy with all sorts of medical emergencies and went back with two of my friends to bring out the guide. What a vacation!" When a stiff breeze blew up from the river, Nathan instinctively reached out to her to keep her warm. "Are you cold? Do you want to go inside again?"

Jessy shook her head, laughing, "How could I be cold in Florida? Back home it's probably ten below zero tonight!" She felt certain she couldn't be in better company. "So you saved your brothers' lives—Mark's and Freddie's. Did you find the guide?"

"Oh, yes, and he was all right, too, snug under a snow fall. Oddly enough, the snow kept the old codger from freezing to death. My friends and I dragged him back to the camp on a sled—a good thirty-mile hike!"

"It takes perseverance to survive, doesn't it?" Jessy asked.

"Perseverance, patience, knowledge, faith, and a good sense of humor! That old guide of ours sends me a Christmas gift every year like clockwork—this past year, a whole smoked salmon! He always asks why I haven't gone back after caribou! Mark and Freddie have. Perhaps someday I will, too. I never did take any pictures on that trip."

In the faint light, Jessy admired Nathan's profile. Thinking it would have been great fun to have grown up living near him, she asked, "How did you spend your childhood?"

From the cheer with which he answered, he loved her question. "Oh, when I wasn't reading and studying rocks and leaves and frogs and secret messages and maps and things, I would go off exploring, swimming, sledding, doctoring—"

"Doctoring? Whom did you doctor?"

"Dogs, mostly, and cats and hamsters and moles and shrews and snakes and a few wild birds who broke their wings and let me catch them. And how, may I ask, did you while away your youth?"

Jessy, holding onto the ornate railing with both hands, looked into the night and said, "Oh, somewhat like you, reading, thinking, sledding, hoping, wishing, praying—"

"What were you hoping, wishing, and praying for?"

Without answering directly, Jessy smiled a mysterious smile that warmed him despite the chill breeze that suddenly whipped up through the palms. "I played Ship!"

"How do you play Ship?"

"I thought everyone knew how! Funny, I hadn't thought about Ship in years, but this fantastic place reminds me of it." Jessy grasped the balcony and leaned back on her heels in the wind, remembering. "The game of Ship requires a balcony, the prettier the better—this would have been ideal for me and my playmates! Ours were plainer, but it doesn't matter, not to children. The balcony could be indoors or outdoors. A tenement can become, for you and your friends, your trusty crew, a ship where you battle pirates and sea monsters and evil princes to reach treasures and wonderful faraway places with unusual names." Jessy glowed with the thought of her childhood dreams.

Nathan grasped the balcony with her now, their hands gently brushing. Together, both of them looked toward the water. "And just which unusual places did you visit, Jessy?"

"Oh, every unusual place! A world full of places! Domed cities, secluded lagoons, golden deserts! Playing Ship, I went around the world and back again, and to other worlds too. The pirates never won. They never stopped me from fulfilling my destiny."

"Congratulations, Captain Flint!" Nathan, bowing graciously to her, turned from the railing to gaze at her. "I suppose I play a form of your game when I row hard and get tired. It helps to pretend I'm crossing vast oceans."

"You row?" asked Jessy.

As Nathan explained he was "a fair rower in college," his father came outside from the glittering ballroom. "My son's rowing skills earned him numerous awards, including more than one silver medal and the job of rowing coach at St. Azarias. And as for leadership, why," the silver-haired gentleman said proudly of his firstborn son, "I've always said you could drop Nathan from a balloon to just about anywhere on earth and he'd find his way home easy as one-two-three! It's a gift of his, one of many!"

When Cyrus Fisher strolled away on the balcony, Jessy said softly to Nathan, "So when you aren't teaching and winning medals, you're saving people lost in the woods and keeping lynch mobs from killing innocent people."

Without missing a beat, Nathan responded, "And you go around rescuing people from vicious storms and the evils of drink and then save their souls by leading them to Christ."

"People have been talking!" Jessy exclaimed.

Nathan stood very close and whispered, "I'm so glad you're here, Jessy. So glad you came." After a pause, he asked, "This Leo Kimball—will he cherish you and love you always, you and only you?"

Before she could answer, Cyrus Fisher returned. "If we want to see Laguna Springs, we'll have an early wake-up call tomorrow, son."

"So we have," Nathan said. He made a move toward the entryway into the ballroom with Jessy.

Wishing for more time with him, Jessy went inside without a word. In a few little days, Nathan would return to his teaching work in Enigma and she would be back in Bethel. She sensed even a thousand-and-one nights would not be enough in this, the closest she had come in her young life to Eden. Perhaps the closest she would come in this life.

CHAPTER 20

❦

The voice of the Lord is upon the waters, thought Jessy, remembering the Psalms as she thrilled to the view before her that glorious morning when the *True Heart* reached Laguna Springs. To the delight of the children, numerous alligators roamed the muddy far shores of the springs, barking and bellowing as passengers left the *True Heart* and boarded a dozen small glass-bottom boats. Jessy, with her family, could not believe their eyes as together they glided over clear spring waters that reflected the huge live oaks dripping with gray Spanish moss looming over their heads. Every day, a half-billion gallons of fresh water flowed up into Laguna Springs from deep within the earth, purified as it came surging to the surface through limestone caverns.

"The water is so clear here!" Jessy reached in to touch the water from her seat in the boat. She could see dozens of fish and turtles swimming beneath the glass at her feet. Long grasses swayed in watery blue lagoons, swirling like strands of green silk, but of fantastic lengths and in a state of absolute perfection. Craggy limestone formations underwater looked like craters of the moon—aquamarine, mysterious, pure. Pebbles shimmered like crystals.

"It's like an aquarium, but gigantic," said a passenger near Jessy.

"And better!" said another. "Sixty-five feet deep and perfect!"

"Look at the force of the water!" Adam noted with grudging admiration.

"The springs are so powerful here they can move a rock twenty-five feet as if it were nothing," their guide informed them.

Pointing beneath the glass, Stephen said, "Aunt Jessy, those snapping turtles are twice my size!" He and Taddy and Martha took bread from their guides and tossed it to the fish swimming in silver hordes, thousands moving and twisting as one, shimmering in the turquoise depths. In a twinkling they swooped up the food and disappeared from view.

More fish swam up together to the boats looking for a free meal: black fish and silver, blue fish and white, and turtles, hundreds of them, massive and ponderous in the clear surging waters.

Seeing Nathan's lordly face so full of love for creation, for God, Jessy said softly, "Thank you, Nathan, for suggesting this trip. I'll never forget. Never. We've loved every minute."

When their glass-bottomed boat reached shore, the passengers cried that the ride was over too soon. Many asked if they could have another turn on the water. Two hours were not enough. The schedule of the *True Heart* remained fixed, but there was time enough for passengers to tour the shore of Laguna Springs on foot. Oscar, the mighty sixteen-foot alligator, old and slow and lazy, lurked about, looking as if he had been roused from a nap.

"Can Uncle Bo wrestle him do you suppose?" Taddy asked his father.

Adam laughed. "Maybe so, but he's out of shape, I think, since he sold his share of Cowboy Joe's!"

The sluggish old reptile scrunched into the mud and refused to budge. Most of the ladies skirted the beast on their way to the souvenir shop. Suzanna and Jessy, remembering their friends back in Bethel, bought salt and pepper shakers in the shapes of oranges and flamingos, while the boys bought alligator teeth, small stuffed alligators, and snakeskins. Martha, groaning at the choices her brothers made, took more interest in the colorful Indian weavings and beadwork.

"For you, Jessy," said Nathan when she stepped outside the shop. He pressed a small package into her hands. "Wait until you get home to open it, when it's snowing and cold. Then remember this place. You'll be glad, I hope, to remember."

Jessy beamed at Nathan. "What is it? A tiny magic carpet?"

He laughed. "I wish it was."

A blast of the *True Heart*'s foghorn shook the earth: time to go. All too soon the *True Heart* had sailed down river and returned to Vitrina in the dark. The Flints and Fishers left the *True Heart* for the last time and boarded the train to Garden Springs.

"When do you leave Florida for home, Jessy?" Nathan asked.

"In three days." Three little days! "My brother's eager to get back to Bethel. He wants to leave for home on Saturday."

"I see. Can you, your family, and the Ballys come to Hope's house before you leave, on Friday afternoon, say, at four? Bo and Beatrice know the place well. My parents will be there too."

"Well, yes, I suppose, but why?" Jessy asked.

The glow of his smile was as warm as a kiss.

❦ ❦ ❦

Jessy could hardly contain her curiosity at Nathan's intriguing invitation for Friday afternoon at four. The Ballys and Flints, all looking their best—the men and boys in suits, the ladies and girls in ivory lace tea dresses—went to Hope's house, a spacious, breezy, inviting home by the sea, filled and surrounded by treasures. The garden, graced with dozens of thriving rose bushes, reminded Jessy of what Nathan had told her on their first meeting: his late wife loved flowers.

In the dining room with its tall windows overlooking the sea, the Fishers poured hot tea for the adults and lemonade for the children, and served all tiny heavily iced pink cakes. Afterward, Nathan led his guests to the living room. Over the mantle was a life-sized oil portrait, painted by a British master, of Hope Ellmont Fisher. Nathan's dear departed wife had been a delicate, dark-haired, dark-eyed beauty. She had posed in an elegant room with velvet drapes. Hope wore a soft white gown with a dramatic black-and-white striped vestlet and matching bustle. She clutched a loose bouquet of roses to her bosom. In the room where she stood were ornate rococo chairs, shelves loaded with books, oriental rugs, and painted images of tropical birds.

Nathan thanked his guests for coming and then said, "As you know, when Hope died, so did the Ellmont dynasty. While she lived, she continued her family's tradition of building up the community and establishing scholarship funds for worthy youngsters. Hope's parents built the first hospital and school in Garden Springs and the first library. Many have benefited from her family's largesse, but Hope also wanted to be remembered by visitors who loved Florida as much as she did, those who come from faraway to visit, rest, and reflect. I've invited each of you here this afternoon to select a gift that will remind you of Hope and the place she loved best, this last frontier of America—Florida—a place to rest and reflect on the glory of God's great creation, with its mysterious springs and wondrous birds and beasts, its glorious waters, blossoming flowers, and succulent fruits."

"Why, Nathan," Beatrice Bally said. "We couldn't. We shouldn't! Hope's things belong to you now, and someday might benefit a museum! I knew her well."

"I've either shipped or stored what she would have donated to museums," Nathan said. "Everything else in this house will be given away or sold. Hope valued your friendship, Beatrice, and I'm sure she would have wanted you to have a treasure to remember her by. If she hadn't died so suddenly, you know she herself would have given you what you desired. Please—" Nathan stretched out his arm to Beatrice and the other guests. "Please look and see what interests you most."

Slowly, bashfully, the guests wandered through Hope's house, admiring the books, the furnishings, the views through broad windows. The house was light and bright, with a profusion of cheerful pillows and chintz cushions. In the sunroom, the children searched through baskets full of shells of every size, shape, and color, from large conchs to tiny scallops. Adam was drawn to a set of tinted views of natural wonders of scenic Florida. Bo found a good book on Florida fishing habitats. Beatrice, with Nathan's encouragement, selected a pair of silver souvenir spoons. Suzanna chose a small candleholder.

Jessy, aware Nathan was following her at a discrete distance, turned to say: "You generous soul! What would you select?"

"Let me show you something." Nathan pulled a small but choice seascape framed in gold away from the wall to reveal a safe. With a few deft turns of the combination, he opened the lock. From inside he removed a bundle wrapped in dark velvet. "Look."

Jessy gasped at the sight of so much gold and so many emeralds wrought in the forms of rings, necklaces, bracelets, earrings, belts, and more. A horde of gold coins had been impressed with the cross of Christ. "Oh, Nathan!"

"In the seventeenth century, a Spanish ship sank not too far from here.

It went down in a hurricane with a king's ransom on board." Nathan held up a golden ring imbedded with three square emeralds.

"How magnificent!" Jessy took a close look at all the treasures.

"Hope's father acquired them. How she and he both liked acquiring things!" Nathan said softly, "When I met Hope she was a rich man's only child and I was an austere-living student bound for academia. I was happy to wander the world and to expand my mind, to sleep in one room with one trunk, one coat, one hat, one Bible. I was content with health and adventure, the stars over my head and the earth under my feet and the sea beckoning to me. But I fell in love with Hope and Hope loved things—jewels and gowns and thick pillows and art and crystal goblets and all the rest, as you see. It's taken a small fortune of Hope's own estate to guard her treasures and tend her gardens while I'm away teaching in Enigma." Nathan drew a massive golden rosary from the Spanish cache. "Would you like to have this?"

"Oh, I couldn't." Jessy gasped at the sight of such a splendid treasure which gleamed bright and rich as the sun. Flustered, she turned to admire Hope's dressing table covered in lace. It was strewn with shallow bowls of rose potpourri and crystal vials filled with shimmering perfume. At last Jessy made her selection: a richly scented paper bookmark embossed with images of roses. Closing her eyes, she put it close to her face. "Mmmmm. Smells divine. A rose is one of God's masterworks, don't you think?"

Nathan laughed at her modest choice. "Of course! But take something more, something of substantial value."

Now Jessy looked at this splendid man who epitomized the psalmist's declaration of all humanity: *a little lower than the angels.* "Hope had many treasures, but the greatest of all is—" She couldn't quite bring herself to say the word. "The greatest treasures on earth are not things but rather—" Still she couldn't say what was deepest in her heart. Her ivory face flushed soft as a rose. "I'm no flirt. I don't know how to flatter, but I do know what the real treasure is on this earth." Her gaze at him never wavered. A tender wordless undercurrent passed between them before he detected her meaning.

"What?" Incredulous, Nathan pointed to himself. "Do you mean me?" Still, his warm gray eyes lit with thanks for her heartfelt compliment. "Here." He started to put the heavy golden rosary into her hands.

205

"No! Nathan, it's far too much! This belongs in a museum for the world to admire." Quickly Jessy returned the rosary to the velvet cache and cast about for something more than a scented paper bookmark but less valuable than a Spanish chain of hollow golden beads the size of walnuts. *Caramba!*

In a hall she came to a kneeling rail before a stained-glass window depicting lavender wisteria against a shimmering blue sea. On a candle stand she saw a small piece of wood. Thinking it gnarled driftwood, she picked it up but to her surprise, realized it was a fragmentary relic, something a lonely Spanish sailor might have carved as he followed the stars to this New World three hundred years ago. All that was left of the sculpture was a head crowned in thorns and a torso twisting in pain against the fragments of a cross. The whole fit easily into Jessy's palm. She looked to Nathan, her warm brown eyes asking for permission.

He answered by closing his hands over hers so that her fingers enfolded the Christ. "This couldn't go to anyone more deserving. It came from that same shipwreck. Hope liked holding it. I imagine the sailor who went down in the hurricane did the same. Hope believed in God. I think she'd be glad to know you're taking care of her treasure. Oh, don't cry now. Hope's with Him, and we'll be with Him one day too. Who could ask for more?"

Jessy thanked him through her tears.

When the two returned to the living room, they saw Adam presenting Mrs. Fisher with the cane he no longer needed. Smiling graciously from her chair at the dining table, she kicked at her hated crutches. "Thank you, Mr. Flint! A cane will be much better than crutches!"

The setting sun shone through the greenery flanking the tall French windows in a way that signaled farewell. When appreciation had been expressed all around, the guests left for home.

Home! Jessy clutched Hope's relic as she nodded farewell to Nathan Fisher. This parting gave her the tiniest glimmer of the pain Adam and Eve must have felt to leave the first Garden.

CHAPTER 21

❦

The Midwest Express sped north into the increasing chill with the Flints on board, each lost in thought. Jessy sat with the children, her arms around their shoulders. She gazed out into the darkness, thinking of Nathan, wondering about Leo, and praying for Emma. The children were busy drawing alligators and palm trees from memory.

"Daddy, will we go back to Florida again?" Taddy asked softly.

Adam, with Suzanna napping against his shoulder, answered, "I don't know, son!" He grinned at his children. "Can't wait to shovel snow, can you, Stephen?"

"I'd rather swim and make sand castles."

"How about you, Martha, ready for your piano lessons?"

"No, Daddy. I'll miss Betty Bally. She's my best friend."

"Well, what about you, Taddy? Dyin' to go back to school?"

Taddy shook his head miserably. "I'll miss Bill and Bob and the tree house and the toys in their attic. See what they gave me?" He dangled a medal on a chain, a trinket from the Bally attic.

Adam sighed. How his family had fought to stay home, and how much harder they had fought to remain at Garden Springs! He'd miss Bo, his best friend—as good a friend as ever—perhaps better. Now their two families were close despite the distance that would separate them. Still, travel was costly and Adam had a farm to tend. He looked like he needed some cheering up.

"It's a miracle they let us check all our bags and bundles at the station without charging extra," Jessy told her brother with a smile. "It's a wonder the handles on our suitcases don't break with all the seashells and pebbles—Oh! And the beach mats and those wooden bowls painted like oranges are crammed inside too! I hope my glass ball filled with lagoon water and make-believe gold dust doesn't break! I packed it well."

"It was all so lovely, darling, so very lovely," murmured Suzanna, drowsing. She shifted against Adam's great warm body, snuggling into his jacket. "Thank you forever and ever."

Adam closed his eyes briefly and pressed his lips against her hair. Softly he told her, "You're sweeter than any mermaid I ever saw, 'know that?"

"But we didn't see any mermaids!" Suzanna grinned with eyes closed. "Can we sit close like this forever?"

Now the children cuddled next to Jessy as they nodded off. She watched Adam and Suzanna, seated across from her, so blissful, both sleeping now, their bodies gently rocking with the motion of the train. They made an adorable couple.

As for herself, Jessy was wide awake and wondering if she would ever sleep again. She stared through the glass windows, but the night was so black all she could see was her own reflection: her oval face, dark hair, and the mulberry wool suit she had worn at the start of the trip and had forgotten during warm happy days at the beach. Jessy had worn that suit when Leo visited her in November. She had written him several times from Florida—breezy little notes on pastel stationery the colors of seashells. At the end of her stay, two letters had arrived at Garden Springs from him about *el beisbol* and the unhurried life lived south of the border.

He mentioned the food—tender roast pork wrapped in flour tortillas spiced with cumin and hot chili peppers—the brilliantly colored flowers, and surprisingly good *beisbol* players with names like Brave Bull and Crazy Champion. Many of his team's opponents scattered throughout Mexico, Cuba, Puerto Rico, Nicaragua, and the Dominican Republic played as well or better than the Trans-Southern Rowdies. Leo thought his team might play ball in Hawaii and Japan. If he knew about Emma's condition, he never alluded to the fact in his letters. Gazing at her own reflection, Jessy wondered why.

"It's four miles in that direction, toward the lake. Past the old boathouse, remember?" said one woman to another.

"Oh? Is that where they go?" The other woman gasped.

"Yes, that's where! They've been going there for months!"

Jessy cocked her head, not meaning to eavesdrop but unable to rise and leave without disturbing the sleeping children. In the seat behind Jessy's, two women were speaking in hushed but distinct hissing tones. On and on they went in their accusations. "He's been seeing that little tart for months! A girl in his office."

"No! Your husband's been cheating on you?"

"This isn't the first girl he's had either." Her voice shaking, the woman whispered, "A brunette this time. There are affairs going on all over that office. They go to the river for their trysts! And they're all married, many of them with children!"

"That's nothing! Last winter a letter came to our house, addressed to Mr. and Mrs. Ridley. Ben was at work at the time so I opened it since it was for the two of us. You can imagine my shock to read a letter from a good hotel downtown that had been undergoing renovation. They wanted to thank us, Mr. and Mrs. Ridley, mind you, for our patronage and patience during the renovation—only Ben never took me to that hotel in my life, not ever! Turns out he'd been going there on his lunch hours with the wife of one of his partners and had the audacity to register that hussy in my name!" Mrs. Ridley began to cry.

"No! It's horrid the way men cheat!" her companion said angrily.

"Not just men. His partner's wife was no saint either, don't forget. She dropped Ben and is seeing another of my husband's partners!"

With that the women went to the ladies' room to freshen themselves before dinner. Jessy watched as they passed, two attractive young women, both victims of adultery. She had seen them board a stop or two down the line. Jessy wondered how their husbands could be so callous, and how another wife could be so boldly sinful, abandoning her marriage vows. After the women had passed, she turned toward the darkened windows, wondering more than ever about her future.

❦ ❦ ❦

The next morning broke, cold and grim, over the stark Midwest. A foot of hard dirty snow covered the ground like asphalt. The Flints' train had stopped for an hour in Chicago. They would be home in Bethel before noon. For now, the children explored the shops near the station with Suzanna. Jessy and Adam decided to take a walk in the opposite direction, toward a line of restaurants and theaters.

"Do you miss Florida?" Jessy shouted over the roaring February winds that blasted them from the very Great Lakes.

Adam, tanned and happy, laughed and fought to keep his hat from flying away in the wind. "Let's go in here!" Adam led her into a theater alcove protected from the wind.

Jessy fought to catch her breath. "I'd forgotten all about the cold."

"Come on, Cinderella," Adam growled in his best mocking voice.

Together they explored the theater lobby where photographs of actors and actresses were arranged behind glass, along with small props and play notes. People came and went through the plushly carpeted alcove, cleaning up after the previous evening's performance or rushing to appointments and rehearsals. A girl behind them was laughing rather loudly.

Turning to see what was so amusing, Jessy was confronted with a surprise. "Mr. Kimball! Why, ah, how nice to see you!"

Adam turned too. "Walter! What brings you to Chicago?"

Together, Adam and Jessy looked at the big, genial red-haired man with his arm wrapped around a girl not much older than Emma Kimball, dressed in brilliant shimmering green. Her cheeks were rosy pink, not from the blustery day but from rouge.

"Afraid I'm not your man," the fellow answered. The girl in green clutched him like ivy.

"Okay, Walter, if that's the way you want it," Adam said warily.

"Come on, Georgie, you promised!" whined the girl in green. "Let's hurry!"

After the woman and the man called Georgie disappeared into the theater, Jessy said, "Could Walter Kimball have a twin?"

Through the side of his mouth Adam confided, "That was no twin. That was Walter Kimball or I'm Georgie Washington!"

"You don't suppose he's cheating on Acacia Kimball, do you?"

Adam looked down on his sister. "He ain't walkin' that chorus girl to prep school, that's for sure!" He stared into the alcove, but Walter "Georgie" Kimball had disappeared with the girl.

"Oh, how sordid!" Jessy whispered. She clutched Adam's arm in the cold.

"Hey, you're shiverin'. Want my coat? Here."

"No, please, Adam, you need it. I'll be all right. It's just a shock to see a man you think you know, someone you can trust—" Still clutching her brother's arm, Jessy returned to the train. She couldn't forget seeing Walter Kimball gadding about with a woman a fraction of his own age.

❦ ❦ ❦

At eleven o'clock that morning The Midwest Express pulled into Bethel. By this time the Flints were either grumpy, edgy, or gloomy. Jessy felt all three. "Back to the pigs," she said, half-smiling at Adam.

"Or worse," he said good-naturedly. "Come on, all of you. Home sweet home!"

"I don't wanna go home," whined Stephen.

"I don't wanna go to school," moaned Taddy.

"I don't wanna leave the train," wailed Martha.

"I don't want to feel so cold," complained Suzanna. "My face feels frozen! Funny. I never minded the cold before."

Adam sighed as he arranged to have their luggage, including all their vacation trinkets, hauled home. Slowly, his family dragged behind him, burdened by their carrying cases. Tanned and sullen, they stood on the frozen, windswept prairie by the railroad tracks.

"Hi, folks! So how was Florida?" asked Burl Everett cheerily.

"Lovely," said Jessy to the stationmaster, Leo's brother-in-law. "Too lovely." Her breath seemed to freeze in midair.

"Didn't miss much in Bethel except eighteen inches of snow."

Nathan's warm smile came to Jessy from that faraway land, his golden voice soothing and dear, the friend she would never see again. She shut her eyes tight and forced the image of him away.

"You okay?" asked Burt. When she nodded glumly, he asked, "Say, where's Emma? Didn't she go to Florida with you?"

"She's staying on a while," said Jessy.

"Hear from Leo lately?" Burl asked.

"Yes. He's fine. He's probably going to Hawaii."

"He made it to the majors, you know."

Jessy nearly dropped her bundles. "No! He did? Really?"

"It was in yesterday's paper—Boston Red Sox. Three thousand a year!"

"No! Really?" Jessy beamed at the thought. Now Leo could announce their wedding. Now he could finish paying for that beautiful ring he had given her and she could wear it. Once they were married, Jessy could go with him and share his life! Jessy's smile could have melted snow, all eighteen inches of it. "Guess what!" she called, running toward Adam and Suzanna. "You'll never guess!"

❦ ❦ ❦

The Flint homestead appeared in good order. Ed Mannon, delighted with the extra choice selection of Florida fruits, among other presents the Flints gave him and his family, had taken good care of their animals in their five-week absence.

Suzanna and Jessy entered the chilly kitchen. With a sigh they tied aprons over their coats and set about preparing lunch. While Suzanna got wood to burn in the stove, Jessy hunted for jars of home-preserved vegetables. She rinsed and filled the kettle once she got the pump going.

"How different everything seems. I feel taller!" Jessy said, laughing.

As they dusted off kitchen counters, Jessy noticed the gloomy view out the windows which needed cleaning. The lead sky looked heavy with snow. While Adam and the porters hauled luggage up the stairs to the second floor bedrooms, the children hollered and ran amok.

From the kitchen Suzanna called out to her brood: "Go upstairs and change your clothes while Aunt Jessy and I prepare your lunch!"

Instead they began flinging sheets off the parlor furniture. "Leave those alone!" cried Suzanna angrily. "You'll shake dust all over everything! Stop it, do you hear me?" Again Suzanna sighed. Home sweet home.

Jessy emptied a sack of fruit onto the counter, one she had handled with care all twelve hundred miles of their trip. She began peeling and slicing oranges and bananas for the family's lunch, fighting hard to put Florida behind her.

Suzanna turned to her, a big spoon in her hand. "We should be grateful for memories to warm us through the winter!" Then she settled down to the practical matter at hand. "We could do with some beans. Do you mind?"

"No, not at all. I'll be right back." Jessy lit a lantern and went to the cellar to look through shelves of homegrown, home-packed vegetables sealed in glass jars, along with bins of root vegetables, squash, and apples they had harvested last autumn.

"Please bring up some onions, too, will you, Jessy?" Suzanna called from the top of the steps. "Just a few!"

"All right!" Jessy, carrying the lantern, made her way through the darkness. She hung the lantern in the center of the main storage room, a cavern of stone under the huge Victorian house. There were dry beans stored in tins, but Jessy surveyed the many varieties of beans in glass jars ready to heat and eat in a hurry: string beans, limas, kidney beans, and more. "Scarlet runners," she decided, picking out a jar of the tasty, mammoth deep red beans she had plucked from vines ten feet high last year. As she turned to the onion bin, she stiffened when she heard a noise.

"Who's there?" No one answered. She put down the jar of beans and took up the lantern. Slowly she paced the cold stone floors, looking at everything in turn—Adam's tools, empty seven-gallon milk cans, a cream separator, brooms, rakes, shovels, and old tins. One sight chilled her bones: a thick bar of scrubbing soap gnawed deeply around the edges. Repelled, she put it down and continued her search.

"Jessy? Is anything the matter?" Suzanna called.

"I'll be right up!" Jessy called out. The contents of a few shelves seemed all wrong. Lightweight items had tumbled over—paper boxes, pencils, a pad of paper, little measuring cups Adam and Jessy used to mete out fertilizers and repellants. Everything was in disarray as if an animal had scampered through. Then Jessy saw the costly sack of ruined seed spilled over the floor. The Flint home had been invaded. She remembered the telltale signs she had noticed on that laundry day months ago, when she had forgotten to alert Adam. Again Suzanna called to her. Jessy grabbed the onions and jar of beans and ran up the stairs with the lantern.

"Took you long enough!" Adam said good-naturedly from the table. He had already changed from his Sunday best into warm coveralls and two thick work shirts. "Ed did good. Barn's all tidy."

Jessy didn't speak at first, not wanting to spoil Adam's lunch, but she knew he must hear the truth as soon as possible. As she set down the food on the counter, she said, "Adam, we have a—a visitor. It might be a squirrel."

"It's probably a rat," Adam said calmly. "And probably more than one."

Jessy turned, alarmed. "What makes you say that?"

"They usually travel in pairs. They like grains and things to gnaw on, like bars of soap. Their teeth don't ever stop growin' so they have to keep chewin' or their teeth'll grow right through their beady little heads!"

Jessy and Suzanna shivered at the thought, but Adam wasn't finished.

"When I brought up the luggage, I thought I heard somethin' in the attic so I went up and saw chewed paper! They been havin' a field day while we been gone. If they've prowled the cellar, my guess is they're climbin' inside the walls. After lunch you can help me set some traps."

"Yes, sir. I mean, no, sir. Why kill them?"

"Why?" Adam sputtered at his sister's naïvete. "They carry fleas 'n' lice 'n' disease, that's why—deadly diseases too. I heard someplace they destroy ten times what they eat, with all their mess. And they're the devil to catch. The sooner we get rid of 'em and plug up their entry holes, the better."

Animal-loving Jessy, thinking of the pelican she had rescued not so long ago, pleaded for mercy. "But Adam, what if it's only chipmunks?"

"They're first cousins to rats. Suzanna, got some cheese?"

"No, darling, why?"

"Eventually we'll need it for the traps—not today, but soon. First we'll lay out empty traps, open ones so the animals will get used to walking over 'em. Then we'll start baitin' the traps, but leave 'em open, so the rats'll get used to that and then . . ."

Adam went into detail about the time-consuming process he would follow. When he saw the dismal expression on Jessy's face, he laughed and said, "Welcome home, sister!"

"Lunch is ready!" Suzanna called out sweetly but loud enough to rouse her recalcitrant children. "Come on, children. Lunch will get cold! Hurry up now! Oh, where did they disappear to now?!"

"Home sweet home," said Adam as he dug into his lunch.

CHAPTER 22

❦

On a late March afternoon too stormy for working outdoors, Jessy decided to clean her room. After straightening her small wardrobe, she went through her bureau. Leo's letters, tied in a bundle with red ribbon, were there with his ring, still too big for her finger and still in its velvet box. He had made no mention of announcing his engagement to Jessy and she had been too hesitant to raise the matter herself.

She looked at the snowstorm raging outside her windows. At this moment Leo was in the sunny South at the Red Sox spring camp in Hot Springs, Arkansas, training for the start of major league baseball in April. She hadn't seen him in months, but he wrote with unbridled excitement about working with professional athletes at the top of their game. Even though he had lost his nickname, Count Smoke, because it was too close to his fellow pitcher's, the great Smoky Joe Wood, Leo was superb on the mound. When word got around about Leo's Crimean ancestry, his teammates dubbed him Crimmy.

Jessy dusted her desk piled with books, magazines, newspapers, and correspondence. Emma's latest letter made her smile. Still with the Good Sisters, Emma was now seven months along and feeling at least as well as the other unmarried but pregnant girls staying with her. She was learning the rudiments of sewing, cooking, and gardening with the nuns who had been explaining their faith. Emma brought these matters to Jessy in letters, asking about life, sin, death, forgiveness, and resurrection. "These are questions about God I could only ask you, Jessy. What does He want from me? Does He hate me? I hope not! I trust you to give true answers. I know you're busy, but please write soon."

And Jessy had always responded, often only after searching her Bible for the most appropriate verse of Scripture, be it comforting, enlightening, or challenging. Of course God didn't hate His children, Jessy wrote to

215

Emma. Quite the reverse—He loves as no human could love, for He is the Creator of love, the Source of love eternal. Sadly, it was His rebellious children who hated Him.

Jessy came to appreciate Emma's letters more than she did Leo's. His, though vivid with details of his budding professional career, pained Jessy with his agonizing slowness of purpose as far as marriage and visits to Bethel were concerned, while Emma's brimmed with love, friendship, and curiosity. With every letter, Jessy could see that Emma's growing hope in Christ was leading her to a new life established on age-old beliefs, the path that brought her peace and led her away from the destructive road she had been traveling.

Emma had been receiving visitors. Bo and Beatrice Bally, in an effort to overcome the loss of their own miscarried child, approached Emma about adopting her baby, but, to everyone's surprise, Emma declined. As much as she admired the Ballys, Emma preferred not to know to which family her baby would go once it had been adopted.

Soon afterward, the nuns contacted a childless couple in Maryland who pledged to arrive at the convent once Emma gave birth to a healthy, normal child. After thinking and praying, as Jessy suggested, Emma signed the adoption papers. Dr. Cyrus Fisher assured her she had made a sound decision.

The Ballys had written to Jessy, and so had Mrs. Fisher who was using Adam's cane and walking more easily. Hope's house had sold quickly once Nathan placed it on the market. Town council members were building the Hope Ellmont Fisher Museum to hold her shipwreck treasures, Florida memorabilia, and other historic items Nathan had donated to the city of Garden Springs in his wife's name. Jessy could easily picture the quaint town square she had seen on vacation, but with the addition of a new museum.

Nathan had returned to his teaching post. Despite his harried schedule after his leave of absence, the professor still found time to mail Jessy an illustrated brochure about the college. How often Jessy had read the course descriptions and dreamed of attending St. Azarias tucked in the mountains of the Mid-Atlantic near a town called Enigma. The tidy green campus looked inviting with towers, pointed arches, and leaded glass windows in the English High Gothic style. Jessy wondered if Nathan was trying, in a roundabout way, to recruit her to enroll at St. Azarias. Though college was beyond her means, she enjoyed seeing the place where Nathan prepared young men and women to do great things.

Nathan's handwriting flashed as bright as his smile. Plato Q had sent Jessy his regards, but according to Nathan's transcription of the bird's boisterous squawkings, he missed her peanuts.

As she rustled papers, she thought she heard a noise, that strange scraping noise. She paused and listened. With a cold shiver Jessy eyed the walls and ceiling that kept their secret from her. She and Adam had plugged a few small holes, hoping they had sealed the invading animals' entry and exit points, but the house was big and the snow was deep and there was no telling where the clever foe were gaining access to the rambling two-story farmhouse.

After doing the hard farm work of springtime, Adam was planning, with the help of Kem Curtis, to install electrical wiring and a coal furnace with vents throughout the house for central heating. *What secrets will this old house reveal then?* Jessy wondered.

Now, nearly finished cleaning, Jessy had saved the best for last. She polished the water globe she had purchased in Florida; it had survived the long trip home in her baggage. She gave it a shake. As the sparkly golden sands began to settle, they revealed tiny palm trees, and, among the waving grasses, hand-painted fish and a wee turtle exploring a miniature treasure chest. How it warmed her to see that reminder of her wonderful vacation.

Hope's wooden fragment of the crucified Christ Jessy treasured above all else, keeping it close to the Bible on her nightstand, but there were those other little trinkets Nathan had given her in a package at Laguna Springs. How eagerly she had opened the package, soon after arriving home to Bethel, and how she had loved what it contained: a tiny but keenly observed alligator family cast in pewter, each piece crafted to represent the bellowing beast in various poses and at various stages of life. The whole collection—two grandparents, two parents, and several alligator tots—fit in the palm of her hand. The grouping sat in a place of honor on Jessy's desk amid a handful of delicate gray Spanish moss Nathan had used as packing.

The mere thought of her friend made her smile. Although she would never see him again, she had written to thank him for the present and to let him know how she was getting on at school.

Since the Flints had returned from Florida, Jessy and Adam had been attending classes two afternoons each week and every other Saturday morning. They and several other Bethel residents, working at their own pace, were taking part in a county experiment with adult education which would lead to high school certification. In addition to studying math, science, and literature as Adam was doing, Jessy was also learning how to use the Qwerty typewriter she had received for Christmas. After a few weeks' practice, Jessy's fingers flew over the keys, making quick work of all her homework assignments, letter writing, and farm business.

With the snowstorm still raging, she decided to work on farming accounts downstairs by a toasty fire in the parlor. Before she left her room, she glanced again at her small treasures, warming at the thought of bright sunny Florida. Soon the snows would stop and winter would end in Bethel and spring would come, and with it all the demanding field work she would do with Adam. Now Jessy lived on spring and hope.

The spring would bring with it a new baseball season. As so many Americans thrived on the promise of a new chance with a fresh team, now so did Jessy. On her way down to the parlor, she passed the telephone which remained silent. How she waited and hoped for Leo to call her! Smiling, she thought, *It's easier to talk with God than Leo Kimball!* Perhaps Leo could work in a visit to Bethel once his team began traveling the country during the regular baseball season, due to start in just a few more weeks.

During 1909, the eight American League teams, including Leo's Red Sox, would play 154 games in a geographically compact area between New England and the Midwest. In addition to New York and Philadelphia, his team would go to Washington, D.C., Detroit, St. Louis, Cleveland, and Chicago. *Surely Leo will visit home when he tours the Midwest*, Jessy thought. *Surely he will.*

❦ ❦ ❦

April came, and with it the start of spring plowing and planting. These days, when Jessy returned to the house from a hard day's work, tired and aching, she still faced homework and stacks of newspapers with their sporting updates. Leo had not pitched often, she knew, but he had done well when given the opportunity. He hadn't phoned and had barely taken time to write. In May, though, two pieces of news reached her.

The first involved Emma. A letter arrived from the Convent of the Good Sisters of St. Catherine, but not in Emma's writing. Dreading the worst, Jessy opened the letter and read:

> Dear Jessy,
>   Sister Theresa is writing this letter for me. I have asked her to because I feel so weak. My Belinda is a beautiful baby girl with soft red hair and happy eyes like Grama Flo's. She was born two days ago and she is perfect in every way, and so dear to hold, with precious tiny hands and feet. She gurgles so sweetly! I cried the first time I saw her. The birth was hard like Dr. Cyrus expected, and at least a dozen times I prayed to die. That must have been a great sin, I know, but I asked God to let me die because the pain was so bad. Later, when I saw my baby, I forgot how much it hurt to have her and I'm so very glad and grateful I did have her, thanks to you, Jessy. But soon (tomorrow, I think) her adoptive parents will be here and then it will be over, and I can come home as soon as I'm strong enough to make the trip. I'll write to you myself when I'm able. Please pray for my baby. Love, Emma.

Jessy's other news came from Adam, fresh from Shakes's barber shop where he had learned that the Red Sox would battle the White Sox at Chicago's South Side Baseball Park for a four-game series. From a *McGuffey's Reader* tucked in his bib overalls, Adam pulled out the scrap of paper on which he had jotted the dates of the Boston Red Sox playing schedule for May. As she read Adam's penciled notes, she said with no little amazement, "Gosh, Adam, Leo's team will be in Detroit, Chicago, St. Louis, and back to Detroit in just a matter of days!"

"The Big Leagues don't waste time when they're on the road. They have to make every day they spend away from their home park count, with all the expenses they got—hotels, train trips, and so on."

"Oh, well," Jessy sighed, "Leo will be much too busy to visit us. Thank you for showing me the schedule, though. Here," she said, handing back the paper to Adam. She watched him slip it back into the reader he carried everywhere these days. "Doing your homework, I see?"

"Uh-huh. I carry a book with me to look at when I got a few minutes. Why, just this mornin' at the barber's I was readin'—" He flipped pages till he found what he was looking for. "You ought to read this book sometime, Jessy, 'specially the story about Omar."

"Wasn't Omar the fellow who, as a young man, made all sorts of plans for his future but he got so bogged down with everyday cares and worries that, by the end of his long life, Omar realized he had accomplished absolutely none of his original goals?"

"Yeah! Pitiful!" Adam nodded for emphasis but then looked more than a trifle abashed. "I keep forgettin' you finished all your readers." Before Jessy could enjoy even a passing glimmer of scholarly pride, her brother called her smarty pants. Still he thumbed through the reader, saying, "I got—I mean I *have* to write a report on three of these stories by next week." He grinned at her, reading her mind. "No, I ain't askin'—I mean, I'm *not asking* you to help me but maybe you could let me use your typewriter?"

Jessy beamed like the sun at him. "Of course!" She took the book from him, glancing over the familiar table of contents: poems, essays, excerpts and more. "Which selections will you pick, do you think, besides Omar's story?"

"I thought maybe the one about Napoleon Bonaparte."

Closing her eyes, Jessy quoted from it, "He worshiped no God but ambition."

"Yeah, how 'bout—I mean *About*—that guy? The nerve!" He took the book from her again. "To balance out my report I thought I'd write about that poem, the one 'bout God bein'—I mean, *beinG* everywhere."

"Oh, what a lovely poem!" she cried, delighted, thinking of its wondrous imagery, the great Lord of the universe guiding the moon through silent skies. "Those three should do nicely, I think, for your assignment." When Adam didn't seem ready to start the work awaiting them, she said, "Nice haircut, what I can see of it." She peered impishly at the perimeter of Adam's fine head under the brim of his battered felt hat.

"Shakes cut it too short, don't you think?" Adam removed his hat and turned around so she could see the barber's handiwork.

"I've decided that Shakes can give only one haircut," Jessy said sagely. "From the back, all the men in Bethel look the same. I notice in church."

Adam, rocking with laughter, turned to her. "And all these Sundays I thought you been prayin'!"

"*PrayinG!*" she corrected, blushing and sputtering a defense: "About the only places farmers take off their hats are at church and the barber shop!"

"True!" said Adam as he crammed his hat on his handsome head. With his green eyes dancing and as casually as he could, he asked, "Think you'd like to see that Saturday game between the Red Sox and the White Sox in Chicago?"

"Oh, Adam! Are you serious?" Jessy was ecstatic.

"Sure! The boys'd love it, and so'd you 'n' me. I mean, you and *I*." Slowly, thoughtfully, Adam rubbed his freshly shaven chin. "Maybe I can convince Suzy and Martha to go along."

Stephen and Taddy were thrilled with the prospect of seeing their first major league game, but Suzanna and Martha had other ideas. They would take the train with them to Chicago, but instead of seeing what they both deemed "a silly old ball game," mother and daughter would spend that Saturday afternoon shopping at some of the most fashionable stores in America.

Before the Flints made their Chicago excursion, Jessy had two unexpected visitors. First, Darlene Kimball Wilcox arrived one afternoon, alone and upset, asking to see Jessy in private. She refused the tea and home-baked pastries Jessy offered.

After Jessy had shut the heavy wooden sliding pocket doors in the parlor, Darlene, carelessly dressed and with her dark hair wispy and fighting from the pins and combs meant to control it, began to Jessy: "I apologize for coming to see you unannounced like this. I hope I'm not keeping you from anything."

"I'm glad to see you!" Jessy, beaming with enthusiasm, asked, "How's your family—Chad and Billy? Well, I hope!" When Darlene didn't answer, Jessy said in a more subdued tone, "I must apologize for my appearance." Though wearing clean clothes, Jessy was prepared for field work in an old brown-checkered cotton dress with frayed cuffs. "I'm sorry you and I don't visit more often. I'd like to but we've had so much work!

We never seem to catch up around here. And we were away in the winter."

"That's what I came to talk to you about—that trip you took. Emma went with you—" Darlene's voice trailed upward, dangling with questions.

"Yes, of course she did." Now, thoroughly subdued, Jessy looked away to the mantle, to the milk-glass lamp, the piano strewn with music sheets, and up to a painting of a young boy and girl sitting together on a bright green lawn enjoying a picture book. At last Jessy faced Darlene. The woman's eyes looked aching, red, tired. Darlene's whole appearance conveyed weariness and defeat. Sensing Darlene's inner turmoil, Jessy asked quietly, "What's wrong?"

"I hardly know how to say this." Now Darlene looked about, her dark-circled eyes roving about but not really seeing the room. She turned back to Jessy and asked, "Did Emma tell you who the father was?"

"Darlene!" Jessy was too surprised to say more.

"In January I thought Emma left Bethel with you because she dropped out of school and was bored staying at home with Mum and Daddy. They've always spoiled her, being the youngest, so I thought the trip was another bribe of theirs to keep her out of their hair but then, when I found out my little sister went to Florida to have a baby, I was shocked, I can tell you! And Mum told me this wasn't Emma's first pregnancy! That was news to me too!" Regaining her composure with effort, Darlene said firmly, "I must know who the father is. Won't you tell me?"

"I can't tell you!" In Jessy's frank, open way, she added softly, "Emma never told me who the father was." With no little satisfaction Jessy added, "I think Emma has done a great deal of growing up in Florida. I'm thankful her baby is healthy and pray Belinda will be raised by loving parents." Her face brightening with hope, Jessy said, "I'm looking forward to seeing Emma when she comes home, aren't you? I think she'll be back in late June. She'll need a great deal of loving support from all of us." Jessy waited a long while for Darlene to speak. The woman grew increasingly more agitated, wringing her handkerchief into fantastic twists. Finally Jessy pleaded, "How can I help you, Darlene? Can you tell me what's wrong?"

In a scalding rage, Darlene blurted out: "My husband's cheating on me! I think he's been cheating on me since Billy was born! Eight years of—"

Sinking back into her chair, defeated, Darlene added, "I never told this to anyone, Jessy. Not a soul. It's been torture for me to face the truth, but when I heard that Emma was expecting a child, well, then, I knew."

For a moment Jessy sat there in stunned silence, digesting Darlene's implications. Emma had admitted the father of her child was married— but to Darlene? Shaking her head, incredulous, Jessy asked, "You don't honestly think Chad fathered your sister's baby!"

"Chad goes off so much, leaving me to run our gun shop and look after Billy. I don't know where my husband is half the time, or what he's doing. He loves to hunt, you know, and he's an excellent shot, whether it's ducks or deer he's after, but so often he comes home empty-handed and not looking like he's been trooping through the woods. I shudder to think what Chad's been hunting for!" Darlene added, "He's always liked Emma."

Jessy smiled kindly at Darlene. "Oh, I wouldn't worry! Emma's easy to like, that's all. Have you talked with Chad about—"

"If I dare question him, he beats me."

"Oh, Darlene! Please stay with us, you and your son, until—"

"No!" Darlene added softly, "No, but thank you. Billy and I will be all right. I shouldn't have come here. I'm not asking for—I don't mean to—" Darlene forced her stress into intense opposing motions of her hands, twisting her hanky into tortured shapes.

Jessy gazed out the triple windows toward the road, the newly budding hardwood trees, and railroad tracks. Thinking of that bitter cold day in February when her train stopped in Chicago and she and her brother had by chance run into the dapper Walter Kimball, Jessy asked, "Does your father—does Mr. Kimball go to Chicago much?"

Darlene nodded. "All the time! And once in a while he asks Chad to go with him—they *say* to see baseball games. Daddy used to take Leo all the time, before he got so busy with college and then left for Texas to play ball. They'd deny it, but I think the whole lot of them see more than ball games!" Nothing but a freight train could stop Darlene's awful suspicions from surging out: "If you're going to marry Leo, you should know what you're in for!" Suddenly Darlene's eyes flooded with tears. "I love my husband so much! I'm tired of pretending it doesn't matter what he does, that as long as Chad and I are married and he doesn't leave me, Chad's womanizing couldn't hurt me, but it does! I can't trust my own husband!"

Jessy's worst fears had been verified: Walter Kimball had set an example of cheating for the younger men in his family. Quietly, Jessy said, "When your father was a young man, he went to Chicago on business for your grandparents, to sell livestock, and that's how he met your mother, wasn't it?"

"Yes." Biting her lip, Darlene's eyes drifted away toward the windows. "Daddy's always loved Chicago and all the exciting things to do. Going there makes him feel young, he's always said. He loves the Cubs, summer concerts, the theater, the elegance. A long time ago, Mum's father owned a lovely place on Washington Street and an estate farther north, on the lake. Daddy told me he wanted to stay in Chicago after he married Mum. He was so happy there. He didn't want to live here in Bethel where he was born and raised, but he and Mum decided to move back here when they had that bad time with—" Darlene paused, unable to mention the unmentionable name.

"Peter?" Jessy asked softly, with understanding in her liquid brown eyes.

Surprised but yet relieved, Darlene said, "Leo tells you everything!"

"Peter's a fine man, I think, and so talented."

"I hardly remember him at all. I went to see him once, years ago—a hopeless case! There was nothing anyone could do for him." Shrugging off the memory of Peter, Darlene said with firmness, "I have to know who Chad is seeing."

"I'm afraid I can't help you, Darlene."

Darlene cried, "If Chad had anything to do with Emma, I'll never—"

"Can you talk things over with Chad? Maybe there's nothing sinister going on at all. Perhaps he's—"

"He's cheating on me all right. A wife knows! You're the only one I can turn to. I wouldn't ask Suzanna; we attended school about the same time but we were never very close, so I had to turn to you, Jessy, don't you see? People in Bethel look up to you. You Flints spent time with my little sister when—well, I've heard that Emma trusts you so she must tell you things. She told you who the father was, didn't she?"

"No. She didn't tell me that." Sighing deeply, Jessy put one arm around Darlene's shoulder and gave her a gentle hug. "I'm sorry to see you so unhappy, Darlene. I don't know what else to say, but I'll pray for you. We can pray together now if you like."

Darlene pulled away from Jessy and stood. "I don't bother about God and He doesn't bother about me."

Jessy stood, too, saying, "There's always hope with God, but no hope whatever without Him."

Darlene, her mind swimming in deep waters indeed, a whirling torrent of confused and fearful thoughts, was unable to face Jessy. For a long moment she stood staring at the closed parlor doors, and then she turned to Jessy, saying, "I shouldn't have come. I hardly know you. I'm sorry I wasted your time, and you're so busy. Forgive me." Darlene headed for the double doors.

Jessy stopped the distraught woman. "You didn't waste my time at all, Darlene! I'm glad you came." Seeing that Darlene was determined to leave, she slid open the doors but said in a low voice, "If I can help you, if you want to talk, I hope you'll come again. If you need a home away from home—"

Nodding, Darlene fumbled with her gloves. Again tears came—the silent, streaming, smothering tears of a woman betrayed.

"Please don't go like this, Darlene!"

Shaking her head and brushing away her tears, Darlene murmured thanks and added, "I promised Billy I'd pick him up after school." The cuckoo clock began rattling in its nonsensical way, making Darlene smile for the first time.

Again Jessy reached out to Darlene. She touched one of her gloved hands, saying, "I won't say a word to anyone about our conversation."

Darlene calmed noticeably at this. She nodded her thanks and left. From the front porch, Jessy watched Darlene ride off alone in a horse-drawn carriage, raising dust in the road and casting a big shadow behind her.

Jessy had hardly come to grips with Darlene's worried visit when, a few short days later, Laura arrived, alone and unannounced. Into the parlor she went with Jessy. Behind closed doors, the fashionable Laura, as glamorous as ever, proved to be in quite a snit but, unlike her sister Darlene, got straight to the point of her visit: "It's Burl. He's cheating on me. With Darlene!"

"Darlene and Burl? Oh, that's ridiculous! Darlene would never—"

"Yes she would." Laura, far from the teary-eyed wreck Darlene had been but still a woman in need, drowned her sorrows with tea. She downed two cups of it before removing one fashionably long kid glove and helping herself to home-baked treats studded with raisins and heavily iced. "These are delicious, Jessy."

"Thanks! Suzanna showed me how to make them. They're called English cream scones. Would you like the recipe?"

"Me?" Laura screeched with unexpected delight. "I never cook! When I was growing up, Mum said I never had to and so I never did!"

Acacia's style of mothering never failed to amaze Jessy. Offering Laura the plate, Jessy asked mildly, "So what do you and Burl do about meals, then?"

Laura wiped her fingers daintily on her napkin before she took another scone and answered, "Oh, this and that. We open cans, mostly, or he tries to cook." This set her giggling too. "Burl's a rotten cook! I don't know how he puts on weight—must be all the fried fish and chips he buys at that stand near the station. He eats lunch there most every day, or else hot dogs, pies, and cakes he gets from the snack man who comes around in the afternoons." With a sigh Laura, momentarily satisfied, sank into the sofa.

"So what makes you think your husband is, ah—"

Laura's contentment vanished, but she didn't rise up from her comfortable position. Still, her fair coloring so like Emma's darkened visibly. With quiet but unmistakable rancor Laura said, "That miserable no-good! The other day I was unpacking. I had just gotten back from a trip to Chicago."

"Posing for more fashion catalogs?" Jessy ventured.

"Swimsuits this time!" Laura squealed, "Divine! Look!" She pulled several different catalogs from her handbag and arranged them on the tea table. When Laura saw that Jessy hesitated to pick up one, she said, "Keep them! I have tons more!" For a moment Laura pouted, trying to resume her original train of thought. Settling back in her seat, she said, "Well, anyway, as I was saying, Jessy, I was putting my suitcase under the bed and I saw this—" Laura leaned forward and whispered, "—this dusty undergarment! And it wasn't mine!"

"A-another woman's garment in your own home?" While Jessy's face flushed scarlet to her hairline, her hands turned to ice.

Laura nodded cooly, the detective in her triumphant. Over steepled fingers she peered at Jessy, saying, "There it was under my bed, but I can assure you it wasn't mine. It was something Darlene would wear, that tramp!"

"I wouldn't call Darlene a—I couldn't imagine she would—"

"I could and she did! I know she came here to see you, and so if she could, so can I." Now Laura straightened up on the sofa, asking, "What did you two talk about?"

"That's confidential," said Jessy, starting to feel like an umpire back at Lumpy Land.

"What did Darlene say about me?"

"Aren't you concerned about Emma?" Jessy asked in wonderment.

Grudgingly, Laura said, "Mum told me Emma's all right." Laura was not to be diverted. "What did Emma say to you about me? You certainly had a lot of time to talk when you went all the way to Florida together!"

"Emma didn't feel much like talking," said Jessy truthfully. "She was in Palm Beach most of the time I was there, and then she went into confinement."

"I thought about adopting her baby, can you imagine? I mean, if Burl and I are never—we've been married nine years already and nothing! I'll be old and gray with no baby to show for being married. I mean, what's the point of marriage if you don't have babies? Burl doesn't like children, I guess. He doesn't like me either. I never should have married him."

Now that Laura had bared her soul, Jessy felt immediate sympathy. With soft emphasis she said, "Some people don't like babies until they become parents. Emma, for instance."

"That's what I said! I said, 'Burl, we could adopt Emma's baby and pretend it's ours, but would he listen? He must hate Emma. He won't even discuss her. On the other hand, when it comes to Darlene—" Laura rolled her eyes. "He thinks she's wonderful—so *round* and *plump* and a good cook too. She studied home economics at school even though Mum told her she'd be better off learning anything else. Oh, Burl's disgusting! I kill myself dieting and for what?" Laura eyed the last of the scones.

"Help yourself." Jessy said, pouring more tea for them both.

"Oh, I couldn't. Maybe a half?"

"All right." Jessy sliced a scone and handed the more generous half to Laura.

"Thanks." Eyeing the thick icing and plump raisins, Laura asked, "Why bother staying attractive for a man who thinks Darlene is pretty?"

"Darlene is very attractive," said Jessy. "I like her a lot."

"How could you? How could anyone like my sister?"

Savoring her scone, Jessy said, "You're fortunate to have sisters. I don't have any."

"Lucky you! Are you sure Darlene didn't say anything about me?"

Jessy said in her soothing way, "She doesn't dislike you in the least, as far as I can tell, and I think Emma would be just like you, if she could."

For all practical purposes, the conversation ended there, though the two women chatted until Laura had managed to nibble away the remaining scones. Just as Jessy did after Darlene's departure, long after Laura had gone, she said nothing to anyone, but she thought about these conversations often. How deep were the troubles of the Kimballs?

CHAPTER 23

On a beautiful Saturday in May, the Flints rushed through their morning work, dressed their best, and drove to the Bethel train station. On the way to Chicago, they enjoyed the panoramic view of the Midwestern countryside in spring—vast but gently rolling meadows surrounding thickets of trees; men plowing with horses; and empty, roofed corn cribs standing like gargantuan bird cages near brightly painted barns.

In two hours the family arrived in Chicago, America's second largest city after New York, looming over the prairie. Chicago fascinated the Flints with so many new buildings raised up from the ashes of the 1871 fire begun, according to legend, by Mrs. O'Leary's cow. Streets bristled with trolleys, cars, and pedestrians. When Jessy saw this vast city with its skyscrapers and telegraph lines, she remembered her dream of the previous Labor Day. As in that dream, the people looked stylish, prosperous, and busy.

The Flints went to State Street with its famed department stores: Louis Sullivan's masterpiece, Carson Pirie Scott, with its *art nouveau* cast-iron façade framing high-fashion window displays and, two blocks north, Marshall Field's and its famed green clock with prominent Roman numerals—a Chicago landmark since it had been installed twelve years before, in 1897.

Swarms of Saturday shoppers surged past the Flints, who began to feel giddy. Except for Adam, none of the Flints, Jessy included, had ever seen so many people in one place. Bethel's entire population could fit comfortably inside one store.

"Oh, darling, this is so exciting!" Suzanna said, just raring to shop. She squeezed Martha's small hand.

"We'll meet you both here under the clock at five." Kissing his wife and little daughter farewell, Adam said wryly, "Have fun, ladies, but don't spend all our money!"

Suzanna, with a coy look, asked, "Do you trust me?"

"Course I do. We pray about money often enough—that we use it wisely and not let it use us." He called to his sister who had wandered off to stare at window displays, "Hey, Bright Eyes! You *sure* you'd rather see a ball game?"

"Of course!" Still Jessy found it hard to tear away from such pretty displays of clothes, stationery, jewelry, and more—everything behind the glass arranged by a stylish hand. Three windows were devoted to bridal gowns, each a shimmering vision of glistening white satin, beadwork, and lace.

"Silly old White Sox. Everybody who's anybody knows the Cubs are better," said Suzanna, still looking coy.

"Boo," said Adam, with a rousing chorus from his boys.

From where they stood, Suzanna scanned the crowded streets for a restaurant. "Martha and I are going to have a wonderful lunch, aren't we sweetheart? And we'd love for Aunt Jessy to come with us!"

Tempted by the pleasures of shopping and fine dining but overcome by a wave of baseball fever made irresistible with the possibility of seeing Leo Kimball, Jessy turned from the glittering displays and went to Adam's side. She couldn't resist giving each of her young nephews a hug. The four bid good-bye to Suzanna and Martha.

"Okay, boys and girl, it's off to South Side Park!" Adam said, leading the way to the trolleys. Streetcars were new to Jessy and the boys, as were the famed Chicago stockyards where the Flints' own hogs were shipped every fall. Here ranged a square mile of pens filled with cattle from all over the Midwest and as far away as Texas. As they rode toward their destination, Adam described the rare, solitary business trips he had made to these stockyards. The boys listened to their father with rapt attention, but in her excitement over seeing Leo Kimball and the Red Sox, Jessy could hardly think about livestock. Arriving at their destination, Princeton and Thirty-ninth Streets, where the Chicago Wanderers played cricket long ago, they saw hundreds of baseball fans heading to South Side Park.

The aroma of Polish sausage wafted on air. "Get your red hot Chicago sausage!" a robust pushcart vendor proclaimed above the steam of roasting meats. "Sausage, sauerkraut, hot dogs, the works!"

"What do you think?" Adam asked Jessy and his boys. They answered by eagerly queuing up to buy their lunch. As they enjoyed their tasty hot sausages on rolls, Adam said, "We oughta do this more often, what do you think?"

"Yes, Daddy!" As Stephen ate, he watched well-dressed baseball fans, male and female, young and old, surging around them toward South Side Park.

"Boys, don't get mustard on your new suits, or your mama'll be mad at me."

"Yes, Daddy."

The Chicago sun was hot, but still there was a distinct bite in the air. "This is delicious, Adam, thank you!" said Jessy as she sipped soda and gazed at an open field where purple and white clover grew nearly waist high. The big city towered directly north of them.

"That was so good I want another one. What about you?" Adam asked. The boys eagerly lined up with him for more Chicago red hots, but Jessy waited to one side as mobs of fans came to the ballpark on packed streetcars.

Soon the Flints were inching along in the line for tickets at South Side Park. While she waited, again she remembered her strange and moving vision of the previous Labor Day. From where she stood she noticed the spires of two churches. A lady waiting near Jessy pointed them out by name to someone else: St. George's was closest to the South Side Park gates and just across the street stood a German church. A small but merry wedding party ambled past. The bride and groom couldn't have looked happier. Jessy smiled a secret smile, her mind on Leo.

Once the Flints reached the ticket seller, Adam splurged and bought the best seats remaining in the pavilion. With the long line of people behind them still waiting to buy tickets, the game would be sold out, all ten thousand seats. Local rooters pined for the new park Charles Comiskey, owner of the White Sox, was building four blocks away.

"Too bad Comiskey Park won't be ready for another year!" Jessy heard one fan say. "If it opened now they could fill it up and then some with this mob!"

On the way inside the old but venerable wooden park, Adam bought a scorecard for a dime. In it were named all players for both teams, but no mention of this day's Red Sox pitcher. It was too much to expect Leo to pitch, Jessy thought to herself, but she felt certain he would be on hand to root for his teammates.

Once the Flints took their seats under the protective deep roof, Jessy was glad she wouldn't be needing the parasol she had brought along. From her shady seat, she squinted to see the playing field shimmering under a brilliant sun. Far from the manicured playing fields of the coming years, pro baseball grounds in 1909 were hardly smoother than Bethel County's Lumpy Land. Recent rains had left South Side field soft and wet. Jessy watched groundskeepers fill puddles with sawdust.

With the aid of a megaphone, a man shouted the names of each of the day's players for both teams, but said nothing about Leo Kimball. Pitchers for both teams were warming up in their respective bull pens, but still Jessy saw no sign of Leo. Peering through Adam's binoculars, Jessy could see players for both teams move in and around their dugouts on either side of home plate. The dugouts at South Side Park were not recesses in the ground but roofed sheds on field level open to the wind, which was at the moment in this, the Windy City, lazily rippling the American flag at the far edge of center field. Infielders and outfielders began warming up at their positions. Each team took time to toss balls around and get the feel of the ground. There was much hollering going on among the players. Every man looked glad to be alive on such a glorious spring day.

Jessy smiled to see the uniforms both teams wore, new this early in the season: blousy flannel shirts with roomy knickers bunched up at the knee, deliberately oversized to account for expected shrinkage with repeated washings—assuming superstitious players would dare wash their uniforms and thereby ruin a lucky streak.

The White Sox wore their white home uniforms with smart black trim: black belts, black shoes, white caps with dark blue visors, and, of course, white sox. On each Chicago player's left sleeve was a bold black capital C. The Red Sox wore their gray road uniforms with black belts, black shoes, red lettering, gray caps with dark visors, and distinctive red sox. Both team uniforms had collars, but instead of wearing shirts that buttoned like those of the White Sox, Red Sox shirts laced up at the throat.

Opposing players wearing white or pale gray could be difficult to distinguish from a distance. Fans craned their necks and speculated amongst themselves over who was who only by the look and size of a player, or his unique movements. No baseball uniform bore a number or the player's name.

While her nephews chatted with their father and fans seated near them, Jessy read signs on the outfield wall advertising Bull Durham tobacco, quality shoes and hats for gentlemen, pianos, cigars, flour, Castoria, newspapers, and a multitude of distilled spirits. In these days before the custom of singing the National Anthem before each ball game began, a loud bell was sounded instead to get everyone's attention. A red-faced umpire in a dark blue suit, baseball cap, and chest protector shouted, *"Play ball!"*

And so it began, a classic game where batters didn't seek hitting home runs as much as getting on base any way they could and, once on, to keep moving toward home by stealing bases and using their sharply spiked shoes as weapons.

For six innings, the Flints in that packed stadium watched the game so like war in its plodding slowness interrupted with sudden, explosive action. Adam's scorecard gradually became a scrawl of partial diamond shapes, shading, and abbreviations. Jessy had hardly seen Adam so excited, and his boys, too, showed keen interest in all the action. Spectators made as much noise as possible with the aid of cow bells, horns, whistles, and even pots and spoons.

She delighted in watching coaches for both teams in perpetual motion, signaling to their men. The coaches' elaborate gyrations—chest-scratching, arm-thumping, potbelly-rubbing, and more—made Jessy wonder if these were baseball signals or attacks of hives. The crowd, too, got into the game with their strong opinions, commands, and even insults which they shouted to the players at ear-shattering volume. The athletes took all this in stride. Both teams were blessed with an abundance of relaxed, nimble athletes who could field and fire the ball with amazing speed and accuracy, as if they'd been born on that sun-soaked field.

The pitchers threw spitters, curves, and fastballs with astonishing speed, seldom pausing between hurls. Their goal was to finish the game in two hours. Everyone winced to see a batter hit on the shoulder by a pitch, and, later, a catcher who leaped about in pain after a ball hit him hard on his instep. In the third inning, a youngster sitting close to home plate who had been looking at everything but the game was hit hard by a foul ball. The game was delayed while the child was carried away on a stretcher.

Adam told Stephen and Taddy: "Let that teach you boys to keep your eye on the ball at all times, even when you're not up at bat!"

A fellow near them said, "That's life. One minute you're all right, and the next, if you don't watch it, you're out cold."

In the sixth inning the Red Sox pitcher tripped over a rut as he ran backward trying to catch a pop-up. The game stopped when the injured pitcher was helped off the field and the call went out for a doctor in the house. Soon the announcer shouted through the megaphone that a new Red Sox pitcher was warming up: Leo Kimball. Everyone with scorecards began looking up his name.

Jessy's elation could not be contained now that she could see Leo in his pale gray uniform with red sox warming up in the bull pen. He looked to be in great form.

"You're right on it today, Crimmy! Better'n yesterday!" shouted the Red Sox catcher. "Two more!" he shouted with a slap of his glove. Leo threw rapidly but with precision.

Leo walked out to the mound, smiled that unmistakable smile, adjusted the brim of his cap, and nodded to his catcher. Peering through Adam's binoculars, Jessy, with racing heart, saw that her Leo looked wonderful. Adam nudged her so she blushed.

"Look at Leo's belt," Adam said to Jessy and his sons. He pointed to Leo's belt, which was angled, not straight, as he went into his windup. "See how his hips rotate when he gets ready to throw? That's one sure sign a pitcher's in top form."

Jessy hoped Adam was right. The score was close. Boston led Chicago by one run. Leo struck out the first two hitters easily but struggled with the third, who reached second base by hitting midway into center field. The fourth batter bunted the ball well, but Leo stuck out his gloved hand to catch it for the out. Looking cool, self-assured, and handsome, he thumped the ball again and again into his glove as he returned with his team to the Boston dugout.

The crowd was getting anxious. Jessy felt as if she were the only Red Sox fan in Chicago, but she heard more than a few other rooters for Boston in the stands. Quietly she cheered on the Red Sox. In two more innings, Boston won the game. As the disappointed throng of White Sox fans surged out of the ballpark, Jessy, with Adam and the boys, rushed to the field toward the Red Sox players, who found themselves surrounded by loyal Boston fans a thousand miles from home. Stephen and Taddy were starstruck to see major league players up close, so real and so powerful, gathering up their gear—bats, bags, gloves, and balls. Jessy, too, felt starstruck. Never had she seen so many handsome, clean-cut, powerfully built young athletes.

"Jessy!" Leo looked astounded to see her. "Jessy! What are you doing here? Did you come all the way from Bethel just to see me?"

Jessy nodded shyly, suddenly and totally embarrassed. She was glad that Adam and the boys stood apart from them. "I'm so proud of you and your pitching! You've reached your goal! Here you are in the majors! A dream come true for you—and a win! Congratulations!"

"Congratulations, Crimmy! Great game!" cried another visitor with a distinctly Bostonian accent. There were noisy congratulations all around.

Leo, perpetually distracted by passing fans, said brightly to Jessy, "I'm glad you came! My dad thinks the American League isn't worth beans, you know. He's always been a Cubs fan. So how are you? I keep meaning to—"

Dazzled by this pitching king, she stood there feeling foolishly bashful as if facing a stranger instead of the man who had proposed marriage to her.

"You got a real knockout there," one of Leo's fellow players told him, admiring Jessy openly. "A peach!"

"Yeah, I know," Leo said with assurance. He smiled boldly at Jessy.

Blushing, Jessy turned her warm brown eyes toward her brother, out of earshot. He and his boys were talking and laughing with some of the other players. She turned back to Leo, saying, "Adam suggested we see this game. He knows how much I miss you! I was hoping I could see you even for a minute and well, here you are! How are you, really? When are you coming home again? It's been ages."

As he cast around for an answer, they were interrupted again, this time by a breathless beautiful brunette in a long hobble skirt. "Leo, honey, there you are! Great game! Al and Louise said to tell you congratulations! They went on ahead; they're waiting in the car for us. After the way I've been raving about the food, they want to have Chinese at that place you took me to last time, just the two of us, remember?" Realizing she had interrupted, she eyed Jessy cooly. "Who's this, Leo, one of your sisters?"

Shock forced Jessy to clutch her parasol as if it was a life preserver and she was sinking into the deepest, darkest sea. Feeling sick all over, she shut her eyes when Leo's teammates catcalled and whistled at this second female visitor, shouting, "That Crimmy's got girls comin' out his ears!"

Speaking calmly to this newly arrived woman, Leo said of Jessy, "She's a friend of mine. She and her family came all the way from my hometown to see me play."

She. Jessy was a *she* now—a friend, unworthy of being named. As if stirring from a nightmare, Jessy opened her eyes, but the nightmare continued.

"Well, just remember, sweetheart, I'll be waiting for you in the car," the brunette purred. "The closest parking place Al could find was on Wentworth near the greenhouses. Don't take too long now!" Clutching Leo's arm, she asked in her silkiest voice, "Still love me?"

Leo didn't answer. He ignored the brunette, also for the purposes of this strained conversation, a woman without a name and not important enough to be introduced. Once the nameless female left, Leo said, "Jessy, look, she's just a friend! Her parents were neighbors of my mother's years ago, when Mum lived in Chicago. Mum expects me to look up her old friends whenever I'm in town."

"I see," Jessy said, wishing she had seen nothing at all. The blood that had drained from her face returned now in hot suffocating waves. Through the corner of her eye she could see Adam watching her, but he kept a distance. Her throat dry as dust, Jessy managed to say, "She's beautiful, that girl."

"Oh, yeah, I guess so. Look, I can break my date with her and you and I can—I'll take you—you and your brother and his boys—to—I know this town like the back of my—ah—we can—"

"Great game, Leo—I mean, the one you played for the Red Sox." All smiles, Adam intervened while Stephen and Taddy continued visiting with the other big leaguers. As tall and powerful as most of the athletes nearby and, in fact, bigger and broader than most, Adam spoke softly, his voice never rising above a normal tone. No one standing a few feet away could have heard, or guessed, what Adam was saying to Leo: "But as for this other game you're playin', my sister's too good for you. I've been standin' over there thinkin' I oughta knock you flat on your can for hurtin' Jessy like this, but I wouldn't wanna risk gettin' arrested 'n' spendin' the night in jail 'n' lettin' my family down. I'd really like to let you have it." Adam rubbed one fist into his other hand for emphasis but continued smiling, as if talking to his oldest, dearest friend. In a way, Adam was, in the sharing of heartfelt advice when he said, "Let me just tell you this, Leo. Life on the road seems great but the way to hell is wide 'n' loose 'n' easy. I've been around plenty, a girl in every town when I played road shows. You'll stick to the straight 'n' narrow, if you know what's good for you." With that, Adam turned and urged his sons to say their good-byes soon or they would be late to meet Suzanna and Martha and catch their train home.

In an unsteady voice, Leo said, "I wish you wouldn't go so soon, Jessy."

"Why should I stay? I shouldn't have come at all."

"We have to patch things up."

From the dark icy brink of desolation, she answered, "Leo, I've had to do with many patched-up things in my life. I've been poor, destitute, homeless, orphaned. I haven't had it all nice and new like you, but a patched-up relationship? It's just too much to ask! How long could you be true?"

Annoyed, he said, "You're making too much of this!"

"That beautiful girl had the idea you love her!" Jessy was quick to remind him. "How could she think that unless you told her you did?" That Leo remained silent left her to think the worst. "You reached one of your three goals—making it to the majors. I hope you pitch a no-hitter, too, lots and lots of them. But I can't see how you'll reach your third goal. I couldn't marry a man who was unfaithful."

"Listen," Leo began, sounding irked, "don't you think I know how tough it's been for you or how hard farm work is?" Leo paused to sign autographs for the children, Stephen and Taddy included. They looked up at him with bright starry eyes. "Listen, Jessy, I can make life easy for you if you stick by me." When she turned away, he drew her aside from the crowd, saying in a low voice, his lips close to her face now in profile to him, "Sweetheart, if my pitching arm holds up I'll be able to afford anything you want. You'll never have to work again. When you're my wife, you can have everything you ever wanted—*everything!*"

Fighting the tremors he always excited within her, the perilous longing she felt for Leo, Jessy remained fixed in reality and maneuvered out of his grasp. She faced him to ask, "What possible good would it be for our marriage if I had 'everything' without what's really important? If I had 'everything' but you?"

Now it was Leo who turned away. "My father's cheated on my mother for years, ever since I can remember. Right in this town, as a matter of fact. It's no big deal."

"It's dreadful! The pain it must have caused your mother, the harm it's done to your whole family!" Keeping her voice down, Jessy pleaded, "Leo, you're probably the most desirable man I'll ever know, but I couldn't share you as your mother shares your father."

Angrily, Leo snapped, "You're old-fashioned, that's the problem with you! In some ways that's okay, but this isn't the Dark Ages, Jessy! Look around!" The impressive Chicago skyline loomed in the distance. "In case you hadn't noticed, it's the twentieth century."

Sadly, Jessy said, "Then we're in for a rough century if your ways are a taste of what's to come." Anxious as she was to leave, still she was struck by that awesome skyline in relation to the churches near the ballpark. In her mind's eye she saw those mighty skyscrapers—monuments to commercial, managerial, and marketing prowess—superimposed with her poignant dream of the struggling, suffering Christ bearing His cross. Envisioning that dreamscape now more strongly than ever, Jessy murmured to Leo: "Strange, isn't it, how churches used to tower over all, and now they stand in the shadows, in the darkness man builds up all around them."

"Why argue with success?" Leo said with annoyance.

Jessy turned to her happy nephews. Stephen and Taddy, with their golden hair and clear green eyes so innocent of the world, waited for their Aunty to finish speaking to the real live ballplayer who had just won a game against the famed White Sox on their home turf. "Success has its price, Leo. Remember that God looks down on you and children look up to you."

"So?"

"Don't confuse success with the joy and peace that come only from God. Now I must go! The next time you visit Bethel, please come for your ring. It's been collecting dust all these months."

"I just finished paying for it!" In a pained voice, Leo pleaded with her, "It's a symbol of my love for you."

"To me it represents your unwillingness to tell your mother or your other girlfriends about us." Seeing the hurt in his face, the peacemaker in Jessy was moved to say, "Oh, Leo, our relationship is at a dead end, can't you see? That ring will never mean anything without your commitment!"

Red Sox players readied to leave the park for their hotel. One tow-haired Adonis with permanent laugh lines etched around his merry blue eyes shouted, "Hey, Crimmy, don't stay out too late with the girls! We gotta catch a train for the game in St. Louis tomorrow, remember!" When the cheerful player tipped his hat to Jessy, a crucifix gleamed at his throat.

Acknowledging his courtesy with a polite nod, Jessy watched him and the others, a boisterous, handsome band of successful young men on top of the world. To Leo she said, "I wish you well, but I fear for your soul. Good-bye."

"When I get a minute I'll write to you. We'll get this behind us and—"

"Uh-oh! Crimmy's got girl troubles! Again!" Leo's teammates exploded with hearty laughter.

Adam swept Jessy and his sons away. She went blindly, burning with humiliation for herself and Leo. The derisive laughter of his teammates echoed in the nearly deserted South Side Park. Two hours before—just two little hours—on her way to the game, Jessy had seen lovely churches and a festive wedding party. What high hopes she had had! Now from the open streetcar she saw a grimmer reality: the stockyards, where countless animals waited, without knowing, for slaughter. Odors emanating from the pens reeked in the air, carried far by the now whipping wind. Men on horseback herded animals to their doom. In the processing plants adjoining the pens, animals were being steamed, pickled, salted, and canned. Whatever couldn't be eaten of them would be made into something, be it lard, soap, cushion stuffing, fertilizer, or glue. From myriad smokestacks a stinking cloud of death rose up to obliterate the grand skyline a mile away, including the spot where Leo would assure a Chicago beauty that, yes, of course he still loved her.

"This is where we get off, boys and girl!" a familiar voice boomed. As if in a dream, Jessy heard Adam speak but she felt too leaden to move. She didn't see the one big work-roughened hand reaching out to her.

Gentle as dew, Adam patted the side of her face. "Come on," he whispered.

Jessy finally roused, embarrassed to see him and half the passengers on the streetcar looking at her. As Adam helped her off the running board and to the busy sidewalk, all the while keeping his boys in tow amid the throng, he said with mocking humor so only she could hear him, "More like 'crummy' than 'Crimmy' if you ask me!"

For a brief moment her mood lifted. Adam took her hand and Taddy's while she reached automatically for Stephen's. As they walked, Adam and the boys discussed the wondrous tall buildings of downtown Chicago, but she retreated once again to her mental haze all the way back to the department store where Suzanna and Martha were waiting, laden with bundles and bursting with details about their shopping expedition. Blindly Jessy went to the railroad station, seeing and hearing little until the family was nearly home in Bethel.

On the train Jessy couldn't stop thinking of the Bible story Jesus told about seeds that fell on stony, thorny places. When the sun came up, some seed was scorched because it had no root. Other seed that had sprouted among thorns of deceitful riches and lusts of other things became unfruitful. Leo began attending church because of her. He even became a member, much to her delight. But what did he believe? He was seed fallen where it could not thrive.

Before the train stopped at Bethel, Stephen, seated next to Jessy, said something to her, but she had been so deep in thought she had to ask him, with her apologies, to repeat himself.

With his cupid's-bow lips and dimples and bright green eyes, the very image of his handsome father, Stephen repeated, "Aunt Jessy, I said that someday when I'm a famous ballplayer like Leo, I'll travel just like him but no matter where I go, I'll always love you."

The dam burst. Sobbing, Jessy held the boy tight, begging him to be good and decent when he grew up. "That would make me gladdest of all, Stephen, for you to be a fine gentleman and a strong Christian."

"But Aunty!" Stephen answered, pouting, "I'd rather be a ballplayer!"

CHAPTER 24

❦

Now her phone rang incessantly. As soon as Jessy returned from Chicago late that Saturday afternoon, a long-distance call came through—Leo shouting his apologies and swearing his eternal devotion over the din at the Chinese restaurant. Jessy listened patiently, thinking and praying all the while, with the children staring and snickering at her, ignoring Suzanna who demanded they leave their aunt alone.

"You're crazy to have anythin' to do with that heel!" shouted Adam. "Hang up that phone!" When Jessy didn't, he roared up to her.

"Adam, please say you're sorry!"

"All right! I'm sorry I didn't knock Leo flat when I had the chance!" Leading with his powerful square chin, Adam shouted defiantly, "Go on and tell the big league big shot that, why doncha? Tell him I oughta—"

"Adam, is this any way for a Christian to behave?" Jessy wailed, covering the mouthpiece and trying in vain to keep their argument from being overheard in Chicago, and all over Bethel via the party line.

At this reminder of his high calling, Adam said in softer, kinder tones, "Well, I should've socked him! The nerve of that guy! Gimme that phone!"

"Adam, stop it!" Jessy gave her brother a shove, but her mightiest effort was futile. Just then the cuckoo clock announced, in a louder volume than ever before, that it was eighteen past eighteen.

"One of these days, somebody—anybody—remind me to shoot that thing!" yelled Adam to no one in particular.

"Adam, sweetheart!" came Suzanna's dulcet tones. "I need you!"

Growling, Adam stomped off but still the children gaped at Jessy, the woman who knew the man who won the baseball game singlehandedly, or so they thought. Ever hopeful, Jessy asked, "Don't you three have homework?"

They shook their heads. "Mama made us do it Friday," Taddy explained.

"Jessy?" Leo was still apologizing, backed up by a chorus of Chinese waiters from the restaurant din Jessy could hear coming over the line.

"Yes, Leo, I'm still here—ah, Stephen? Taddy? Martha? Don't you have a Sunday school lesson to do for tomorrow?"

"No, Aunty. We did that Friday too," said Martha.

"Children! Go upstairs and wash your faces and hands for dinner!" shouted Suzanna from the kitchen.

Once the children had trooped up the stairs, Jessy said, "Yes, Leo, what is it you were saying? Hello? Hello! Operator? We were cut off!"

Leo's calls continued on Sunday and for the following four days while the Red Sox battled St. Louis. On the following Friday afternoon Leo drove up, unannounced and unexpected, after a Red Sox game against the Detroit Tigers. He sat on Jessy's porch waiting to talk to her.

"You're as cuckoo as that clock of Suzanna's if you see Leo anymore!" Adam warned Jessy in the downstairs hall.

Jessy, inwardly dying to see Leo, answered, "I can hardly turn him away."

"I can!"

"Adam, please! Maybe we can straighten things out."

"Not with a guy like that! Besides, you got work to do. Tell him."

"Yes, sir."

"And tell him you ain't wastin' yourself on no two-timer."

"Yes, Adam."

"And—" Adam paused when he saw Jessy begin putting on her hat. "Just where do you think you're goin'?"

Wistfully Jessy eyed her brother's reflection in the hall mirror. "With Leo, of course."

"Oh, no, you don't!" Adam spun around and headed outside, roaring, "Leo, you 'n' my sister ain't goin' no place, understand! No more of them long rides with you to who knows where! Jessy ain't that kind of girl!"

Panicking, Jessy quickly hung her hat on the hall tree and went to the front door which Adam had slammed shut behind him. She could barely hear Leo's voice but could hardly miss Adam's booming bass. She almost got flattened behind the door when Adam flung it open and stormed inside. Jessy's haggard, fretful appearance didn't improve his disposition. "You listen to me," he said, clutching Jessy's upper arm for emphasis, "if you talk to Leo at all, which is pure stupidity, go no further with him than our front porch, you hear me?"

"Yes, sir."

"And we got work to do."

"Yes, sir, I know." Jessy looked down at her hard-worn hands, which she held together in one tight mass against her long, faded denim skirt.

Letting go of her arm, Adam fumed, "I'm tryin' to help you. I hope you know that."

"Yes, of course, I know," she said in her most fragile voice, glancing up. His blazing eyes calmed in her compassionate gaze. "I love you."

"I love you, too, 'n' I don't wanna see you get hurt."

Wordlessly she sniffled her appreciation. As he was about to go off, she said sweetly, "Thank you, Adam, for not punching Leo in the nose."

Adam grrumphed off, his Christian principles battling mightily with the warrior in his bones. Jessy took a deep breath before stepping outside.

Leo stood and removed his hat when he saw her. He looked leaner, stronger, better than ever, with his smooth olive skin, brilliant blue eyes, and dazzling smile. His suit was new and rich, his shoes of soft good leather, his cravat rich but not gaudy. Once she had nodded hello and had taken her seat, he sat down again and handed her a golden box of Belgian chocolates tied with red silk ribbons.

"How lovely, Leo. Thank you."

Although she opened the box and offered him first choice, neither of them tasted the treasures within, nor did they speak for a long while. Instead, they sat together, gazing across Jessy's front yard to the unpaved road, the cemetery, and the railroad tracks. Filling much of their vision was an unkempt field of billowing yellow grasses, Queen Anne's lace, and wildflowers. Bees murmured about under the hot sun, searching for pollen among Suzanna's flower beds lining the walkway to the house.

Still gazing at the landscape, Jessy spoke first. "My brother thinks I'm crazy to see you."

"Oh, yes, I know all about what he thinks. He told me flat out." In a sweat, Leo ran his index finger between his starched white shirt collar and his neck. "The question is, what do you think?"

"That Satan wants nothing better than for us to do things he claims will make us happy—things that can only bring our downfall."

"You didn't answer my question," Leo said.

"I'm trying to!" Jessy turned to him at last, saying softly, "I'm one in a long line of conquests for you, and nothing more. You don't know me."

"I love you! Don't you have any confidence in me?"

"You have an overabundance of confidence and an underabundance of values. You think more about home runs than running a home!"

Leo eyed the big Victorian house Jessy shared with her once-riotous brother. "I bet Adam cheats on Suzy all the time. And vice versa."

"Neither of them cheats! Regardless, I wouldn't live my life in accordance with the foolish things I think other people might be doing. Wrong behavior in others doesn't require or excuse wrong behavior in ourselves."

"I love you, but I'm a free man. I was born free and I'll die free."

"Doing what you like isn't true freedom, Leo. Freedom carries with it responsibilities: honor and a clear conscience. Honoring God and submitting to His will."

Leo stiffened at this, saying, "I'll *never* submit."

Jessy's eyes washed over Leo, taking in his grand good looks and wonderful face that exuded the fire and mystery of distant Crimea. "The Lord offers us two choices—to follow Him or go our own way—but there's only one proper, sensible choice, Leo. If you won't submit to God, there's no hope for you. Or for our love."

"I'll be a good husband to you, Jessy, a good provider. You'll never lack for anything, I promise you."

She shook her head. "How little you understand me, Leo. I don't long for things, although things make life convenient in some ways. If I marry, what I would want more than things is a loving, faithful husband who believes in God."

Leo snapped his fingers. "That's it! You're angry because I don't go to church any more."

"I've been wanting to ask why you began attending church."

"To make you happy. Why else?"

Jessy bit her lower lip before saying, "That's not much of a reason."

"I didn't get anything out of church and it took too much of my time.

I'm busy." Leo shrugged his shoulders as if the matter was settled now and forever.

"We don't go to church to please each other, or to 'get something out of it,' but rather to please the Lord and give Him the praise He deserves and to have communion with other believers. We are blessed through serving and worshiping God. Surely, with every good thing He gives, and the fact that He sent His Son to die for us, we all have time for the Lord."

Leo folded his arms across his chest. "I'm on the road too much. I don't have the time for church."

"You have time for socializing," she reminded him, thinking of his brunette in Chicago, and all the Als and Louises there must be in Leo's life.

"I don't go out much," Leo said in his own defense.

"Last week your teammates gave me a very different impression."

"I'm under a lot of pressure. Between games I need time to relax."

"I see." Jessy reached into her skirt pocket, then held out the velvet box containing the ring he had given her months ago. "Here."

Leo wouldn't take it back. "I want you to have good things."

"*Things* again! Have you ever thanked God for your success? Your health and talent? Your nimble mind? You have much to praise God for."

"I made it to the majors on my own ability. I wanted to get away from here." He waved at the dusty road, the cemetery, and fallow land before them. "There was nothing here for me and it's the same for you. If you don't marry me you'll end up stuck here in Bethel for the rest of your life, an old maid. A dried-up spinsterish old maid!"

Undaunted, Jessy answered, "I'll be what God wants me to be. If I'm to remain single, fine. If I'm to marry, that would also be fine. I'd become a pilgrim and walk thousands of miles barefoot if He asked me." She glanced to the table beside them, at the morning newspaper filled with bad news. "If I looked only at circumstances, I would despair. But when I look up to God, everything good is possible. It was the same for people thousands of years ago as it is today. True happiness doesn't depend on the world or its riches and entertainments but rather upon our relationship to God."

"Maybe for you, that's true," Leo answered, "though I don't see how you could be happy cooped up in Bethel with nothing to do but work and pray. Me, I'm happy the way I am, doing what I like."

"We can choose to live in the light or stumble in the darkness."

"Don't worry about me. I know what I'm doing."

"Then pray with me now! Worship with me on Sunday!"

"Can't. Got a train to catch at three and a four-game series starting in Philly tomorrow. I came here hoping we could work things out."

"I want to so very much." Just then, a railroad crew came along, mowing down the tall grass on each side of the tracks across the road. Jessy asked, with her eyes on the mowing crew, "What do you see in our future, Leo?"

He closed his eyes and smiled with utter contentment. "A big wedding for you—because women like them—and then off to a big house in Boston with servants to tend the place. Maybe a second house on the Cape—you like the beach. And nice cars."

"And then?" Jessy asked.

"Me making twelve or fifteen grand a year—at least—for a good ten years, and making investments that pay big dividends. I've been playing the stock market for trends that could pay well. We ballplayers hear good tips in sports bars."

"And then?" Jessy asked.

"Well, whatever you like. Visit Europe? I think you'd like that!"

"And then?"

He shrugged. "Kids."

"And then?"

Frowning, Leo stared at her. "What else could you possibly want?"

"Haven't you forgotten Someone?"

"Who are you talking about?"

"Let me ask you, Leo: what happens after you acquire all you want?"

"Then I retire."

"And then?"

Leo didn't want to answer. His contentment faded with the picture in his mind of aged Leo Kimball, worn and frail, his black brows turned ashen, his strong build shriveled and weak, his pulse feeble, his step uncertain—for indeed, what waited for him was an empty casket. "I know what you're trying to get me to say and I won't say it. Why, the idea is ghoulish, Jessy!"

"Life is best planned knowing we're all headed to eternity. It's best now to think of the end of our lives, to know all along that God is waiting for us, and to plan to live lives that are pleasing to Him."

He sighed impatiently, "I don't think like you."

"I know. That's why it's so hard for us to work things out. Even if we did, Adam doesn't approve of my marrying you, not after what happened last week at the ballpark. He's talked of nothing else since. He wasn't happy about me even seeing you out here on the porch!"

"We don't have to have a big wedding. We could elope."

Jessy nodded. "I suppose we could, but I wouldn't want to hurt Adam by doing that."

"If you loved me, you wouldn't care what your brother thought."

"If you loved me, you *would* care what my brother thought, and our heavenly Father." After a moment, Jessy said, "You might as well know, Leo, that ever since last Labor Day, I've been concerned about how I could ever fit in with your family." She sighed heavily. "There's so much unhappiness." All at once she covered her face with her hands, trying to wipe away her own agonized childhood, the pain her parents caused each other. "I couldn't deliberately walk into more family strife after all that's happened to me."

Leo leaned close. "We wouldn't live here. I told you long ago I don't expect you to befriend my family." Leo sat at the edge of his chair, whispering, "I'll tell my folks about the ring on my next visit, when I have more time." Leo ran one hand through his thick, waving hair. "I'll tell Mum about us. I promise. And everything will be fine. You'll see." Leo pulled out his pocket watch. "Two-thirty already! I've got a train to catch. Will you write to me?"

Jessy nodded. "And I'll pray for you, as I always do."

"Suit yourself! I love you, you know. Do you love me?"

Jessy nodded again, her coltish brown eyes smiling at him. She really did love Leo! He turned to go, making a striking figure as he rushed to his car. How handsome he was. Perhaps there was hope for them yet, she thought, for he did say he loved her and he did sound sincere.

Still, Jessy wondered why she didn't feel cherished. In his eyes she was a one-of-a-kind trophy, not a woman with hidden depths and powerful convictions. He proposed the second time they met. How brash he'd always been! That sultry summer day during threshing she was so surprised and flustered just thinking of how he had looked at her that she chipped Suzanna's best serving dish. He stirred up charges in her that crackled like summer heat before the storm.

He hardly knew her, but how well she knew him. Even before Leo's footsteps faded down the gravel walk, she prayed with all her might that he would choose wisely to follow Christ. That one, genuine, heartfelt step of faith would go miles toward clearing their differences and establishing the best possible foundation for their marriage. Would Leo turn to Christ, not for Jessy's sake, but for his own?

Off Leo went in his fabulous car, the Simplex convertible that only Leo drove, and only when he was in Bethel. His tires stirred up dust as he sped off. Across the way, the railroad men were still mowing grass in the hot sun. They were far along now, nearly past the cemetery.

One lone cloud blotted out the sun. A chill shivered through her. Jessy's heart pounded the psalm proclaiming *they are like grass which is cut down, their secret sins consumed by His anger, they who fail to number their days and apply their hearts to wisdom*. Sick with fear, she who feared nothing but God, Jessy sensed she might never see Leo again.

CHAPTER 25

❧

Afew days after Leo's visit, a letter from Emma arrived. "Dearest Jessy," she began, still at the convent,

Soon I'll come home to Bethel, but not Mum and Daddy's house. Grandpa Roy and Grama Flo will let me stay with them until I know what to do with my life, my strange new life. After much prayer, I must tell you something, Jessy. I can't stop thinking about my baby's father. Now that Belinda has gone to her new home, I can hardly bear to think of her without crying. Whatever happens, I don't want to have anything to do with her father ever again. I only tell you, Jessy, that Burl Everett and I did what should never be done, and it's my fault—all mine! There's a line we studied in school from Shakespeare. It was Hamlet, I think, who said to his lover, "Be all my sins remembered." I have sinned, Jessy, and I've paid dearly. I just don't want any trouble with Burl when I come back. I can't contact him because I don't want Laura to find out. She must never know. I love Laura! I must have been crazy to hurt her the way I did, going after her husband. She was my idol—another sin of mine, having idols. I can't trust this mission to anyone but you, Jessy. Would you and Adam talk to Burl before I come back, to clear the way?

There was more to the letter, but Jessy felt too sick to read any further just then. She sank down into the nearest chair. Martha spotted Jessy first, looking ashen. She immediately called for Adam who took the crumpled letter from Jessy's hand and read it. Once he sent his young daughter out of hearing, Adam said, "Another louse! Two in one family. I'll go talk to Burl."

"I'm coming with you," Jessy said, feeling suddenly stronger. She took the letter from him and hid it in the folds of her skirt.

"I'll talk to Burl alone, man to man."

"Emma's my friend. And I know Burl, don't forget, and his wife."

"And don't forget Burl's big shot big league brother-in-law," snorted Adam. Towering over her, Adam noticed the look of resolve on his sister's face and said, "Well, come on, then. Hope you have a strong stomach."

Off they went in the family car to the train station, but Burl had already left work for the day so they drove on to a small, square two-story building at the far end of Main Street. Burl and Laura lived on the second floor above a vacant store shaded by a green-and-white-striped awning and fringed with bushes so overgrown they obscured the shop windows. Before Adam banged on the door that led into the stairway to the second-floor flat, he said to Jessy, "Wouldn't you rather wait in the car?"

"No, I wouldn't." Jessy looked straight ahead, through the glass pane of the door, to the empty stairway. "I'll be fine, really I will." While waiting for Burl to come to the door, she noticed, on each side of the entry, flowerpots with no flowers, just dry soil, and planters along the walkway with the stiff, brittle remains of plants.

Adam knocked again In mid-bang, the door knocker loosened so much it dangled from a lone rusty screw. "Regular handyman, that Burl!" sneered Adam.

"Burl does work long hours at the station," Jessy said in his defense.

"He's got time enough for trouble. Otherwise, we wouldn't be standin' here knockin' on his broken knocker!" snapped Adam. Despite his annoyance, Adam dug through his overall pockets for a screwdriver and attempted to reattach the knocker. The screw was so rusty it crumbled when Adam pressed it between his work-toughened fingers.

Just then Burl, barefooted, his suspenders pulled up over his sleeveless undershirt, came padding down the steps. "Well, hello, folks!" he said cheerily. "I was just finishing a can of beans. What brings you two here? Jessy, if you're looking for Laura, she's out of town again. She'll be back Thursday."

"It's you we're here to see, Burl. May we come in?"

"Sure you can!" Burl looked puzzled but he padded back up the stairs, with Jessy and Adam following behind him. "Don't mind the mess."

Jessy wanted to cry just being there, but remained quiet, prayerful, sick at heart. The place was small and dimly lit. It was furnished with a few choice wedding presents from Walter and Acacia Kimball but things were in general disarray and everything needed a thorough cleaning. There was a tiny kitchenette with a table and chairs, and a few side rooms, all shuttered and cool in the rapidly approaching evening. Burl hastily put on a shirt and cleared the table. He looked at them with those dreamy, sultry dark eyes of his, drinking both of them in, but his voice was friendly. "I just got off work. Sorry for the mess." He brushed crumbs from the oilcloth table cover. Adam and Jessy stood near the table, watching him in silence. "Please. Sit down. Here, if you like, or there—" He gestured to the parlor chairs heaped with papers and laundry.

"Here's fine," Adam said, sitting at the table.

Jessy sat with him, the letter still hidden in her pocket.

"It's about Emma," began Adam bluntly. "She's comin' home soon and she don't want no trouble from you."

"She's all right, isn't she?" Burl asked, looking terribly worried at the mere mention of her name. "I heard she had the baby. It's all been hush-hush, but I heard she wrote to Acacia. Laura told me Emma was all right."

Jessy stammered, "Em-Emma's all right, Burl, as far as her medical situation, but she's upset. She only just wrote naming you as the—and she doesn't want to see you ever again, that's all."

"Thank God!" Burl sighed in relief. "I thought she'd have me arrested! I've been worried sick! You don't know what I've been through."

"What *you've* been through? What about Emma? She nearly died!" Letting Burl mull over that thought for a moment, Jessy looked around his place, wondering why Laura didn't spend more time with her own husband in their own home. It looked untended, unloved without her, and her husband looked so lonely, so empty, and forlorn. "Are you always alone like this, Burl?"

He nodded miserably. "Laura's never here anymore and when she is all we do is argue." Looking chagrined, he asked, "It was a girl, wasn't it?"

Sick at heart of yet another reference to *it*, Jessy said with emphasis, "*Belinda* is a perfect, healthy little girl. She weighed more than six pounds when she was born!" From her pocket Jessy retrieved a tiny sepia photograph. "See? She was just a half-day old then! Isn't she beautiful?"

Burl took the picture carefully, as if it were made of metal more precious than gold. "Oh, my, yes, she's so—aw!" Burl had to pause to gain control of his emotions. For a long time he stared at the picture, his thoughts racing too fast for speech, his eyes streaming. Then he wiped his face with the back of one hand and said, "Laura wanted to adopt Emma's baby, but I said no. Just the thought of—" Burl looked again at the picture of his daughter born of adultery and living with strangers on the other side of the continent. "I wish now I had listened to Laura. Maybe our taking in this baby would improve things for us."

As he spoke, Adam unfolded and refolded his long legs and uncrossed and recrossed his arms against his chest. "Burl, I doubt that takin' in your girlfriend's baby would do much for your marriage!"

Burl laughed at himself. "It was a crazy idea, I know, but this is my kid! Gee, she's sweet." Burl's own chin curled like his baby's in the picture. "Laura doesn't know I'm the fath—say, you're not here to—"

"We won't tell Laura or anyone else," Jessy assured him. "And neither will Emma."

Burl nodded to show he had heard, but he couldn't take his eyes from his baby. Gazing at her picture, he asked, "She went to a good home, I hope?"

"Yes, Burl, we think so," Jessy answered. "We pray Belinda will be in good hands all her life."

"Good. I'm glad Emma didn't have an abortion. She told me she would, if she got pregnant, and frankly, I didn't care, not then. But later—"

Adam was in no mood to listen patiently. He took the photo away from Burl and snapped, "Just what in blazes were you doin' with a fifteen-year-old kid? I ought to wring your neck!"

Burl, about two-thirds the size of Adam, looked alarmed. "I-ah, now listen, the two of you." He took both of them within his glance. "There's two sides to every story. I don't know what Emma told you, but at least hear my side of it before you make snap judgments!"

Grudgingly, Adam nodded, but the look on his face meant business.

Burl took a moment, trying to collect himself, and then began. "Kids come to the railroad station all the time after school. It's fun for them to see the trains coming and going. They like the switching station and all, you know. Around September some time, I think it was, right after Labor Day, Emma began coming by."

Jessy immediately thought of that Labor Day she went to the train station with Leo and Emma, and how Emma lingered with Burl, waiting for the railroad employee to come and relieve him so they could go to the Kimball cookout. Jessy pictured the train station vividly: the passenger waiting room, the ticket window, the big clock, the private office where Burl did his paperwork—the office Jessy had seen from the waiting room but had never entered.

Burl continued: "I asked Emma how she was doing and she would always say she hated school. Every afternoon about four she'd come by. I'd ask her why she wasn't home studying and she'd just shrug. She'd show off all the time, looking at me over her shoulder. Every day she'd come by. It got so she knew my work schedule. She'd linger after the other kids went off. She'd wander up and down the tracks. Aimless, you know, anyone could see that. She'd come by on Saturdays, too, on that red bicycle of hers.

"It was October—I'll never forget—a beautiful day. I'd been busy my whole shift and half another employee's too. I was shorthanded and had to work the ticket window alone. Well, finally, the four-ten left. For the first time that day, I had a breather. Things quieted down and I headed for my office. I thought it was odd the door was closed. I usually leave it ajar. I walked in and there was Emma, sitting on my cot. The train master has a cot for bad weather, when we can't get home or get a replacement. Anyway, I demanded that she leave at once. 'Don't you like me, Burl?' she asked. 'Everyone either ignores me or makes fun of me. Everyone but you.'"

Ten months later, Burl was still in a sweat at the thought. "I told her I was going out for some air and when I came back she'd better be gone. Emma had left all right, but she came here to my place! She knew Laura was out of town for a week and that we hid a spare house key under one of those flowerpots outside the door. That reckless kid!"

Burl looked thoroughly ashamed. "I didn't make her leave and I've paid the price ever since. I figured sooner or later I'd go to prison, her being a minor, but what's the difference? I'm living in prison now!" Burl looked ashamed but relieved to have confessed his wrongdoings. "I'm glad Emma's all right. Will you tell her that? And tell her—"

So. Burl wasn't a heartless brute. He was one of the few in the family who truly liked Emma, but their relationship would be forever tainted with this tragedy of their own making.

Adam snapped, "A man's supposed to control himself or he ends up bein' controlled by his weaknesses, whatever they are—sex, liquor, power, money. You'd better stay straight from here on out or you'll answer to me personally. I got a daughter to raise, and a wife and sister too. And stay away from Emma."

"She was dying for attention. That's why she came to me," said Burl.

Adam snapped, "That don't excuse you from what you did."

Jessy intervened. "You gave Emma the wrong kind of attention and you know it!"

"Don't you think I haven't paid for my sins? I live with them every day, every hour," Burl admitted. "My folks raised me right, you know. I don't know where I went wrong. Nights here alone I try thinking of where things soured for me, and why. I just don't know." He shook his head in frustration.

Jessy remembered hearing Nathan tell of the advice he gave his students about living with the consequences of their actions. It was clear that Burl and Emma would have tremendous problems in that regard.

"When Emma comes home, we want you two to keep away from each other," warned Adam. "That's all Jessy 'n' me came to say."

"You can count on me," said Burl, offering to shake Adam's hand. "I don't want any more trouble." To Jessy he said, "If Emma cares to hear it, tell her the baby's beautiful. I'm thankful she let her—our daughter—be born. I only wish—oh, just tell her I'm sorry. That first day she came on to me I wish I'd have dragged her to her house instead of doing what I did and I've been sorry as I can be."

Jessy stared at Burl for a time, thinking of Emma's house, of the unfaithful Walter and unhappy Acacia, of Laura's and Darlene's woes, of Leo and his liaisons, and Peter, shut up for life in an institution. Without revealing all she knew of the Kimballs, Jessy wondered what good it would have done if Burl had succeeded in returning Emma to a place with so little love or guidance and so much unhappiness. "If it's any consolation, Burl," said Jessy kindly, "Emma is sorry she interfered with your marriage. She regrets what happened as much as you do, and she's sorry she hurt Laura."

"She is?" Burl looked penitent as a child.

Now even Adam softened a little. "Maybe there's a way you 'n' Laura can make up. Start out fresh. It won't be easy, not after all that's happened, but if you love your wife—"

"I do, but—" Burl shook his head hopelessly. "My love's not enough for Laura."

"But Laura thinks you don't love her!" Jessy said.

"Burl, it's your business to show your wife you care!" Adam said. "Take care of this place. Fix it up! Pull yourself together and take an interest in your wife! Laura might stick around if she knows you love her."

"She wants a baby, Burl. She told me she did, not that having babies is a cure for troubled marriages," Jessy said. "No matter what, though, Laura needs to know you love her."

Burl laughed without mirth, saying, "It would take a miracle to save our marriage."

For the first time, Jessy could smile. "Then believe in miracles," she said joyously. "Trust God! He can do anything, you know, anything!"

"He don't know Laura!" Burl snorted.

The look on Jessy's face said, *Oh, yes, He does.*

CHAPTER 26

❦

"**W**hen will you be done?" wailed Suzanna over the din of hammering in her upstairs hall that late June afternoon.

"I don't know, sweetheart!" Adam yelled merrily as he pounded a hole through the wall. "Will you hand me that level?"

Suzanna hunted through his tools, all the while ducking out of the way of Kem Curtis who was trying to climb the stairs with a ladder. Once Kem reached the second-floor landing, Suzanna cried, "Supper will be ready soon!"

"What?" Adam shouted, still pounding away.

"Supper!"

"You'll love having electricity, Mrs. Flint!" shouted Kem over the din.

"I'm sure I will, Mr. Curtis!" Suzanna pealed in return.

Jessy appeared from her bedroom with a pencil over one ear and a book and notepad in hand. Over the hammering she shouted, "Math isn't easy with all this noise!"

"Daddy, the tire's gone flat!" Taddy stood in the downstairs hall, looking up.

Adam stopped cold. "Have you been foolin' with the car again, son?"

"No, sir."

"Well?" Adam towered over his boy. "What tire?"

"For the bicycle, Daddy."

"Oh." Adam resumed hammering, but more thoughtfully. "Sorry, Tad. Can't fix it right now. After dinner I will."

"Ask Gina to help you," Kem suggested. "She helped me fix up an old bicycle the neighbors gave us."

"Okay, Mr. Curtis," said Taddy. He ran off, shouting for Gina.

In her lilting voice, Suzanna, still standing in the middle of her torn-up stairway, asked, "So, dear, should I plan for dinner at seven?"

257

"What?" shouted Adam. He gave his wife an enthusiastic wink but never ceased making a racket.

Jessy's head began to throb from doing homework in such noise. She watched Kem and Adam happily tearing out walls to install electric wiring. Suzanna drifted off, still wondering when the six Flints and Kem Curtis with his five children might be able to sit down to their evening meal together. Meanwhile, Kem and Adam went up into the attic pulling a trail of wiring behind them. It was then a familiar face appeared at the front door.

Jessy peered down the stairs, not entirely sure she was seeing clearly, but then she put aside her homework and flew down the stairs, lightly skirting the wires and tools Adam had scattered about the steps. "Emma!" she cried, not taking her eyes off the bright blue shadow she could see through the curtain across the glass in the front door. "Is it really you?" She flung the door wide and rushed forward.

"Hi!" shouted Emma. The two girls hugged a long while.

"Look who's here!" Jessy cried loud enough through the open door so the whole household could hear, but Adam and Kem were making so much noise in the attic no one heard her. Jessy, flushed with excitement, turned back to Emma. "Oh, my, but you look well! I'm so glad! Did you just get in?"

"Uh-huh. My grandparents met me at the station." The mere mention of the Bethel train station had an immediate and sobering effect on Emma. She whispered, "Burl was there, behaving really nice, but he didn't say much except 'welcome home.' He tipped his hat to me and made sure the porters helped me with my luggage."

"Good!" Squeezing Emma's hand, Jessy answered in confidence, "Burl doesn't want trouble. Laura doesn't know about you two, but she's suspicious about her husband. Please promise me from now on you'll respect their marriage."

Emma nodded vigorously. "I've learned my lesson, believe me. I'll never see Burl—or any married man—ever again, I promise you."

"Good! We must respect everyone's marriage vows as Scripture teaches: 'Let the marriage bed be undefiled.' Oh, my, but it's great having you back!" Hugging Emma, Jessy radiated confidence. "From now on life should go better for you if you've become the prudent girl I think you have." Jessy drew back a bit to see Emma's face.

Looking contrite, Emma whispered, "I'm not the person I was a year ago, I know that for sure. I'll never act wild again! I've got some good news for you. I've become a Christian! When the priest came to baptize Belinda at the convent hospital, I asked him if he would baptize me too. Oh, how I miss that child!" She paused, her face wet with tears. "My dear friend Jessy, the best friend I've ever had! How can I ever thank you and your family and friends for going to so much trouble for me? Last year I was so out of control I didn't have the sense to be ashamed. Sister Margaret said Jesus took my shame on Himself! Well, I just had to thank you for everything, for putting up with me all this time. You, and your family, and the Ballys, and the Fishers! They send their love, they said to tell you, all of the Ballys and Dr. and Mrs. Fisher. They saw me off at the train when I left Garden Springs."

"I'm so glad you're home! How are you? You look positively beautiful!" Jessy saw how really lovely Emma had become, but she could also see that her friend was, beneath her shimmering façade, torn by conflicting emotions. Jessy said with assurance, "Now that you're a Christian, you can rejoice deep in your inmost heart! The past is over."

"Thank God! Oh, Jessy!" Again, tears overwhelmed Emma.

"It's time for the beautiful new you to shine!" Jessy said brightly. "Oh, look at us standing out here on the porch. Please come in!" Seeing three sacks brimming with wrapped packages but no suitcases or trunks, Jessy asked, "Where's your luggage?"

"At my grandparents' farm. I'll be staying there indefinitely. Mum and I don't get along well—we never have. She thinks I've been 'duped' into Christianity. She just doesn't understand at all. I don't know how to make her see. Maybe someday." Emma gathered up the sacks and came inside, looking hesitant with all the noise being made above the ceiling. In a moment Adam and Kem trooped down from the attic and appeared on the second-floor landing.

"We're getting central heating and electricity," Jessy explained to Emma. Calling to Adam and Kem, Jessy said, "Look who's here!"

"Hey, there, Emma Kimball!" shouted Adam. "Welcome back!"

"Thank you. Hello!" Emma greeted the children, Adam's and Kem's, as they raced through the hall playing Ship, with Stephen as captain. "I've brought you presents, one for each of you!" Emma glowed at the sight of them all, but then frowned. "Only seven?" she asked after counting them as they waved to her and zipped past. "I thought there were eight children to buy gifts for."

With her index fingers to her lips, Jessy led Emma into the parlor where Kem's youngest child lay napping on the sofa, barricaded by pillows and oblivious to the noise. Emma leaned close to the girl she had first seen the previous December.

Jessy stood at the parlor entryway, smiling at the picture they made, Emma and Dana, two comparative strangers looking for all the world like mother and daughter. Kem came along wiping attic dust from his hands onto a rag. "Is Dana fussing again? She's had a cold."

Emma leaned over to touch the child's forehead. "She isn't feverish."

"No," he said, smiling, "she's over the worst of it." He watched Emma straighten up in one fluid motion, looking fresh and elegant in her trim royal blue dress with bright square buttons and a small matching hat. Kem, feeling the contrast between them as he stood before her in his soiled work clothes, said with heartfelt pleasure, "I've missed seeing you, Emma. It's been months! I've been wanting to tell you again how much your Christmas gifts meant to the children—the toys and Christmas decorations and especially the storybooks. You were so thoughtful. I've been wanting to thank you again." Kem glanced at Jessy. "Whenever I ask about you, the Flints have said you've been out of town."

"Visiting friends in Florida," Jessy said, giving Emma an out.

"I wish my trip was as innocent as all that but people in Bethel will guess the truth sooner or later. The fact is, Mr. Curtis, I went to Florida to have a baby. It nearly killed me to give up my Belinda for adoption and I prayed to die, but God let me live. Not because I was good, because I'm not, but because of the prayers of so many people who care for me." Emma was too distraught to continue.

Jessy took the sobbing Emma into her arms. "Everything will be all right now, Emma, really. I've missed you so much."

Kem, rather than walking away as might be expected, gave Emma his handkerchief.

"This smells like motor oil!" she said, laughing as she dried her tears.

"Oh, I'm sorry! Adam and I were working on his car earlier today." Kem laughed too, but then added in a serious voice, "I had no idea why you left Bethel, Emma, but I'm sure glad you've come home again. Is there anything I can do for you? You've helped us so much."

Returning his handkerchief, Emma shook her head. "I don't know how I can show my face back here in Bethel! Maybe I shouldn't have come back at all, but I had to see my family and especially to thank Jessy for being my friend."

Kem said, "Why, Emma, I couldn't stand to hear anyone in Bethel or anyplace else say a word against you!"

Emma's face revealed her surprise and gratitude for Kem's forbearance.

In the intervening lull, Jessy said, "Kem, do you know that Emma was baptized in Florida? Isn't that good news?"

"It sure is!" Kem brimmed with enthusiasm. "I hope you'll visit the Church of Bethel. You'll find that people will meet you more than halfway!"

"That's where my grandparents worship!"

Joy bubbling up in him, Kem said, "I know Roy and Flo well. Many good folks belong. I don't know how I would have survived—me and my children—without the church pitching in all these months helping us out after my wife died. Let me know what I can do to help you."

Emma wasted no time taking him up on his offer. "This may sound silly, Mr. Curtis, but right now more than anything I'd like to hold your child, if you don't mind. Doctor Fisher told me it might help to fill the void—holding babies, loving other people's—" Again Emma broke down. Sobbing, she tried to explain, "You see, once a woman gives birth she has a real, physical need to nurture that child and if that child can't be held and loved, then—"

Without a moment's hesitation, Kem went to his youngest, his daughter born the day her mother lost her life in childbirth. "Dana," he whispered as he lifted his sleepy child in his arms, "there's a lady who wants to see you."

"A lady!" Emma laughed harshly at herself but melted at the sight of Dana Curtis. "Gosh, she's sweet." Emma took the toddler from Kem.

"Dana is heavier than she looks! I think you should sit down with her." Kem steered Emma to the sofa and sat down with her. "My motherless daughter needs holding as much as you need to hold her! Look, she likes you! Dana doesn't always take to newcomers." Together they gave Dana her bottle.

Jessy took in this new scene before her, a trio now—man, woman, and child. A thrill ran through her but she shook a thought away as far-fetched. She strolled to the kitchen and back to the parlor to visit with Emma, but Emma and Kem were deep into conversation, with the child singing sleepily between them.

"Adam?" Jessy looked up to the second-floor landing where her brother was kneeling on the floor hammering nails. "Shall I get the cows and start the milking without you?"

"Is it that time already?" he answered in surprise.

Jessy smiled wryly at her brother. "Didn't you hear Mr. Cuckoo say it's forty-and-a-half past sixteen?"

"Oh, yeah!" Adam said slowly, his dimples appearing in his rugged face. He rubbed his grimy hands on his pants. "Ask Stephen to help you. I'll be along in a few minutes. Stephen? Stephen! Help your Aunty! And Taddy and Martha, it's time to start your chores too!"

His children appeared from nowhere beside Aunty, one pirate and two Indians, with a band of gypsies following. "Can Gina and Tom and Cathy and Brad come with us?" Martha, in war paint, asked on behalf of her new friends. "They want to see our barn with the snowflake windows!"

"Oh, by all means! No two windows alike! Everybody should see our barn! Come on!" As Jessy trooped out the front door with her band of merry marauders, she noticed that Kem had stood and was taking his leave of Emma, but Emma remained seated, still holding young Dana.

❦ ❦ ❦

"For what we are about to receive, oh, Lord, make us truly grateful," intoned Adam Flint. "We thank You for this day, for these our friends and family, and for Emma's safe return, and for all Your gifts. Help us be the people You want us to be. In Christ's name we thank You. Amen."

"And thank You for Gina who fixed the bicycle," added Taddy in solemn tones, his eyes closed.

"Amen!" said Adam, nodding his thanks to the cheerful, clever Gina.

At the head of the long dining table, Adam began passing plates. "So, Kem, when will we be done wreckin' the house, my wife wants to know."

"Two weeks?" Kem ventured. "Getting in the furnace and duct work is the hardest part. Should go fast from then on out. Of course, once we seal up the walls, the wallpaper will need to be replaced."

"That's needed doin' since we moved in here." Adam mounded mashed potatoes on his plate and passed the bowl. "Do you put up wallpaper?"

"I do, but I know a fellow in Blue Forge who works better and faster than I could and he doesn't charge much. I can see if he's available, if you like."

"I'll be goin' that way myself on Wednesday. Auction June 30."

"Oh? What will they be auctioning off?" asked Suzanna eagerly.

Adam looked at his wife with his shrewd green eyes. "Not antiques. Farm equipment, mostly."

"Oh, pooh!" said Suzanna. "But I can begin picking out wallpaper, can't I? I just love looking at patterns."

"I s'pose!" said Adam over his pot roast. "This is good, sweetheart."

"Yes, ma'am!" said Tom Curtis, Kem's seven-year-old.

"Delicious," added Kem and Emma together. Giggling, Emma added, "In Florida, Sister Frances taught me to make pot roast. She was such a good cook! And she showed me how to bake bread too. At first I refused to try, but when I did I was surprised to find that I really liked kneading dough!" Emma ate heartily, grateful to be able to speak honestly about her past and, despite the trials, to remember the good in it. "I'm so glad to be back in Bethel."

"Emma, would you please pass the pepper?" Stephen asked.

"Certainly!" As Emma handed the pepper shaker along, she grew thoughtful. "At the convent, we boarders were expected to serve each other. At first I was really annoyed. Being the youngest, no one's ever expected me to do much at home, but after a month or two at St. Catherine's I decided it was good to serve others—to serve and be served, as Christ taught us."

Everyone regarded the girl who had grown so much in the past few months. In Jessy's estimation, Emma was a far lovelier young woman now than when they first met, her natural beauty buoyed by the redemptive love of God. Accepting a bowl of tender green beans from Suzanna, Jessy took a portion for herself and with a wily look asked Adam, "What sort of equipment?"

"At the auction, you mean? There's a list on my desk someplace. Seed drills, loaders, posthole diggers, disks, harrows—the usual. The equipment of three farms will be liquidated at once. Might be some other things, too—household stuff." When Suzanna perked up, Adam said, "You can come with me if you want, just as long as we don't go antiquin'!" When Suzanna deflated, Adam explained, "We've blown the budget two months runnin' buyin' gear for all this home improvement! Can't afford any more flights of fancy!"

"In that case, I'm not interested," said Suzanna airily. "Take Jessy."

"You interested?" he asked, fully expecting his sister to decline.

"Yes, sir," said Jessy, delighted. She dared not mention why, but she knew that the ride to Blue Forge would give her the opportunity to ask her brother to reconsider his low opinion of Leo Kimball. Jessy turned to say something to Emma, but Emma and Kem Curtis were talking to each other.

CHAPTER 27

❦

"**T**hat trousseau of yours keeps gettin' bigger all the time," Adam told Jessy as the two jostled along the deserted country road toward Bethel in their old but sturdy horse-drawn rig. He glanced over to her latest acquisition, a wedding-ring-patterned quilt. "But that Leo's not your type. If and when Leo settles down, he'll have made an old woman outta you. Old before your time." When Jessy frowned, Adam said, "He's already started! Look at yourself."

Jessy looked straight ahead as they headed home to Bethel from the Blue Forge Auction. Adam was right. Jessy's heart was no match for Adam's logic, but she did say: "Leo just needs time, I think, before he's ready to settle down. I keep praying for him."

"You can't save everyone. Not everyone wants to be saved."

Jessy nodded. Her recent exchange of letters with Leo had become intense theological debates. "After Leo's visit I wrote him that everyone needs to submit to a higher authority."

"And what did Leo say to that?"

Jessy had sunk so low in her seat and had paused so long Adam whoaed his team to look at her. "Well?"

Straightening up with effort, Jessy answered, "Leo wrote that he'd die first, rather than submit."

"Oh." Adam clucked the horses onward. "Can't make a man see what he don't wanna see, especially when he's got the world at his feet—and the best-lookin' women in it, at the moment."

"I wrote back that no sensible traveler would sail alone in a little boat deep into the darkness without a star to follow and a chart mapping the course." Jessy's voice grew wistful, but no less convincing. "That's how life is for people without faith and direction, no matter who they are or what work they do in their lives—without faith they might as well do nothing! We all need faith to live our lives to the fullest, even famous baseball players. Success is no substitute for faith."

"If I tell you never to have anythin' to do with him again, I'd probably succeed in makin' you go runnin' off with him, just to show me you know better. I'm prayin' you do the right thing, that you use your head as much as your heart."

Jessy sank down in her seat while the ruts in the unpaved road rocked her from side to side. She hugged her new quilt to herself, but even a comforter offered cold comfort to the lovelorn Jessy Flint. After a while she decided it was too fine a day to be spoiled by matters beyond her control. She was glad Adam had decided to go to the auction in the rig rather than the car. As it turned out, Adam needed the broad flatbed to haul home the three heavy pieces of used equipment he had bought.

She picked up the operator's manual that came with Adam's portable, nearly new three-horsepower gas engine and began reading aloud to her brother: "'It will do the work of a crew of hired men. It can be hitched to a wide variety of farm machines and save hours of backbreaking work. This quiet gasoline engine powers wood saws, cream separators, grindstones, washing machines'—wow! You won't need me anymore now that you have a machine to do all the work!"

Adam found this most amusing. "But can machines laugh at my jokes?"

Referring to another of his purchases, Jessy said, "Suzanna will love that oriental rug you weren't supposed to buy for her." As she expected, Adam turned crimson, which made them both laugh.

"I'm spoilin' that girl!" he admitted happily, the tough-talking husband having splurged a bit in an effort to please his wife.

Jessy patted Adam's splendid purchase, a beautiful hand-knotted thick carpet in rich red, blue, and ivory wool, rolled up so that its fringe fluttered in the breeze. "All the way from Persia, just think! A handmade magic carpet for one dollar! It's hardly a dent in the budget and someday I think it will be worth much, much more, don't you? Besides, Suzanna has been looking for a pretty rug for the front hall ever since we moved into that house."

"She sure has. I'm glad no rug dealers came to the auction or I would've been outbid for it." He turned to Jessy with a sly grin. "You didn't do so bad yourself. That quilt was a bargain and that barrel's heavy enough." Adam groaned and rubbed his back in mock agony.

Jessy cheered at this remark. "It must be the heaviest thing anyone ever bought for a quarter! What a deal!" Jessy leaned back to dip into her latest acquisition, a big cooper's barrel loaded with old books no one else at the auction bothered to bid against her for. "I can't wait to look through them all, except the ones at the bottom are soggy."

The bottom of the barrel was damp, as if it had been left standing forgotten in a leaky basement too long. From the top Jessy retrieved a slim but pretty, navy blue leather-bound book. "Here's a nice one: *The Majestic Night Sky*. It might make a good present for Nathan Fisher. Do you know the entire senior class at St. Azarias College voted him Best Teacher? Not *favorite* but *best*! Beatrice Bally wrote and told me." Jessy looked through the pretty little volume filled with astronomical diagrams. "Nathan probably knows everything in this book by heart, but it's awfully nice. Look: the Pleiades cluster. Such a lovely name, *Plee*-ah-dees," Jessy repeated, enjoying the musical sound.

"Got anythin' 'bout roofin' or sidin' or plumbin' in that barrel?"

"No roofinG, sidinG or plumbinG books. Sorry!" Jessy laughed at her down-to-earth brother and reached for another book.

"Then how 'bout rat catching?"

"I don't think so! Sorry again to disappoint you." Jessy corrected herself as she browsed through an especially heavy volume. "This one might be about the bubonic plague, except it's written in an oriental language of some sort." Jessy peered at the obscure but exquisite type. Diagrams illustrating insects and small mammals including rodents abounded. "Anyway, I think the rats—if that's what got into our house—may have left us for good. I haven't heard a squeak out of them for—"

"Don't be too sure," said Adam. "I found one day before yesterday."

"You did?" Jessy sounded forlorn. "I know they shouldn't be inside the house, but it's so sad when one gets trapped and dies."

"I wasn't plannin' on tellin' you. I know how it upsets you."

"Thank you, Adam," Jessy said sweetly to her brother, then dug for more books. "Here's a really nice-looking history of British literature. Too bad this one's so damaged: *European History in the Arts*. Gorgeous pictures! Mmmm." Taking out another handful, she continued: "This one's in

French, and here's another in German. I like these engravings! There are maps too." To herself Jessy calculated a long string of Roman numerals indicating the year the book was printed. "Seventeen hundred and sixty-eight!"

"Hey, now, maybe they're worth somethin'," Adam said hopefully.

"Maybe! It's my good fortune no book dealers came to the auction." She strained for more books, but couldn't reach them from her seat. "I can't wait until we get home and I can empty my barrel!" She peered down into its dank, dark depths. "Oh, Adam, I think I see some sheet music down there! Won't that be fun?"

Sure enough, Jessy's barrel contained sheet music: a ragged but popular collection of German etudes for piano, yellow with age but of enormous interest to music-loving Suzanna and Martha. With Jessy, the three emptied the barrel in the sun and set out the books and damp sheet music to air. Some of the old books were too damp to open just now, but still Jessy was astounded with her treasure, and all for twenty-five cents: histories, biographies, poetry, and even a Spanish-French dictionary, with not a word of English in it. Some of the books were printed in languages so obscure Jessy couldn't guess their countries of origin. Others had bindings so damaged she decided to save only their illustrations and frame them as she could afford to do so. Her favorites were meticulous views of bustling northern European port cities in the eighteenth century, and vast Italian landscapes sketched by itinerant artists, the ruins of ancient Rome enduring on every hillside with no one taking notice but the occasional goat.

"The world is filled with surprises, isn't it?" she said to Suzanna.

"Oh, yes! Treasures galore." Suzanna was busy unrolling the oriental carpet Adam had bought for her. "It looks as if it were made for our hallway! A perfect fit! Isn't Adam a love? He knows how I've wanted one!"

"Look here!" Adam came in the front door waving the newspaper that had just been tossed on their porch. "Yesterday Leo pitched a no-hitter against Washington!"

Leo had reached his second goal. Jessy wondered if he would ever reach his third—to marry her.

CHAPTER 28

❦

Not only Bethel but the entire baseball world was rocked by Leo Kimball's sterling performance on the mound for the Red Sox. Sportswriters glowed in the telling of Leo's feat, a one-hundred-and-two-pitch masterpiece including fifteen strikeouts, two walks, and a spectacular running catch Leo made to prevent a sure hit. His teammates had given their all both in the outfield and infield, supporting Leo with superb catching and fielding. The newspapers were full of praise for the new right-handed sensation.

Jessy read and reread accounts in the *Bethel Journal* and then more and more stories as papers arrived from distant cities. There were pictures of Leo being surrounded by his teammates, hailed as a hero, lionized by all. One reporter noted that at the end of the game Leo cried for joy.

The evening of his victory Leo had written to her with an excited hand, a note exploding with the thrill of his accomplishment, but with a faint tremor about the future, a hint of the pitcher's life after a no-hitter: "It's grand, Jessy, being King of the Mound, but tomorrow—" Ah, tomorrow, with all its uncertainties. "As much as I wanted to play since I was a kid, to show the world I could pitch with the best, now—don't think I'm crazy—I kind of dread having to pitch. On the bench, my record is safe, but on the mound . . ."

Leo limited his letter-writing now with his hectic playing and travel schedule and all the attention given him by the press. The Red Sox were in a three-way race with the Detroit Tigers and the Philadelphia Athletics for first place in the American League, but the fun of the game was over for Leo. The never-ending work and worry of it remained. His movements became so closely watched, in fact, fame began taking its toll on him in a curious and pained way: Leo began losing games. The hero was fast becoming the goat. Jessy, railing at the unfairness of it all, kept him in her prayers. If Leo was praying, he never admitted to it in his letters. Jessy, reading her own Bible in her upper room in Bethel, wondered about the Bible she had given Leo the previous Christmas. A Bible's treasures could not be discovered if it remained closed, collecting dust. Did Leo even have it any longer? *Leo, dear Leo, now more than ever you need strength and courage to face life and live it to the fullest as God intends for you to do!* Jessy thought.

A knock at her door disturbed her contemplation. It was Martha, dressed in white with red and blue ribbons in her curling hair. "Daddy and Mama are taking us to the Fourth of July parade. Are you coming?"

Stephen and Taddy popped into Jessy's doorway, ready for the celebrations too, with fistfuls of sparklers they couldn't wait to ignite. "Afterward there'll be a picnic and fireworks at Lumpy Land!" they reminded her.

"Ah, dear Lumpy Land," Jessy said with a flashing broad smile, her dimples showing as she recalled her triumphant home run the previous September. "A pyrotechnics display," she said thoughtfully. "It just wouldn't do for me to miss America's birthday bash, now would it?"

❧ ❧ ❧

The festive Sunday afternoon proved eventful indeed. After the parade, with everyone in Bethel either in it or on the sidelines cheering, there was a town picnic—a combined fishfry and ox-roast—at the park with games and cakewalks and prizes, climaxed by an evening fireworks display. Long before dark, hundreds of people surged into the grandstand of Lumplyn Memorial Park to see the show. For a full hour beforehand they searched for the best seats and chatted with friends. The park was festooned with red, white, and blue bunting.

"Laura Everett!" Jessy greeted Leo's fashionable sister.

Laura reached for Jessy's hand with a friendly smile. "Can you talk a minute? I'm so excited!"

"Of course!" Jessy called to her family, hunting for seats, "I'll catch up with you in a minute!" Jessy turned to Laura, a contrast indeed to the distraught picture she had made in the spring. "I'm so glad to see you. My, you look happy!"

"I am! We are!" Laura could hardly refrain from bouncing about as she spoke. She squeezed her husband's arm happily.

"Miss Jessy," Burl Everett said mildly with a tip of his hat.

"Hello, Burl," Jessy said with cautious optimism considering the circumstances of their last conversation, one she prayed would never become common knowledge to anyone in Bethel, especially to Laura Kimball Everett. "How are you both?"

"Just fine! Wonderful! Oh, Jessy!" Laura took her aside, even from Burl, to say in what for Laura was a rare, subdued but yet excited voice, "I'm going to have a baby! After all this time. Me!"

"Oh, that's wonderful! When?"

"February! Burl's been so sweet lately." Laura paused while a crowd passed them on their way up the bleachers. Laura continued, whispering, "Back in May, about the time I came to see you, well, after that Burl became so—so loving in lots of little ways like talking with me, going for walks after supper, and holding my hand. He said he wanted to recapture the love we felt when we were courting! And now, well," Laura lifted her pretty shoulders in delight, squealing, "in a few months, we'll be parents! We've been fixing up our apartment, you know, sprucing it up and making room for the baby, but we're thinking about buying a home of our own."

"Oh, how wonderful for you both! And you thought your husband didn't love you!" Jessy, bubbling with joy, looked from Laura to Burl and back again.

"How silly of me to have said such a thing, but our marriage had reached rock bottom for a while." Laura's ethereal beauty clouded for a moment, but then she chirped, "Oh, it doesn't matter about the past. I'm so happy about the present—and the future!"

Surge after surge of people came by them looking for seats. Laura told Jessy, "Burl's expecting a promotion. If he gets it we'll move to Chicago."

"Oh, then you could continue your career in fashion modeling without having to travel?" Jessy ventured.

Burl entwined Laura's arm in his own. "Perhaps. But I'd like to enjoy my wife's company as much as I can, and our baby's too." He looked to Jessy. "We want you to be godmother, if you would do us the honor."

Surprised and delighted, Jessy said without hesitation, "Certainly! It would be my honor! Are you hoping for a boy or a girl!"

"We don't have a preference," Laura and Burl said together.

Now more crowds surged in. The afternoon light was fading. A color-guard paraded the grounds, followed by a band playing patriotic airs and stimulating marches. Jessy loved the sounds of brass and drums. While Jessy scanned the bleachers for her family, Burl and Laura said so long to her and took two seats on the bench just in front of Darlene and Wild Billy Wilcox. In the rapidly descending twilight, Darlene yoo-hooed to Jessy while her boy brandished his popgun. Waving hello to mother and son, Jessy wondered where Chad might be, but the thought fled as she hurried up the crowded stone steps to the wooden bleachers where Adam, Suzanna, and the children were munching popcorn. In the rapidly descending twilight Jessy pressed through to her seat, trying not to jostle anyone, but she did jar loose Adam's straw hat.

"Oops! I'm sorry!" Jessy murmured as she retrieved his hat and handed it to him. Even in the fading light she noted with delight how much Adam's sons resembled him, each wearing flat-crowned straw boaters, white suits, and ties. Seated next to Suzanna and Martha, the three females garbed in white squeezed together, Jessy surveyed the packed bleachers. People were waving small American flags or fanning themselves in the heat. After she smoothed her long white cotton skirt, Jessy shared Suzanna's popcorn. It was suddenly very dark.

A loud pop echoed through the park, commanding everyone's attention. The first of the fireworks had been set off, a powerful salute—a sudden, resounding white light that punched the air overhead with a blinding flash. A few more noisy salutes followed without generating a colorful tumble of lights, and then came a spectacular round of pink bursts which fizzled into sparkling green streamers. Amid the ooohs and aaahs of the crowd, golden lights lit the sky next, broad wisps of color streaking down, trailing red tails. When a whistling blue bomb went off, a half-dozen red and white mini-bursts blasted within it. While the crowd sighed in wonder at this three-dimensional display, another even more spectacular vision appeared: a noiseless gigantic yellow starburst with a dozen silver bursts gyrating within it. A series of red, green, and pink explosions followed, then twisted apart like a showering mist. The silent crowd looked up in awe.

From the bleachers below Jessy, a mild disturbance could be heard. Voices wafted up in the direction of the Flints, but the words were unclear.

Another salute silenced the crowd, a heart-pounding blast of white light. A rapid succession of lift charges were fired upward followed by blasting second charges—breakers spewing brilliant red and blue star-bursts, long silvery teardrops oozing golden tails, spiraling white comets—all punctuated with more heart-pounding salutes. In the short pauses between rounds, the disturbance continued in the crowd below Jessy's seat. A popgun went off, and a child shouted. "That sounds like Billy," Jessy said to Suzanna.

"Billy Wilcox gets in trouble at school all the time," Stephen answered. "He never minds our teacher."

Jessy regarded her nephew in the bursting pink light. "What kind of trouble?" she asked him.

Stephen shrugged. "Oh, you know, Aunty, forgetting his homework or missing class and not bringing the teacher a note from his folks, carrying his gun to school even after he's asked to leave it at home. Things like that."

The pyrotechnics reached their crescendo of noise, the loudest birth-day greeting to America that Bethel Township was capable of making. The sky burst with color: brilliant blue, red, and silver explosions fired rapidly and loudly in the deep blue night sky. Soft white lights sifted down like handfuls of pure falling snow. Whistling golden suns radiated over silver, shimmering weeping willows.

"Gosh, that's nifty!" sighed Taddy. Much as he was enjoying the show, he snuggled close to his father all the same.

Martha began nodding sleepily between Suzanna and Jessy but contin-ued twirling her little American flag.

The sky resounded with a fleeting outline of the United States, a red-white-and-blue mass of lights that glowed and lingered and then puffed away into the night mist. The show was over. For a moment no one moved, all hoping for more. Then parents began lifting sleeping children into their arms and the crowd began heading to the exit ramps.

"You need to keep your son under control, Chad, for his good and everyone else's!" Burl Everett's voice rang out distinctly now, as the Flints reached the lower bleachers. "It's your duty as his father!"

Adam, holding the sleeping Martha against his left shoulder, took Stephen's hand in his right. Suzanna followed with Taddy. Jessy walked directly behind them until a throng of people separated her from the rest of the Flints. "We'll wait for you in the car!" Suzanna shouted over the crowd to Jessy.

"It's none of your business how I raise my son, and I'll thank you to keep your eyes off my wife!" Chad Wilcox sounded livid.

Jessy stopped to see what was happening at the edge of the empty field. Burl and Chad were having a row. Beyond the two arguing men, young Billy ventured deep into the grassy parade grounds that smelled like spent dynamite. Darlene, torn between reasoning with her husband and brother-in-law or following her mothering instinct, waivered a moment before running after her son. "Don't touch those!" she cried as she rushed toward Billy.

"Look what I found, Mama!" Billy held up a shredded red paper wrapper from a spent charge. A blown fuse, empty tube, and charred wooden spike dangled from the burned-out fireworks display in his small hands. "There's lot of them on the grass, Mama! See?"

"Billy, put that down or you'll get hurt!" Darlene shouted. "Those aren't toys!"

Clutching Jessy in a panic, Laura whispered, "Chad showed up late and began picking a fight with Burl for no reason!"

"I could hear them arguing," Jessy replied, her eyes fixed, as Laura's were, on the two men who now began shoving one another.

"Stop it, Chad! You know Burl's right!" Laura demanded.

The men only waved her off. Nearby, boys were torching cherry bombs and firecrackers of their own. Explosions were being set off all about the park.

"Burl and Chad have never gotten along," Laura continued whispering. "Billy was acting so restless tonight! He was sitting behind us, pointing that gun of his at Burl and kicking our bench the whole time. Chad wouldn't say a word to Billy to make him stop. Darlene tried but she can hardly manage him."

"And who's going to manage Chad?" Jessy wondered aloud. "Oh, no!" She cried with alarm when she saw the handgun Chad pulled from the holster under his white sport coat. "Please, stop! No!"

A few men in the crowd saw what was happening, but too late to stop Chad Wilcox from firing at his unarmed brother-in-law. Laura and Jessy screamed as Burl Everett crumpled down in the blast. Billy came running and crying toward his family. Laura fainted into the arms of two total strangers.

Jessy reached Burl first. "Burl. Burl!" As she kneeled and took off her jacket to prop up his head, she called for a doctor.

"Dr. Grady's on the way," a lady near her answered, "and the pyrotechnics crew is coming with the first-aid kit. They got enough medicine on hand at these shows to tend an army!"

Three men had taken hold of the shooter who continued shouting. As a fourth man disarmed Chad and joined in the attempt of getting him under control, he said, "Chad Wilcox, I believe you're drunk!"

"No, he's just impossible!" said Darlene in a stone cold fury. Speaking to her husband who was now being locked into handcuffs, she said, "Now you've done it! You'll go to prison! You and your guns! How utterly stupid of you!"

"I did it to protect you, Darlene!" Chad answered back.

"I'll have you know, Chad Wilcox, that I have never needed protection from Burl Everett, who has always been a perfect gentleman! I need protection from you! How could you accuse me of—I love you and only you and always have! How stupid of me!" With that, Darlene burst into tears. Billy tried to console her and go to his father, but she clamped hard on his wrists to keep him from straying. She pulled him toward her sister, crying out, "Oh, Laura, I'm so sorry! How could we have let things reach such a sorry state?"

Jessy strained in the dim gaslit park to see if Burl was alive. He was sprawled on the grass. The oval gathered around him was lined with faces, concerned bystanders looking down to him. With the help of another woman, Jessy unbuttoned Burl's crisp linen jacket and loosened his tie. His pulse raced so fast it scared the women. A dark stain widened slowly at his shoulder, seeping through his white clothing. "The doctor's on his way, Burl. Can you hear me? It must hurt awfully bad." Jessy adjusted his head on her jacket. "Are you cold?" Three or four men took off their jackets and handed them down to cover him.

"Jessy? Is that you?" In the darkness Burl reached for her hand.

"Yes, Burl. I'm here." Jessy sighed in relief as he squeezed her hand.

"Don't Chad beat everything?" With his eyes closed he whispered, "I never went near Darlene, not ever. Where's Laura? I'm worried about Laura, in her condition!"

Calmly, Jessy answered, "She fainted but she's being looked after."

"She's coming around! Keep her down!" shouted those who attended Laura with a nasty but harmless tube of smelling salts pressed to her nostrils.

"Eeaarrgh!" Rousing abuptly on the lowest level of bleachers, Laura screeched her familiar screech. "Get that stink bomb away from my nose!"

"Ah, that's my girl! How I love her!" Hearing Laura's inimitable screech, Burl smiled and closed his eyes. "She's all right, that wife of mine."

"Yes, she is." Jessy started crying at the irony of it all. No sooner had this troubled twosome begun resolving their differences and growing together in love when Chad had to go and spoil things. Darlene sat with Laura now. The two sisters were holding one another and having a good cry together.

Someone was coming through the crowd toward Burl. "Make way for Doc Grady!" Jessy got halfway to her feet.

"I heard there was shooting." Dr. Grady went about his examination with businesslike dispatch. "This man must be moved immediately. My house is only two blocks from here. Someone bring up a car and a stretcher." The doctor made a quick examination of Burl who by now had drifted into semiconsciousness. Laura came close, in total disarray, for once not caring a whit for fashion. "Missed the lungs, I'm sure of it, and the shoulder bone. He's a lucky fellow," said the doctor. "Of course, I'll need to make a full examination at my place." The doctor did his best to pack the wound and stem the bleeding with the limited means at his disposal. "Where's that stretcher? Hurry up!"

"Oh, Burl, don't die! You can't die now! I love you! I've always loved you!" Laura screeched to the world. "Oh, Burl, oh, ohhh . . . "

"Watch her, watch her! She's going to faint again!"

"I am not! I've never fainted in my life, before now. Oh, Burl, please live and we'll move to Chicago! We'll be happy if it kills us!"

"Poor Laura," said Jessy, half crying and half laughing, glad to see Laura feeling strong enough to take her rightful place by her husband. To the doctor, Jessy said, "Burl is going to be all right, isn't he?"

"Hmmm? Oh, yes, yes, the man should pull through if we can just get him out of here. Hurry up with that stretcher!" the doctor ordered.

"What's goin' on!" demanded a familiar booming bass. "I got the car all cranked up and rarin' to go!"

"Hi, Adam," Jessy called out. At last the stretcher had arrived and Burl was being rolled onto it. Jessy picked up her grass-stained jacket. "There's been a shooting."

"Suzy 'n' me heard noises but we thought it was just kids playin' with fireworks." Looking about, Adam boomed, "Burl Everett, is that you?"

From the stretcher, Burl raised one limp hand in greeting.

Adam went to him, speaking low. "Hey, pal, you okay?"

"Oh, sure, sure," Burl answered as stretcher bearers carried him to a truck that had been pulled onto the grassy parade ground. "Say, Adam, thanks! Nice of you to stop by."

"Don't mention it, Burl," said Adam, scratching his head in wonder. Would the Kimball clan never live in peace?

CHAPTER 29

❦

"**I** think I'm going to be traded," Leo wrote to Jessy as the 1909 baseball season drew to a close. He had fallen into a slump after his triumphant no-hitter. Jessy, ever faithful, continued to correspond, always with uplifting replies, but where once Leo could do no wrong on the mound, now he could do no right. "Most of August my throwing shoulder hurt so much I had to ease up on my game. It looks like there's no hope for our team to win the pennant, but I'll attend the World Series no matter who plays it this year."

The tone of their correspondence had changed. In the weeks following his impromptu visit earlier in the summer, which concluded with Jessy's chilling premonition, she had exhorted him, in letters, to see the light. Failing to move him, Jessy retained a neutral attitude until, by late summer, their letters were reduced to impersonal exchanges between two mere acquaintances. It was as if Leo regarded Jessy as a sympathetic listener, which she was, even though she longed to be so much more.

"There's a time for everything under heaven," Suzanna had reminded Jessy often enough. "I've known Leo a long time, longer than you have. I watched him grow up, him and my baby brother, Matthew. Leo's never been the introspective type. Sometimes I think it's harder for a man than a woman to submit to God," she added thoughtfully, looking at her own husband and remembering his long struggle and hard fall before coming to Christ. "Men are so self-reliant, so bent on success, on doing things their own way. Obedience, submission, and serving come hard to some, especially those who are driven to reach the top of their professions."

"If they only knew the Lord wanted to go with them day by day in their walk, wherever life takes them," said Jessy. "If only they knew that God has so much more to offer them than they can ever hope to find on their own."

"Sometimes it takes a hard knock for a man to listen," said Adam, speaking from his own experience. "Maybe more than one." He laughed at himself. "How stubborn I was. I'm glad you women showed me the way!"

Suzanna and Jessy basked in his acknowledgment, for the proof was evident in the Flint home. How close the family had become in the year since Adam took his fateful step to rely not on his own understanding but on God. All they could do was pray that Leo would one day join their family and the larger family of the faithful.

Yet, the news could be cruel, and come when least expected. On a quiet Saturday afternoon in early October, Jessy walked from home to the Bethel Pharmacy which had recently been enlarged and renovated. Much to Jessy's delight, the druggist had begun carrying newspapers from some of the larger cities. After she paid for a Boston paper, she saw a feature story that hit her hard as a club: for two months Leo Kimball had been seen escorting the lovely Regina Mason to social events.

The divorced Boston heiress had been seen with the Red Sox pitcher on a regular basis. The charming twosome had been noticed together attending a museum gala, sailing along the North Shore, and rooting for their favorite horses at the races. Regina Mason had been seen cheering Leo on whenever he pitched for Boston. After the regular season ended, the twosome attended the World Series when the Detroit Tigers traveled east to play their foes in Pittsburgh. With the story was the caption: "Wedding bells for Leo and Regina?"

Jessy felt numb all over, there in the drug store. It was over between them. Jessy had been betrayed. In the last two months, while Leo had been seeing Regina so regularly, he had written not a word to Jessy about his social life, just one letter after another about his game, his sore shoulder, and his fears for his future in baseball. Between these penned lines of Leo's, Jessy understood that Leo was also saying that he must delay their wedding until he could establish his career on firm footing. Leo had failed to realize that though a vast distance separated him from Jessy, he was no longer a struggling nobody. Leo's private life was no longer private. The Lord saw, as always, but now so did the press.

A *divorced heiress*, Jessy thought, her heart aching, as she studied the beauty's picture. Despite Leo's, and indeed his entire family's enchantment with modern life, new ways were having dubious effects upon marriage and the family, Jessy could see. "It will be remembered that Miss Mason's difficult and trying divorce from financier Howard Hudson shook Boston society only a few months ago," went the news account in Jessy's hands.

"I'll buy you a soda," came a familiar voice. Jessy turned to see Darlene and Billy Wilcox. "Leo's my brother and I love him, but I know him only too well." Darlene put a friendly hand on Jessy's arm. "Bet you ten dollars he won't marry Regina Mason!"

Fighting tears and unable to speak, Jessy fumbled with the newspaper until she had refolded it into a small neat bundle.

"Billy and I have come here for a treat! We need one after the day we've had, don't we, son?" Darlene patted her youngster's shoulder. "Billy and I have just come back from visiting his father."

Sighing deeply, Jessy nodded sympathetically to Darlene. "How is Chad?" Everyone in Bethel knew that after the shooting, Chad had been speedily tried and sentenced to eight years in the state penitentiary for attempted murder.

"Oh, under the circumstances, Chad's better than I am! Come on," she urged, guiding her son and Jessy to the new ice cream parlor within the drug store, a vision of white marble counters, gilt-framed mirrors, revolving stools, and shiny chrome fixtures. Newly wired for electricity, the counter had some of the prettiest lighting in town and a ceiling fan to circulate the air.

Once Darlene and Jessy helped Billy up onto his seat, they sat on either side of him. The soda jerk took their orders and began filling clear glass serving dishes with decadent concoctions—a chocolate soda for Darlene, a strawberry sundae for Billy, and a root beer float for Jessy. While their order was being filled, the trio stared at their collective image in the wall of mirrors before them: Darlene in her good traveling suit and hat; Billy in a red shirt, ball cap, and short pants; and Jessy in a plain blue-striped shirtwaist dress and straw sun hat, with her newspaper on the counter beside her.

"We need a treat as much as Miss Flint does, don't we, Billy?" Darlene roughed up and then smoothed her son's stick-straight blond hair. "Billy looks like Chad, don't you think? Not a bit of me in him."

"I see you in Billy." Jessy studied mother and son in the vast mirror across from their swivel stools. "Children change so much when they're growing up. My own niece and nephews look different to me every day." Jessy's face brightened with this gentle diversion, but soon turned glum again as she noticed the newspaper at her elbow on the counter.

Darlene said wisely, "Leo's escapades must be awful for you, but he'll tire of Regina, believe me. He falls in love faster than anybody I know."

"Here you go, folks," said the soda jerk. He placed napkins, long-handled spoons, and water glasses beside their orders, big dreamy concoctions with generous scoops of old-fashioned ice cream that steamed in the afternoon heat. Billy's sundae was covered in whipped cream, nuts, and a cherry.

"Can we eat sundaes on Saturdays?" Billy wondered. The boy had made his mother and Jessy laugh.

"Thank you both," Jessy said as she dipped into her float. "This looks wonderful." For a moment she watched Billy as he spooned up some of the rich topping on his sundae. "Say, Billy, where's your popgun?"

"I'll never carry a gun again!" Billy answered solemnly. "It was a gun that hurt my Uncle Burl. I don't like guns anymore. They hurt people."

"It was your daddy who hurt your uncle, Billy. Guns make suffering too easy to inflict! We learned something on the Fourth of July, didn't we, Billy? And so did your father, but at such a price!" To Jessy Darlene murmured, "Chad will be lucky to get off in five years with good behavior!"

"How are you managing?" Jessy asked.

"Not well—until I found a buyer for our store. Two days ago I was given some earnest money and a contract to consider. Chad didn't want to sell, but he signed the contract today. I don't like dealing with guns. 'Chad,' I told him today, 'the boating and bait side of our business is fine with me, but no more guns!' I've been thinking about moving back home for a while; my parents have offered to help me. The church has helped, too, with bags of groceries every week and train tickets to visit Chad, and spending money as I needed it. Chad left us with debts, I'm afraid."

Inwardly Jessy felt pleased that she and her family were helping Darlene and her son through the church. It had been a good farming year and the Flints had been generous with donations of all sorts. Financial success had its distinct benefits, when money was earned and shared with the right spirit, for the right motives.

While Jessy pondered these things, Billy turned to her, saying, "I miss my daddy. Today I asked him to come home with us on the train but he said he couldn't for a long time. How long is a long time?"

Jessy put her arm around him. Her problems, as much as they hurt, seemed pale by comparison. "Your daddy loves you very much, even if he can't be with you now. He'll come home just as soon as he can!" After she sipped her float, she tactfully changed the subject. "We heard Burl Everett got his promotion."

"Yes! He and Laura are moving to Chicago! The first day Burl was able to get around after the shooting, he and Laura came to see Billy and me. They have never been by before. I was shocked, especially when they offered to help me any way they could, and Burl had every reason to despise me after what happened on the Fourth. I'll never forget the way they put it to me. They said, 'God has been good to us so we want to be good to you.' Can you imagine? I don't know why Burl has changed but he has, I suppose because of the shooting. Anyway, he told me he's so grateful God spared his life. How easily Chad could have killed him with that stupid gun of his!" Seeing Jessy's face in the mirror rejoicing over the news of Burl's changed nature, Darlene's own face brightened. Now Darlene enjoyed her soda, especially the dark, rich chocolate ice cream. "It's odd, you may think, but since the shooting, Laura and I have become closer than we've been in years. It's a miracle!"

"Sometimes it takes a tragedy to wake people up," said Jessy.

"Sometimes," Darlene nodded. She reached around behind Billy, to say in confidence to Jessy, "Listen, thank your family for helping us. Tell Suzy and your brother I'll pay them back as soon as I can."

"There's no need for that! Adam and Suzy would ask you to help someone else sometime when you're able. In the meantime, please let us know what else we can do. And thanks for the treat! I needed it!" Jessy slipped off the stool, said her good-byes, and headed home with her newspaper.

❦ ❦ ❦

"That rat!" Adam snapped as he read Jessy's paper after supper.

Jessy said nothing, but she prayed the phone would ring. Perhaps Leo had a logical explanation about Regina. Jessy paced the kitchen while Adam continued reading her paper, fuming aloud the whole while. To occupy herself she decided to catch up on her ironing, but still Adam fumed. "Any mail?" she asked, hoping to divert his attention.

While waiting for the trio of heavy irons to heat on the stove, Jessy went to the hall table where the incoming mail had been left. Jessy flipped through the stack of circulars, flyers about farm equipment, and a new catalog of winter clothes and sporting gear. Jessy paused at a letter for her postmarked *Enigma*. Nathan! She was just about to tear open the envelope when the telephone rang.

"That's probably Mother! I'll get it!" Suzanna came running but turned to Jessy after she answered the phone. "It's for you." Leo! Jessy couldn't move. Suzanna covered the mouthpiece and whispered, "It's Emma."

Jessy sighed audibly, feeling relieved and yet sorrowful that Leo failed to call. Taking the phone from Suzanna, Jessy said, "Hello, Emma? Yes, I saw the newspaper. I'm sorry too." Unexpectedly, Jessy smiled. "You mustn't call your brother a rat! Yes, I was looking forward to being your sister-in-law, too, but it probably never was meant to be." Jessy listened a moment and then burst out, "Oh, how wonderful!" Jessy looked around excitedly. She waved Suzanna and Adam closer and said in a rush, "Kem's asked Emma to marry him but they haven't set a date yet!"

Adam and Suzanna said together, "They'll make a good couple!"

"It's unanimous, Emma. We're thrilled!"

After a bit more conversation, Jessy said good-bye, put down the phone, and said to Adam and Suzanna, "Walter Kimball has offered to help Kem start a home renovation business here in Bethel. Acacia's not too happy about Emma marrying 'below her station' as she put it, but she can't put up much of an argument, seeing that Emma had—well, you know." Jessy blushed thinking about little Belinda born out of wedlock. "Well, I think Kem Curtis is quite the gentleman for her."

Although Jessy rejoiced for Kem and Emma, she hurt all the more because of Leo's cavalier treatment of her. In silence she ironed, wondering how Leo could hurt her so. How many other women had he hurt? She raged within, just thinking of that rotten heel.

Jessy went upstairs with her hands full of freshly ironed clothes. In the twilight she lit her lamp and remembered Nathan's letter, still in her pocket. On his college stationery he had written:

My dear Jessy,
    During the upcoming fall recess at St. Azarias College, I am planning to deliver a series of lectures in the Midwest. I have been asked to speak to the faculty of your state university and wonder, if it's not an inconvenience to you and your family, if I could stop in Bethel for a visit with you.

Delighted at such a prospect, Jessy ran to ask Adam and Suzanna if he could stay with them. Dr. Isaac Nathan Fisher coming to see her! She had never seen the state university, more than a hundred miles from her home, but had heard it was the best of its kind in the nation. Returning to her room, she wrote,

We'd be honored to see you. We have plenty of room, so please plan to stay with us as long as you like. Best wishes for a safe and successful lecture tour. Your friend, Jessy.

After she addressed and sealed the envelope, she saw the books she had purchased at the auction. The soggier ones had dried completely and now could be handled without damaging them. She began turning pages of a heavily illustrated volume bound in red leather with gold tooling. She had no idea as to its subject. She couldn't even determine the language but thought it might be Greek. She turned page after page with special care, sensing that although the book was old and had been forgotten in a damp barrel, it had seen little use. After turning pages and studying illustrations for a long while, she paused, stunned by one engraving. No, it couldn't be. Jessy shook her head. *My eyes must be tired. They're playing tricks on me!* she thought.

She checked the date the book had been published, the series of Roman numerals stamped clearly on the title page: MDCCCLXI. Jessy peered at the engraving again. What was Leo Kimball's picture doing in a book printed in 1861, more than twenty years before he was born?

CHAPTER 30

❦

Supper was over, the dishes washed, and evening chores completed for hours at the Flint homeplace that bitter cold Friday evening in November. Jessy, having changed into her best winter dress, her hair pinned up in a soft pouf, had gone to the front windows a dozen times looking for Professor Fisher. Nathan had written that, after delivering the final lecture of his series, he would take the train to Bethel and hire a cab from the station to her home, but under no condition was she or any member of her family to go to any trouble on his account. Of course Jessy had gone to enormous trouble, and gladly.

The guest room on the main floor was ready. Earlier that day Jessy had seen to every detail herself, even to scrubbing the adjoining bathroom from top to bottom. Now in the soft glow of an electric lamp—the newest addition here and throughout the house—she checked the guest room with its fresh linens and soft pillows, a pitcher of water and drinking glass by the bed.

Along with the benefits of electricity, the entire home was evenly heated now, with the new coal furnace working beautifully, thanks to Adam and Kem's hard work. The toasty fire burning in the fireplace was hardly necessary, she knew, but it added immeasurable charm to the guest room. *Now, where is the guest?* she wondered.

After dinner, Jessy had spent the evening with Adam, Suzanna, and the children as they usually did, in the sitting room. She and Suzanna had darned socks while Adam and the children did homework. Jessy smiled at the thought: her big burly brother and his little sprouts studying together. As for Jessy's own studies, she had already completed the program and was awaiting receipt of her high school certificate with honors.

Once she bid the family good night, she tidied the already tidy parlor

285

for her honored guest. She glanced at all the books in the room. On a table by itself, in all its majesty, was the massive family Bible, well thumbed and beloved. On groaning shelves were her own books: an ever-growing collection of histories, travelogues, ancient art and archaeology, reference works, collections of fables, biographies, poetry, and the treasures of world literature. Her own room had become so crammed with books she had begun filling the parlor with them as she finished reading them.

She jumped when she heard someone pulling up the drive. Soon car doors were being opened and shut. Nathan's distinctive voice rang out in the crisp night air. She peeked through the lace-curtained windows in the parlor to see Nathan standing in her yard, settling the fare with the cab driver who had brought him here from the train station. While the driver helped Nathan with his luggage, Jessy ran to the hall. The illustrious professor, voted the very best by his students, had come to see Jessy Flint! With a shiver of delight she flung open the front door.

"Hello, dear Jessy! How good of you to have me!" Nathan cried as he came up the steps with his things.

"A thousand welcomes!" Jessy answered. Once Nathan was safely inside out of the cold, she reached for his hat, coat, and scarf. "Your room is there, to the right, past the parlor. Did you have a good trip? Are you hungry? You must be exhausted!"

Nathan beamed with delight at her enthusiastic welcome. "Oh, I'm sorry to arrive this late! My train stopped everywhere along the route!" He gave her a most engaging look.

Smiling, enchanted, and momentarily speechless in the presence of her marvelous friend, Jessy helped him with his greatcoat, a heavy tweed with a worn but rich black velvet collar. His dark big-brimmed hat suited him, she thought, graphite with a matching band around the crown. The dark gray of it brought out the brilliance of his eyes. He wore timeless but comfortable clothes. His strength and charm radiated within the hall. Remembering the first time she had seen him, looking pale and mournful by the sea, she couldn't help but rejoice on his robust appearance, saying, "You look well!"

"I *am* well, thank you." He flashed her a dazzling smile, his even white teeth glistening, his large gray eyes twinkling with humor. "And you?" He looked about for a moment in apprehension, then said softly, "This house is mighty quiet. I suspect I'm disturbing your family."

"Oh, no, not at all! Everyone's gone upstairs. They'll see you in the morning. Suzanna's planning a country breakfast in your honor." Jessy hung up the professor's coat and tucked away his hat in the hall closet. "We've kept some supper warm for you—beef stew."

"Yes, thank you, I would like some supper, if you don't mind."

As Jessy led Nathan down the hall toward the kitchen, she paused at the doorway of the guest room. "All for you. Please let me know if there's anything else you'll be needing." She watched from the hall as Nathan carried in his valise and leather briefcase bulging with books and papers.

"This room is splendid, Jessy, but I get the feeling I've put you and your family through a great deal of trouble."

"Nothing but the best is good enough for the best professor at St. Azarias College!" she said with a grin. "Congratulations again!"

"That's kind of you to say, Jessy." He washed his hands at the sink and, after a quick glance in the bathroom mirror, smoothed his thick head of hair. He noticed the small vase of flowers she had grown, dried, and arranged on the vanity: fall mums in rust red, brilliant yellow, and snow white, hardy sunbursts that suited him well, she thought. As if reading her mind, he said, "Perennial symbols of love, truth, and cheerfulness under adversity?"

"Why, yes. How did you know?" She laughed at herself. "Oh, but you know everything!"

"Well, not *everything*!" He laughed at himself, too, as he joined her in the hall. "What a grand place you have."

"Thank you! Glad you like it." With a wry look she added, "The Webbs—Suzanna's parents—gave it to us after disaster struck. The kitchen's this way. We could eat in the dining room if you prefer, but on such a cold night I think it's cozier in here."

"There's nothing more inviting than a big country kitchen!" While admiring the proportions, scale, and design of the place, Nathan said, "1870s, I'd guess."

"Yes. This house was built in 1876." As Jessy ladled hot stew and a colorful array of vegetables onto a generous deep-rimmed dish for him, she asked, "What would you like to drink?"

"Water, please." When Jessy set a plate at his place, he said, "This looks heavenly."

"Thank you. I'm heating up some hot chocolate too."

Once Nathan helped her into her seat and had taken his seat across from her, he opened his napkin over his lap. Bowing his head, he prayed, "Dear heavenly Father, thank You for a safe trip to this place, and especially for the friendship Jessy and I share."

As Nathan prayed, Jessy's heart couldn't help but squeal with delight: the honored Dr. Isaac Nathan Fisher praying here in her own home, over the tasty stew she had helped Suzanna prepare from foods the family had raised with love. He offered the bread basket to her, but she declined. "Aren't you going to join me?"

"I've already eaten, thank you. We usually eat around six-thirty or so."

"I'm sorry for disrupting—"

Jessy laughed good-naturedly. "Don't be silly! We're so pleased you could come and see us. You'll be staying a while, I hope?"

"My train leaves tomorrow morning at eleven."

"Oh, so soon?"

"Yes, I must. Classes start again Monday." Though he was sorry to have to leave so soon, he looked pleased to know he was welcome to stay longer.

Jessy liked watching Nathan break bread. As he did, a spray of crisp crumbs crackled about under his long fingers. He was a careful diner. He ate slowly, in his courtly way, with a respect for food, savoring each morsel to the full. "You've had a good trip, I take it?" she asked as Nathan ate. "Your lectures went well?"

"Excellent trip! I do think the lectures went over rather well."

There was nothing flashy about Nathan Fisher, nothing false, nothing pretentious, Jessy decided, and yet he had so many gifts he could have appeared pretentious about. She propped her delicately dimpled chin on one upright fist. Dreamily she said, "I wish I could have heard you speak at college. I'm fortunate just to have finished high school!"

"Oh, you did, did you? Good for you! No easy thing, to work as hard as you must and find time for study too. Congratulations!"

With eagerness she asked, "What were your lectures about?"

"Church Renewal since the Middle Ages," he answered.

"Oh, how I wish I could have heard you!"

"I have a spare copy of my lecture notes with me, if you're interested."

"Oh, my! Yes, of course I'm interested." After a moment she asked, "What's your conclusion? About the church as a whole, I mean?"

Nathan smiled so his dimples appeared. "I like to compare the church to a forest: despite inevitible decline in some places, there's new growth cropping up in other places all the time."

"I agree!" Jessy's eyes narrowed in thought. "Some say the church is dying and will soon be obsolete, but I say that God is always reaching out toward His loved ones, always calling His children, always sending His word into the hearts of those who seek Him."

"Exactly. If the church was nothing but a man-made institution—" Nathan paused to take a sip of water.

"—it would have died out ages ago!" Jessy said with a flourish.

"Precisely!"

They paused a moment, enjoying each other's presence. Seeing that Nathan had nearly finished his stew, Jessy said, "There's more! And apple pie."

"Sounds wonderful but I'll pass. It's getting rather late and—"

Just then Mr. Cuckoo went mad in the hall. Nathan laughed with Jessy over all the noise, a nonsensical array of needless notes and whistles.

After the claptrap concerto ended, Nathan exclaimed, "My heavens, what a production! Twenty-two after seventeen, is it?"

"Oh, that silly clock!" Jessy hoped Nathan wasn't too tired to stay up and talk a bit, but would never have intruded upon the comfort of her illustrious guest. All she said was, "It's only about nine, I'd guess."

Nathan took out his pocket watch, a glowing thing of old, well-worn gold, and snapped it open. "Nine-oh-five." As he closed and put away his watch he said, "My father bought one of those cuckoo clocks from a catalog."

"So did Suzanna!" Jessy led Nathan into the hall, saying, "Suzanna's Folly, that's what Adam calls that clock of hers. It's not worth shipping back to the company, they decided. We think one of these days the poor thing will just kick up its heels and squawk its last."

For a moment Nathan listened to the clock's mechanism whirring madly. "Shall I have a try with it? I fixed that clock of my father's."

"You know how to fix clocks?" Jessy said in wonder.

"I like clocks." Giving the errant clock a sidelong glance he added, "When they behave, that is." Nathan took the clock from the wall and headed for the parlor where he took a seat. He placed the clock on the tea table before him. "Do you have a screwdriver?"

Jessy ran out of the room and soon returned staggering under the load of one of Adam's tool boxes crammed with all sorts of hardware. As Nathan began unfastening the back of the clock, he said to it, "I'll tell you what time it is, you poor old thing—time for your operation!"

Jessy put another log on the fire and, excusing herself, left the room again. Soon she returned with two cups of hot chocolate. She sat beside Nathan on the sofa, marveling at his endless expertise. In a few moments the clock's wayward innards were spread about the tea table. With an impish grin she confided, "Adam has threatened to shoot that clock."

Nathan found this amusing. "Ah, there's the problem! Just as I thought." Nathan fiddled with the mechanism, and then reached for another of Adam's wide range of tools. "Your brother must be quite handy, like all farmers I know!"

"Yes, he is, but Adam couldn't fix a clock!"

"I like to tinker. I have a complete workshop and laboratory at home." Nathan glanced up at the lamp.

Without being asked, Jessy drew the lamp closer for him.

"Thank you, Jessy. Workers accomplish nothing in the dark, eh?"

"We work while we have the light," Jessy answered.

"So true, so true! There, I think that should do it," Nathan said. He held the clock close to his ear, listening.

"That cuckoo has an awful voice, don't you think?" Jessy asked.

"We can fix that too. Down, bird, down!" Nathan made more adjustments.

"Speaking of birds, how is Plato Q?"

"Faculty's probably spoiling him rotten. He told me to tell you *bbrraawkk!*" Nathan's perfectly raucous imitation of Plato Q set both of them laughing. He took a moment to reach for the cup of hot chocolate Jessy had put before him. "Mmmm. Delicious. Thank you." He made one last adjustment and said, "There. Let's see how this bird does now." Together they returned the clock to its rightful place in the hall.

While Nathan made sure the clock was balanced, the cuckoo appeared and sang a perfect two-note toodle. Nathan checked his watch. With satisfaction, he said to Jessy, "It's 9:30, and the bird sounded twice, as it should."

When they heard someone approaching, the pair turned up to the top of the staircase to see Adam in a long woolen robe with a book in his hand.

"Good evening, Adam! Hope I haven't disturbed you," said Nathan.

Looking puzzled, Adam said sleepily, "No, not at all. Glad you could stop by and see us. Don't mind me." Adam rubbed his temple. "It's funny. I thought I heard the hall clock just now, workin' right for a change. Guess I must've dozed off while I was readin'."

Jessy beamed proudly. "You weren't dreaming, Adam! Nathan fixed the cuckoo clock!"

Adam's sleepy green eyes widened. "No kiddin'! Well, thank you, Nathan!" To Jessy he said, "Don't you stay up too long, now."

"I won't. We're just going to have hot chocolate and say good night."

Adam eyed the pair, his face saying, *That's all you'd better do.*

Nathan and Jessy, innocent as doves and intending to stay that way, bid Adam a peaceful night. Once Adam walked back to the master bedroom, Jessy and Nathan returned to the parlor. There Jessy ventured: "Nathan, before we say good night, I have some books I'd like to show you this evening, while the house is quiet."

Nathan, his charming face and deep gray eyes brimming with insatiable curiosity and uncommon intellect, nodded respectfully to her. Over deep mugs of hot chocolate, in the stillness of the cold winter night, Jessy and Nathan sat together before the fire. She handed him a slender volume. "For you, if you don't think it's too elementary. I bought it at an auction."

"*The Majestic Night Sky*! Great heavens!" Nathan, looking positively delighted, explained, "A long time ago I lent my copy of this wonderful book and never got it back. I tried to buy another, but it had gone out of print."

Pleased at his reaction, Jessy said, "Perhaps your book has gone all around the world and here it is back again in your hands."

"And to think I fully expected never to see this wonderful little book again! How very thoughtful of you, Jessy! I can't thank you enough."

With sudden and profound appreciation to the Lord for this moment and for all His countless tender gifts of love, she said gently, "Nothing can keep our good from us."

"How right you are!" Nathan leafed through the slender volume, admiring astronomical diagrams of his beloved starry skies. Jessy couldn't have felt happier. For a few moments they sipped hot chocolate while Nathan looked through the book, expressing his thanks again and again.

The clock sounded correctly once more, this time a three-note melody indicating that the third quarter of the hour had arrived. Her evening with Nathan Fisher was fast slipping away. Soon, very soon, Adam and Suzanna would be expecting to hear Jessy's footsteps climbing the stairs to her room.

Swallowing hard and taking a deep breath, Jessy stood all of a sudden. With the glow of the fire behind her she said quickly, "There's something else, Nathan, another book I bought at that same auction. Would you look at it for me and tell me what you think? Would you mind terribly?"

Nathan put down the astronomy book and said without hesitation, "I'd do anything for you, dear Jessy, anything within my power. What is it? You look so troubled. That's not like you."

"No, it isn't. You're right. But perhaps I'm upset over nothing at all. I've said nothing to anyone until now. When I first made this discovery—if anyone could call it a discovery—I didn't know whom to ask about it, but when you wrote you were planning a visit, I knew I had to ask you. I trust you to help me get to the bottom of this mystery—that is, if it's a mystery at all." She went to the shelf where she had placed the book printed in 1861 with the red leather cover. Before she handed it to Nathan she stood between him and the fire, looking as nervous as anyone had ever seen her. "You'll think I'm silly asking you about such a thing."

He shook his head. "Never. They—whoever 'they' are—say there are no silly questions—just silly answers!"

Jessy handed him the book. "Here." As she settled beside him on the sofa, she said, "I think it's written in Greek."

Nathan opened the book carefully. "Extraordinary," he said quietly, "but this isn't Greek." Fully absorbed, he turned page after page with his smooth strong hands. As he read in silence, he smiled a knowing smile.

She watched Nathan, a rare scholar with a rare book in his hands—a rare sight indeed. The crackling mellow fire surrounded his wise face and broad form in a golden glow. He looked so comfortable and so pleasant there in her parlor, with his casual tweeds, giving the impression of scholarship mingled with rousing good humor. Jessy's nervousness faded completely as she watched Nathan's grand profile, his large gray eyes radiating wisdom—all in all, the very face of love.

Jessy felt herself falling deeply in love with Nathan Fisher. *Impossible*, a voice cried within her, *but yes, I love you, Nathan Fisher. I think I always have, since I first saw you that day by the sea!*

Turning to her at last, Nathan asked, "Do you know what this book is?"

She shook her head. "I haven't got the foggiest idea."

"You say you found this at an auction?" When she nodded to him, he flipped to the cover page, explaining, "My Russian's a bit rusty, but what you have here is a set of short stories: Russia's most intriguing true mysteries."

"Mysteries?" Jessy's deep brown eyes glistened in the rosy light. "I love a mystery, especially one I can solve."

He turned a few pages, explaining as he went, "Yes, it's a collection of stories about strange sightings, disappearances, missing persons, unsolved crimes, sinister plots, disgruntled heirs looking for lost fortunes—that sort of thing. But why would such an entertaining but obscure book trouble you?"

A shiver ran through her. "This picture—here." She turned to that oddly familiar portrait of a handsome Russian at the height of his manhood with a full bushy moustache, thick waving dark hair, light dazzling eyes, and high sculpted cheekbones. She peered as she had done a hundred times before at the mark on the distinguished gentleman's left cheek. Was it a beauty mark or a stray spot of ink? Confessing her ignorance, she said, "I can't read the caption. Does the book say who this man is?"

Nathan scrutinized the Russian text a moment before answering: "Otto Illyanov, a sort of private secretary or administrative aide to this gent—" Nathan tapped at another engraving connected to the same story. "The worthy Count Alexsei Vostolokov."

Jessy studied the picture of a portly, elderly man standing in a resplendent military uniform with a sword at his hip, an ample sash and swags across his chest, glittering medals and shining buttons down his jacket, and hefty epaulets at his shoulders. His plump, cheerful face was accentuated by closely cropped comma-shaped curls.

"Illyanov. Vostolokov. These names mean anything to you?"

"No." Jessy shook her head, but asked, "Did they live in the Crimea?"

"Yes. The Count owned several large estates, one near Yalta, in the Crimea, and another along the Don. Russia has controlled the area for centuries. If I recall correctly, Rostov-on-Don was, once upon a time, under consideration to be the new Russian capital, but nothing came of the political machinations involved. The Crimea is rich in ores, steel mills, and the like. It's a beautiful country, and fertile too. The peasants raise figs and pomegranates and tend sheep. There's a fishing industry, too, by the river that empties into a nearby sea."

Noting the trouble that persisted in Jessy's face, Nathan searched the volume for a map to show her the region in question. "Here's Yalta, in the the Crimea, and not too far to the east, the Don River. You can see that at Rostov-on-Don the river empties into the Sea of Azov. Why?" He beamed at her, trying to reassure her.

Taking the book from Nathan, and returning to the troubling picture, Jessy tipped her head and gave him a sidelong glance, whispering, "This Otto Illyanov looks like Leo Kimball."

"How *is* that young man of yours?" Nathan asked.

Jessy's soft eyes widened and her pale rosebud lips parted, but no words came forth.

"I read about that no-hitter of his. Quite a feat!" Nathan glanced at Jessy's slender fingers. "I halfway expected to see a ring on your left hand by now."

Jessy hid her bare hands from view, and her troubled face as well. Wishing not to admit that Leo had betrayed her, instead she stammered, "L-Leo's not r-ready to settle down, I don't think. Not yet. He didn't have a good year after that no-hitter. Sh-shoulder problems. There was talk he'd be traded, but I haven't heard for sure."

"Baseball's a worrisome business. I'm not prone to offer advice, particularly to one so level-headed as you, but I wouldn't want to see a good woman marry the wrong man." Nathan leaned back and tucked his thumbs into his vest pockets. "Do you love him?" Nathan's question took

Jessy by surprise. She hardly knew how to answer. "I can see you have strong feelings about him. But are they love?"

Avoiding Nathan's eyes, Jessy stammered, "I u-used to think so, but I-I'm n-not sure." She looked at Nathan, adding, "He's far from me. He leads a life so different from my own."

"And what, if I may ask, other than a similarity in facial features, does this Russian mystery have to do with your baseball pitcher?"

"I don't know! Leo's family has a photograph of his grandfather, Count Dimitri Alexandrov. The Count and Leo resemble each other strongly—they could have been twins. Leo's grandfather came to this country from the Crimea around the time of the American Civil War, that's what Leo told me. He married and settled in Chicago, where Leo's mother, Acacia, was born. Leo's grandfather must have liked the weather, I think—cold and blustery—with flat open prairies good for growing things. Perhaps Illinois reminded Leo's grandfather of his homeland.

"He was wealthy, from what Leo and his sister Darlene have told me. He owned a home on Washington Street and an estate just north of Chicago on the lake. He raised horses, too, I think, and Leo's father, Walter, managed the estate after he married Acacia. She had a pampered childhood in Chicago, from what I understand. She loved the theaters and concerts and fine arts, all those things."

Jessy paused to gaze at the picture of Otto Illyanov who resembled so much the photograph Leo had shown her. "This man looks so much like Leo and his grandfather, except Leo's grandfather wore a military uniform and had flat, short curls like Count Vostolokov. Leo's grandfather had a mole on his left cheek just like this fellow Otto Illyanov does." Confused, Jessy paused. The fire began to fade.

Nathan stood and adjusted the logs on the grate. They blazed and crackled under his deft touch. He leaned against the mantle and asked, "I take it you know nothing of the story printed in this book?"

"Nothing."

"And you've said nothing about this book to anyone?"

"No." Not wishing to appear the gossip, Jessy avoided telling Nathan about the troubled Kimball household, the dark side that had struck her so forcefully in so many ways, but she did look intently at Nathan, saying, "I've told only you about this book."

"That was wise, Jessy. Very wise." Nathan paused a moment to collect his thoughts, take his seat, and begin in his casual but lucid way, "You see, Jessy, according to this book of yours, Otto Illyanov left Russia under mysterious circumstances in the 1850s during the Crimean War. Otto was an aide to Count Alexsei Vostolokov, a retired military man who had a son fighting in the Crimean War—a war that pitted Russia against the combined forces of England, France, and, for a time, Italy, over custody of and access to the Holy Places in Jerusalem. Well, according to your book, the old Count developed a serious zymotic disease."

Jessy's face looked quizzical. "A what?"

"Oh, a sort of fermented contagion—a gastric fever of some sort. The text is obscure on that point. My guess is that the old count was being poisoned!" Nathan glanced at the text before continuing. "Well, as old Count Vostolokov was breathing his last, home comes his son who had been wounded in the war. Now, the son resembled Otto Illyanov—they were about the same age, height, and weight and had the same foppish look. You see?" Nathan showed her yet another picture connected to the story. The young Count Vostolokov did vaguely resemble Otto Illyanov in youth and vitality.

"So what the book author suggests is that Otto Illyanov tired of the work he was doing for the elder and younger Vostolokovs. He was also at odds with the political situation in Russia, which at that time was a police state under the Romanovs." The honorable professor paused, staring into space for a moment. "Yes, you see, Jessy, Otto Illyanov was a sympathizer with the revolutionary Decembrists, a poorly organized lot who failed to take over the government in December of 1825. The Decembrists dreamed of a world without czars, with all rule and property in the hands of the people. According to this book of yours, Otto Illyanov was politically frustrated and immeasurably ambitious. Ambition is a dangerous thing. Have I lost you entirely with this story, Jessy?" Nathan asked, smiling at her.

Jessy laughed and nodded. "Yes, but please tell me more!"

"All right. We have a sick old count in bed with a fatal bellyache, his young son home from the front severely wounded, and this serpent Otto in their midst—an ambitious upstart who wants to overthrow the government or, at the very least, to advance his own position. If there was to be no freedom through a revolution, Otto might turn to other drastic measures. According to the author of this book, Otto killed the injured soldier and his aging father, and made off with the family jewels, the military medals, the epaulets, the sword, et cetera, et cetera."

"Otto Illyanov was a murderer and a thief?" Jessy exclaimed.

"So says your book." Nathan tapped the picture of the man who so resembled Leo Kimball. "This Otto Illyanov, bearing stolen treasures in a peasant's knapsack and dressed in rags, was believed to have made his way south before his crimes were discovered. He joined a host of Russian peasants for a pilgrimage from Russia due south to the Holy Land. Each year, thousands of Russian peasants still go by the boatful to see the glories of Jerusalem. It wasn't too hard for Otto Illyanov to hide his identity and slip away undetected."

"Then how did his picture end up in this book?" Jessy wondered aloud.

"Ah. Heaven sees our deeds—good and bad. And the Russian secret police are no slouches, either. Since 1825, when the ill-fated Decembrists made their haphazard and unsuccessful bid to rid Russia of the monarchy, the czars, starting with Nicholas the First, began to keep a tight watch over all their subjects by means of a ruthless secret police. A handful of these human bloodhounds followed Otto Illyanov to the Holy Land, but Otto eluded them in the Crimea, where the war was still going on. Before or during the bitterly contested, hand-to-hand battle for the port at Sevastopol— " Nathan peered at the book and then looked up at Jessy, "—it's uncertain, but it is thought Otto Illyanov hired a private yacht with part of his ill-gotten fortune and made his way to the Dardanelles— lovely, those Dardanelles—and beyond to the Mediterranean. The trail grew cold after that but according to this book, it was believed that Otto continued westward, perhaps to America. Of course, by the time this book was printed—1861—we were well into our not-so-Civil War and I suspect Otto Illyanov, still in possession of the Count's fortune, got lost in the crowd of other immigrants to America carving out a comfortable life for themselves."

"In Illinois perhaps?"

"In Illinois perhaps."

Gazing at the pictures in the book, Jessy said, "I smell a rat."

"So do I." Nathan asked, "What are you thinking?"

"That Otto Illyanov is Leo's grandfather. The name he went by, Count Dimitri Alexandrov, is made-up. Leo's grandfather was no Count at all, but a—" Jessy, unable to say the words thief and murderer, did say, "I know for sure that around 1885 in Chicago, something bad happened to the Kimballs, so bad and so sudden that Walter and Acacia moved away. They both loved Illinois yet they left. About that same time, something happened to their young son Peter." Peter Kimball's haunted face flashed before Jessy and held her, but before saying or doing anything further, she knew she needed time to think and to pray.

Nathan stood and went to the fireplace. For a moment he gazed at her before saying, "You're still troubled. How else can I help?"

At that moment the cuckoo clock chimed a perfectly correct ten times. Jessy rose from her seat and stood by her guest, saying from the heart, "You've done so much! I can't thank you enough. You told me when we first met that you liked untangling things! Before you leave tomorrow, would you mind dictating a translation of this story for me to keep? There are people who must know—"

"Promise you won't get into any danger over this business."

"Danger?" Jessy looked at Nathan with her gentle, doe-like eyes, but in her heart she knew that, at all costs, the truth must overcome darkness.

Nathan said solemnly, "Extreme caution must always be observed whenever there's a fortune involved and desperate scoundrels who aren't afraid of doing violence. Promise me you'll take every precaution, no matter where this mystery leads you." When Jessy gave no answer, he asked again, "Promise me?"

As a red-hot log tumbled into the ashes, the two gazed into each other's eyes, their shadows flickering in the night.

CHAPTER 31

❧

The following morning, after the Flints enjoyed a hearty home-cooked breakfast with Nathan Fisher, they saw their guest to the railroad station. The family stood at a little distance while Nathan, with Jessy beside him, waited near the tracks for his eleven o'clock train. Their breath puffed in the cold November air. Jessy was reluctant to say good-bye.

"I'm so glad you came to see me," she said, blushing in the cold.

"I wouldn't have missed our time together for—for the world." The normally gilt-tongued professor was as aware as she that his inmost feelings were making him stumble in his speech.

Jessy noted this rare and precious little slip of his with feelings too private to make known on a busy railroad platform. He valued her friendship! Casting her lovely brown eyes downward, she clutched her tapestry bag with her gloved hands. Nathan must have read her mind.

"You'll use caution, Jessy, about that Crimean business? You promised!"

Jessy looked up to her dear friend, in the prime of life, a strong, well-made man of God with a courage few possessed, and yet he fretted over her. That this outstanding gentleman would express concern for Jessy made her beam with pleasure. "I'll be fine, really I will! After our talk last night I thought and prayed a long while. This morning I wakened knowing what to do." Despite the warmth in her voice, she renewed her tight-fisted grasp on her bag, the contents of which were precious. The translation Nathan had written out for her could mean the downfall of some and the vindication of others.

From a distance they could hear an approaching train. Its deep sounding whistles echoed over Bethel Township. Soon—too soon—the black behemoth came chugging into the station. Nathan sighed audibly. "Too short!"

Jessy looked up to him, her face a delicate question mark.

"Our visit—it was far too short!" He took off his glove and grasped her hand. "You'll take care?"

"I will." Reluctant to let go of his hand, she said so only he could hear, "And you'll take care, too, won't you? Enigma is a long way off."

"Ah, Enigma. It's a place I think you'd find endlessly interesting. Have you read the brochures I've sent?"

"Oh, yes, several times over!"

"Do you think you'd like to see the place for yourself some day?"

Jessy laughed nervously. "Me? I'm not college material! But St. Azarias does sound like a grand place to study. To grow."

There was no time to say more. Passengers were exiting the train while others boarded it. Railroad men unloaded bundles of newspapers, sacks of mail, and crates. Suzanna presented Nathan with a going-away basket of her best home-baked treats to enjoy during his long ride to Enigma.

"Oh, you shouldn't have gone to so much trouble, Mrs. Flint!" he exclaimed.

"It's the least I could do! I'm so glad you fixed our clock!"

"Not as happy as I am," said Adam with a sardonic grin. He wrapped one all-encompassing arm around his beloved and extended his right hand to Nathan, saying, "Come back 'n' see us any time."

"Oh, yes, Dr. Fisher, please visit us again!" Martha asked with merry eyes. "Will you please?"

Nathan was about to respond when a railroad man hollered, "All aboard!" and a pack of noisy bystanders crowded the platform.

Nathan turned away to climb up the steps into the passenger train. Jessy moved forward into the spot where Nathan had been only a moment before. Despite the crowd, she felt the emptiness Nathan Fisher left behind him.

From the top step, Nathan turned to smile at her. In a reluctant farewell, he raised his hand. Raising her own hand, Jessy's mind at that moment became a camera, forever capturing this final, parting image of Nathan Fisher, those deep-ranging gray eyes of his radiating a world of unspoken thoughts and feelings. Were any of those thoughts and feelings about her?

Inwardly chastising herself for reading too much into Nathan's friendship, she waved again. Nathan did the same, waving first to her and then to her family, and back to Jessy again, but then he turned one final time and was seen no more. The train chugged off, gaining speed as it went. As it rolled off, taking Nathan Fisher far away from her, Jessy reconsidered the question he had put to her moments before: Would she like to see Enigma? Had she understood correctly and responded appropriately? Too late. Now Jessy would never know. Worse, from nowhere she was gripped by Suzanna's long-gone fear of trains going amiss and taking lives.

"Oh, Father!" Jessy prayed in frozen silence, "Dear Father, please watch over Nathan and all who—"

"Nice guy." After failing to get a response, Adam said, "Ready?"

With her heart aching, Jessy glanced wordlessly at her brother.

"Time to go." He gestured toward the road.

"Oh, I feel like walking, if you don't mind. Please go home without me. I have an errand in town." When Adam showed reluctance to leave without her, she added, "I won't be long. No more than an hour." As Adam and the family headed home, Jessy hurried from the station in the opposite direction, fiercely clutching her tapestry bag.

ლ ლ ლ

"And that's the whole story, Mr. Webb, as far as I can tell. See for yourself." From her bag Jessy took the Russian book and Nathan's English translation and placed them on George Webb's desk. Then, for the first time, she sat back and relaxed a bit in the lawyer's guest chair.

Behind his desk perpetually strewn with papers, seals, stamps, and open law texts, George Webb, Suzanna's father, took up Jessy's documentation and leaned back in his chair, too, deep in thought. Inclined to stoutness, George Webb was of middle height, with thinning gray hair and gold-rimmed eyeglasses. He studied Nathan's translation and examined the pictures in Jessy's book.

As he did, she regarded the man who had so helped the Flints after the tornado struck. The Webbs had given Adam, Suzanna, and Jessy a home, farmland, and loans to rebuild their lives. Before George Webb spoke again, he read and reread Nathan's translation of the Russian text.

After a moment of deep thought, he said, "Though I've never handled this sort of matter before, I suppose something can be done—not that I'm convinced anything should be done, mind you. Medical experts and the staff at Fair Haven would have to be consulted and there'd be a great deal of paperwork involved, but nothing can be done without the knowledge and consent of Peter Kimball's parents. You know that."

"Yes, of course." Jessy sat erect again, adding, "I plan to talk with the Kimballs as soon as I can. I wanted your advice first. In confidence."

"In confidence," the attorney said, assuring her their conversation was private and privileged. His law office was quiet today, this Saturday noon. "Now, let me see if I understand you," said George Webb as he slowly filled and lit his pipe. "You think Walter and Acacia are hiding something—that perhaps they knew her father wasn't a count at all but the renegade Otto Illyanov who was stalked by the Russian secret police all the way from the Crimea to Chicago, and that this business somehow triggered Peter's mental breakdown. You think the Kimballs are keeping their own son confined without cause."

Sighing heavily, Jessy answered, "Yes. I'm not sure of the details, exactly, but I feel something wrong is being done against Peter Kimball."

"Aren't you being rather melodramatic, Jessy?"

"I don't think so, Mr. Webb! The day I met Peter, he seemed troubled but sane. I think Peter knows something his parents don't want made public. Why else would the family have so quickly left Chicago—a place they loved?"

"Are you a doctor?" Webb asked her. "Are you trained in mental health?"

"No, of course not. I just have this feeling that—" Jessy sank back in her chair, feeling uncomfortably like a fool.

"A feeling!" Webb chided. Pulling deeply on his pipe, he added, "Peter had a complete mental breakdown shortly after his grandfather's death. The two had been very close. After his grandfather died, Peter went 'raving mad' according to Walter Kimball. I spoke with Walter at length once he settled back here in Bethel. By that time, he and Acacia had already given up their boy to the hospital. Walter asked me to draw up papers that would ensure that Peter would be well cared for no matter what happened to them."

"And Peter has been locked up at Fair Haven ever since!" Indignant, Jessy leaned forward, pleading her case. "I've met Peter. He's as sane as—"

Mr. Webb eyed her warily. "I've met him, too, when he was hospitalized. No doubt about it, the boy was seriously disturbed. Ranting, in fact. Peter had to be locked up for his own safety."

"He isn't a boy anymore, Mr. Webb. Peter Kimball is a grown man. I don't see why he should be confined like a prisoner! I intend to talk with his parents. I'll show them my book."

"Preposterous! This book has nothing to do with the Kimballs. You'll only offend Walter and Acacia by showing it to them. If you take my advice, Jessy, you'll keep this foolishness to yourself and toss that book into the fire!" Webb turned to look at the snapping fire burning in his office, the brilliant glow of it reflected in deep red tiles and the polished cherry mantle.

Jessy, refusing to give in to the rational arguments of the attorney, gazed instead at one of the hunting pictures in his well-appointed office. "What happened to the Count? Was there an investigation?"

"Oh, yes," said Webb, pulling gently on his pipe and emitting a small cloud of blue smoke in the process. "The police decided it was a felony murder—a death resulting from a robbery gone wrong. The Count was a wealthy man murdered during the commission of a robbery."

"Murdered?" This was news indeed to Jessy.

"You didn't know?" Webb eyed her through the haze of his pipe smoke. "The Count was murdered one twilight near his boathouse on Lake Michigan. Acacia came on the scene just before Peter did. Someone was seen running away from the boathouse and into the fog coming off the lake. Problem was, the crime was so unexpected, the light so poor, and the weather so heavy no two witnesses agreed on what they had seen. One neighbor thought he saw a man and a woman running away. Another claimed he saw two gypsies, both men."

"*Gypsies?*"

"I know it sounds preposterous, but that's what one fellow said! A neighbor swore that earlier that day she saw a vagabond in the neighborhood who looked Bohemian. So much for eyewitnesses! There were various reports, no two alike, but in a city as big and diverse as Chicago, there are all sorts of people moving about—immigrants and otherwise—most of whom are perfectly within their rights to do so.

"Regardless of who was responsible for the crime, Acacia was profoundly disturbed by the murder of the noble father she adored. A woman of her wealth and prominence would fear adverse publicity, understandably so. Walter was all for staying put and riding out their troubles, but Acacia begged him to move away. They had a young family at the time. Peter was the oldest but not the only child they had to consider. Acacia, sensitive, artistic soul that she is, wanted and needed her serenity. She was badly frightened.

"That's why they decided to move to Bethel where Walter's family has lived for generations. In the end, Walter agreed with Acacia that they couldn't risk more trouble. That's all there is to it, Jessy. It's unfortunate, but I have to agree, with everyone else, that the shock of his grandfather's death was too much for Peter. The attempted robbery ended with two victims—the Count and his grandson."

"Oh, I'm so sorry," Jessy said with feeling.

"So if you'll take my advice, you'll just forget that book of yours and let the matter go. You can't help anyone now, dragging up this old, sordid affair. And if you'll pardon me for saying, it's none of your business."

"But it *is* my business! I care about Peter. No one in his family seems to, but I do!" Jessy clutched her book and Nathan's translation. "Let justice reign though the heavens fall."

"You can only do harm opening old wounds. Walter is a friend of mine. Acacia's a fine, delicate lady."

"Of course I don't wish to hurt anyone," Jessy confided. "But I do care that justice is done. That the truth be known." *The truth*—what had Peter said about the truth? As Jessy put her book into her bag, she mused aloud. "I wonder what was stolen."

"Hmm?" George Webb turned abruptly from the fire to Jessy.

"What was stolen from the Count's boathouse? The police thought the murder was secondary to a robbery. What was it the vagabonds were after?"

Avoiding her eyes, Webb knocked the ash out of his pipe. "As I recall, nothing was missing from the boathouse."

"And from the main house? The Count was a wealthy man. What was taken from his home?"

304

"Nothing." George Webb shook his head. "The Count surprised the robbers. He must have gotten a good look at them so they killed him but were forced to flee before taking anything. It happens more than you'd think, Jessy, a robbery gone wrong, innocent bystanders killed, and no loot taken."

"Still—" Jessy, her mind racing, gazed once more at the colorful hunting scenes on the wall behind George Webb's desk. In the central scene, a lively fox eluded the bloodhounds. Glancing back to him, she said, "Mr. Webb, I think the police might have missed something in their investigation. I won't rest until I've done what I can to help Peter."

George Webb held her fast with his eyes. "You're determined to confront Walter and Acacia Kimball despite my warnings?"

"Yes. Surely after all this time, they could discuss this matter in a reasonable way, don't you think?"

"Perhaps. But if I were you, I wouldn't confront them alone."

"I don't dare tell Adam or Suzanna."

"Because you know they'd try to stop you!" Webb declared.

"Perhaps." Jessy stood and picked up her tapestry bag. "Thank you, Mr. Webb, for talking with me. Perhaps you're right. Perhaps I'm wrong. But, feeling as I do, I can't simply do nothing. I think Peter deserves better."

"Then again, perhaps you're right and I'm wrong!" Now Webb smiled kindly at Jessy. "Regardless of what's in that book of yours, perhaps Peter's condition has improved. Perhaps it's time the Kimballs thought about having Peter's condition reevaluated. Perhaps it's time he came home."

"Perhaps!" Jessy said with a triumphant smile.

"Perhaps I'd better go with you." George Webb picked up the telephone. "Operator? Please ring the Flint home. Yes, thank you. Suzy? How are you, daughter? And Adam? How're my grandchildren? You all coming to dinner tomorrow? Good! Listen, Jessy is here with me. We have a matter to look into that may take us a while and I wanted you to know. Yes, she's fine. Don't worry. We'll get some lunch first and then run our errand." Webb grunted sharply. "Now, daughter, you know better than to ask a lawyer questions about confidential matters!" At this George gave Jessy a wink. "Must run, now, Suzy. See you tomorrow."

Grinning bashfully, Jessy asked, "Don't you think we should call the Kimballs too?"

"Surprise is one of our best weapons, my dear. Let's go!"

❦ ❦ ❦

Acacia Kimball, dressed in lavender and wrapped in a pale blue woolen shawl, sat in comfort on her luxurious gold-satin striped settee. "Gracious, where did you find that piece of junk?" she asked Jessy Flint.

Jessy, seated pertly with George Webb across the tea table from Walter and Acacia Kimball, passed the water-stained leather-bound book toward Acacia's delicate hands. "Then you haven't ever seen this book?"

"No, and I'm not sure I want to! Such a moldy old thing!" Acacia made a halfhearted effort to reach for the book.

Red-haired, accommodating Walter helped by handing the book to Acacia, explaining to his guests, "My wife hasn't been feeling well since lunch."

"I'm so sorry," said Jessy. "Nothing serious, I hope."

"Nothing life won't cure in time," Acacia answered weakly, her intensely blue eyes, so like Leo's, taking on a faraway gaze.

"Acacia told me a few minutes before you came that her arm felt numb." Walter shook his head. "I wanted to call the doctor, but she wouldn't let me."

"I'm perfectly fine!" Dismissing her husband's comments with a serene lifting of her head, Acacia limply scanned the Russian tome. Clearing her throat, she said finally, "This means nothing to me. Nothing whatever."

Before Acacia could return the book to Jessy, Walter took it, asking, "Mind if I look at it?"

"Of course not," Jessy said at once. "And here's the translation. May I take a picture down from your hall? There's something I'd like you to see."

Acacia frowned, but Walter nodded out of curiosity. Off Jessy went to the hallway to get the photograph of Count Dimitri Alexandrov. When Jessy returned, George Webb was asking Walter and Acacia, "After all this time, do you think Peter should be reexamined to see if he might be released from the hospital? Shouldn't he be reevaluated?"

With her eyes on Jessy, Acacia snarled to George Webb, "You've been listening to her! She went to see him! Don't think I don't know what's been going on behind my back!"

"Is it true, Jessy?" Walter looked up from the Russian volume and took the picture Jessy handed to him. "Did you visit our son in the hospital?"

"Why, yes, I did. I wanted to see him." How well Jessy remembered the day she, Leo, and Emma had driven to Fair Haven.

"You miserable—" Acacia's eyes narrowed as her voice rose.

"No, don't, Acacia." With heartfelt enthusiasm, Walter said, "I'm touched that Jessy would take an interest in our boy."

"Interested as only a nosy troublemaker would be!" Acacia snapped.

"Mrs. Kimball! I only sought to do the right thing! I wanted to see your son because he was in the hospital and because Christians should—"

"A *mental* hospital! You had no right! You Christians want to change the world! I won't stand for your interference!" Regaining her dignity, Acacia wrapped the shawl tightly around herself and perched daintily on the settee. "I wish you would go!"

"I was about to say I'm glad you've come!" Walter intervened. "I'm ashamed to say it's been years since I've seen Peter. How was he, Jessy?"

"Your son seemed fine—until it was time for us to leave. I suppose it was to be expected that he didn't want us to go without taking him with us." Jessy glanced to the piano in the parlor. "He plays beautifully, Mr. Kimball. It's such a shame to know he's locked up, cut off from the world—"

"That's where he belongs! We know best!" Acacia snapped. "He's not well enough to have visitors! You probably did a great deal of harm to him!"

That her visit to Peter Kimball might have caused harm overwhelmed Jessy. Feeling anxious, she wondered if Leo had been correct in not wanting to see or even discuss Peter with her, and that perhaps George Webb was right in advising Jessy not to pursue this matter now. Silently she prayed God would forgive her folly and grant the right outcome. *Not my will but Yours*, she affirmed. Then she remembered Peter's outburst: *Truth is a killing gypsy.* A chill rushed over her. What had Peter been talking about? Was he raving mad or not?

Walter patted his wife on the knee with one hand but retained his grip on the book with the other. At the moment he was comparing the photograph from his own hall to an illustration in the book. "Look at this, dear."

Acacia refused to turn her head. She sat in a rage, stewing silently.

"Don't you think Peter might be released after so long a time? Perhaps he's over his mental ailment," Webb repeated.

For the moment more absorbed with the pictures and translation than George Webb's comment, Walter exclaimed, "This is very interesting! Acacia, I could swear this fellow Otto What's-his-name looks exactly like your father! He was certainly bright, nimble, and daring enough to pull off such a feat and elude the czar's police for so many years, don't you think?"

Acacia tore at the book with a force that surprised everyone. "Lies, I tell you! My father was a nobleman! Dimitri Alexandrov, a land-owning count!"

Walter, a big, powerful fellow, easily kept Jessy's book safely out of Acacia's blind rage. Now all attention focused on Acacia, the well-groomed woman in lavender. Avoiding their stares, she unwrapped and rewrapped the pale blue shawl around her gracefully curving shoulders.

Slowly, levelly, Walter asked his wife, "Why are you so angry that someone resembles your father down to the mark on his cheek?"

Acacia gazed off into space, saying as if from a dream, "My father was a great man. People were jealous. Little people will try to steal what they can't have by rightful means." With this Acacia glared at Jessy as if she, too, were another in a long line of jealous little people.

Walter tapped the engraving in the book. "Otto and your father were one and the same man, isn't that right, Acacia?"

"How dare you?" Acacia avoided looking at Walter and their visitors.

Softly, Jessy said, "Mr. Kimball, your children have told me that their brother Peter was a normal boy until he reached the age of ten and then—"

George Webb sought clarification. "What exactly did Peter experience that unhinged his mind?"

Walter sighed deeply before answering. "My boy found his grandfather's body." Walter looked at his wife and added, "I wasn't home at the time, but Acacia was. From the house she heard screams."

"Peter was screaming?" George Webb asked.

"My father was," Acacia answered. "I heard my father calling in agony and I ran to him."

"You never told me that before," said Walter, surprised.

"Certainly I did. My father called out and I ran to him, but someone got to him before I did."

"Peter?" Jessy asked.

Acacia didn't respond yes or no. "He was shouting 'Granddaddy, don't die!'" With her hands, Acacia closed her ears to the offending sounds of years past. "I tried to silence Peter, but he wouldn't let me near him. He thrashed about, screaming the gypsies warned him. He said the gypsies told him the truth. Oh, what rubbish he babbled that terrible day, as if my pain wasn't enough without his lies!" At last Acacia took her hands away from her ears and shouted, "My son is a liar! My own son, a liar!"

From the look on Walter's face, this was a revelation to him. He thundered, "Why didn't you tell me this before? Why?" He looked to George and Jessy. "At the time, Acacia told me our boy had found the body and became a raging maniac at the sight. From that day forward, his mind was not the same. 'Make him stop saying those terrible things!' Acacia told me again and again. She told the doctors, too, the specialists we called in to cure our son. For days and nights our boy ranted about gypsies. We kept him locked in his room, but there was no stopping him. He was disturbing everyone. We had to put him away for the sake of the family."

At last Jessy knew: Peter, as a boy, had seen assassins disguised as gypsies who told him the truth. When he proclaimed the truth, he was locked in an insane asylum. How unjust! Jessy was too appalled to speak.

"Liars, all of them! They were all against my father! They knew he was a great man and they killed him!" Acacia cried in her father's defense.

"Perhaps it was a case of mistaken identity," ventured George Webb, in an effort to reconcile the story in the picture book with the strange facts surrounding the murder. "Perhaps the czar's secret police came to America searching for a murderer and mistook your father for Otto Illyanov?"

Walter, still studying the picture in the book and comparing it to the photograph of the Count from his own hallway, said, "I'd swear this is one and the same man." He had read Nathan's translation carefully. "The age, the physical description, the pictures—Otto and the Count were the same man!"

"Peter wouldn't stop repeating those lies!" Acacia began mumbling incoherently at first, but then more audibly. Walter, George, and Jessy exchanged concerned glances as she muttered, "I had to make him stop! He would have ruined everything. There was no other way of stopping him." Blood pulsed a livid purple through Acacia's throat and temples.

Walter asked Acacia, "What would Peter have told us?"

"You fool!" Acacia turned her hard blue eyes on her husband. "He would have ruined everything. He would have repeated what the gypsies told him. I had to make him stop. I had to!"

Walter ventured, "Peter would have told the story in this book, isn't that right, Acacia? Peter came upon the 'gypsies'—the czar's secret police in disguise—as they assassinated his grandfather. They spared the boy's life but they told him the truth: that his grandfather was a fraud and a murderer, isn't that what you've been meaning to tell me all these years?" Now Walter grabbed his wife by her delicate but iron-framed shoulders, shouting, "Is that what you never told me all these years, Acacia? That our son Peter was telling the truth, but you couldn't bear for anyone to know that your father was no great, noble count after all, but a thieving murderer the secret police had orders to assassinate?"

George Webb leaped from his chair to stop Walter from hurting Acacia who had become hysterical. Her face was distorted nearly beyond recognition.

"Yes! Confound you, yes!" Acacia raged. "My father called to me and told me, with his dying breath, that the secret police had caught up with him at last! I couldn't believe he had run away from his homeland like a criminal! I never will believe it, but then I saw Peter standing there, seeing everything, hearing everything! And he wouldn't shut his infernal mouth! Why should Peter make me, his own mother, suffer so? How could I allow my father's good name to be dragged through the dirt by scum like—"

"—like our own son Peter," finished Walter, exhausted. He let go of her. "All these years I never knew. You lied to me to save your own selfish skin, your own miserable, haughty reputation! From the start, before our son was born, you never wanted him so you took the first opportunity to be rid of him and all these years you had me believing you! And you have the gall to call him scum! You vile—"

"Calling me vile? What about you?" Acacia hissed. "Don't think I'm ignorant of your dalliances."

Nodding slowly, as if his head were made of the heaviest iron, Walter let go of Jessy's books and papers. "Yes, it's true. I've wronged you. I've wronged our children. But you wronged us first."

"That's it! Blame me. Blame anyone but yourself!" Then to Jessy Acacia shouted, "Are you satisfied? Have you gotten what you came for?"

How could she have hurt Peter all these years? Jessy thought. Then, with a shudder, Jessy remembered Acacia's sinful advice to the pregnant Emma. Now Jessy saw firsthand the hatred a mother could feel toward her own innocent child.

George Webb wrapped a fatherly arm around Jessy's shoulder as he again appealed to Walter and Acacia Kimball. "If you sign this release, the doctors will reevaluate Peter's condition to see if he can come home now." George Webb pulled a fold of papers from the inside pocket of his suitcoat.

Without hesitation Walter crossed the room and went to the writing desk to sign the form, with Acacia sobbing the entire time. "Stop it, Acacia. You'll get no pity from me. Putting your own selfish skin before our son! I ought to throw you out in the street!"

"Put me out of my own house, will you? It was my father's money that got you this place, Walter, the best farm in Bethel Township! Don't forget that. Don't ever forget!" Acacia slumped forward in a contorted heap.

Walter returned the papers to George Webb. He looked at his wife, a twisted lavender heap on a gold-fringed settee. "Can the Lord forgive us?" he wondered aloud.

Seeing that Acacia appeared to be coughing or choking on her tears, Jessy said, "Perhaps a drink of water would help." As Jessy ran to the kitchen, George and Walter tried to prop Acacia into a sitting position. When Jessy returned to the parlor, glass in hand, George Webb was phoning for a doctor.

Jessy could hardly believe the change that had transformed Acacia Kimball. The tall, elegant woman was twisted now, her face, left arm, and torso contorting violently despite Walter's efforts to help her.

"Yes, Doctor, hurry, I think Mrs. Kimball might be having a stroke," George Webb said. "I'll tell Walter." When George Webb hung up the phone, he turned to Walter, saying, "The doctor will be here in a few minutes. He said to keep her warm and elevate her legs."

"There are blankets—" Walter Kimball was too shaken to say more.

"I'll find them." Jessy covered Acacia with her warm winter coat and then turned away, not knowing where to go, unfamiliar as she was with most of the house. She wandered out of the parlor and back into the hall. Just then the front door opened.

"Grampa! We're back! Grama! We saw an aeroplane!" Billy Wilcox came running into the house, fresh from a long walk, his mother close behind him.

"Oh, Darlene," said Jessy with a feeling of combined relief and dread. "Oh, Darlene, thank heavens you've come. Your mother—we need blankets."

"What's going on? What's the matter, Jessy?"

"Your mother's ill, very seriously ill," Jessy murmured to the daughter of Acacia Kimball. The hating illness in Acacia's soul had done countless years of damage. Jessy wondered where such a river of evil would end.

CHAPTER 32

❧

"So after I brought Suzy and the kids home from the station and did some work around here, I went back up town for a haircut, you know, my usual Saturday Special," Adam explained to Jessy. He stood at the kitchen counter chomping on thin slivers of raw carrot between sentences.

"Shakes cuts Adam's hair too short, don't you think, Suzanna?" Jessy asked.

"Yes! But will he listen?" Suzanna complained with a lighthearted voice. She continued rolling out dough for the evening's beef pasties while Jessy and the children scrubbed potatoes at the sink.

Adam took a seat at the kitchen table with his feet propped up on a chair. "So while I was there—say, why don't you kids go practice the piano?"

Suzanna turned her pretty profile toward him, one eyebrow raised.

"I know they're helpin' you but I got somethin' to say to Jessy."

Suzanna nodded and continued rolling out dough, and the children scampered off. Jessy girded herself, saying, "Adam, this has been a strange enough day without—"

"You might as well hear the news from me," he said.

"Gossip, that's all you men do at the barber's, and you think *women*—" An outraged Suzanna had stopped rolling out the pastry dough.

"A woman holdin' a rollin' pin's a danger," Adam said lightly before continuing his story. "You know Leo Kimball said he was plannin' on marryin' that Regina Mason, the divorced heiress he met in Boston."

Flinging a dishrag onto the counter, Jessy fumed, "No, I hadn't heard, not officially anyway!"

"No, I guess not, but well, accordin' to the papers it seems that now he won't be marryin' her after all." Adam paused while this seemingly disjointed story of his took hold.

Suzanna railed, "Adam, if this is your idea of a joke—"

"Would I joke about a thing as serious—as potentially dangerous—as marriage?" Adam automatically covered his head to protect himself from the wrath of Suzanna, but this time Suzanna didn't pause in her dough-rolling. When he felt it safe to continue, Adam chomped on a few more carrot sticks and said, "Leo can't marry Regina Mason. He won't be marryin' nobody."

"What do you mean?" Jessy asked in a hush.

Suzanna turned now, hanging on Adam's every word. "What is it?" she asked. "What's happened?"

Only when Adam could hear his youngsters safely out of earshot, laughing and singing around the piano in the parlor would he continue. "Leo's got some—some kind of disease."

"What disease? Where is he? I'll go to him!" Jessy cried.

"No!" Adam stood and took hold of her. "You can't help Leo. No one can. He's in Mexico. Where he is, no visitors are allowed."

"Mexico?" Jessy asked, straining against her brother for release.

"He was spotted bein' carried into a special clinic they got down there, but, well," Adam renewed his careful grasp of Jessy who continued struggling against him.

"Why wasn't something in the papers? Why wasn't I told?" Jessy cried. "I was at the Kimballs today and no one said a word!"

"There was a story in one of the out-of-state papers that came in by train late this afternoon, while I was in town. Paper said Leo's problem is one he didn't want known—it's not the sort of thing polite folk talk about in their pretty parlors, if you get my meaning." Ever so gently, Adam continued to hold Jessy who struggled against him. "Listen to me, Jessy. Leo's got a disease people get when—well, when they misbehave. A disease with no cure." Adam eyed his good sister. "I'm sure glad you stopped seein' Leo. No tellin' what harm would've come to you."

Suzanna came to stand close to them, tears welling up in her eyes. "I've known Leo since he was little. How dreadful!"

Adam reached out to include his wife in his comforting arms. Tenderly he said, "There's not a thing we can do for Leo but pray by some miracle he pulls through."

Both Suzanna and Jessy nodded as they cried together.

"I warned him, didn't I?" Adam asked Jessy. "That Saturday at South Side Park I warned him, but he wouldn't listen. In his place, I probably wouldn't have listened either."

"Trapped by his own sin," Jessy murmured, her grief over Leo's plight more wretched than any pain she had ever known. She ran up to her room, her one great desire to shut out the world and be alone with this dreadful news. In her room she tried not to look at her hope chest containing her trousseau, things she had been amassing for the day she would marry, with them the wedding-ring-pattern quilt. No use for any of it now! *You got what you deserved, Leo Kimball!* Immediately she regretted such bitter, vengeful thinking.

A sound disturbed her disturbing reverie: light scratching in the attic above her room. Jessy froze, listening, with her heart throbbing. The noise stopped and then continued directly over her head. Light scampering followed, and then a loud, cracking *snap!* that echoed through the ceiling. A high-pitched scream from above pierced Jessy's ears. The rat that had evaded them so long was trapped at last.

Jessy ran from the room. "Adam, come quickly! Hurry!"

Adam was already climbing the stairs two at a time, shouting triumphantly, "We got him!" Without a pause he hurried up to the attic. Soon all was deadly quiet.

Jessy could only think of Leo, lured by the devil and broken by sin. She felt sickened to her very soul. Would Leo ever recover? Would she?

315

CHAPTER 33

❦

In the chill December air so good for putting up the family's meat supply for the coming year, Adam said in a low voice to Jessy, "You're awful quiet these days. I want to talk to you."

In an equally quiet voice, her breath puffing in the bitter cold, Jessy answered, "I don't feel like talking." Slaughtering time was painful enough for animal-loving Jessy without having to talk about Leo. Jessy had been quiet, not communicating with anyone in the weeks since the news of his illness reached her. She had withdrawn from the world.

"Then I'll do the talkin'," Adam said.

Sensing another lecture, Jessy snapped, "I wish you'd leave me alone!"

Adam stopped sawing a carcass. "You've been mopin' around here feelin' sorry for yourself for weeks! You're makin' everyone feel bad."

Through silent tears, Jessy stammered, "I can't help how everyone feels! I can't even help how I feel!"

"Leo wasn't right for you, and you should be glad you didn't marry him."

"I know." Feeling as broken as the hog she was helping Adam carve to pieces, Jessy admitted, "Still, it hurts for me to think about Leo."

"He was no good for you! Can't you get that into your head?"

"My head yes, my heart no. From the start I never could be sure that Leo and I could be happy together, but I was so attracted to him! What girl wouldn't be?" At that moment and during all the moments in the month since she heard the terrible news of Leo's illness, Jessy fervently wished the frozen earth would swallow her up. The look was plain enough in her face.

"I wish you'd snap out of this sour mood of yours."

"Perhaps I should go away. I've been thinking of moving out."

"What?" At first serious, Adam's face soon flushed with humor. "Where, to the old mule shed out back? Spinster Hollow?"

Not amused, Jessy said, "I've been thinking of building a place on a corner of our farm, a cottage with a big fireplace and a garden and lots of books to read. What do you think?" When he didn't answer, she said, "I suppose I could move to Chicago and look for work. I can type and keep books."

"You alone in Chicago? Over my dead body!" With tenderness, Adam added, "You'll always have a home wherever I am. You know that."

"You're a love!" Jessy said, smiling warmly despite the coldness of the morning and difficulty of the work they were doing. "Maybe I could join that convent in Florida if they'd have me, except, except—" Except Nathan told Jessy that Christians were needed outside as well as inside convent walls, and Jessy knew this to be true.

The two worked with a will, both speaking brightly now. As they did, Jessy explained, "Every year at this time I wish I could do something other than raise hogs for slaughter."

"It pays well," Adam said. "And you know it."

"So does popcorn. And mint."

"What do you mean?"

"For one thing, nearly everyone likes popcorn. The other day I started reading a library book about mint farming. Did you know that mint grows well in marshes? I got to thinking that it might do well in that wet ground of ours out back. We're not using our marshland for anything and mint flavors all sorts of things—medicines and candies and jellys and herb teas."

"Maybe you're on to somethin'. I'll think about it," Adam promised.

Jessy sighed in relief. At last the work of slaughtering was over for the year. A light snow fell as together they hauled meats to their curing and smoking sheds. While Adam cleaned up the yard, Jessy arranged the choicest cuts of meat to cure in one of the sheds. Her hands and feet were stiff from cold even though she was wearing nearly everything she owned—long underwear, double socks and shirts, her heaviest wool skirt, lined boots, sheepskin jacket, wool hat and scarf. She recalled the previous winter's trip to Florida, glorious warm Florida. Since then so much had changed, so very much! She would be single now, a spinster.

As she worked in solitude, she resolved to continue looking for alternative sources of farming income. Raising hogs might be just the thing for her brother but it was not for her; she'd rather have a pig for a pet.

Maybe Adam would let her try her hand growing mint and popcorn. She felt a growing confidence that regardless of circumstances, whether she married or was meant to remain single, she could continue in God's love, grateful for all she had. After four weeks of sheer misery, Jessy's mood was beginning to lighten.

"Your brother said I'd find you here!" rang a familiar male voice.

"Nathan!" Shocked, Jessy breathed in the cold winter air. "Nathan!" she said again, softly but with no less surprise.

"Oh, I've frightened you. I'm sorry!" Nathan's cheery smile, rosy cheeks, and dimples paled at the sight of her. "Mind if I come in?"

"Of course not!" Jessy said, making room for him to enter the small wooden shed hardly bigger than a closet. "But look at me!" she said in horror. She glanced down at her oldest, most thoroughly hard-worn clothing spattered from slaughtering.

"You look wonderful!" he assured her, his noble face glowing rosily in the cold. "I would have written to let you know I was coming, but I wanted to surprise you—surprise certainly, not shock. Forgive me?"

As the reality of Nathan Fisher's presence sank in, Jessy began to glow with pleasure. "I'm so happy to see you. You don't know how happy!" She wiped her hands on a rag stiff with frost. "Are you on another lecture tour?"

"No, not this time," Nathan said, his kind gray eyes saying: *I'm here about something one doesn't write in letters*.

"How's your family? Your parents? Well, I hope?"

"Fine, just fine. They send you their love."

"And Snaggletooth?"

"He's down in Garden Springs, warming his old bones in the heat—which reminds me! He gave me a message for you. Now where did I put it?" Nathan began searching his pockets. Soon he pulled out a bit of bright paper which recalled the vivid hues of sunny Florida. "Here you are."

Jessy looked at the brilliant slip of multicolored paper and then said with surprised laughter, "But this is blank!"

"Well, you know, despite my efforts, Old Snaggletooth has terrible penmanship. If I let him, the rascal would chew up every pen I own! But I think I can recall what it was he wanted to ask you." The professor studied the blank scrap, the lime and pink and turquoise of it looking like a little rainbow in the drab shed. "He wants to know if you enjoy sea voyages."

"Sea voyages?"

"Snaggle spent a good bit of his baby birdhood at sea, you may recall." While she pondered this curious question, Nathan opened his coat and searched the pocket closest to his heart. He held out something familiar.

Without reaching for the treasure, Jessy looked at the ring he had first shown her in Florida, the wide gold band set with three flat square emeralds.

"You see, Snaggle was wondering—well, actually, I've been wondering, seeing you and I have such a grand time whenever we're together, as we were on that riverboat—if you would like to cross the Atlantic with me and explore Europe and the Holy Land. I have this treatise to write about ecclesiastical architecture which will require a lengthy stay abroad. It would be a shame to go alone, not that Snaggletooth isn't company, but he's so avian and you're so human and humane—delightfully so—and you above all women would so much appreciate seeing such wonders. I've been wanting to ask you for a long time. I made up my mind to when news reached me that Leo Kimball was out of the picture."

"Oh, so you've heard about him," Jessy sighed.

"Belatedly, I did, yes. I'm afraid that this time of year I seldom keep up with the papers. End of term is like that for me. I'm always swamped with work—giving and grading final exams and reading term papers and so on and I only just two days ago wrapped things up at college for the semester and it was then I finally got around to reading some back issues of the papers and as soon as I did I knew I had to drop everything and come to see you." The ring still glinted in Nathan's hand.

Looking from the ring to his eyes, Jessy stammered, "Y-you're s-serious, aren't you?"

"Never more serious in my life."

"But look at me!" Jessy exclaimed.

"I am looking! And I love what I see."

"B-but I'm not your calibre at all!"

"Of course you are. You live on a farm; you know cream always rises!" Nathan's exuberance softened as he added, "In so many ways it is I who am unworthy of you, dear Jessy."

"How can you say that?"

"You are a lady in every sense, with a good mind, a loving heart, a pure soul. I'm certain I could search the world my entire life and never find another one so fine as you. We're right for each other." When Jessy shifted her weight from one foot to another like a bashful schoolgirl, Nathan beamed with high enthusiasm, "You want me to be happy, don't you?"

"Of course I do, Nathan, but I'm just a plain old—"

"—wonderful darling I'll love always, all the time God gives us to love!" Nathan scanned the dim, cramped shed packed with cuts of meat before adding with an infectious grin, "I think under these conditions I'm supposed to say something like, Let me take you away from all this."

Jessy's laughter rang in merry peals.

"You have such a wonderful laugh, dear Jessy. You should always laugh. I want you to be happy! And you have such a splendid spirit! Will you be my wife—my lovely, lovely wife?"

She stood in awe of this man with brains, courage, and faith who loved her so. What more could she ask for in a husband? Still she couldn't accept the fact that Nathan would do her such an honor as to propose marriage. Haltingly, she admitted, "We do make a good team, I think."

"I think so too!"

Jessy remembered their rescue of the pelican and their solution of a mystery. "What a joy your friendship has been, right from the start!" she said with enthusiasm.

"My thought exactly! Time and again, I've seen that it is so. We think alike, we believe as one, we were meant for each other. I would have broached the subject of marriage with you sooner, but saw that you were committed to Leo Kimball, a man who was not so committed to you as it turned out—and, I might add, so unlike you and so unworthy of you in spiritual terms. And it is a sharing of spiritual values that matters most in marriage—a meeting of two minds—two souls bound together in God."

"Of course, you're right. Absolutely and totally right!" Overcome, Jessy looked away. "Leo wasn't right for me at all. I know that now. I always sensed he wasn't, but I had such hopes for him and me. I prayed so hard, but the answer in so many ways was always no."

Genuinely moved, Nathan said solemnly, "What a shame! I pity him

The newspapers didn't seem to indicate—I hope he'll come through all right."

"I don't know. In all this time, I haven't heard a word from him. Not one word," she answered. "All I can do is continue to pray."

"I see. But if Leo didn't have the good sense—the means, the will—to hold you, well, I certainly do!" Nathan Fisher said with unbounded cheer, "A woman with your sensitivity, your faith, your mind, a splendid woman who appreciates the finer things—including my jokes—and who loves God as you do, well, how could I let you go? Quite frankly, you're the most remarkable lady I've ever met. I love you."

Remembering the stunning, distinguished portrait of Nathan's deceased wife, Jessy confessed, "I could never take Hope's place."

"I don't expect you to. Hope was unique in all the world, but then, so are you, for where you go, a great light goes. The Lord, in His infinite wisdom, has drawn us together. Let's be glad for the gift of love He's given us to share. Let's pool our resources to serve Him in love. I'd be most honored if you would agree to be my wife." When still she hesitated, he added, "If you don't think me too presumptuous, I believe you love me."

"How did you ever know that?" Jessy blurted out, adding with a bemused grin, "Oh, but you're a genius!" As growing belief in his proposal took root in her, she said with subtle pleasure: "I must confess I was drawn to you at once; perhaps it was love at first sight."

"Will you love me until the stars lose their mystery?"

"Longer than that!" Jessy's smile beamed in the dim light, knowing deep in her heart Nathan was the man for her. "My mother once told me that when two people are meant for each other, God shakes the world to get them together."

"She was right!" With bottomless joy, Nathan said, "Then here. For you."

"I should wash my hands first," Jessy protested as Nathan slipped the ring onto her finger anyway. "Oh, my, it is such a lovely ring!"

"Fits perfectly too! I thought it would!" Nathan admired her hand, then bowed to kiss it. Drawing to his full height, which wasn't a simple matter in such a small shed, he said, "Now I trust you don't mind being married to a man ten years older than you. You don't? Excellent! And you won't mind having a husband who holds a modest teaching position? You won't?

Good! And you know I don't think much of worldly goods and that I couldn't offer a girl the excitement a handsome young ballplayer could but—" Nathan extended his arm to her. "But I could offer you the world, at least as I've come to know it, and as I wish to explore it with you. I offer you adventure, romance—steady, faithful romance, naturally—and learning, if you so desire. You who enjoy schooling could take all the courses at St. Azarias that interest you. You love books and I have access to more books than we both could ever hope to finish reading in two lifetimes and there are battles to be fought—great battles against spiritual corruption in high places and low, even in such a charming place as Enigma. I need you, Jessy. My family loves you and wonders why I've waited so long to propose! And Old Snaggletooth does love your peanuts!"

They were interrupted when Suzanna and the children began making a ruckus at the back porch, ringing the bell that indicated lunch was ready. Nathan offered her his arm—his protection. Nathan was all Jessy could hope for in a husband: earnest, sincere, kind, loving, optimistic, good-looking, gentle, witty, brave, bright, faithful, and good. Still, a girl had to be careful. Before she reached out to him, recalling all too vividly the many stumbling blocks the Kimball family had tossed her way, Jessy asked coyly, "You don't by chance have any skeletons in your closet, do you?"

Nathan laughed his marvelous laugh. "As a matter of fact, I do have a skeleton I keep around for the occasional anatomy lecture."

Laughing, too, still Jessy had to ask, "And just what do you believe? In summation?"

"Well," Nathan pursed his lips as he always did when he was about to emit great oratory. "In summation, I believe the Divine Incarnation—Christ's visitation and resurrection for all civilization—was and is God's revelation for our salvation, for our redemption, so we may give Him our adoration and avoid temptation and damnation which would mean ruination, for without Him we would suffer eternal separation from divine communication."

Jessy asked, "Is it your assumption that our sin caused the lamentation which led to the crucifixion—the Son of God's unjust execution—but His resurrection was for our consecration, our emancipation, our transformation—"

"Precisely, Jessy! The resurrection—God's invitation to participation in His revelation—is certainly cause for celebration! And as for celebrations, won't you say yes to my invitation to a collaboration?"

"Well," Jessy said, submitting at last, "we do make a good combination!" Laughing, assured beyond doubt Nathan indeed was the man for her, Jessy grasped the strong, capable arm he offered. Their shared, heartfelt joy abounded on that cold day, the coldest day of deep December. As they made their way toward the rambling farmhouse, Jessy looked up into Nathan's face more than once, always seeing there the very face of love. He kept her close to his side as they walked over crusted snow. She sensed that no matter where life took them, Nathan would never let her stumble. New snow kept falling until their hats and coats were coated with the stuff. "White as a bridal veil," Nathan remarked, admiring the effect on her. "Aren't we the fortunate ones?"

❦ ❦ ❦

The house was redolent with the aroma of fresh-grilled sausage flavored with fennel and red pepper. At the big cast-iron stove, Martha was stirring her mother's pot of sweet spiced apples laced with fresh butter and cinnamon. A tray of hot buttermilk biscuits was cooling nearby. Stephen and Taddy were grinding fresh pork for more sausage. Jessy washed her hands, but for the moment kept the emerald ring on her left hand from view.

Soon Adam came in to clean up for the meal. He nodded to Nathan. "So. What brings you to the frozen tundra? Another lecture tour?"

"Yes," answered Nathan, "the most important lecture I'll ever give. I've asked your sister to be my wife. To my delight she has agreed."

Adam responded without hesitation. "Good!" As he scrubbed his hands at the sink, Adam said, "You know, Nathan, I think that girl has loved you from that first day you two met in Florida."

"How wonderful for you both!" exclaimed Suzanna. "When's the wedding?"

Nathan said, "We haven't decided, but I hope June, as soon as the upcoming semester's over. The *Steadfast* leaves New York for England the second week in June. I have some business in London, Canterbury, and

323

York, after which we'll have a Channel crossing and a connection by train. I haven't quite decided which route we'll take, but we'll cross the Alps over to Italy and down to Brindisi for a sailing to Greece and eventually to Piraeus, after which—"

The entire family paused at this. Everyone looked at Jessy, their own, leaving them forever for the other side of the world in a little more than six short months. Jessy herself looked overwhelmed at the prospect.

"You did say the Holy Land," she murmured to Nathan.

"Yes, I did. It will be an amazing trip for you, Jessy, meaningful in every respect," Nathan said in reassuring tones.

"You've been there? Where Jesus lived and walked?" she asked in a hush.

"Jesus, Paul, Joshua, Moses, David, Solomon, Pilate—why, yes."

Everyone in the room seemed transfixed, transformed at the thought. "Think of it, to see the land of the Bible," Suzanna said, enthralled. "To walk where Jesus walked."

Smiling at them all, Nathan said, "And what's even more remarkable is to behold His living presence in the shining faces of His loved ones, believers like you. All of you."

"Will you and Dr. Fisher be going on a big ship, Aunty?" Stephen asked.

"Yes. It does sound romantic." Still Jessy looked to Nathan for answers.

"Ah, you mustn't be carried away by the romance of the high seas and forget the danger, Stephen! The sea is glorious more in the memory of the going than the going itself, once the wanderer has safely reached home! Sea-going is fraught with peril." With his face close to Jessy's, and offering his hand, Nathan asked, "Are you interested in an adventure?"

"Yes!" Come what may, she had courage. Her eyes sang with romance; her heart sparkled with love as she took Nathan's wonderful hand in hers.

"I'll sure miss Jessy, no question 'bout that—she's become my right hand! But even if she were to stay on here, she knows farmin's dangerous work." Adam nodded encouragement to his sister, even though it was apparent he hated to see her go so far away.

Nathan interjected. "I've sailed on the *Steadfast*. It's a fine vessel. I'll pray we have a safe, smooth crossing—restful, uneventful, and dull!"

At this everyone smiled and relaxed. "We'll pray too!" they said.

"I hope everyone's hungry," Suzanna said in the intervening silence.

She urged the children to set the table and make room for their unexpected guest, the newest addition to their growing family.

"You're as happy as I've ever seen you," Adam said to Jessy as he patted her hand. Then Adam reached out to Nathan and shook hands again.

Together they gathered around the big table arrayed with magnificent foods. After giving thanks for the good harvest and plump animals that provided wholesome meat, Adam invoked over the family a blessing of God's unfailing love. Come what may, including the perils of worldy separation, the cord of eternal love binding them together could never be broken.

CHAPTER 34

❦

Once the weather warmed up, the Flints made a thorough inspection of the house exterior from top to bottom. While Jessy stood at ground level, holding the ladder for Adam who was examining the roof, she became transfixed. "Adam," she said, not moving a muscle, her eyes fixed on a spot, "I think I see where that rodent might have come in."

"Good! Hey, Stephen! Taddy! Bring me some of that wire mesh, will you?" To Jessy Adam said, "We'll pack up that hole soon as I come down from here."

"No more intruders!" Jessy said with a shudder. "Not in our house!"

"With a house this nice and cozy, you always have to be on guard," Adam told her. "Here I come!" Slowly Adam made his way down the three-story ladder. "Glad that job's done," he said as he stepped to the walkway.

"I shouldn't say this, but the house could use a paint job!" she told him with a grin. The pretty yellow paint was beginning to show signs of wear.

"Don't remind me," Adam laughed. "Keepin' up a house this size is a full-time job." As she helped him move the ladder, he said, "Don't you worry. We'll have the place all slicked up for your big day."

Jessy felt overwhelmed at the thought: her June wedding was only three months away.

"Look's like we've got company," Adam said. He gestured toward the road.

"That's Mr. Kimball's car!" Jessy ran to greet him.

Mr. Kimball, red-eyed but happy, was with Darlene, Billy, and a tall, rail-thin redhead who strongly resembled Walter.

"Peter!" Jessy cried. "Is it really you?"

The gangly thin Peter stepped out of the car.

"It's so good to see you again!" Jessy hugged him with joy.

326

"Peter insisted on coming here first, straight from Fair Haven! He kept saying, 'I wonder if Jessy will remember me,'" Walter said. Standing on either side of him, Darlene and Billy held Peter's hands.

"Of course I remember! How could I forget you, Peter?" Jessy cried with happy tears. "Please come inside and meet my family!"

Tinkly piano music floated from the parlor to the hall where the Kimballs stood with Jessy and Adam. Stephen came in with an armload of wire mesh.

"If you folks'll excuse us just a minute, there's a hole we'd better plug up," Adam explained with a bemused grin. "Make yourselves comfortable!"

"Good to meet you," Peter said after shaking Adam's hand. "Who's playing?"

"My niece, Martha," Jessy whispered, to the tune of off-notes. "May I take your coats?" While she hung up coats, she called out, "Suzanna, look who's here! It's a miracle!" Once she led her guests to the parlor, she asked Walter, "Peter's home for good, isn't he?"

"Oh, yes indeed, at long, long last. Darlene and I will be looking after him until he gets his bearings, however long that takes." For a moment, emotion overwhelmed Walter so he couldn't talk, but then he told Jessy out of everyone else's hearing, "A slew of doctors have been examining him since November. They say he has a long period of adjustment ahead, but that he should do well, once he settles in at home."

Home! Jessy murmured, "I'm so sorry about Mrs. Kimball." Acacia Kimball, bedridden since November, had suffered another stroke a few days ago and had to be taken to a nursing home for around-the-clock care.

"It doesn't look good for her or Leo!"

Leo! Jessy's eyes widened at the mention of his name. "I haven't heard a word, not one word since last fall."

"I'm told we wouldn't recognize him. He's suffering a sort of bone deformity." Clearly it pained Walter Kimball greatly to speak of Leo's condition, but he added, "So far there's been no damage to his heart and brain. The doctors have stabilized his condition but can't seem to heal him. I only hope he won't lose his sight."

Jessy closed her own eyes at the thought of Leo Kimball blind.

327

Just then Suzanna breezed in to join them. "Well, this is a delightful surprise," she said, making Peter Kimball's acquaintance.

For a moment Peter looked unsure of himself in this new social situation, but then he stood to take her hand politely. "Mrs. Flint."

"Peter Kimball is a wonderful musician and composer," Jessy said to Martha, who kept tinkering at the piano.

"You are?" Martha asked, turning and regarding this newcomer with interest. "Can you show me how to play? Sometimes I think I'll never learn how, no matter how much I practice."

Peter Kimball laughed and joined the girl on the piano bench. Soon his fingers flew over the keys with a fierce and vibrant joy. After a few moments of uninterrupted bliss, he reached around and put his long, tapered fingers over Martha's little hands. "Your fingers are so short! Just wait till they grow a bit more. You'll do wonders!"

"I will?" said Martha eagerly. "Do you promise?"

Peter laughed. "I can't promise, but I'll pray they do."

"Pray my fingers grow as long as yours!" Martha said. She squealed with glee to hear the music their four hands together made. "Mama, just listen!"

"I am, darling, I am! Oh, Adam, come and listen!"

"I am!" said Adam, returning with Stephen. "I didn't think that piano of ours had that many good-soundin' notes in it!"

"Is that Martha?" said Stephen. "I can hardly believe it!"

Just then the cuckoo clock announced the time: four o'clock sharp. At this, Darlene took notice. "The last time I was here that clock made no sense whatever! After I went home I laughed just thinking about it, Jessy."

"It was silly, wasn't it? Nathan Fisher—my fiancé—fixed it," Jessy said with restrained but obvious pride.

"He must be a genius!" Darlene said.

"He is!" said Taddy. "Professor Fisher knows everything! He built us an entire model train for Christmas. He can even read Russian!"

Tactfully, smoothly, Jessy changed the subject. She rubbed her gold and emerald ring as she spoke. "You're coming to the wedding, I hope? All of you?"

"Wouldn't miss it for the world," Walter Kimball said.

"Burl and Laura are planning to be here too!" Darlene added.

"They sent us an announcement from Chicago about their babies!"

Jessy said, laughing. "Congratulations on being a grandfather again," she told Walter, "twice!"

"Twins! Who would have believed it, after all their childless years?" he said, laughing at the thought of his squeaky daughter and her railroad man.

The impromptu concert resumed full force. Jessy excused herself a moment to help Suzanna and Taddy with the big tea tray of sandwiches cut into triangles.

As they all took up their cups, Mr. Kimball surprised everyone by offering a toast, saying, "To Jessy: may you live a long life filled with joy. And to my son Peter, who I gave up forever as lost, now found. It's a privilege to know you, Jessy Flint."

Once conversation resumed over the ample tea, Peter excused himself a moment. Soon he returned from the car, holding what Jessy assumed was a puff-ball. Curious, she sat up tall on the sofa, wondering why Peter would show them a paperwasp's nest, for that is what it resembled.

Flustered but undeterred, Peter entered and crossed the room full of people. When he reached Jessy's side, he said, "Please inscribe it to me, Jessy. Since you visited me in the hospital, it's been a source of endless knowledge, my greatest joy."

With infinite care Jessy took this strange object from him, unrecognizable but vaguely familiar. Only when she held it close did she see. "Why Peter!" she cried, tears brimming in her warm brown eyes. "Can it be? Is it possible?" When she tried closing the book to see the cover, she knew.

Peter stood over her with head bowed. "I read it, every page. Every word. And then when I finished, I thought it was so wonderful I read it over again."

With shaking hands Jessy held the Bible she had given Peter months ago. How often had she wondered if he had glanced at it, much less read it from cover to cover until the pages had puffed and fluffed from hard use.

"This morning when I saw it, I offered to buy Peter a new Bible but he likes that one just fine," Darlene said, smiling. "On our way here, Peter told us you gave it to him and that made it all the more special."

The stains of Peter's sweat, his tears, his struggling pen, had all left their marks on the precious book Jessy now held. Taddy, closest to the writing table, brought pen and ink to his aunt.

"Thank you, honey," Jessy whispered to her nephew. Then, looking up to Peter still waiting patiently at her side, she asked, "But what shall I write?"

"Anything you wrote—why, just your name alone—would be honor enough."

"You amaze and humble me!" Moved again to tears, Jessy remembered the eagle she and Nathan had seen on the Florida river, denied, for a time, of its rightful prize. She knew in her heart that, despite obstacles, despite evil, the eagle would triumph over injustice.

In the Bible, Jessy wrote: "Peter Kimball, the truth has indeed set you free. No one can take your joy from you. Your sister in Christ, Jessy Flint. March 1910."

Having read the inscription, Peter smiled from his heart and touched her shoulder. "Sister," he said softly, "you are my sister."

Jessy patted his hand, then glanced around the silent room so packed with loved ones. Merrily she said, "Well, I think this calls for a celebration!"

"There's some of that cake of yours from lunch," Suzanna reminded Jessy.

"Lopsided, I hope?" asked Peter. "That's the best kind—Jessy's homemade choclopsided cake!"

"I'm glad you like it," Jessy confessed, "because that's the only kind I know how to make!"

As Jessy's cockeyed devil's food cake was being cut, Martha scrambled to the piano to play a not-so-very-lopsided *Here Comes the Bride*.

CHAPTER 35

❦

That Saturday in June rose up warm and clear, perfect in every way. Jessy wakened later than usual, weary but happy with all the preparations and festivities that had gone on so long. The whole week had been spent cooking up a feast with Suzanna, Mrs. Webb, Darlene, and Emma, and a host of other women and not a few of the men. Yesterday afternoon Jessy, Nathan, and the wedding party had adorned the church with garlands and fresh flowers the Ballys had brought up from Florida by train, packed in ice to stay fresh. In the evening the Flints and Ballys had partied with the Fishers, the guests having arrived a few days earlier to reside in their rented summer home on Lake Bethel.

Jessy started her day, as all days, in prayer, and then donned her work clothes for the last time in this place. She rushed downstairs, knowing she was later than usual.

Adam was outside already, chatting with the mailman. Once the fellow rode off, Adam greeted his sister. "Mornin', Sleepin' Beauty! I mean morninG!"

Jessy rubbed the sleep from her weary face and murmured her apologies.

Adam leafed through the stack. Amid the usual flyers and circulars he noticed an official-looking envelope he tore into at once. It contained his high school certificate which he proudly showed to Jessy.

"Congratulations," said Jessy, wide-eyed at last.

Adam handed her an envelope nearly as light as air.

"From Mexico!" she gasped. "It's Leo's writing!" Jessy trembled all over. "Aren't you going to open it?"

"Yes, of course," she said, feeling shaky. "Of all days!"

"Not a word from him in almost a year!" Adam barked. "Oooh, look at this: Day's Pharmaceutical Corporation." Adam waved a business envelope in her direction, then tore it open. "I wrote them like that book of yours suggested. Wow! Look." Adam handed her his good news.

She read with growing interest. "They'll buy all our—your mint!"

"Now I wish we had planted more," said Adam.

Jessy grinned at him. "One acre of mint seems like a hundred of corn!"

"Sure smells nice, don't—*doesn't* it!" Adam whistled as he read and reread the list of revenues the pharmaceutical corporation had projected. "A few years at these rates and I'll be able to retire! Pack up the wife and kids for Florida and golf every day with Bo!"

"Retire?" Jessy regarded her handsome brother who had yet to sprout the first gray hair.

He rubbed his chin. "Well, maybe not quite yet, but, you know what?" Adam's rugged face softened as he beheld his sister on this day of all days. "You've always brought me good fortune. Right from the start. I'm going to miss you!"

"Oh, Adam," she said bashfully, fighting a lump in her throat.

Fighting a lump in his own, he hugged her close. "You won't forget to write, now will you?"

"'Course not!" she murmured into his old cotton shirt.

"And you'll stay healthy and keep Nathan happy?"

"Of course!" she exclaimed, starting to laugh. "And you'll take care of yourself and look after Suzanna and the children?"

"You know I will!"

Together they made for the barn, where Adam's sons and daughter had already started the morning chores, the endless round of feeding livestock, milking and driving out cows, and the cleaning up afterward.

Only after Jessy returned upstairs for her long, luxurious bath did she unseal Leo's letter. It read:

Dearest Jessy,

Soon you'll be married. I wish it was our day, not yours with some other mai.. What a fool I've been! Can you forgive me? I've lost everything, you know. My career, my health, and perhaps my life, through my own folly, to syphilis. My throat always hurts and sores come and go. My spine aches so much I can hardly sit up most days, and often my eyes hurt from the light, but today is one of my better days so I want to write and tell you some things before you slip away from me forever.

It's strange that this is the first summer since I was five years old that I can't play ball. I've been alone, helpless, and crippled, and for a long while I didn't understand why. I railed against God. I blamed Him for my own stupidity! His laws are for our protection, but I learned that too late.

I can hardly believe my brother Peter has come home and I'm the outcast now. What a turnabout, a strange twist of fate! Funny about life, isn't it? Peter comes home and my mother is institutionalized. I never really understood that woman until now. A dark, dirty secret eats away inside of someone—a secret so grim I refused to believe it at first, when Dad wrote to me.

But there is a light at the end of the tunnel. If that's true for someone as wayward as me, then it's true for everyone. One of the few things I brought with me when I left Boston in such a hurry was that Bible you gave me one Christmas, do you remember? I carried it around with my athletic gear and had forgotten all about it, to tell you the truth. I used to think your way was too hard, but my way was hardest of all, for look at what it's brought me!

Once I got here, I can't tell you how alone I felt. Even with all the doctors and nurses and other patients around, I felt so utterly hopeless. I don't know much Spanish and there was nothing here to read in English. Out of desperation, I dug out that Bible. At the time, I confess I knew nothing about how to read it or make sense of it, but I discovered a list of Scripture verses in the front of the book and I began looking them up—verses about feeling afraid, hopeless, lost—until gradually I learned some things I never knew before. The Bible is nothing like what I thought. It's so good.

I'm sorry I didn't listen to you sooner, my sweet Jessy! I'm paying for my sins, but I have hope now in Christ. I won't always be in this condition. I'll see resurrection and new life, for I've been saved by the grace of God. That I may never see you again in this life hurts me more than words can tell, but you should know your prayers and your gifts weren't wasted . . .

Jessy set down Leo's letter and looked up to the high windows in the bathroom flooded with the light of this glorious day in June—her day, Nathan's day, the most momentous day of her life—and she cried to God as she had never done before.

CHAPTER 36

❦

After one long final bout with the jitters, Jessy stepped from the family car like a princess, leaning on her brother's arm with one hand and, with the other, lifting her long white skirts out of harm's way.

As soon as Jessy's small feet sheathed in fine white kid touched the gravel, Suzanna began fussing with her veil, the one she had made with love. In the sunshine it sparkled with frosted bits of silver. From this cloud of virginal white veiling, Jessy smiled brightly to her family with her one bit of color: her small rosebud of a mouth. Suzanna couldn't stop fussing over Jessy. The snowy white orange blossoms encircling her crown had to be just right.

Jessy reached to her lace stand-up collar. With relief she felt, through the veiling, the long strand of pearls Nathan had given her, but still her hand searched. "It's still there, isn't it, Suzanna? Your cameo?"

"Yes! Something borrowed!" Suzanna began to cry, thinking of distant Italy where her cameo had been crafted. "You must let me know what Naples is like, when you get there! I'll miss you more than I can say."

Her stomach churning, Jessy nodded.

"Oh, now Jessy's crying again!" wailed Emma.

Jessy tried to dab her nose, but couldn't for the veil. With her satin ribbons fluttering in the light breeze, Jessy stepped from the knot of females around her toward Adam, resplendent and handsome as ever she had seen him. With gloved hands she straightened the flower in his dark lapel. He patted her hand and held it a moment in an effort to reassure her, but his own hand was shaking. Bells high in the steeple began ringing. A flock of doves made a noisy retreat from the belfry.

"Remember when I fixed that roof after the tornado?" Adam asked his wife and sister.

"You did such a fine job," they answered. And he had.

334

They began to chatter nervously before entering the holy place. In truth, all seemed holy today, down to the last detail: the happy crowd that hurried up the church steps, friends of the timid bride lingering outside, and the rich, moving strains of Bach enhancing the still late morning air. Everyone but the bridal party slipped inside to their seats.

The time had come for Jessy Flint to put her girlhood behind her forever. She took the fateful steps toward a new life, praying as she had a thousand times she would always be worthy of the one waiting for her at the altar. With all her family going before her, Jessy and Adam closed ranks, taking slow, measured steps to the crowded altar where the minister, attendants, and the noblest, brightest, dearest man in the world stood waiting.

The music stopped. The minister asked who gave this bride.

Adam, in his best voice, said, "I do, with much love." He gave Jessy a kiss, a hug, and a tearful smile before stepping away from her.

The bride and groom knelt together. In a voice ringing with joy, the minister uttered the familiar, ancient, binding words of ritual: to have and to hold from this day forward, for better, for worse, for richer, for poorer, in sickness and in health, to love and to cherish, till death us do part, according to God's holy ordinance.

Once both rings were blessed and exchanged, the whole gathering shared communion. Then the bride and groom's lifelong promise was sealed with a kiss—Jessy's first—and as warm and sweet as ever a kiss could be.

With wondrous joy Nathan, and then the entire congregation, beheld his exquisite slip of a bride, the new Mrs. Isaac Nathan Fisher. The silent crowd now exploded with noisy good cheer.

❦ ❦ ❦

"For a long time I've prayed I would get along well with my mother-in-law and my prayers have been answered!" Jessy told Grace Fisher at the first opportunity. The excited, merry bride squealed, "And as for Nathan, why, he's perfect!"

"Oh, no, he's not," Grace Fisher answered without hesitation, smiling wisely as she did.

"Not perfect?" Nathan looked indignant but gave his wife and mother a wry smile. He came alongside Jessy and took her hand in his.

"Ah, but not to worry, son," Grace replied with serene confidence. "Jessy is just the girl to see that you become perfect!"

That Jessy nodded gingerly caused Nathan to chide both women: "Am I a man or-or an old house that needs renovating?"

"Oh, dear love," Jessy said with delight, "the Lord will transform us from glory to glory into what He wants us to be."

Nathan, brimming with love and good humor, nodded and took both her hands, now, into his own. "Quite a party, isn't it?" he said.

Out on the lawn of the Flint home, the crowd enjoyed the punch and thin-sliced roast beef and herb-roasted chickens and crisp savory nuts and honey-baked ham and raucous good music. Everyone looked forward to the cutting of the cake, a white Eiffel Tower of a confection frosted with cream-laced marzipan.

Nathan and Jessy strolled around the yard, admiring all the presents. One of her favorites was from George Webb: a fine old English oil painting of a fox confronted by a hound, and a note saying, "Hats off and cheerio!"

When Jessy sat in the shade with Nathan, she said, "This is the first moment we've been alone since you arrived four days ago!"

Nathan scanned the vast throng with his mild but gleaming gray eyes. Summer lightning flashed through his face. "Soon we'll have a party of our own. Just the two of us."

Jessy shifted nervously in the lawn chair. Avoiding the gleam in his eyes, she busied herself with her full white delicate skirt.

"Our train leaves at three," he reminded her.

Days ago she had shipped her belongings to Enigma, all but the essentials she needed for their extended trip abroad. Suzanna would ship the wedding presents to Enigma after this day of days. Jessy looked more than a trifle faint.

"You've hardly eaten a thing today. Let me get you something."

Before Jessy could protest Nathan was off, filling a plate and punch glass for her. Soon he returned, with two hefty, bearded young men in unaccustomed finery on either side of him. "These two think we need an escort, my baby brothers! What do you think, Jessy? We'd be crazy to haul them all the way across the Atlantic with us!"

"We'll stow away. We want to go with you!" said Freddie Fisher.

"But we'll settle for cake," added his brother Mark.

Nathan easily rapped their heads together. A lovely girl, Violetta Fisher Parks, so unlike her brothers—and with the most remarkable violet eyes—joined them. The dark-haired young woman clutched the arm of her husband, Edmond. "You're always welcome to stay with us!" she told the bride.

"The next time we happen through California, we'll definitely come calling," Nathan promised his young sister. He winked to his bride.

The crowd, Jessy and Nathan with them, grew restless for cake, for the tossing of the bouquet, and the last round of toasts. Adam and Cyrus Fisher wished the couple a long, happy life with absolutely no regrets.

While Nathan waited downstairs for her, Jessy returned to her room for the last time. She changed into her new, fawn-colored traveling suit, checked the contents of her handbag, and glanced at her image in the mirror. As she smoothed her hair, she saw the unfamiliar gleam of new gold. Her simple wedding band was identical to Nathan's. The antique Spanish emerald ring glowed with it on her left hand. She rubbed them a bit, just to assure herself they were real, and looked around one last time: the room seemed bare without her straw hats and other simple belongings, and all her books. Jessy picked up the last thing to be packed, her Bible. The truth that had served her so well she slipped into her bag. As she glanced around her room for the last time, she remembered her dream of Labor Day and the voice that called to her. She would not follow Christ alone. She now knew who had offered to follow Christ with her.

Downstairs, Peter Kimball was playing the piano. Martha's little hands accompanied him with more skill than Jessy had ever heard. When Jessy at last opened the door to her room, the guests crowded the staircase. Jessy walked down in a rush, hardly able to bear waving good-bye to them all: the Ballys, the Webbs, the Fishers, Walter Kimball with Peter and Darlene and Billy, Laura and Burl with their matched set of babies, Emma Kimball with Kem Curtis and his happy brood, good neighbors including Ed Mannon, even Shakes the barber and Dr. Grady, and at least half the residents of Bethel Township.

Emma stood with the single women, hoping to be lucky enough to catch the bouquet. Jessy, fair-minded as ever, closed her eyes as she prepared to toss away her flowers with their white satin ribbons streaming and fluttering, but in truth she did aim in the general direction of Emma Kimball.

"Let's have another home run!" Emma said with a mischievous grin.

Amid cheers that shook the hall, Jessy opened her eyes and delighted to see the happy girl clutching the bouquet. Jessy couldn't help but applaud Emma's good catch. Kem stood close to Emma, glad for the good omen.

"But I wanted to catch the bouquet," Martha wailed.

"Your turn will come soon enough!" Suzanna said, clutching her daughter with a sudden burst of mixed feelings, dreading that day as all mothers do. "Such joy and such sorrow!" she murmured as she kissed the newlyweds good-bye.

The crowd surged out the front door behind the joyous couple.

When Adam said good-bye his lively green eyes betrayed his deepest feelings. He shook Nathan's hand and kissed Jessy on the top of her head. "Wherever you go, you know I'll always love you. May God keep you safe and sound!"

Jessy was crying too hard to answer. Nathan helped her into a waiting car while a hundred voices gave all sorts of marital advice, nonsensical and otherwise, and two hundred hands threw birdseed.

Soon Jessy and Nathan were off in a car streaming with old shoes and tin cans. The best man, Nathan's best friend, Zachary, sped the couple to the Bethel train station and onto the three o'clock express to New York.

The passenger car was nearly empty. Alone at last, seated snugly together, the couple leaned against one another, exhilarated but exhausted.

"Happy?" Nathan asked.

"Jubilant!" Jessy answered without hesitation.

As the train began picking up speed, they glanced at the lovely June day unfolding beyond the windows but turned back to each other, preferring to gaze into each other's eyes.

Nathan reached into his valise. "For you."

"Not another present! I've given you so little!" Jessy's budget had been strained to the limit, with her trousseau and wedding draining her coffers.

"You've given me more than words can say," Nathan assured her. "Here."

Reluctantly, Jessy took the pretty package from him, a thick rectangle wrapped in silver paper and tied with a shimmering pale blue ribbon. Within the wrapping she found a book with a dark blue leather binding. The pages were edged in gold.

"Oh, how exciting! A new book!" Jessy opened it, but then paused, wondering. "But Nathan!" she laughed. "These pages are all blank!"

"Yes, and won't it be wonderful to fill them up with the story of faith God will write through you and me! What amazing things does He have in store for us?"

As the train sped on, God's guiding hand led Nathan and Jessy Fisher into the grandest adventures of all. No matter where life took them, they would be guided by His greatest gift, the gift of love.

About the Author

Chris Drake grew up in Lawrence, Massachusetts, and earned her B.A. at Mount Holyoke College. She did graduate work and married in Michigan before migrating south. She and her husband live and worship in Atlanta.

The Gift of Love is her second inspirational novel. Chris is most grateful to readers of *The Price of Love* for their moving testimonies and kind support and she wishes all of you God's blessings.